A Pair of Kings Beats All . . .

"Richard?" Noel came near to strangling on the name. "*King* Richard? Of, you know, England?"

"Aye, and Duke of Aquitaine as well!" the red-haired giant roared. "And if you know me for a king, why do you stand in my presence?"

The dark man at Richard's side could not repress a slight smile. "I would not insist on ceremony too much with this youth, were I you. Who shall bow? The king, or the sorcerer who freed him from the Jewel?"

The dark man made a low obeisance before a dumb-founded Noel. "Had I the lands and men I ruled in life, Noble One, I would lay the half of them at your feet. Failing that, you must accept only the humble thanks of Salah-ed-Din."

"But how can you be here?" Noel squeaked.

"Black treachery, blacker sorcery, a dying mage's curse . . ."

▼ DEMON ▼
BLUES

ESTHER FRIESNER

ACE BOOKS, NEW YORK

This book is an Ace original edition,
and has never been previously published.

DEMON BLUES

An Ace Book/published by arrangement with
the author

PRINTING HISTORY
Ace edition/May 1989

ISBN: 0-441-14309-1

Ace Books are published by The Berkley Publishing Group,
200 Madison Avenue, New York, New York 10016.
The name ''ACE'' and the ''A'' logo are trademarks
belonging to Charter Communications, Inc.

PRINTED IN THE UNITED STATES OF AMERICA

10 9 8 7 6 5 4 3 2 1

This book is for Roy Alexander Jaruk,
Officer, Scholar, Gentleman,
With thanks.

AUTHOR'S ACKNOWLEDGMENT

Besides Roy Alexander Jaruk, I would like to thank the following members of the Barony of Dragonshiphaven for their very informative and helpful input:

JON DOUGLAS SINGER

DAVID KATZ

JEFF GEDNEY

Prologue:

Daddy's Little Girl

THE DEMON SQUATTED on the sands, a black fire of rage against the golden burning of the desert. Claws crept up to shade tiny scarlet eyes, glowing with the hideous cold of knowledge, merciless knowledge lacking any shred of innocence to lend its warming touch. What there was to know of flesh and earth, of here and now, of all things firm and fact-ridden and stone-hard practical, the demon knew.

And he knew that he was prisoner, here in the heart of the desert.

The black rock reared itself out of the sands, a woodblock wave caught in stone by the hand of a greater master than any artist of old Japan. It had no equal in all the dun and gray and yellow cliffs beyond the Nile that sheltered the tombs of Pharaohs. It was a unique splinter of creation, irrational by all man's knowledge of geology, completely out of place. Yet it was there.

The demon crouched free of its shadow, sidling from the shadow as it swirled slowly over the sand in its daily sun-driven compass. He knew what lay beneath the black rock, the blacker shadow. It was the gateway to what had been his kingdom. He, Murakh, its exiled lord, must linger a beggar at the gate forever.

Forever . . . or until he fed the lords of Hell a soul.

Murakh's lost realm was not Hell. It was a place called Parvahr, a refuge and a torment for souls still embodied, souls clinging to the gray realm between good and evil. They were not dead, having never lived, and they were Murakh's chattels. He was too young a demon, as demons reckon time, to have been granted an infernal principality. Too much of the mortal world still colored him. He actually thought that some of humankind's stabs at wickedness showed real inspiration. He believed in the perfectibility of man.

Time would show whether he was right to keep such faith. Meanwhile, he was banished.

Murakh sighed and dived into the sand. He emerged spluttering, the thighbone of a monk in his claws. By rights, the bone should have been dark with age, if over a thousand years beneath the sand had spared it far enough for it to remain whole. But it was white and whole and perfect. Though flesh was consumed, after the natural order of things, little else perished in this small space of Egyptian earth. Some special grace still clung to it. Black sorcery, some would say, and the stink of old demonic magic. Others would smile and shake their heads and meditate upon the holy life of Quintus Pilaster, founder of the ill-starred monastery where Murakh's snack once had prayed, sung, and died.

Murakh didn't care. All he knew was that he was grateful to whatever power so preserved all that he found in his new territory. He was a very picky eater, and he liked his midday munchies clean.

His double rows of savagely pointed teeth ground through the thighbone with the same dispatch that its previous owner had used to bore through heretical doctrines. There was not much taste to the relic—the marrow was a memory centuries old—but it was better than nothing. Murakh was sick and tired of chasing lizards for his lunch.

A flutter of wings in the heavens made him look up sharply from his dust-dry feast. On silvery pinions like a giant swan's, a figure robed in white and light dropped slowly earthward. A palm frond was in the being's outstretched hand, and its androgynously beautiful face beamed with serene joy as it lit on the sand and knelt. Its curls were gold, its voice music.

"Hail Murakh, Lord Prince of Parvahr!"

"Lysi, I'll give you two seconds to shuck that obnoxious get-up and then I'm taking a paw to you!"

The shining visitant thrust out a luscious red underlip. The magnificent wings slumped. "Oh, *Daddy!* You never let me have any fun."

"I'm warning you. You may be a demon grown, but I'm still your sire."

"Honor thy father and thy mother?" Lysi quipped, still in angelic guise. Murakh slammed her across the wings with the well-gnawed thighbone. It splintered as it sent her sprawling in the sand.

"I didn't send you to college to have you use language like that to me, my girl!"

Lysi pushed herself up and sat cross-legged opposite Murakh. The robe, the wings, the palm, all props and vestiges of her offensive costume melted away. Her black hair stood out from her head in impossible spikes, each a half-yard long, the ends tipped with razor-sharp iron points. Her four bare breasts winked their eye-nipples saucily. At her tiny waist she wore a short kilt of leather strands that did more to accent her private parts than to conceal them. Her dainty feet were black and webbed, and in her modestly clawed hands she held a cup of gold studded with chrysoprase. It brimmed with blood.

"The Akron chapter sends you their best regards," she said, passing the cup to her father.

Murakh seized it without thanks and drank greedily, scooping the inside dry with his prehensile tongue. When he had finished, he made a face.

"Cows' blood."

"Well, honestly, Daddy, what *did* you expect from Ohio? At least you don't have to be there to listen in on all the silly gibble-gab they go through before they make the offering. It's nothing but a bunch of singles' bar strikeout artists and bored hausfraus who use us as an excuse to get naked and commit adultery. In the missionary position only, mind you. They serve cheese balls afterwards. You can't be evil with cheese balls, but do they know? Do they care? Will they even listen when I materialize in the middle of that wretched pentagram and try to give them a word of healthy advice? Oh no!"

"Oh, shut up," Murakh mumbled. "You sound just like your mother."

Lysi had her father's eyes. They kindled from red embers to the incandescence of white-hot iron. "Precious little you know about my mother," she said, glowering.

"Don't you start that again."

"It wouldn't have killed you to pay a little more attention to Mother. You used to respond every single time she summoned you, she said. That was before you knocked her up. Even then, you'd still show up every other call."

Murakh dug his chin into his chest defensively. "Didn't use the right materials." His words were barely audible.

"Well, pardon me if I just keel over laughing. You expect a pregnant woman to tear open the throat of the sacrifice with her bare hands just because you prefer it that way? The most she could manage was a chicken.''

Murakh looked just like a sulky three-year-old under his daughter's harangue. ''Yeah, well how about after she had you? She let herself go, that's all. That's always the way, once they think they've got you hooked. There was no excuse for sloppy spellcasting on that scale from a woman who was forever reminding me that *she* was a professional, *she* had worked her way up to five familiars and two genuine imp slaves, *she* didn't need me to get where she was.'' Most bitterly he concluded, ''*She* had a career!''

''Daddy, you are such a pig!''

At once, Murakh's sullen look flashed into a smile that went from ear to ear and then some. He embraced Lysi fervently. ''Ahh, now that's my sweet baby girl.''

''Yowch! Daddy, be *care*ful. You almost jabbed your claw in my eye!'' She shoved him off her and pointed an accusing finger at her left top nipple. It was blinking madly, Hellish tears already striping Lysi's ribs with their searing acid trails.

Murakh retreated into his snit. ''Some daughter. You got your mother's blood, all right.''

''The town of New Ramah, Massachusetts, got my mother's blood, and you know it. It wasn't any sort of a trial to compare with the carryings-on in Salem Village, but those poor bastards might've had the satisfaction of knowing they got the one real witch in the whole damned colony!''

''Now, Lysi, you're not going to get into *that* old story again. . . .''

''Why not? Because it reminds you that you could've saved Mother if you'd answered any one of her last *seven* summonses?''

''I was waiting for eight; 'smy lucky number.''

Lysi rolled right over her sire's weak excuse. ''Then should I shut up because you know damned well that my poor brother and I had to take to the woods to avoid going up on the same gallows with her? Children of Satan, they called us. I should be so lucky! The Princes of Hell take care of their own. We had to live like animals until you deigned to show up again and claim us!''

''As I recall it, you *were* animals. You were a raccoon and Raleel was a wolverine. He nearly tore my throat out when I cornered him.'' Murakh closed his eyes, carried away by fatherly nostalgia. "I wonder if I've still got the plaster casts of your tiny little paw prints in the palace?"

Lysi was not satisfied with her sire's reaction. It was always the same. No matter how many times she took him to task for past defaults on family matters, he never seemed to show any remorse. "Mother *died* because of you! Doesn't that mean anything?"

Murakh chuckled and tried to stroke his daughter's cheek. She pulled her head away, her spiked hair scoring his temple perilously close to the eye. "Hey! Watch it! You think everyone's got spares like you?"

Frustrated past bearing, Lysi began to weep from all six eyes at once. The lowermost pair got the worst of it as burning streams from both upper sets trickled down. "All you care about is yourself!"

Murakh leaped to his feet and shouted, "Of course I do, you dumb applebait! I'm a demon!"

Lysi wiped her eyes and nose with the back of her hand, which only added to her pains. "Maybe I ought to be more of a demon, then," she said. "Maybe I should just forget about you the way you forgot about me and Raleel and Mother. Maybe I should leave you here to rot. At least then I could keep the Hell out of Ohio."

"Now, baby . . ." Murakh made another swift dive under the sands and came out with a tatter of sackcloth, more plunder from the ancient monastery's graveyard. He dabbed at his daughter's eyes, taking especial pains with the two lower sets until she smacked him.

"You know you're not telling the whole truth, Lysi." He sat beside her again and spoke cajolingly. "When I did come back, didn't I avenge your dear dam? By the time I was through—what with fires, plagues, crop failures, massacres, wolves, slaving raids—no one could remember that there'd ever been a New Ramah, Massachusetts. There's a Burger King built on the site now, and the French fries always scream when you first stick 'em in the hot oil, but aside from that, *nada*."

After much maneuvering, Lysi managed to rest her quilly head on her sire's shoulder. "I know. I'm sorry, Daddy."

"I don't know what I'd do without you, Lysi." Murakh squeezed her, but kept it more properly paternal this time. "Raleel hardly ever comes to see me since he hit the big time. I guess the old saying's right: *A son is a son till he snags him a soul, but a daughter's forever under control.*"

"Speaking of souls, Dad, any luck?"

Lysi realized immediately that she had asked the wrong question. Her sire's claws dug into her arm. She heard his double rows of fangs grinding together rapidly, with a shin-shivering sound like a dentist's drill. The desert shook and the black rock trembled. Magic pulsed from his body, throbbed deep into the earth.

Five pillars of sand erupted from the waste, melting into molten glass as they grew. Shaping magic in a blood-red cloud gusted from Murakh's flared nostrils, molded them into the forms of demons, three male, two female. Lysi heard her sire growl the despised names as each took shape:

"Lura!"

Her small body would have been entirely human, utterly enchanting, except for the tail that twined itself up between her legs. Glass turned black, flowed from her head, braided itself into countless plaits that tinkled together on the wind of sorcery.

"Atamar!"

Nothing so handsome in all the earth, no face so angeli-cally flawless as Atamar's. But his glorious perfection was marred by the huge batwings springing from his shoulders, and though glass is scentless, Lysi caught a whiff of dung wafting from his statue.

"Horgist!"

The glass glowed yellow, sagged into the picture of lazi-ness. One absolutely circular eye seemed to droop shut even as it took shape.

"Gerial!"

Deep blue flushed the melting sand. Tusks and a tail sprang into being, and the indelible badge of mortal birth, a navel on a demon's belly.

"Melisan . . ."

This last name Murakh uttered with a loathing steeped in contempt, though Lysi could not understand why. Golden hair, exquisite naked limbs, wings like Atamar's, and liquorish eyes taunted any living man to resist their combined charms. The succubus Melisan appeared to be no better or worse than her companions.

The glazy figures shimmered in the sun. Murakh's magic

withdrew. Still they changed. The one-eyed male called Horgist sank back into the desert, slumbering. Gerial shed blue skin for mortal form and vanished into a bank of cloud. The male and female, Atamar and Lura, flowed into a single form, lust softened past the point of recognition in their joining, mutated horribly into love. Then they were laved in a golden light whose source drew them far from earth, farther still from Hell.

Only Melisan remained. The lushly naked curves of a succubus in her prime disappeared under a prissy tweed skirt, a high-necked linen blouse. Glasses perched on her nose, her golden hair was pent in the stranglehold of a bun, and her wings weren't even a memory.

"Euw!" Lysi squealed. "Gross!"

"Behold, my child, and learn from the mistakes of others," Murakh intoned. "Those five were once demons, even as you and I. Oh yes, like you! Don't think your mortal blood's a bar to full demonhood. It's all a matter of attitude. Gerial was once a full mortal, albeit a rather special one. The Princes of Hell entrusted these creatures with a simple task—so simple! They had but to take the soul of a so-called holy man of the desert, one Quintus Pilaster. The temptation of desert holy men was all the vogue in those days. Well, they failed."

"Failed? I thought desert holy men were a piece of cake. If straight temptation draws a blank, you slip on an angel suit and read them a list of lies. Mortals will believe the darndest things if you claim you've got a hot line to . . . that place." Lysi pointed heavenward. "How could they fail?"

"That doesn't matter. Suffice it to say, they did, and for their failure were condemned to roost here at the site of their debacle until they might bring down another soul. The fools! In all the centuries that passed, they muffed one chance after another! Even Atamar, and he was so grandly beautiful that he once must have been in the ranks of the Firstfallen."

"Well, Daddy, this really isn't a very well-traveled part of the world; not the best place for soul-snagging."

"Do you make excuses for them?" Murakh thundered. "You won't when you learn. They were *tainted!* Demons born and demons made, they were flawed within. From the beginning they were destined to fail, and all Hell hates a failure."

"Flawed? Tainted? You don't mean . . ." Lysi could hardly

bring herself to pronounce the shunned word. ". . . love?"
Murakh nodded. "Ucky."

"See how far the taint took them! They lost their very
demonhood, and gladly. They went their separate ways, and
for my part in failing to keep them here—exiles from Hell but
demons still, according to the will of the Princes—I was
condemned to take their place. I could bear that, child. Yes, I
could bear that. But one thought galls me day and night:
Melisan." He thrust a claw at the lone statue left standing.

Lysi studied the smooth surface. "She turned mortal."

"Worse, she made her choice for love of a mortal, a man
named Kent Cardiff. Melisan is Marguerite Cardiff now,
taken in"—he gagged—"holy wedlock. She went so far as to
bear him young; a boy-pup. I swear on the scales of Scylla, I
wish I had Marguerite and her brood here right now! I'd give
Hell such a harvest as the Princes never saw since the
Crusades!"

A rock materialized in Murakh's paw. He flung it at the
glass figure, shattering it back into its component grains of
sand.

Lysi looked thoughtful. "Marguerite Cardiff, did you say?"
A datebook fanned open in her palm as she materialized a
red-tipped vulture's quill from behind her ear. "How do you
spell that?" she asked, scribbling.

"Lysi, why do you want to—?"

She tapped her sire lightly on the lips with the quill.
"Daddy needs a soul, Lysi will help out so Daddy can kiss
this Lawrence of Arabia gig bye-bye."

"But—but—" Murakh was sputtering like an overheated
radiator. "But you can't *give* me a soul! That would be an—
an unselfish action. The Princes would have your ass!"

"What makes you think they haven't had it already? No
fear, Daddy dear. The Princes of Hell are O.K., but they're
strictly Old Country. Real stick-in-the-brimstone types. Raleel
and I were born in the U.S.A., and good old American
ingenuity counts for something. First I'll grab that soul for
you, then I'll come up with a justification that even Mephisto
will swallow." Lysi winked, but only above the neck. "A
soul, Daddy . . . a Cardiff soul. Maybe even Melisan's. Why
not take it? The first one's free."

"You would never get hers. It's too new, and therefore too
precious. She doesn't take it for granted yet."

"Her mate's, then."

Murakh was still doubtful. "Kent Cardiff is highly educated, well-read, and keeps an unbelievably open mind. It was part of the job requirements for working as a host on PBS. Also, he's Canadian. All that fresh air and unspoiled wilderness warps a mortal, makes it almost impossible to get a purchase on his soul."

"Daddy, you're not being much of a support network. Of course"—Lysi looked thoughtful—"there is still the child. Is he at the age of reason yet? I mean, has he got full sale rights to his soul?"

Her sire snickered. "It's his to dispose of as he wills. But as for the age of reason . . ." Murakh scooped up a pawful of sand. It glowed red-hot, smoke escaping through his fingers, then cooled. When he spread his hand, it cradled a crystal ball.

Lysi knelt close. She gazed into the smoking crystal and saw a great castle. Scores of young people scurried in and out of the titanic twin doors, their minds obviously as burdened as their arms.

One of them caught his foot on the steps and fell flat on his face. Books took to the air. A fellow-scurrier set down his own load and helped the fallen one to his feet.

C'mon, Noel, quit fucking around.

Lysi got a good look at the boy's face as he was hauled upright. He had his mother's bright hair, thick and gold and slightly curling, with sea-color eyes beneath dark brows.

"Oooo."

Murakh did not hear this. "There is your prize, my dear," he said. The crystal crackled, liquefied, then seeped away between his claws. "That is, if you still have a mind to help your old sire. Now you know where to find Noel Cardiff."

"Disneyland?"

Murakh cuffed her. "Idiot! That's no castle. It's a library; Sterling Memorial. Our little Noel has gone to college. Oh, but not *too* far from Mummy and Dad and New York City. Just far enough to give him the illusion of independence. Connecticut." Murakh leered, again prey to pleasant memories. "*Yale.*"

Lysi tittered. "I always did want to complete my education."

"I think you'll teach more than you learn, child."

"Oh, *Daddy!*" Lysi gave her sire a playful shove. "Then I

guess this means we have a deal? You won't object if I bring you the soul of Melisan's brat? Then we could tell her we've got him, and maybe she'd come after us, begging to have him set free, offering her own soul in exchange, crying, pleading for mercy, tearing her hair, scratching her face until the blood flows, getting runs in her stockings?''

Murakh's laughter filled the empty sky. "You do know how to tempt a body, child!'' He patted her on the backside.

"Of course I do, you dumb sulfur-sucker!'' Lysi shouted as she slapped his hand away and leaped up. "I'm a demon!''

She crossed her arms over her chest, claws sunk in her own shoulders. There was a rending sound. Her skin split open from the soles of her webbed feet to the crown of her spiked head. Minor lightnings played around the fissures. With the casual elegance of a lady stepping out of her bath, Lysi stepped out of her demon's hide.

She emerged as a slim, small, seventeen-year-old girl whose jeans fit just snugly enough for simultaneous comfort, style, and innuendo. Her black hair hung straight and shining down her back. Murakh examined the pile of books that had appeared at her feet.

"Nietzsche?'' he asked her Frye boots.

"I'm going to major in philosophy,'' Lysi said. "No sense running the risk of forgetting entirely that I'm hellspawn. Well, I'm off, Daddy.''

Murakh detained her. "Aren't you forgetting something else?''

He pointed at her chest. There were four distinct curves pushing out the front of her panda-print sweatshirt.

"Oops. Silly me.'' With a wave of her hand, Lysi consolidated her assets. The effect was gratifying. "He won't have a chance,'' she said, smiling at her sire. A curtain of sand rose up to hide her. When it fell, she was gone.

"That's my girl,'' said the demon, and sank back to wait.

1

Man Who Searches for Roots Must Get Down and Dirty

"I CAN'T BELIEVE it!" Marguerite Cardiff trilled as she bustled around the apartment. "I simply can't believe that our darling boy is coming home for the weekend."

Kent Cardiff looked up from the library fireplace. One of the electric logs was on the fritz again, and Marguerite was insistent that everything be just so for her son's return. "I don't know why you should be at all surprised, my dear," he said in his mellifluous British accent. "He's come home for a visit every weekend since matriculation."

"Oh, but isn't it dear of him not to forget us?"

"My love, how can he? You call him every day."

Marguerite's back stiffened, and her voice along with it. "Every *other* day."

"I stand corrected." Kent Cardiff went back to fiddling with the plastic kindling. He extracted the shattered remnants of a meerschaum from the tangled wires backing the offending log.

"I say . . ." He screwed up his mouth and gave his lovely wife the one-brow-up quizzing look. It never failed to extract the truth from waffling guests on his show. That look, coupled with his Oxonian intonation and backed by a custom-shabbied tweed suit, always put folks in mind of Empire, pukka-sahibs, chota pegs, puttees, solar topees, Lord Kitchener, "Chinese" Gordon, the White Man's Burden, and no-demmed-nonsense-out-of-you-me-buck. A few lesser souls also recalled the Falkland Islands.

Unfortunately, "the look" had no such effect on Cardiff's wife. "Why are you doing a Mr. Spock imitation at me?" she demanded.

Kent dropped the look immediately and took the direct approach. "I have been searching for this pipe all over. Now I find it destroyed and hidden away. I wish to know who is responsible." He gave Marguerite a hard stare that told her he *knew* who was responsible and the guilty party might 'fess up at her earliest convenience.

Marguerite laughed and snatched the white shards from his hand. "So *that's* where I threw it! You'd left it smoldering on the end table again, after I'd asked and asked you not to do that. So I lost my temper and smashed the silly thing, then tossed it away." She let the remnants fall. "I certainly have enough to do in my life without forever picking up after your clutter. The Women's Club alone could give Beelzebub lessons in eternal bondage. And just the other day the Museum Committee called me and asked—"

"That was a priceless antique!" Kent raised his voice, an unheard-of proceeding. He usually kept it level, rational, and well-modulated. When he lost his temper, his dearly acquired British accent slipped and his vowels skidded all the way back to Toronto.

"Then you should have taken better care of it. It's not as if you weren't warned."

Kent's mouth opened, then shut. He sagged on the hearthrug. "What's the good of arguing with you, Marguerite? Your people have a justified reputation for being able to argue black into white and back again."

Marguerite's large eyes grew wickedly narrow behind her gold-rimmed glasses. "Are you speaking of demons . . . or Democrats?"

The urbane host of *World Insight* bit his lower lip. He had plunged headlong into deep trouble, and he knew it. There had been no living with Marguerite since she'd taken that accursed Jane Fonda exercise program at the health club and come home with a tightened derrière and a raised consciousness. She had changed her voter registration that week, and fruitlessly attempted to make him give up his beloved pipes. He failed to follow how she linked shag tobacco to the crisis in Nicaragua, but she managed. He gave himself ten minutes of life before she started blaming him for the slaughter of baby harp seals.

"I referred to the former," he replied, crawling backward into an invisible shell. "You know I'd never stoop to mud-slinging on the political level."

"Merely on the racial."

"Really, my pet, you can't very well tell me that demons form a uniform racial group."

"Ethnic, then."

"Hardly. And don't say 'religious.' You know it won't wash. Your folk are an unclassifiable minority group."

Marguerite laughed. "Minority? That's all you know of the world!" She flung herself down on the rug beside her husband and threw her arms around his neck. "My poor innocent, no wonder I love you so much!"

Beneath her oxford-cloth blouse and corduroy skirt, eighteen years of mortal life had been very generous to Marguerite-Melisan. She had lost nothing of the expertise her centuries as a succubus had brought her, and she had even managed to add some tidbits to that vast store of information, from a subscription to the Frederick's of Hollywood catalog. Though Kent's hair was now as tweedy as his wardrobe, his whilom-demon wife still managed to startle his senses into surprising reactions.

He did not remember the meerschaum fragments on the floor until it was too late.

"Why is Dad in the library, eating off the mantelpiece?" Noel asked his mother at Friday night supper.

Marguerite cleared her throat and did not look up from the shallow bowl of chilled watercress soup before her. "It's a new diet, darling. If you dine standing up, you won't eat as much."

"Oh, for—" A loud snort erupted from the direction of the library. "Gad, Marguerite, must you *always* shelter the boy?"

Kent Cardiff came ramping into the dining room, ignoring its breathtaking view of Park Avenue by night. "If you want to know why I'm eating on my feet like a bloody carthorse, Noel, it's because I got jabbed by a broken piece of my favorite pipe right in the—"

"*Kent!*" Marguerite strangled her napkin, a warning.

It was too late. Noel was chortling. "How'd you manage that, Dad?"

Kent dared to give his wife a wry smile. "Most enjoyably. Don't pry into the affairs of your elders too far, son. You might find out we're human." He fetched a downy pillow from the living room sofa and lowered himself gingerly into his usual place at the head of the Queen Anne table.

"Well, I hate to contradict you, Dad—"

"You mean you've proof we're not human after all?"

"Kent, you're not being funny." Marguerite's napkin was twisted into a Turk's-head knot.

"—but that's exactly why I've come home this weekend. I've got a load of prying to do."

Kent poured himself a glass of Zinfandel and offered to serve Marguerite. She slapped her hand over the top of her glass and scowled at him. Imperturbable before most wifely snits, Kent shrugged, sipped, and said, "And here I thought you enjoyed our company. You know, I do think Yale stays open on the weekends. Why don't you stay over once and find out? There must be lots to do—movies, football games, subversive organizations, girls. . . ."

Noel became enraptured by his watercress soup.

"Don't fret, son. It's early in the year yet. Your social life will pick up, but I think it would improve all the sooner if you hung about campus more."

"Noel's social life is all right!" Marguerite snapped, clearing the bowls. She brought a covered dish from the sideboard and unveiled cold poached salmon in aspic. She did not give a plate to her husband, who had to fetch his own, at great personal pains. This was a snit of the royal breed.

"Marguerite," Kent said between clenched teeth. "Marguerite dear, you would find no fault with Noel's social life even if he became a monk."

"Over my dead body!"

The dining room atmosphere froze. Ice crystals could almost be seen forming between Kent and Marguerite. Noel looked from one parent to the other, completely bemused.

"Hey, Mom, don't worry," he said, trying to lighten the air. He did wonder why his mother was so vehemently against the conventual life. The only monks he'd ever encountered were on bottles of spirits and olive oil or jars of preserves. "I'm not planning on getting measured for a sackcloth suit, y'know? I mean, I'm not even taking Religion this term. Anthro's enough of a pain. You know what our assignment for Monday is? We're studying kinship systems, so Dr. Paulinus told us to trace our own family trees back at least four generations, then document it. I might as well be a monk, with a load like that to do over the weekend. Anyhow, that's why I'm here. I kinda hoped we could get the names down tonight and I could bop over to the Public Library or some-where tomorrow to get any proof you can't give me.''

Marguerite rose from the table. "Out of the question," she said, and left. Her husband and son heard the front door slam a few moments later.

"What's wrong with Mom?" Noel asked.

"The French nuked another whale this morning. It was in all the papers," Kent replied blandly. "Pass the salmon."

Kent sat up in bed and switched on the light. "About time you came home," he said. "I was considering calling the police."

Marguerite shucked off her London Fog and let it drop across the banquette at the foot of the bed. "You know I have no worries on the streets," she said wearily.

"I do, though I've never fully understood why it should be so."

"The dower laws of Hell." She sat down and removed her shoes. "Each demon that escapes the ranks still carries a little of the infernal aura away with him. It's like being sprayed by a skunk. You never can get away from it entirely."

"Ah. That explains that little incident at Noel's christen-ing. I remarked to Father Jonathan that it must be beastly hot weather for the font to bubble. He, being a gentleman, urged me to give it no further thought."

Marguerite sighed. "The aura is a warning to other de-mons, like the leper's bell. They can sense it, and are advised to take immediate evasive action. We renegades are a bad influence." She smiled wanly. "It has its uses, though. For some reason it also seems to warn off the more hell-bent among ordinary mortals. I could walk naked through Central Park with a pot of gold on my head and no one would touch me. They'd be seized by irrational fear and they'd run away."

"Is that where you were? Naked in the park?"

If Kent were trying to establish his reputation as a come-dian, he did not make the cut. Marguerite covered her face with her hands and began to cry.

"Oh, I say!" He caught his feet in the sheets and almost fell out of bed in his haste to embrace her. "Dearest, what's wrong? Tell me."

Marguerite lifted her chin. "You know very well what's wrong! Oh Kent, you know what a diligent student our son is. He won't be content to leave this nasty, snoopy, muckraking anthropology assignment half done.''

"I daresay not. It's more than half done already. We spent a very interesting evening, Noel and I, tracing the Cardiffs back more than the required four generations. I was able to shake him off the scent just before we got to my less reputable relations. They were wreckers on the coast of Cornwall in the eighteenth century. You know, the sort of folk who put up false beacons to lure ships onto the rocks, then butchered all the passengers and crew unlucky enough to survive? Less unpleasantness over the salvage that way.''

"Oh, hang your Cornish ancestors!''

"They did.''

"What are we going to do about *me?*''

"Mmmm, yes.''

Marguerite clung to her husband, waiting for him to say more. When a good stretch of silence had passed, she became restive. "Well? Haven't you any ideas?''

"My love, at the risk of sounding Manichaean, I'd say we have two choices: Tell him the truth or lie like the—the dickens.''

"The truth's impossible. You'll have to help me make up a plausible set of ancestors. He knows my maiden name was Gounod. . . .'' Marguerite steepled her fingers and knit her brow in concentration.

"I wouldn't suggest claiming kinship with the composer. That would take you over very thin ice indeed. Darling, don't lose sleep inventing your pedigree. As you said, our son is diligent, and the second part of his assignment was to substantiate the genealogy. He'd accept not being able to find the fourth-generation-back Gounods, but when you tell him you can't even produce evidence to prove that you had parents—''

"All the records were destroyed during World War II!''

"Good. Nice improvisation. Where?''

"A small town in France. I'll pick one out of *Michelin.*''

"Make sure it has a good hotel. We might have to leave town in a hurry when the boy disowns us. Your passport says you were born in the United States, and Noel's seen it. If your parents emigrated from France, there would be records of their arrival at Ellis Island or some other port of entry.''

"They were stowaways!''

"I don't think you'll get Noel to swallow the notion of French wetbacks."

"My grandparents were the ones who came over."

"Then where are your parents' birth records, their school records, their Social Security records, their income tax records? Where and when did they die and where are they buried?"

"Montreal!" Marguerite sounded both shrill and desperate.

"I hate to shatter your illusions, but we Canadians have been known to keep track of our citizens, too. Give it up, Marguerite. The time has come to tell the boy the truth, that's all."

Marguerite sank back against her husband. He could smell the strange perfume she always wore, a mortality gift from her old companion Lura. It had last been distilled by the holy prostitutes of a sand-lapped temple near the black rock. The ersatz American passport for herself and some vital documents for the infant Noel had been Atamar's tokens of good wishes and farewell. From their new positions, Marguerite's former associates were able to pull some very substantial strings.

"Kent, I'm afraid. How shall I put it? How will he react?"

He gave her a bear hug. "I can't predict Noel's reaction, but I'll tell you this much: You won't have to do it alone. I'll stand by you, never fear."

"I wish now we'd told him earlier. Children are so much more flexible than adolescents. I suppose it's no worse than learning you're adopted."

"Not at all. I'll wager you ten dollars, cash on the barrel head, that he's less shocked by this than he was when he heard I voted for Nixon."

Marguerite smiled wholeheartedly for the first time that night. "I'll take that bet, Kent. And I'll tell him tomorrow morning."

After Noel stopped pacing back and forth through the apartment, from foyer to butler's pantry, repeatedly shouting "You're a *what?!*" every time he passed his mother, Kent handed Marguerite a ten-dollar bill. She let it fall to the floor, where Noel soon trampled it into the Karastan.

At last she reached out and grabbed her son on one of his

passes, pushing him into a wing chair with so much force that the upholstery studs threatened to pop.

"You're kidding. You've got to be. This is a joke, right? You're not what you said. How could you be? There's no such things! You're a *what?!*" Noel's babbling subsided eventually. He slumped back in the chair, arms flopped over the sides, and sought his father's face.

If he hoped Kent would give him the good news that Mom was merely insane, he was soon disappointed.

"Your mother is telling you the truth, son. She was—mark me, I said *was*—a demon."

"This is the stupidest joke I ever heard. Come *on*, Dad, get real. A demon? Yeah, sure, right. And I'm the Easter Bunny."

"Don't be silly, Noel," Marguerite said briskly. "You've known since you were six that there's no such thing as the Easter Bunny."

"There are no such things as demons!"

"How do you know?" Kent took the chair opposite his son and crossed his legs. With brows raised and fingertips lightly touching, he needed but a camera or two to complete the picture of talk-show host in pursuit of quarry.

"*Everyone* knows there's no such things."

"Ah." The fingertips played pat-a-cake. "There is no less reliable source than *everyone,* and it's about time you learned that. *Everyone* has been responsible for the tale of the chicken-fried rat, the exploding poodle in the microwave oven, and the popular soft drink used for birth contr—"

"*Kent!*" Marguerite was scandalized. She positioned herself behind the wing chair and seized her son firmly by the shoulders. "Please don't be so graphic. Noel isn't interested."

"Well, the method of birth control in question wouldn't affect him, my love, and he only drinks Dr. Pepper."

Noel tried to squirm free of his mother's protective grip and failed. "Hey, look," he said. "I don't know what all this stuff's about or why you're messing with me like this, but it's pretty weird, you know? And I don't like weirdness. You want to drive me crazy, you're gonna have to prove your facts."

Kent glanced at his wife, still hovering behind Noel's chair like Merlin's pet owl. "Here's a wrinkle you never thought of, darling. The lad's a conservative."

Marguerite sighed. "I suppose I knew the day would come

when the truth would have to be told, but I never expected so much resistance to it. Proof? What sort of proof can I give you, Noel, beyond my word?''

''If you're a demon, what good's your word?''

''Don't get snippy with your mother!'' Kent's frown wiped the smug grin from Noel's face. ''And above all, don't start spouting paradoxes at this hour of the morning. It's not only juvenile, it's boring. We shall be hearing the old omnipotent-God-and-the-immovable-rock one next.''

Noel became truculent. ''I don't need this sh—this stuff. I should be at the library right now, getting some *real* answers. I've got work to do! I only took Anthro for the distribution requirements. Now I wish I'd taken Linguistics or something.''

''Perish the thought.'' Kent rose from his chair and checked his Rolex. ''You want proof, do you? Very well. The library should be open about now. Why don't we all take a little stroll down the avenue? It will be most enlightening.''

Kent kept a watchful eye on his son and heir as Marguerite slowly turned the pages of the huge folio volume before them all. His muscles tensed, ready to clap a hand over Noel's mouth the moment they got to *that* page.

Kent knew *that* page. He'd come across it himself some dozen or so years back while researching an interview with Dr. Pandolfo Francati, author of *The Philistines: Pagan Pacesetters of Palestine*. One look at *that* page, and Dr. Francati's attempt to squeeze Goliath into the mold of an antique yuppie with gland trouble was forgotten.

A leaf turned. *That* page surfaced. Noel leaped from his seat, and Kent clapped the suppressing hand down hard. No one else occupying the reading room paid them any mind. Marguerite just shook her head.

''He never did get my good side,'' she said.

Noel peeled his father's hand from his mouth. He pointed one trembling finger at the sleek, glossy photograph of an ancient fresco from the temple of Dagon near Ekron. The band of merrymakers captured in the act were showing a lot of enthusiasm, though their activities were more proper to Astarte's cult.

Maybe it was part of an ecumenical movement, Kent reflected. To his son's unasked question, he replied in a library hush, ''Yes, Noel, that *is* your mother. Amazing likeness, even without taking the local artistic conventions into account. She doesn't have the wings anymore, but there's no mistaking the face.''

Noel shook his head violently. He was not an easy party to persuade. Kent understood what the boy was going through. He recalled how he'd come near to getting booted out of the reading room himself when he'd come across the incriminating photograph. He had stormed home and confronted Marguerite with the evidence.

She had looked up from the L.L.Bean catalog in her lap and calmly said, ''You knew I was no angel when you married me. Do I come round chucking your past at your feet like a terrier with a dead rat to show off? And I don't see what's bothering you. That's all ancient history! You know I'm far too busy these days to go mucking about at orgies. Besides, no one invites us, and I wouldn't go if they did. Uncontrolled sexuality is always the inadequate hostess' excuse for serving second-rate food. Even the Philistines knew that.''

Somehow, Kent thought, Noel wasn't going to be as easily pacified.

Marguerite took Noel's arm and steered him from the reading room. Too well-brought up to violate the holy silence of the library, the boy kept his peace until the three of them were outside, gazing down the tiered steps at the broad white backs of the huge stone lions. Marguerite marched him down until they reached the left-hand lion's plinth and there she made him sit.

''Yes, that was me in the fresco.'' She planted hands on hips. ''I can show you a half-dozen additional examples, though none with as good a likeness. There were others too, but they've yet to be unearthed. Even back then, I did my best to encourage the fine arts, and I've heard I was an inspiration. I have sat for Sumerian, Egyptian, Persian, Assyrian, and Babylonian painters, sculptors, and—''

'' 'Sat' might not be the word for it.''

''Oh, shut up, Kent.'' Marguerite's eyes flashed behind their gold-rimmed glasses. She took a seat beside her son and continued in a gentler tone. ''But that was a long time ago, sweetheart. Biiiiillions and biiillions of— Well, thousands of years ago, anyway. And it's all over. It's done with. I renounced my demonhood when I met your father and had you.''

Noel spread his hands and stared at them. "You can't do that. I mean, once you're damned, that's it.'' He raised his eyes to his mother's. "Isn't it?''

She put her arm around him and felt him shudder, then relax reluctantly. "Let's go home, dear. I'll tell you all about it.''

As they wended their way crosstown, she released her hold on the boy to fall back a few paces and speak to her husband. "That wasn't so bad after all." She had the radiant smile of a person recently relieved of a great burden. "You were right, Kent. I'm glad the truth's come out at last.''

"Told you so." He squeezed her hand.

Well ahead of his parents, Noel paused before the window of a croissanteria on Forty-second Street. He stared glumly at the rows of horn-shaped flaky pastries set out to tempt the public appetite to new excesses of socially approved gluttony.

Horns . . . he thought. *Temptation . . . appetite . . . gluttony, wrath, sloth, envy, pride, avarice . . . What was that other one?*

"Damnation," he said aloud.

It was well for Marguerite that Mother's Day was still some eight months away.

2

Behind Every Great Man

NOEL SPRAWLED ON the shopworn sofa in the living area of his dormitory suite. He had all the *joie de vivre* of a half-cooked pancake, but he didn't feel like keeping his misery pent up in his tiny bedroom. Life had dealt him a blow of great magnitude, a shock and disillusionment from which he might never recover. It was not unthinkable that eventually he would be forced to turn to drink, or worse, in order to forget what his mother's past had done to him.

Taking all this into consideration, he decided that he owed it to his four roommates to let them know that their cramped little world was about to turn into a den of irredeemable, self-destructive, concerted, and conscious vice and decadence.

Who could tell? One of them might even know some upperclassman old enough to buy liquor in one of the New Haven "packies" and offer to split costs.

Alas for Noel's dreams of sensual abandonment, his roomies had other fish to fry. Decadence was all right for the weekend, but Luis was pre-med, Jonathan a computer freak, and Bradley was already studying the entrance requirements for the top business schools in the country. They flashed through the living area like fireflies, offering little more than a grunt of greeting and farewell as they went about their own business.

Only Roger lingered.

Roger Tagliaferro was a six-foot-two green-eyed blond with shoulders so broad and muscular that when he'd first shown up at the suite, the others took side-bets as to whether he'd have to tilt sideways to pass through the narrow doors. He soon showed them that whether or not he had to do an Immelman to get in and out of his bedroom, he never lacked for female companions to help him execute this and other, more complicated maneuvers. When the phone rang and a soprano voice was on the line, no one bothered asking who she wanted. The receiver was passed to Roger by reflex.

Now, Roger poked his damp head out of the bathroom door and inquired, "Still here, Noel?" He pronounced the name to rhyme with *bowl*. Roger's Midwestern accent was the only thing more developed than his libido—the Curse of Kokomo, he called it.

"Yeah." Noel heaved a deep sigh. "Still here."

"Thought so." The blond head ducked back into the bathroom and an electric razor buzzed to life. Roger was not much given to the *60 Minutes* bloodhound style of investigative living.

"*Damn it!*" Noel jerked the sofa pillow out from behind his head and threw it at the fireplace. It hit the mantel, where it sent Bradley's three sailing trophies and Luis' Yale mug crashing down.

The electric razor was turned off. Roger opened the bathroom door again. "What is it, you cutting classes or you're unhappy or you're just fucking around or what?"

"It's nothing." Noel slumped farther back, a move made easier by the missing pillow. "Leave me alone."

"Oh." Roger nodded. Naked, damp, and half-shaven, he flopped himself down on the sofa beside his roommate. "So what's her name?"

"*Her* name? How do you know it's a *her?*"

The shoulders that haunted inventive dreams shrugged. "I don't, but I figured it was a good place to start guessing. Unless you're gay?" Noel denied this vehemently, and in the process admitted that his melancholy thoughts did indeed center on a woman. "O.K., I guessed right. Who is she? The one you go back to New York to see every weekend?"

Noel tried to utter a bitter laugh, reeking of world-weariness. He did a commendable job, for a novice. "You might say that. Yeah, you might."

"I just did. So how about an answer?"

"She's my mother."

"Whoa!" Roger tried to jump away, but his bare flesh had adhered to the corduroy-covered cushion under him. He raised his hand to ward off unnecessary weirdness. "Look, I know I'm no expert or anything, but you don't look like someone with parent troubles. You look like you found out your girlfriend's been shopping around behind your back."

"Perceptive, Roger; very perceptive. You got it."

"You mean your mother's been . . . ?" Roger liked less and less of what he was hearing. Where he came from, you could still depend on America to hold fast to the old values of Home, Family, and Covered-Dish Church Suppers. The only people who committed adultery were characters on *Dynasty, Dallas,* and *Knot's Landing,* and in songs like "You Tried to Make Me Take a Credit Card for Love in the Cash-Only Checkout Lane of My Heart." (Show business types no longer counted as potential adulterers. So few of them got married in the first place.) "Your *mother?*"

Noel nodded.

"Holy shit." Roger sat back, stunned. When his high school guidance counselor had said that Yale would be an educational experience, had this been what he meant? Feeling very edgy near so sensitive a topic as a mother's sins, Roger asked, "Your dad . . . How's he taking this?"

"Oh, he doesn't care."

"Wow." So this was what living in New York City did to people. It made them blasé in the face of immorality.

Ta-ta, darling, I'm off to have an affair!

Mind popping by Zabar's on your way home and picking us up some pâté?

Roger could not visualize his own father taking similar knowledge so cavalierly; nor himself, for that matter. What good was the sanctity of marriage if you couldn't go apeshit when you learned your mate had been cheating? Roger made a mental note to live nowhere more exotic than Muncie when he graduated, where adultery still counted for something.

"My father knew all about it when he married her," Noel went on. "He says its all in the past, it's over with, and he loves her, so why should it matter?"

"The past? You mean she hasn't done anything since?"

"Hey, what do you think my mother *is?*" Noel glared at his roommate.

"Hold it; rewind. You're telling me your mother hasn't done anything *recently,* but that she—uh—*did* stuff in the past? Like, before she was married to your father?"

"I'll say she *did* stuff."

"And you found out about it, and that's why you're upset? Because of something she did before she was married?"

"You got it."

"Uh-huh. I see." Roger nodded sagely. "Noel, you are possibly the biggest jerk it's ever been my privilege to know."

"*Hey!*" Noel sprang up, intending to belt Roger a good one, but midway between leaping from the sofa and landing on the floor, the side of the brain governing self-preservation and good sense took over. Roger was a good five inches and forty pounds up on him. Noel's fists uncurled, rage died, and moping reasserted itself. "You don't know what I'm going through," he said miserably. "This is my mother I'm talking about."

"Noel, I've seen pictures of your mother. She's a real classy-looking lady. You ever really think she didn't have any social life until your father came along?"

"She had a social life like you wouldn't believe."

"O.K., so what's the problem? Look, I know it's tough for a kid the first time he learns the facts—*My* parents did *that* to have *me?*—but that's for twelve-year-olds! Don't tell me every girl you ever dated was a virgin."

Noel kept quiet. Virginity was a touchy subject with him, especially when the conversation might so easily turn to the subject of his own carefully hidden lack of experience. Roger did not pick up on his friend's silence and continued, oblivious.

"You probably won't marry a virgin, either. If you're going to call everyone to task for their pasts, you're going to live a mighty lonely life, man."

Noel flumped back onto the sofa and covered his eyes with an upflung arm. "You don't understand. You can't. And I can't explain it, either."

"That," Roger said, peeling the adherent cushion from his behind as he stood up, "is your problem. How do you know what I'll understand? Look, forget it. I'm here if you ever change your mind about talking it out, but I've got a class in fifteen. See you." He vanished into his own cubicle and shut the door.

Noel sighed. He wished he could talk about it. It wasn't the fact of his mother's past that had him so upset right now. He had gotten over the initial shock by Sunday brunch. Something there was about sufficient quantities of smoked salmon and brioches, consumed in the tastefully understated peach-and-green environs of one of Manhattan's finer hotel restaurants, that made any revelation palatable, even the fact that Mom had been a succubus. But then, just as he had come to terms with Marguerite's supernatural origins, she dropped the other shoe.

It's just as well you finally know the truth, Noel, she said, toying with her caviar omelette. *You're still fairly young, but you won't be a child forever.*

He's not a child now, Marguerite, Kent broke in. *Everyone but you seems to realize that.*

Marguerite shot her husband a brief, chilling glance and continued as if he had not spoken at all. *When you were born, I was still . . . what I was. I did not lose my original nature until shortly after your birth. Therefore, while I am no expert on the laws of genetics, I have always been aware of the possibility that you—that you—* Her fork described complex arabesques as she searched for the proper words.

That you might be half a hellspawn; genetically speaking, that is, Kent finished for her. *With all the occult powers and abilities pertaining thereto.* To her yip of outrage he replied, *Dear girl, don't carry on so. You and I both know how silly such a theory is. So does Noel. He's a sensible boy, and he's no more touched by demonic magic than I. It's all your ridiculous pussyfooting around the subject that makes it seem more significant than it is.*

Of course it's significant! Since Noel knows what I used to be, he should know the whole story. It involves him—deeply, perhaps.

Noel set down his own fork. *How deeply?*

Son, don't worry about it, Kent said, stuffing shag in his pipe for a post-brunch puff. *I'm no expert, but I'd be willing to wager that sorcery's a recessive trait. Like blue eyes, don't y'know?*

Sorcery? Noel's voice shook. He had blue eyes.

Now who's making things sound worse than they are? Marguerite put an arm about her son's shoulders. *Darling, you mustn't pay any attention to Daddy. He hasn't a Republican's idea of what he's talking about. You just listen to me. I've seen more than one human-demon match in my time, and statistically speaking, the odds are two-to-one in favor of your not showing any aptitude for magic at all.*

I always thought it was a learned skill, Kent remarked, tamping in more tobacco. *Like football.*

Marguerite hugged a progressively stiffer and stiffer Noel. *There, that shows you exactly how little he knows about it, precious. Anyone can learn to play that nasty old game, but it takes a true travesty of birth to make fullback material. You can fool around all you like with mumbo jumbo and pentagrams and goats—and I do hope you will not associate with anyone who bothers with goats, Noel—but in the end, it takes that certain spark in the blood to make a real wizard, witch, or warlock. It goes way back, all the way to Lilith's time, in fact. Her mortal descendants by Adam have the hidden potential for sorcery that study only brings out and develops; Eve's never had it, never will.*

Noel did not seem reassured by his mother's merry chatter. He stared straight ahead, eyes fixed on his father's briar pipe. Kent had finished stuffing it to his satisfaction and was now patting the pockets of his jacket for matches. His hand-ballet distracted Marguerite from her recitation.

What are you looking for? she demanded irritably.

I'd like to light my pipe.

Well, here! She tossed him the paper book of matches with the restaurant's name embossed on the cover.

Kent ignored them. *You know I only light my pipe with wooden matches. Paper makes it taste almost as revolting as lighter fluid.* He continued searching his pockets, while Marguerite scowled. *I could have sworn I had them—*

A pinpoint of red light kindled on the briar's lip, gleaming like an insect's eye. The light became a tiny diamond, sending strands of fire lacing through the tamped tobacco. A thin trail of smoke squirmed out of the pipe bowl and twined toward the ceiling. Kent saw it rise, drew in his breath sharply, and choked on a lungful. While Marguerite pounded him on the back and fended off overeager Heimlich-trained diners from adjacent tables, Noel stood up from his seat.

I thought it was worth a try, he said glumly. *Not bad for someone with no training, huh? Thanks, Mom; Dad. Thanks a whole lot.* He went straight from the brunch table to Grand Central Station and took the next train back to New Haven.

"Excuse me, Roger," Noel said to his roommate's closed door. "I've decided to talk about it. I'm a little upset because I'm half demon and I can set fires with my eyes and I'm not sure what other little goodies are hiding in my DNA and I didn't even get my Anthro homework finished. Think you can help me deal with all that? Sure you can. Sure."

The sounds of Roger's class-preparations seeped through

the door. Heavy objects slammed and drawers squealed. Noel could just imagine Roger searching the slag-pile on top of his desk for the appropriate texts and notebooks. The class was American History, one of the survey courses that Noel himself had considered signing up for. Now he was glad he'd changed his mind. It wouldn't do to take the Salem Witchcraft Trials as a family insult.

He hauled himself off the sofa. He too had a class scheduled shortly. He'd been thinking about cutting it, but now he no longer cared enough to take even that much action. He would go, sit through it, make a few notes or doodles that had nothing to do with what the teacher was saying, in general behave like a piece of meat with eyes. And since it was a freshman English course, he doubted very much that the instructor would even notice.

"Might as well," he sighed. "What the hell else could happen to me?"

She saw Noel in the last seat of the back row and smiled. She had been searching the campus for him since her arrival, perching on battlements, playing camouflage corps with the stone grotesques decorating the Law School buildings, fluttering invisible around the towers of Sterling Memorial Library, even lowering herself to human-form socializing with the apartheid protesters camped out on Beinecke Plaza. At last she spotted him leaving his dormitory on Old Campus.

She cursed the necessity that forced her to seek him using mortal senses alone. A short phone call to Raleel, telling him her plans for the Cardiff sprat, had elicited a slough of unasked-for advice. Nonetheless, it was wise to heed Raleel. You didn't get to be a demon in his powerful position by being stupid.

"Don't use your magic to find him," he'd cautioned. "Magic always leaves some sign it's been there. It's like setting off the smoke detectors for one lousy cigarette when you could be burning down the orphanage. Dis knows what sort of detectors are hanging around Melisan's brat. The bitch had connections, and she might've set up some sort of protection around him before she went mortie on us."

Lysi listened to her twin brother. There was no sense in taking chances. It was more work to find Noel by the disdained "mortie" senses, but she had time enough, and here was the payoff. Phase One complete: prey *en passant*.

"Excuse me, but I believe you're in my seat."

The lecture hall was just settling down before the grand entrance of the very bored grad student charged with pounding *Beowulf* through forty skulls. The young man seated next to Noel Cardiff treasured his back-row seat, a safe haven for undisturbed slumber, and wasn't about to give it up—not even for a girl as lovely as the dark-haired vision now bending over him.

"No assigned seats," he growled.

"It's still mine," she replied, her smile and voice sweet enough to dust the ear with powdered sugar. "Won't you be a dear and move?"

"There's plenty of other seats. Try the front row."

"You try it."

The young man opened his mouth to speak, then snapped it shut. His face turned crimson by degrees. Helpless, panic-stricken, he slowly looked down at his lap. He could not understand it. He didn't like *Beowulf* that much.

Very, very softly Lysi said, "Now I'm going to give you one more chance to move, and then I'm going to say your girlfriend's name. When I do, you will experience one brief moment of ecstasy followed by an incredibly long walk back to your dorm room, with everyone staring at you and knowing exactly what happened—such being the risks of wearing light-colored jeans. But don't worry; you won't have to put up with such an embarrassing situation again. Not ever. Not for as long as you live. We are talking a lifetime one-shot here. Get my drift?"

"How can you . . . ?"

". . . promise so much? The same way I did *that* to you." An eloquent lift of the eyebrows indicated the lad's precarious condition. "Trust me; you don't want to know more. Now *will* you be so kind as to give me my chair?" She batted her eyelashes with charming abandon.

Hunched over to conceal his state, with a looseleaf binder shielding his interests, Lysi's victim scuttled out of his seat and into one of the vacant slots in the front row. Noel watched him go.

"How did you do that?" he asked as Lysi slipped her slender derrière into the vacated seat.

"Sshhh." An almond-shaped nail was laid to her lips. She nodded toward the front of the room where the instructor was riffling his index cards and clearing his throat for attention. Her spiral notebook was open, her face uplifted to drink in the wisdom of the ages. She did not take her eyes from the barrel-shaped man at the podium for the duration of the class, and Noel did not take his eyes from her. If there was a lecture, or if the instructor stripped naked and did aardvark imitations, Noel never noticed.

When class ended, he tried to take up the conversation. "How did you *do* that?" he insisted.

"Do what?" She was utterly guileless, and her innocent expression made Bambi look like a pimp by comparison. Noel had the impression of standing on the brink of a dark, bottomless pool and seeing how far over he could lean before he tumbled in. Then her eyelashes fell in a silky curtain and cut off the spell. "I haven't the faintest idea what you mean," she said. "All I did was ask for my seat."

"But there aren't any assigned seats."

"Really?" The miraculous eyes went wider. An invisible fist punched Noel in the chest. "Silly me." She gathered up her books.

"Uh . . . Do you have another class after this?" Noel shoved his own things together. It was getting stifling in the classroom, even though most of the other students had already left.

"I'm not sure. I'll have to check my schedule. You see, I'm not familiar with anything yet. I've just transferred here from Smith."

"Gee, Smith, huh?" He fell into step beside her as they followed the trickle of students out of the lecture room, down the oak-paneled corridors, and out into the bright fall sunlight. "Smith . . . How about that. So, um, how did you like Smith? I had a friend in high school who went to Smith. Just a friend-friend. Did you know . . . ?"

Lysi let him babble. She was enjoying this. Her appearance was calculated to reduce a young man of Noel's age to ninnyhood, and she was pleased to see it working so well. She stopped in the middle of the street, flipped open her notebook, pretended to study something in it and said, "Oh. isn't that nice? I don't have a class right now."

Noel almost bit his tongue in his rush to ask, "Would you like to go get a cup of coff—"

"I can go to the library and work on my paper. That *is* Sterling over there, isn't it?" She pointed at the pseudo-medieval pile dominating the next block.

"I can walk you over!" Noel blurted.

"If it's not out of your way." She broke into an easy stride and Noel scrambled after her.

"Maybe I can show you around the library. If you just transferred here, it can be hard finding what you want. What's your paper about? What class is it for?"

She stopped short at the corner, ostensibly because the traffic light had turned red. Noel bumped into her well-rounded rump and jumped back. Lysi's mouth quirked up slightly at one corner. This would be too simple! The boy showed all the classic symptoms of virginity, and male virgins were such desperately easy prey that the more sporting succubi limited themselves to bagging no more than two a year, to preserve the species.

"It's for another English class I'm taking," she said. "American Verse. I'm doing a paper on the role of Satanism in the poetry of Walt Whitman."

The color left Noel's cheeks.

"Oh, I see you've read Whitman," Lysi said.

"No, I—That is, *O Captain! My Captain!* in junior high, but—Satanism? In *Whitman?*"

"Mmm-hmm." She threaded her arm through his. "You can find Satanism in everything if you've got the right sort of mind and you look hard enough. I think it's just the most fascinating thing. I've always been drawn to evil. It's exciting. Very exciting." The light changed and she bore him across the street, skillfully allowing his forearm to brush the generously curved front of her sweatshirt. By the time they reached the far curb, Noel was in a light sweat.

"But evil—" He tried to protest and found his reasons wanting. "Evil is so—so—"

"Wicked?" Lysi gave a throaty chuckle that raised goosebumps in the darndest places. "Wickedness can be very educational. Does the idea of sin frighten you? Of evil? Of demonic influences?" *Because if it does, I'm out of your life right now, wimp, and you'll spend forever kicking yourself for letting me go,* was what her tone conveyed.

"Of course not," Noel said. And suddenly he believed his own lie. Gaining courage, he added, "I could tell you stuff about demonic influences that would scare the pants off—that would scare you pretty bad."

"I doubt it." Lysi snuggled closer. "We witches don't scare easily."

"You're a witch?"

"Don't stare at me like that. The warts are all undercover. Surprised? Did you think all witches were hideous old hags?"

"No, but I sure didn't think any of them went to Smith."

Lysi's lips parted in a smile that could only be called tempting. "Why do you think I transferred?"

3

Fresh Air and Filthy Minds

LIKE MANY A freshman with dangerous leanings toward the Humanities, Noel circled the topic of choosing a major cautiously, occasionally poking it with a stick to see which way it lunged and which way he should jump to avoid it. All that changed with the advent of Lysi. (Or Lysistrata Damon, as she styled herself in the student directory.)

"I want to major in Religious Studies," Noel informed his freshman advisor. "Here are my transfer cards."

The advisor shook his head dubiously. "It's a little late in the term. Are you sure you can catch up with all the work?"

"Trust me." Those had been Lysi's exact words to him when she'd advised him to make the commitment to his new program.

"You don't have to choose your major yet, you know." The advisor wasn't used to so much decisiveness on the part of a student whose program thus far was best exemplified by the scholastic smorgasbord principle.

"If not now, when? That's Maimonides," Noel condescended to add. The advisor surrendered. They didn't pay him enough to fight with the clientele.

Lysi was waiting for Noel outside the advisor's office. She gave him a hearty kiss when he emerged, then asked, "Did you do it?" in much the same way Lady Macbeth must have demanded a progress report from her husband.

Noel affirmed this. "I don't understand why I have to do it, though. Religious Studies? Isn't that kind of going against everything you—we stand for?"

Lysi chuckled. "That's why I love you. You're so naive!"

Noel bristled. He had read somewhere that naiveté was not one of the Ten Top Qualities women looked for in their men. Probably it had been in one of Marguerite's clandestine copies of *Cosmo*. The source didn't matter. "Masterfulness" was up near the head of the list, as was "Intelligence," "Initiative," "Nice Eyes," and "Kevin Costner." Unless you could lump naiveté in with "Sensitivity—But Not Too Wussy," it was nowhere.

Lysi was quick to catch her prey's displeasure. She laced her fingers in his and tickled the palm of his hand. "I'm just kidding, babe. You don't need me to explain why it's smart to use a great cover like Religious Studies when you're going to be the greatest damned wizard the world has ever known."

Noel was mollified, though a little uneasy about the emphasis she'd put on "greatest *damned* wizard."

He thought about her expectations for him as they strolled under the great trees of Cross Campus. Though only a block away from Yale's original confines—now called Old Campus and sacred to the care and keeping of the freshman class— there was a world of difference between the two. Old Campus was a separate world within the Yalie universe, walled in secure by the buildings themselves, complemented by iron gates to keep out the boogiemen of contemporary civilization (symbolically, at least). Despite the wide open central space the walls and gates defined, there was still the sensation of being protected and watched over, whether you wanted it or not.

Cross Campus was more accessible, a broken box of space with one of its shorter ends completely missing, open to College Street and possibilities. At the end opposite, separated from Cross Campus by a laughably narrow street, Sterling Memorial Library raised its imposing façade—cathedral and castle combined—and dared Harvard to do better in the pseudo-Gothic Status Olympics. You could *do* outrageous things on Old Campus, but only on Cross Campus did you feel that you could get away with them.

Not that there was anything especially outrageous going on there at the moment. The autumn weather still held fair, and the grassy rectangles flanked by golden-brown stone buildings bore a bumper crop of sunbathers, Frisbee players, and people pretending to study as they checked out the traffic.

"Don't pin your hopes on me so much, Lysi," Noel said as they walked along holding hands.

"Why not? You've got the talent. You told me so."

"I might not pan out. The only thing I know I can do is light tobacco." He still cherished the memory of how calmly

she'd taken his revelation of inborn magic. It was either her
own affinity for witchcraft, her unflappable personality, or
the remnants of Smith training at work. Whatever, she hadn't
screamed and run, and Noel at last had the perfect confidante.
However, he had omitted to mention the source of his powers, namely his mother's former nature. A girl who studied
Satanism in Whitman might still draw the line at Diabolic
Mendelianism in Cardiff. It was best to go softly.

"That's because that's all you've tried." Lysi found them
a prime spot under a huge elm and pulled Noel down beside
her. She drew up her legs and rested her chin on her knees.
"Seduce me, Noel."

After a while she said, "You'd better have a dentist check
out that back molar, baby. I think the filling's a little loose."

Noel snapped his mouth shut, but continued to stare. "I
can't do that!" he protested.

"Force yourself."

"Seduce you?"

"That's what I said. Don't you want to? It's a lot more fun
than lighting pipes for Daddy."

"Yeah, but— I thought— I mean, about us—"

Lysi knew what he thought. He was hoping that their
supposedly mutual attraction would gradually ripen into love,
at which point—but not before—they would go to bed together. Romantic boob was written all over his face. It was a
nice face, too, with high cheekbones that could be brought
along to look really Mephistophelian someday, through a
proper course of debauchery, applied cynicism, and regular
diabolic care. Such a pity that tenderness and noble passion
softened up the whole picture. Lysi was willing to bet that the
boy even cherished respect for a woman's feelings. Not for
him "I'll call you," "Of course I still respect you," or
"Hey, I need more space." Like a good dictionary, love
would always come before sex in Noel's life.

But that was before Lysi, who well knew there was no
book so good that it could not be made better for a little
judicious editorial work.

"I think you've got the wrong idea about me, Noel," she
said pleasantly. "I didn't want to hurt your feelings by coming right out and saying this, but it looks like I'll have to. I'm
only interested in you as a friend. And as a potential ally, of
course."

She tried not to display too much satisfaction at the way his whole being sagged. For his part, Noel thought he showed no visible sign of disappointment. He was trying to act as if this were old news. He gravely underestimated the lady's powers of observation.

"Yeah, I knew that," he said, jamming the right note of disinterest into his words. "That's how I feel about you, too. That's why I was so surprised when you told me to seduce you. I mean, why should I want to?"

Because it's only what you've been praying for the past eighteen years, razzhead! Lysi thought.

"That's just why you should try it: To see whether you can do it. I don't want to go to bed with you and you don't want to go to bed with me . . . Perfect test conditions!"

Noel eyed her askance. "Are you sure? I wouldn't want to force you into something you didn't want to do."

Scruples! Lysi ground her teeth together and made herself smile. *Mortie scruples are the migraines of Hell.*

"The whole idea of magic is force, compulsion. Wizards do not go with the flow; they are the flow. But you've got to direct the flow within you or it'll just sit there. Nobody likes to work, and that includes cosmic forces. You've got to show your magic who's boss, and the best way to do that is to make it do something it wouldn't do on its own; like force me to go to bed with you."

"Couldn't I just try making my roommates do my laundry?"

"You could, if you're more interested in socks than sex." Lysi was peeved. She folded her arms across her chest—no easy task—and frowned. "If you're serious about joining us, Noel, we're going to have to get honest with each other, icky though it may be. I don't have your gift for magic, don't ask me why—"

"Oh, that's because your family didn't descend from Lilith and—"

A scowl fit to crisp skin shut him up.

"I don't have your gift; you do," Lysi went on. "But I do know the rules of magic, the conditions that enhance and stifle it. I can teach you a lot."

Noel again heard his father's lightly amused comment when interviewing unmarried marriage counselors and childless family therapists: *Those who can't do, teach.*

He didn't think it would be polite to ask Lysi to share the humor, so instead he said, "I'd be very grateful."

"You'd better be." Lysi was unimpressed with his humble attitude. "I've been studying witchcraft for ages, and there's one basic rule you'd better learn right now: There ain't no such thing as a celibate sorcerer."

"Merlin—"

"—looked like an old goat and acted like an old goat and the ladies loved it. Why do you think he came up with the whole Grail-quest scam and made it look like Arthur's idea? To get the husbands out of the way! Babe, just because it never made it into print in *Le Morte d'Arthur* doesn't mean squat. Who cared if the old thaumaturge had a little sugar on the side? But the *Queen's* adultery—! Now *that* sells newspapers! Lesson one: With wizards, the best and the brightest are the raunchiest and the randiest."

Lysi stood up, towering over Noel. She was an even more striking young woman when viewed from that angle. "You've got your assignment—take it or leave it. I'll give you lesson two whenever you're ready." Her retreating hips traced wondrous wave-patterns on the air. A Frisbee player missed an easy catch and rammed into an ivy-decked wall for the sake of one lingering glance.

Noel remained planted on the green. Chin in hand, he pondered his options. He didn't know quite what to make of this bizarre, contradictory creature who had seemingly popped into his life at random and might now be about to leave it in just the same style. And how did she come to speak of Merlin with a kid sister's familiarity? He put it down to a toxic combination of hermeneutics and Malory.

This was nothing like the mild flirtations of his high school days. Then, when the going got even one degree above tepid—when his mother's comments about the girl in question went from belittling jokes to biting critiques—he was always able to find something fascinating in his schoolwork to distract him until the whole business died of apathy and the girl found someone else.

In his heart he knew that it wasn't going to be the same with Lysi.

Those who can't do, teach. Noel needed guidance, and he decided to get it from an expert with some hands-on experience. He would go back to the room and ask Roger.

En route from Cross Campus to Old Campus, he paused only long enough to try setting the in-play Frisbee on fire with his eyes, just to check if he still had the knack. Something went wrong, and a very startled player got an individual size green-pepper-and-anchovy-extra-cheese pizza full in the face.

"I must be hungry," Noel said to himself, skirting the crowd of gawkers. He thought it best to get some lunch before asking Roger for advice and help with the fair sex.

About an hour and a half later, as the pizza oven bakes, he let himself into the room. He found Roger sprawled on the sofa, a poleaxed look in his eyes and a terrycloth bathrobe doing its pitiful best to cover his body. There was something horribly mindless about young Tagliaferro's happy expression as he turned to meet his roommate's inquiring stare. Had he announced that he felt much better since the lobotomy, Noel would not have been at all surprised.

"Uh, Roger . . . can we talk?"

"Gorgeous," Roger replied. "Incredible. Awesome."

By this, Noel took it that Roger wouldn't mind a chat, so he sat down beside him. "It's about a girl."

"Yeah. That's what it's about. That's what it's all about. Always." Roger broke into the theme from *Alfie* and was only persuaded to stop when Luis stuck his head out of his own bedroom and threatened to chuck part of his fetal pig at the songster's head if he didn't shut up.

"He's been like this for the past hour," Luis informed Noel, dark eyes blazing. "Lying on the sofa, swilling Ovaltine, grinning, and singing stuff from movies. This isn't going to be a safe world until we can keep the score from *Camelot* out of amateur hands. Whoever or whatever he's got in there—" he nodded toward the closed door of Roger's bedroom "—I'd love to do a paper on it. She had him maybe fifteen minutes and this is the result! I don't know whether to chloroform him or go for seconds."

Noel's eyes slewed around to rest on the mysterious door. "If she's so great, why is he out here?" he asked with some trepidation.

Luis shrugged eloquently. "*Qué va!* The human body is programmed for survival. My guess is Roger's instinct for self-preservation kicked in. If you're going to be here awhile, keep an eye on him. Let me know if he goes back in. I hear

the fetal pig calling my name.'' Luis went back to his homework, leaving Noel alone with the semidead.

Noel looked at Roger. The big blond had fallen asleep with
his head thrown back, smiling through his snores. The door to
his room remained mute, fascinating. It would be a shame not
to inform Roger's guest that her swain was temporarily out.
More, it would be discourteous to keep the lady waiting for
a repeat performance that did not seem imminent.

Noel rapped on the door very, very lightly.

"Come in."

He knew the voice, and Lysi's disarming smile did nothing
to lessen his anger when he flung open the door and found her
in Roger's bed. "Ready for lesson two yet?"

Noel slammed the door and locked it. "How could you?"

"That would be lesson four. Lesson four is big on
'how-to.' "

"You know what I mean!"

"Yes, and I'm trying to inject a little humor into the
situation before you make yourself into a total asshole and
lose my respect forever."

"How can you talk about respect? What did you do? Just
waltz up to the first guy you met and drag him off?"

"Certainly not." Lysi shifted on the swaybacked mattress,
causing the sheet that covered her to cover a little less. "I had
to make sure he was your roommate."

"You *deliberately*—" A thought gave Noel pause. "How
could you find one of my roommates so fast?"

Lysi picked up a copy of the student directory from Roger's nightstand and waved it languidly. "This is a remarkable
convenience. I wish I'd known about it sooner." *Like when I
was freezing my buns off playing gargoyle and looking for
you all over this campus, my poppet.*

"That would only give you his name, not where to find
him. This is a big campus and you're only a transfer . . ."
Noel's objections trailed off. A theory sparked. "Magic?"

Lysi nodded.

"But you said you couldn't work magic!"

"I said I didn't have your gift for it. Not every ballet
dancer is Baryshnikov, but that doesn't mean they're not
good enough to play Poughkeepsie. You have an edge, that's
all. If you don't use it, the lowest hedge-witch can spell
circles around you. As for me. I can work the odd bit of

sorcery when I choose. Remember that kid in the lecture hall?'' Lysi made a *sproinnnng* gesture with one finger.

''But why did you do this with Roger?''

''An object lesson for your sake. He didn't really want me any more than I wanted him, but I thought you should see a seduction spell in action. See? No big deal. We teachers make the damndest sacrifices in the name of education. It galls me to think of your wonderful gift going down the tubes unused. You're still balking over all that good-versus-evil shit, aren't you? You're afraid.''

Noel blushed. Lysi's uncanny knack for guessing how his mind worked made him feel diminished. Since she was just his age, yet so much more knowing than he, he figured that he truly must be incredibly backward and—let it be said and forgotten—naive.

''Well, what are you afraid of? You didn't ask to be born with magic powers. It's not your fault. Who's going to blame you for using what you've got? Everyone else does.''

''I . . .'' The rest of Noel's response was strangled.

''Look, babe, I don't have all century. Either you're going to get serious about sorcery or you're going to die of terminal self-righteousness. Which'll it be?''

Noel remained silent.

A sly smile curved Lysi's tender mouth. She began to speak with all the patronizing sweetness of a child-hating kiddie-show host. ''Tell you what, I'll make you a deal. If the idea of evil's making you wet your pants, we'll forget all about it, O.K.? I'll just teach you how to use your magic and you can apply it however you want. I'm sure you'll come up with something. Oh, but not something *evil!* Not Noel. Noel's a *good* boy, so you can use your magic for good alone. Good is *so* nice. Why, you can use good magic to make the ickle bunny-wunnies dance by moonlight. You can use it to grow yourself a pair of pretty purple butterfly wings and go swippety-swooping off to Fairyland. You can even use it to leave darling little bunches of violets on your mommy's pillow every single morning. Won't that be a delight? Won't she just clap her hands together and say 'Isn't my Noel the sweetest little boy any mother ever—'?''

Lysi's words snapped off as sharply as breaking glass. She sat up straight in Roger's bed, unable to stir a limb by her own will. Inwardly she gloated, feeling the angry power rippling from Noel's body, thrilling as it grew ever stronger. The sheet flicked off and crumpled itself into a ball in the corner. The mattress rose up to conform to her body. Somewhere below her knees was a tentative warmth.

Come on, come on, she willed him silently. *I got you mad enough to give me more than a pair of mildly horny shins!* The warmth increased, gaining inches and degrees as its kindler gained confidence. Lysi took care to keep her own powers in strictest check while Noel's burgeoned. It wouldn't do to let him learn that she was capable of withstanding his assault. She made sure that her face showed no fear—that might spook him—but only dewy-eyed admiration and mounting desire.

It worked. By the time Noel's first spell of compulsive surrender hit her where she lived, it was a blaze that would have incinerated any mortal girl's resistance. It even melted a little of Lysi's professional detachment.

She couldn't help herself. With a thought, she turned his clothes to fine white powder. He was too far gone to notice, and she would find time afterwards to restore them with a sprinkle of water. The mattress leaped from the bed, Lysi and all, and scooped up its master. With two aboard, it was cleared for takeoff. A yard below the high ceiling, Noel got lesson number two. Several times.

"Hey! Let me in!" Roger rattled the doorknob insistently. "Quit jerking me around, guys! I've got to get dressed for dinner."

"Uh-oh." Noel looked from the shambles he and Lysi had made of Roger's room to his partner in exuberance. "He's going to kill me."

Lysi laughed. "You could turn his eyeballs inside out with a wiggle of your little finger—and *he's* going to kill *you?*" She pressed her body against his. "Turn him into a toad," she suggested. "You can't beat the golden oldies."

"I can't do that! I mean, I'd rather not." In the past few hours Noel had learned that *can't* no longer held its old pride of place in his vocabulary. "It's bad enough what I did to him with you, and in his room!"

"You didn't like it?" There was too much evidence present for Noel to lie and deny.

"I just feel bad about it. He was— I think he was in love with you."

"Nonsense. That was just the aftereffects of the spell I used to snare him. He's forgotten all about me by now, I promise."

Noel's brows came together. "You haven't forgotten about me, and I used the same kind of spell on you . . . didn't I?"

"That's different." Lysi's long nails traced an invisible dragon on Noel's chest. Like many blonds, he was smooth there, the skin more sensitive and responsive to teasing touches. "You see, spells don't work the same way on mortals as they do on demons."

Her smile was filled with the illusion of nothing but canine teeth. Noel froze. Lysi allowed her nails to curl into understated talons as they continued their titillating course over her lover's naked skin. She tossed her long black hair and let him see two tiny horns in bud. Something prehensile with a delicate spearhead point snaked beneath the bedclothes; a tail. Lysi was leaving nothing out. She'd been in the business long enough to know what inexperienced morties expected their demons to look like.

"What's the matter, sugar?" Her hands stroked Noel's face, the talons retracted. "You said you wanted to be a wizard. Only the best have commerce with demons."

"You—you—" Noel tried to leap from the bed, but a second thought made him check to see whether it was still in flight. In that moment of prudence, he lost the urge to flee. "You said you were a transfer student!"

"I studied in Paris during the Reign of Terror—you wouldn't believe my senior science project. I was also present at the battle for the University City in Madrid during the Spanish Civil War. Then there was Berlin in the 30's—I left when they stopped being decadent and started acting too beastly even for me. I also did a short stint at Berkeley in the 60's." Her pale shoulders shrugged. "A transfer student. Did I lie?"

"You said you were only a witch, not a demon!" Noel was deaf to Roger's increasingly persistent rattling of the knob. Five minutes ago he had been en route to bliss, and now he was prisoner in a nightmare based on his mother's worst Health Ed. lectures (*Don't get involved with the wrong sort of girl, dear.*)

"What's so 'only' about witches? And I am half witch. Mixed marriages can be made to work. I don't know what you're so upset about, honey. Wizards can command demons. You have the power to control me completely, which is more than you could ever do with a witch; or a Smithereen, for that matter.'' She raised one foot prettily and ran her toes up the back of his leg. She hadn't included cloven hooves in her transformation; they were too tacky. "I'm all yours; trust me."

By the time Roger got Jonathan, the computer freak, to use his expertise on the lock ("That's a hardware problem!" "Yeah, but you've got the only screwdriver in the suite!"), Noel had tried his fledgling powers of demonic command on Lysi and ordered her to clean up the premises. He was delightfully surprised by her instant compliance and by the results. The door opened on a scrupulously neat room and two dedicated young Elis, chastely separated, poring over their copies of *Piers Plowman*.

"Oh, hello." Noel did his best to look surprised by the invasion. "Is it time for dinner already?"

From her place as far from Noel as the small room permitted, Lysi squeaked, "Oh my gosh! I promised I'd meet Cathy at the Beinecke before it closed!" She shot past Roger and Jonathan, bubbling excuses. Roger did not appear to know her from the proverbial hole in the ground.

"Did he believe you?" Lysi asked across the dinner table. She and Noel were eating in Commons, a building with the length of a football field, the height of a zeppelin hangar, the acoustics of a boiler factory, and the cuisine of the Dis Drive-In ("Over 666,666,666,666,666,666,666 Served"). She felt right at home.

"He said that any time I wanted to use his room for ahem-ahem-ahem *studying*, as he put it, to go right ahead. It was the best the place looked all year."

"And he didn't remember me either, did he?"

"Nope." Noel pushed a forkful of sauerkraut around his plate with all the respect due a potent enemy. "You know, this magic's not as bad as I thought."

"Not bad? It's wonderful . . . Master."

Noel blinked.

"Well, I am your familiar, amn't I? Very familiar," Lysi added.

"I thought only witches had familiars, and they didn't get them until . . ."

Lysi saw his lower lip shake. She suspected what must be going through his mind: *until they sold their souls to the devil.* She clamped her hand down firmly over his, just in case he tried to make a break for it.

"There's so much misinformation going around about us," she reassured him. "What people don't know, they make up. It's scandalous. You've had your powers right from birth, but that doesn't mean you were born with your soul in hock to Hell, does it? That makes no sense and it isn't fair."

"My father always told me that life isn't fair."

"That's just the sort of thing parents say when they make their kid follow a house rule no one else has to obey. Parents will say anything to shut up the whining."

Noel relaxed. He smiled at her sheepishly.

"Of course, parents aren't wrong all the time," she continued, toying with what might once have been a sausage. "When they say that everything in this life has its price, you'd better believe it."

Noel set his fork down. "What price?"

"Smile, baby. You don't owe me a thing . . . yet. I'm not talking souls here. We demons never take what isn't given; we can't. I'm only talking about increasing your present powers. They're O.K. as they stand, but they could be better."

Noel was nettled. "You didn't have any complaints about my powers before."

"The only magic you used before was the seduction spell. The rest was Mama Nature's own. Just think of what might have been if you'd known about spells of . . . stamina? Enhancement? Aerobic summons of the dead? The great lovers of history can all be called up to inhabit your mind and body temporarily. Their spirits can give you some swell ideas for what to do next when you've run through your own repertoire," she explained. "There's nothing like calling up expertise in a tight spot. And they are *so* grateful for the chance to drop in on life again."

To his own surprise, Noel was not horrified by Lysi's words. He knew himself well enough to realize that had she spoken of these matters a scant six hours earlier, he would have rabbited out of Commons. Much had changed in the last six hours. Instead of being scared by talk of bringing back the ghosts of Casanova, Romeo, Don Juan, Vatsayana, Byron,

Lothario and that crowd, he was intrigued.

"Well, teach them to me; the spells."

Lysi batted her eyelashes. "Can't."

"Why not? I—" He glanced covertly around the table to see if any feminists were within hearing range, then dropped his voice "—command you to teach me the spells."

"Sorry, Master, no go. I could tell you the words to say, I could tell you the rites to perform, but even if you followed my instructions to the letter, all you'd be left with would be a twisted tongue and a lot of frog eggs on your face."

Noel was far from comprehension. Lysi patted his hand and quoted that fine old saying about never teaching pigs to sing. "You don't have the inborn force to use such spells, my tasty little lord. You can't power a Plymouth on penlight batteries. You could acquire the power you need for those spells, add it to your own, but that is what I meant by everything having a price. I can give you an estimate, no obligation. Interested?"

"It wouldn't be my soul, would it?"

"If it were, you could always say no."

"All right, then." Noel took a deep breath. "What's your price? For just a *little* more power," he emphasized.

"It's not *my* price, pet. Rates are set by the Necromantic Regulatory Commission. But for just a *little* more power all you'll need is a *little* payment."

She reached under the table and pulled out a book. It looked pretty old and sorrowful, which might have been why Lysi suggested putting it out of its misery.

"Destroy this," she said. "Set it afire with your magic and I guarantee you a 6.9 percent increase in your powers."

Noel picked up the book. Inside, it was marked as the property of the Beinecke Library. The Beinecke, as every Yalie soon learned, was the sectioned marble cube that gave Beinecke Plaza its name, though that same plaza held such equally important monuments as Commons, Sprague Hall, and the President's Office. But Yale was a university, and those entrusted with such matters knew that cafeterias, concert halls, and presidents could be replaced. What the Beinecke Library contained could not. It was the repository of the rarest books on campus, every one precious, many unique, irreplaceable.

"I can't," Noel said. He tried to close the book and push it back at Lysi, but she clamped her hand down on top of his and let her talons grow just the teensiest bit—enough to remind him.

"You can. The only coin my superiors take is wickedness, and offing a book is small change to them. Look, it's just some dumb Latin thingie by—" She lifted his hand from the text and checked out the title page "—Abdul Alhaz-somebody, translated from the Arabic, whoopdedoo. Damn thing's hand-written, hardly legible. You'd be doing the world a favor. Ash it."

"I don't want to!" He made another stab at shoving the open book back at her, equally unsuccessful.

"Oh, yes you do!" Lysi's brows came together. A needle-thin ray of green light shot from between them, a spell of domination.

A disc the size, shape, and color of a styrofoam packing chip sprang up between Noel's eyes and caught Lysi's spell in its shallow cup. The light swirled, bubbled, and arrowed back across the table straight into a dumbfounded she-demon's face. With a meep of distress, Lysi compressed into two dimensions, dwindled to paper-doll size, and fluttered in between the pages of the disputed book. Noel slammed the cover on her.

"I didn't know I could do that," he breathed, and sprinted from Commons.

Shortly after depositing the book safely in his room, he was on the train for New York. There are times a boy just has to have a serious adult discussion with his mother.

4

Phone Home

RALEELRALEELRALEELRALEELRALEEL—

Yo. Stop shouting, little sister. I copy.

GET ME OUT OF HERE!

Y'all excuse me if I laugh—

MENTALLY?

Hey, girlie, a good chuckle-n-snort goes on all frequencies. So how'd you manage to screw up so bad this time?

WHAT DO YOU MEAN, 'THIS TIME'? WHEN HAVE I EVER DROPPED A DEAL BEFORE?

Get real, Lysi. This is your brother Raleel you're hooking up with. Coming in at a piss-poor time, too. We're in the middle of a broadcast.

NO KIDDING? WHO'S HELPING YOU THIS TIME?

Bob is. If you could call it help. Swear to Shaitan, honeybun, that imp's near as big a klutz-case as you. Left the last sucker too damn soon, 'fore I even got warmed up.

MY SYMPATHIES. IF YOU DON'T WANT BOB, SEND HIM BY TO SEE ME. I CAN USE HIM ON MY CLIENT JUST FINE.

How're you gonna use anything, all locked up?

YOU *MIGHT* LET ME OUT. YOU MIGHT CONSIDER PITCHING IN, TOO. THIS IS OUR DADDY I'M TRYING TO HELP, RALEEL. NOT JUST MY DADDY, YOURS TOO!

Says who? Twins are a sure sign of adultery in many cultures. Remember that Indian shaman used to hang around Mother's cabin? Big, good-looking sucker who could turn himself into a varmint on the full moon? Another mental chortle from Raleel hit Lysi's mind. *Sometimes I like to wonder whether I changed myself into a wolverine 'cause it felt so good or 'cause I had to. Heredity; nothing like it.*

TELL ME ABOUT IT. MY CLIENT INHERITED A

HOG'S LOAD OF MAGIC FROM HIS MOTHER'S SIDE. I
WOULDN'T BE SURPRISED IF HE HAS WIZARDLY
BLOOD COMING IN THROUGH HIS FATHER'S VEINS
TOO. I WASN'T EXPECTING HIM TO TURN ON ME
LIKE THAT, UNTRAINED AS HE IS. I'M GONNA KEEP
CLOSER TABS ON HIM FROM NOW ON.

First you'll have to get loose.

COME *ON* RALEEL! I DON'T LIKE THIS BOOK. IT
FEELS CREEPY IN HERE. Lysi brushed away a questing
tentacle, product of one of her strange prison's more purple
passages.

Figures. It's the infernal aura you're sensing.

RALEEL . . .

*I'm not doing a thing for you, Lysi, in case you haven't
guessed by now. Why should I?*

BECAUSE I'M YOUR SISTER AND IT'S FOR DAD-
DY'S SAKE!

And you expect fellow-feeling from a demon? *Which is
what I am, Lysi; what you are, too, in case you've forgotten.
What's the matter with you? We don't help one another; we
just help ourselves.*

I'M NOT ASKING FOR THE MOON.

*The moon I could deliver, postage paid. Dick around with
the tides, plunge the nighttime world into darkness, yank the
doormat to space out from under NASA, mangle three quarters of all the love songs ever written— Now there's evil on
the heroic scale! I can dig it. But help you? You're not
catching me taking one microstep out of the Me-First line, no
way. That's how you chalk up trouble points with the
Underlords. Look what happened to Dad. You want my help?
You pay for it!*

Lysi considered. WHAT DO YOU WANT?

Guess.

YOU PIG! STICK IT IN YOUR EAR, RALEEL.

*I've tried. O.K. Give my regards to Alhazred and his
octopoid pals, Lysi. You'll be bunking down with them for a
good long time.*

Raleel broke the connection, leaving his twin to ponder the
wisdom of her bargain. She swatted off a pesky shoggoth and
sank into glum contemplation of what she would do to Noel
Cardiff if she ever got out of print.

5

Perhaps Rolfing Would Help

"YOU'RE NOT TAKING this seriously, Mom!" Noel smacked the mantelpiece for emphasis and got a tingling hand for his trouble. Across the room, bargello spread across her lap, Marguerite continued to stitch and nod her head calmly.

"I know you're upset, dear. What I told you the last time you were home isn't easy to accept. I'm very, very proud of you for coping with it as well as you've done. Do you know that I'm always very, very proud of you?"

Noel pressed his lips together and blew out all his exasperation between them.

"Darling, don't do that. You sound like a horse." Marguerite set her needlework aside. "Do you remember how you used to beg me to take you riding in Central Park, and when I finally said yes, you froze in the saddle? Oh, you looked so cute up on that big old horsie, clutching his mane so tightly! We bought you your own little riding togs, but you never wore them after that first time up."

Noel felt his face flush. The adorable miniature riding togs—custom-made boots included—haunted him more persistently than any murder victim's ghost. Marguerite always smiled when she mentioned them, but a mother may smile and smile and still be sticking the knife in. In fact, the best mothers specialized in the subtlest ways for reminding their offspring just how beholden they were to the parental largesse.

He decided to let the discussion slalom around the expensive, wasted riding togs. He tried to fight his way back to the main topic. "Mom, I said I'm a wizard!"

"No, dear. You just think you are."

"I've got a *familiar!*" How familiar, he didn't want to say. When he had begun this confrontation, he held back mentioning Lysi's name, sex, appearance, and skills. Better his mother should imagine him with the typical black cat or owl in attendance than the lissome she-demon. Although Marguerite had retired from the field, who knew how deeply the roots of professional jealousy ran?

Noel was wise and insightful beyond his years.

Marguerite dropped the canvas back into her embroidery bag. "I can see I'm not going to get anything done around here until I set you straight, Noel." The weariness of a world full of ungrateful children had come to rest squarely on her delicate shoulders. She folded her hands in her lap. "You are not a wizard. You are a magic-wielder. There are differences."

"What?" Noel hated to hear his voice regress to the belligerent sulkiness of early adolescence, but his mother both provoked and evoked it.

"The prime difference is that were you to confront one of the true wizards—Virgilius, for example—he would reduce your brains to ash, set worms to gnaw your marrow, replace your eyelids with Lucite, and flay your epidermis to a single layer of cells, and all merely because you had the nerve to rank yourself with him."

Marguerite spoke so matter-of-factly about the great Virgilius that Noel had the creepy feeling they had been on a first-curse basis. He licked his lips. "This—this guy's dead now, right?"

Marguerite shrugged. "Death is such a fragile thing. Who knows? I've heard rumors, but you can't depend on anything these days. The greatest wizards of antiquity turn up with less warning than Hamptons houseguests. You see why you mustn't give yourself airs?"

"Yeah, well, Virgilius wasn't *born* a wizard, was he?"

"Dear me, no."

"Then why couldn't I become a wizard someday? If I study, I mean."

Marguerite gave her child a reproving look. "I thought you wanted to be a lawyer, dear."

"I've changed my mind."

The news did not appear to please Noel's mother. "Sweetheart, I know there's a glut in the law field right now, but by the time you pass the bar—"

"I want to be a wizard."

"You'll have a terrible time filling out your tax returns."

"I won't have to pay taxes! I'll be able to turn the whole IRS into toads if I feel like it! You can't beat the golden oldies." Lysi's face winked in his mind, blew him a kiss.

Marguerite's mid-brow frown line deepened into the Marianas Trench. "Just where have you been getting these ideas?"

He hadn't heard her sound like that since the time she'd caught him at age twelve reading SF film novelizations under the covers. He never could forget her lecture on the evils of intellectual self-abuse. That cranky Grand Inquisitor tone of hers could still make him jump, backpedal, deny, and swear reformation immediately.

"Nowhere, Mom, Honest! I mean, it's my own idea. Sort of. Hasn't everyone wanted to turn the IRS into toads?"

"All the more reason for you to come up with something less *jejune*. Striking them leprous—now that would be worthy of an independent mind. I think, Noel, that you have a lot of unresolved hostility towards me, and you're acting out in a very inappropriate manner. I can understand your feelings, though I wish you could. You resent me for lying to you all these years. You saw me as perfect—what child does not view his parents that way, at first? When you learned the truth, you wanted to punish me. Why can't you see that you'll only be punishing yourself?"

"I don't see how becoming a wizard is going to punish me." Noel's lower lip assumed a suspiciously juvenile pout. "Anything I want, I just say the words and there it is!"

"Then you know as little of magic as you do of life."

Marguerite rose from her chair and strode over to the small French Provincial desk in the corner. She flipped open the dreaded Month-at-a-Glance calendar and scribbled a note or two. Noel went cold. His mother was never more dangerous than when she was *organizing* something, and that something invariably included him.

"What're you writing, Mom?"

"I am reminding myself to invite Dr. Fitzgerald to come over for drinks tomorrow night," she said. With a guileless smile she added, "Why do you look so upset? You knew we were having several friends over for cocktails. They may be a trifle surprised to find you here in the middle of the week, but they always enjoy seeing you. They won't pry."

"The h—heck they won't! Dr. Fitzgerald? Give me a break! He's a *shrink!* He's paid to pry. And I bet he wasn't on your guest list until five minutes ago."

Marguerite could look as artless as a debutante when she chose. "An oversight, which I'm happy to correct."

"If he comes, I go! I don't want him here."

"Dr. Fitzgerald is a dear, dear friend of ours, Noel. I had no idea I had to ask your permission to invite him. But if you wish to storm off just as rudely as you did the last time you visited, I can't stop you. I'm only your mother. I'm just the person who spent six months trying to pound algebra into your head. I missed an entire season of the American Ballet Theater to do it, but I didn't mind. You just run back to Yale without a word, if that's what you want. I'll have to pack up your things and mail them to you again, but so what? I'll simply tell the Museum committee I can't be there to help promote culture in New York because I have to stand on line in the post office with my son's—"

"All *right!* All *right!*" Noel surrendered. "I'll stay. I'll talk to Dr. Fitzgerald. He's going to think I'm crazy, but who cares? You can come visit me in Bellevue when you're not working on the Museum committee."

Marguerite returned to her chair and took up the bargello again. "Whyever should he think you're crazy, dear?"

"How many people say they want to be wizards?"

"He'll just think you mean computers. Or that you're overly involved with one of those little role-playing games. Should you explain what you really mean, he won't be unduly disturbed either. He's up on all the latest trends, you see, and the newest school of therapy recommends ignoring the client's concrete problem in favor of treating the underlying motivations. I can vouch for the effectiveness of his technique personally."

"You, Mom?"

"Darling, do you think it's been easy, blending in with the New York intelligentsia with *my* background? It took me ten years before I could see the humor in Woody Allen movies! It got so bad, at last, that I went to Dr. Fitzgerald and told him everything. He pointed out that I was harboring a great deal of unresolved sexual guilt, complicated by my honest love for your father and you, plus a residual nostalgia for my previous erotic freedom. Seven sessions later, I was cured."

"*How could you?*"

"Well, I made amazing progress after only two dunks in the sensory deprivation tank, and then he made me read the autobiography of Linda Lovelace while wearing Estee Lauder body oil and Saran wr—"

"How could you tell a shrink what you were, when you didn't tell *me?*"

"He was licensed."

Noel ramped from the mantel to his mother's chair and back, rage swelling. "You actually told this total stranger that you used to be a demon? You risked telling him everything, left yourself wide open to maybe getting locked up forever as a lunatic, and you couldn't even give your own son a hint about your past?"

A thin skin of yellow mist began to pulse around him. It grew darker, more golden, more opaque. Marguerite had to strain her eyes to make out Noel's body within the enveloping fog generated by his anger. Hairline purple lightnings crackled over the surface of the cocoon. The floor of the apartment shook, the mantelpiece rumbled, and a Lladro sculpture fell and smashed on the hearth.

The harsh sound worked a wonder. Noel's manifestations vanished. He came out of the evaporating mist looking shamefaced. Marguerite knelt to hold up the slivers of porcelain, for guilt-inspiring display.

"Your father gave me this for our tenth wedding anniversary. It was a limited edition. I hope you're satisfied."

Some time later, Noel found himself having promised to invite Dr. Fitzgerald personally, to hand around hors d'oeuvres at the party, and to come back into New York to man the telephones at the next PBS fund raising drive.

"You know about my mother?"

Dr. Fitzgerald helped himself to more sashimi and nodded. "One of my most successful cases. Of course, she wanted me to succeed. You can't force a person to get well when he's determined to stay sick." He gave Noel a meaningful look over the rice and seaweed.

"Your mother tells me you've changed career-paths, Noel. Care to talk about it?"

Noel wondered just how much his mother had told the doctor. Knowing Marguerite . . . Abruptly he realized that he didn't really know Marguerite at all. He decided to play it close to the chest. "There wasn't much to change. I haven't actually decided what I'm going to be."

The doctor commanded an astounding range of skeptical looks, each graced by a nuance of its own, all designed to make his clients start gabbling justifications for the plainest statements. "Is that so?"

"Sure. I mean, I know Mom says that not deciding is a decision too, but I really don't know what I want to do with the rest of my life and—"

"Not with any aspect of it? Not just career?"

"Oh, well, yeah, sure, uh-huh, you know, being healthy and all that, but—"

"Health is more than physical."

Noel raised his lacquer tray and assumed a defensive stance over the seaweed rolls, the still-quivering slabs of raw tuna. "My mental health is as good as yours. Doctor."

Dr. Fitzgerald laughed easily, dipping another tidbit into the green horseradish with the flair of man whose life insurance premiums are all paid up. He swallowed the hellpaste without flinching. Having thus proven his status as the Alpha-male of the cocktail party herd, he said, "That's a rather bold statement, seeing as you know nothing about my mental health. We shrinks have a reputation for needing therapy almost as much as our patients; perhaps more."

Noel was about to fall for the old I'm-more-neurotic double-dog-dare gambit, but his words were lost in the arrival of his father. Kent Cardiff's hale and hearty greeting of Dr. Fitzgerald gave Noel the chance to pull back and clam up.

"I say, Fitz, if you're looking to use my boy for research purposes, you'd best clear it with the A.S.P.C.A. first, what? Prevention of Cruelty to Adolescents, that is. There are things lurking beneath the pre-adult skull that would send Jung ga-ga. Peek at your own risk."

"I would say that an eighteen-year-old is an adult already." Dr. Fitzgerald gave Noel a conspiratorial wink, but the boy was not having any of it. He might not feel totally allied with his father at present, but neither was he about to take sides against Kent Cardiff just yet; definitely not with Mom's shrink.

"I'd agree with you, but I know the case intimately." Kent took up a piece of sashimi from Noel's tray, studied it, and replaced it with a subtle shudder. "Adulthood is not just gauged by years survived. An adult is able to act independently, to resist manipulation, to make his own decisions. And to take the consequences." He looked right at his son.

"I'm sure Noel is capable of all that."

"Capable?" Kent pursed his lips around an invisible pipe-stem. "Oh, assuredly capable. But when has he ever had the opportunity to show his capabilities? If we want Noel to reach full adulthood any time soon, we'd better find Marguerite another hobby."

"I'm not a Freudian." Dr. Fitzgerald pronounced the word as if it were *axe-murderer*. "Blaming the mother for all the child's ills is reactionary."

"I'm blaming Marguerite for nothing. She's done a wonderful job raising our boy—and you wouldn't believe the cultural handicaps she had to overcome to do it."

"I think I might." Dr. Fitzgerald ate a piece of yellowtail sushi and looked knowing. In that instant, he reminded Noel of a soap opera villain: the wicked, amoral, lecherous slimeball who cheats everyone and sleeps with anything slow enough to catch. Now he confronted the virtuous innocent (Kent) whose wife he had lately seduced (mentally, but on the couch none-theless) and gloated over a most private joke.

Noel didn't like it. Inwardly he decided that he'd be damned before he told the sushi-gobbling shrink any of his secrets, only to see them add to that insufferably knowledgeable smirk. No, he would say nothing of wizardry, nothing of magic. This man would reduce all the wonders of the other-world to symptoms. Noel determined that he would not sub-mit to therapy. But there was nothing to stop him from practicing a little of his own unlicensed medicine on the doctor.

Noel directed his gaze to the remaining pieces of sushi and sashimi on his tray. There was one sliver of tuna left. His father hated tuna sushi. Noel half-closed his eyes and concen-trated his powers on the instrument of Dr. Fitzgerald's comeuppance.

Meantime, the great motherhood-vs.-adulthood debate veered back and forth between the two men. ". . . just that she's on top of him too much. She doesn't give him a chance to make his own mistakes or enjoy his own successes. The world is not a laboratory, nor life a controlled experiment."

"Rousseau is not my style, Kent." The doctor's long fingers picked up a fishless rice roll. Noel continued to stare down the tuna.

"Nor is he mine. I don't advocate letting children run hog wild. When they set fire to themselves, people talk, even in

California. But you must cut the tether some time. If you were to tell Marguerite that it's well past the hour for snipping Noel free, she might listen.''

Dr. Fitzgerald shrugged. "I don't preach. And I think Marguerite doesn't appreciate people who do." He polished off the last nibble of rice.

"Have another, Dr. Fitzgerald?" Noel lifted the tray, smiling brightly. "Just got one tuna left."

"Oh, no thank you, Noel. I think I've had enough."

"Noel, darling!" Before he could push the ensorceled snack, Marguerite was upon him. She grabbed him by the arm and whisked him into the kitchen, where a dull-eyed caterer shoveled a fresh assortment of Japanese fish-knishes onto the almost empty tray. The fateful tuna blended into the crowd of newcomers with the adeptness of Mike Hammer shaking an amateur tail in a crowd.

"Now go mingle, love." Marguerite propelled her son back out onto the floor.

Noel tried to hide himself behind the schefflera and bring his supernatural powers to bear on the tray. He knew nothing of how many kinds of sorcery there were in the world, but he had heard plenty of run-of-the-mill psychics claim that they could use their powers to "find" things. If finding-magic existed, he should be able to tap into it. Surely if they could pinpoint missing persons, he could sift out one tampered tuna! He focused on the tray until his eyes crossed. He got a headache.

"Noel, what are you doing back there? We have guests!" Marguerite had him by the biceps again. She hauled him out of sanctuary and dragged him around the room, making introductions that featured "Yale" in the first five words. Noel didn't know half the people now cramming his parents' apartment, though he would have bet hard cash most of them were either fine arts types or fine arts promotion types. Once Kent had slipped an insurance salesman into one of Marguerite's soirees. He was the hit of the evening, sold fifteen policies, and caused Kent to sleep on the couch for a fortnight thereafter.

Artists or actuaries, all of the Cardiffs' guests had good appetites. Noel watched horrified as his tray emptied itself by purely mundane means. He tried the stratagem of dipping the tray out from under the guests' questing fingers; this failed. He tried putting them off the tuna bits with whispered hints of bad fish, but he forgot that these were people who could not take a hint. Within minutes he was down to three pieces, two of them tuna, and his mother was still soldered to his elbow.

"I'll just go back into the kitchen and get this refilled." There was a brittle urgency in his voice. The odds and the gods seemed to have favored him thus far—either the enchanted sushi was one of the two tuna leftovers or his magic had fizzled out. Did sorcery have a shelf life? Whatever the case, he wasn't going to stand around and press his luck. The kitchen Disposall beckoned with the lure of the Holy Grail. He would dump his tray and breathe freely again. "Won't take a second to get more."

"Yes dear, that would be nice." Marguerite released his arm. "I'll just make it a little lighter for you."

She seized one of the tunas.

"Delightful. So will I." A liquid-eyed older man in a bad New Wave haircut snagged the other. "Where did your son get that marvelous blond hair?" he asked as he chewed.

Noel stood frozen in place, eyes darting from his mother to the man. The remaining piece of tuna-free sashimi on his tray went begging.

"Oh, Smitty, *I'm* a blonde." Marguerite's light laugh grated Noel's nerves raw. "And so was Kent before he grayed out on us."

"So much more appropriate to his calling. Oh, for the freedom to grow old!" Smitty finished his munch and rested one hand on a bony, denim-sheathed hip. Discreetly he wiped the other on his open-necked Hawaiian shirt. It only improved the pattern. "In *my* line of work, age must be kept off at any cost. What price youth?" He chucked Noel under the chin. Noel never felt it. "Would you sell me yours, Noel? Your wonderful, golden youth that you are far too young to appreciate properly? I'd give it only the best treatment and return it when I was quite done." He leaned lightly on the boy's shoulder. Noel was too far gone to notice or care.

Not so Marguerite. She giggled nervously. "Now, you just leave Noel alone, Smitty. He's not interested."

Smitty looked at her askance. "Thus speaks the conventional mother. I had higher hopes of you, Marguerite. Free-minded in all else but the sex life of your child, *neh?* And your own, to be sure."

"My sex life? For your information, my sex life—"

Noel stiffened. He'd heard the deep intake of air, the sure sign that Marguerite had gotten the tuna of doom. The notion of a shrink pouring out his personal life before witnesses, rather than the other way around, had seemed amusing when he'd cast the Sodium Pentothal spell over the fish. Now that it was his mother about to Tell All publicly, it wasn't so funny. Former succubi like Marguerite had a distinctly kinky bit of All to Tell. How would the Arts establishment welcome an ex-demon? An ex-demon whose specialty had been sex? None too warmly; not since *Time* decreed that sexual promiscuity was *passé*.

He closed his eyes, waiting for the confessions to spill out and his mother's social life to go ashcan.

"—isn't half up to mine," Smitty said. "Do you think it's easy being gay? Yes, everyone in this crowd accepts me—either that or be labeled a prude—but is acceptance enough? Not for me. It's always been this way. If you could have seen the look my father gave me when I came out! My sister came out the same night . . . in the traditional sense. There Daddy sat, propping up the Plaza bar, learning in one evening that he'd sired a debutante and a deviate. Oh yes, that's what he called me. Whenever you see us together in photos, or in interviews, he's always spouting the proper stuff about how he loves his son no matter what, he wouldn't dream of interfering in his children's lifestyles, anything goes so long as we're happy. But in private? I never knew there were so many synonyms for 'freak'! When my mother died, he said I'd killed her. Charming man. You ought to be a fly on the wall when talk comes round to my career, too. A gossip columnist! An old hen, that's what he calls me when he's not calling me a vulture. No matter that a *word* in my column can make or break you. When he was tupping that sleazy little showgirl—Mother still alive, though just barely—*then* he couldn't kiss up to me enough, all for a nice mention of her in print. She couldn't act her way through an orgasm! But I was nice, for his sake. Nearly ruined my reputation for it. Then she ran off with her leading man and Daddy laid that at my door too! Oh God, oh God, I've done all I can for that man! Why can't he see that I'm still the same person I was before? I still love him! Why can't he still love me? Why?"

Smitty's voice had risen inexorably throughout the course of his recitation. Now it scaled off the high end of the staff and melted into hysterical sobs. A crowd had gathered—small wonder—and were loud in their offers of comfort and consolation. Several of them who shared Smitty's lifestyle now came forward with revelations of their own, no less depressing. Those who subscribed to more conventional manners of pairing spoke up to give testimony that it wasn't all roses on the straight side of the street. Dr. Fitzgerald ran out of business cards within ten minutes.

Marguerite cornered Noel in the kitchen. He had slunk off midway through the fourth monologue.

"Congratulations. You've turned a nice little cocktail party into a sexual perversity revival meeting. I half expect one of my guests to leap up screaming, 'I is cured, I is done seed de light, praise Jeeeee-zus.'" Marguerite's tone was deadly flat and measured, even while speaking in dialect. It lent a sinister note to her accusations.

"I didn't do anything!"

"Do you think I'm a fool, Noel? I have no powers left, but I still know what's what. I can sense when sorcery's at work, even if I can't stop it. You should be ashamed of yourself, picking on Smitty!"

"I meant it for Dr. Fitzgerald."

"That makes it better? Noel, I am your mother. I forbid you to go on with this black magic nonsense. You are going to forget all about sorcery and being a wizard and—"

"The hell I will!" Noel flung the empty lacquer tray into the wall. The caterer picked it up, tsking, and absented himself.

"You don't have the right to run my life. I've got this power and I'm going to use it or not, because *I* want to—not because you tell me what to do. It's all up to me. For a change, I'm making my own choices."

Marguerite got no chance to reply to her son's declaration of independence. He was out the door, out of the apartment, and nearly to Grand Central Station before she could articulate her feelings or even get her jaw to close.

Later that evening, Kent congratulated her. Everyone was saying she had given *the* cocktail party of the season. Confession with canapés was good for the soul and the social life, it seemed. Not even that could console her. She had lost her son.

6

A Wizard Is a Sometime Thing

"THE BOOK! WHERE'S the book?"

Noel tore his desk apart. Index cards fluttered like wounded pigeons, notebooks sailed aloft like albatrosses, and other tomes—but not *the* book for which he searched so wildly—clumped into the walls like dodos on a downdraft while Noel himself neatly completed the avian scene by going plain raving cuckoo.

Roger leaned against the doorjamb, watching his roommate's mental dissolution with a jaded eye. "What book? The one from Beinecke?"

Noel dropped the desk drawer he'd yanked out and seized Roger by the front of his Bill the Cat T-shirt. "Yes, *that* book! Did you see it? I left it right here on top of my desk and now it's gone!"

"Jon took it back." He detached Noel's grip with insulting ease and flicked off metaphysical cooties.

"He *what*?"

"Hey, you know what a stickler he is for rules. I think it's got something to do with learning programming languages. A computer doesn't understand situational ethics, and neither does Jon. You're not supposed to take stuff *out* of Beinecke. Period. Which reminds me, how'd you manage that?"

"Never mind!"

Noel shoved past Roger and ran most of the way from Old Campus to Beinecke Plaza. The scraggly flaps of the South Africa protesters' tent city snapped in the breeze of his passing. He only slowed down an arm's length before the glass doors in order to compose himself. It wouldn't do to show up looking desperate. University librarians, when compared to the ordinary run, always seemed more suspicious of potential borrowers, and those at Beinecke all but strip-searched you with their eyes.

The woman guarding the desk this time was the exception that proved the rule. There was nothing of the dragon breed in her at all—at first glance—though her surroundings were, in themselves, impressive enough to cow the unwary. The walls of the great marble cube rose up around her, light from outside picking out the dark veins in the translucent stone. It gave the casual visitor the uncanny sensation of having been swallowed by a Rock Mutant. Behind her stood the cube-within-a-cube, the glass enclosure where floor after floor, stack after stack, the rare books were kept. There was no obvious way to enter this sanctum, no door Noel could see. Immediately behind the librarian was a thick metal panel with some dedicatory sentiment—*Give Yale Money and Live Forever* perhaps; Noel couldn't be bothered to read it—but that was all.

Maybe there was no way, short of magic, to get books out of this huge glass display case, Noel thought. From his experience with librarians, he was sure that this was just the way they liked to have it: All the pleasures of possessing an infinite number of books, none of the hassles of people continuously clamoring to *read* them. Beinecke was a bibliophile's paradise.

"Yes? May I help you?"

Noel was momentarily taken aback. Usually those words were uttered as a sullen challenge, if voiced at all. The one other time he'd been in Beinecke, he'd run up against a silver-haired specimen who made it clear that he was an unwelcome distraction in her life, irrupting between scribbling phone messages, running back and forth with the same packet of books, and going on her lunch break.

The librarian on duty now actually sounded as if she wanted to help him. More, she smiled as soon as she spoke.

"Uh . . . yes, thank you. I'm after a book." He showed her his Yale I.D. and stared at her while she examined it. She was fairly young, and more than fairly pretty. In fact, she looked like all those dowdy secretaries in 1940's vintage films, the ones who loved the boss from afar. When he tired of the cheap showgirls, he called the secretary over, tenderly removed her glasses, requested her to take her hair out of that unbecoming bun. She shook its abundant silky waves down over her shoulders and melted into his—

"I said, which book? We've got more than a few." It was spoken as friendly banter, not sarcasm.

Noel snapped out of his daydream. The librarian was waving at the wall of books under glass.

"It's Latin."

"Yes. Go on. Do you know the title? The author?"

Noel worked over his memory and uttered a frightfully garbled version of both, but it was enough. The librarian blanched. "That's . . . quite a book, from what I've heard. Are you sure that's the one you want?"

"I need it for a class paper."

She looked only half-convinced, but she was a professional. "If you go down those stairs to your right and behind you, you'll be in the catalog room. Here's the proper spelling of the title"—she wrote it in a flowery hand that shook only slightly—"and if you give it to someone at the big desk, they'll get it for you."

"Oh, I could get it myself," Noel said eagerly. He figured once he had the book in hand, it was small enough for him to stuff up under his shirt and escape undetected.

"I'm afraid not. Only Beinecke personnel can go back there." She jerked a thumb at the metal panel behind her.

"How do they get in?"

"We can walk right through the wall. Didn't you know? It goes with the job." She laughed quietly, stood, and touched a spot beside the panel. The metal slid back like the secret-passage door in a Gothic novel, though no nightgowned governess trembled on the other side. "Pretty neat, isn't it? Reminds me of *Star Trek*." The panel slid closed again.

That is, it tried to. Halfway there, it jammed.

"Now that's funny . . ." The librarian hit the controls again, to no effect. "I'd better call Maintenance."

Her hand stopped an inch from the phone, no more responsive to her will than the big metal door. Fear, surprise, disbelief, and a terrible suspicion took turns playing with her face. She looked up sharply at Noel. "Then you *are!* What do you think you're do—?"

Her lips froze around the word. Noel redoubled his concentration. The warm carmine aura laving her body turned a cool violet as his will overrode hers. It was hard work, holding a full-grown Yale librarian in cold storage while keeping the door to the stacks open at the same time. Noel could feel himself begin to shake under the strain of juggling spells. He'd never tried running more than one at a time before. It was like overloading an electrical outlet. There were even a few sparklets crackling along the perimeter of the librarian's aura. He finally saw what Lysi meant about the advantages of obtaining more magical power, and resolved to apologize to her as soon as he got her free.

Slowly he edged himself toward the open panel. The twin beams of command streaming from his mind tugged at him like St. Bernards on short leashes. His feet stuck to a hundred unseen wads of chewing gum with every step he took. It cost him ages to reach the narrowly gaping entrance, and only then did he realize that he had no idea of where to seek out Lysi's book even if he did slip into the Beinecke stacks.

Very carefully he tried sending out a strand of power to locate the book and bring it to him. It was one strand too many. The panel slammed shut on his shoulder, the librarian defrosted, and Noel's sinuses jammed with the pain of magic backlash—all in one go.

"Help me!" Noel flailed his free arm about. Pinned with his back to the jamb, there was no way he could reach around and press the button that would release him. "Help!"

"*Shhhhh!* This is a library." Rebuke administered, the librarian hit the panel control. Noel stumbled back from the glass cube, rubbing his left shoulder and arm as the door slid fully closed. "Well!" The librarian sat down hard in her chair. "I haven't had an experience like that in—in—in never mind how long. It's a part of my life that doesn't bear rehashing. Young man, are you really a Yale student?"

"You saw my I.D."

"Yes. Is that your real name? Or have I got Merlin Ambrosius on my hands?" His uncomprehending look made her add, "King Arthur's sorcerer. He was supposed to have been the child of a nun and a demon, which accounted for his magic powers. What's your excuse?"

Noel took a step backward, still massaging his shoulder. Much as he wanted that book back, he wanted more to be gone. This woman spoke with too much knowledge of demons and sorcerers for his comfort.

"Of course, if you were a sorcerer, I suppose you'd have your own demonic familiars about to fetch you all the Beinecke books you wanted." She shrugged, and broke eye contact.

Noel took another step away. He could see himself calling home to tell his folks that instead of making the Dean's List he was going to be burned at the stake. The librarian pushed her glasses up the bridge of her nose and went on talking, riffling through a small stack of file cards on her desk as she spoke.

"Yes, I daresay if you had any true magical powers, you wouldn't be wasting your time getting a liberal arts education. I know *I* wouldn't. You'd be surrounded by a harem of succubi—they don't have too much common sense, but that's not their job—and you'd probably have your own copy of that book you claim to want. And you'd have had the brains to let go of the door-holding spell and concentrate all your efforts on keeping me paralyzed."

Noel paused in his backpedaling course. This woman had just come up with the first good suggestion for wizardly self-actualization he'd heard; one without a spiritual price tag, too. He decided to linger just a little more.

"Focus." the librarian went on. "That's the true secret of any halfway competent wizard's power. That's what Don always used to say, anyhow; when I listened to him."

Noel ran his tongue over his lips and found them bricky. "How do you know so much about magic . . . ma'am?"

The librarian's dazzling smile had lost its effect to charm. "Oh, I used to dabble in the paranormal. It's a common affliction among you young folk—a silly affectation I picked up in college, after a summer that was . . . not exactly what the brochures promised. ESP, white witchery, tarot, scrying . . . My goodness, what foolishness *didn't* I try? All harmless fun, for some. I even came to believe I had some powers of my own." Her smile went out. "I was wrong."

Noel drew nearer again. "What kind of powers? What did you do to get them?" His voice was hoarse with intensity.

The librarian shrugged again. "I deceived myself. Mild hypnotic powers, if that, that's all I had. Just because I could get someone to do whatever I said, I thought I had true magical compulsion at my fingertips. Like what you did to me, just now. Snakes charm birds into paralysis the same way, and there's nothing magical about them. A similar power is exercised over supposedly rational men by women with the biggest damned pair of—" She stopped herself and stabbed an index card through the heart with a Bic extra-fine point.

Noel wanted to protest the verity of his own powers, but a tardy inner voice of caution shut his mouth. Instead, he only said, "I'm sorry if I upset you, ma'am."

" 'Ma'am'?" The librarian's lightly arched brow went up. "Doesn't *that* age me properly! Next you'll be expecting me to have the fantods and need my smelling salts. And I'm only thirty . . . something. No, don't worry, you haven't upset me at all. In fact, I'm happy we met, Mr. Cardiff."

"How did you know—?"

"ESP." His eyes flew wide. "Oh, stop that. I'm joking. I saw your I.D., as you yourself said. Noel Cardiff. And I am Amanda Rhodes. How do you do?" She shook hands with him formally. "I know your father."

"So does most of the East Coast."

"And your mother."

The tone of her voice had changed abruptly. She was no longer joking. Behind her glasses, Amanda Rhodes' eyes met Noel's with a steady gaze that told him her remark about Merlin Ambrosius had been in earnest after all. Noel wouldn't exactly call his father a monk, though PBS made a pretty intellectual cloister, in a pinch. But there was no doubt about what his mother had been, and somehow Amanda Rhodes knew it.

"Yes, Noel, I know her." Her soft words confirmed his worst fears. "I was there when you were born. I don't like to think about it too much these days, though."

"Why? The surgery got rid of the horns and tail," Noel replied bitterly.

"Stop talking like a fool. You were born hornless and tailless, not brainless. I'm your friend, not someone you have to fight. When I first saw the name on your I.D., I wondered whether you were any relation to Kent Cardiff. I owe him a lot. Your father's an intelligent, sensible man, a person of great resource. He and I shared a hard time, but we got each other through. No, not *that* kind of sharing."

Noel protested his innocence. "I never said a word!"

"There are some minds it's impossible not to read. Listen, Noel, I don't believe in the occult—not the dime store demonism all the right people are barking about. They see devils everywhere but in the mirror, and they raise such a hunting howl about it that they distract attention from the real evils. What I do believe is that there are great powers walking this world—forces for true good, forces for evil we can't begin to imagine. Too many of the small-souled can only feel good by proving how bad everyone else is. They find it easier to turn a searchlight on some imaginary wickedness outside than to strike a single inner spark that might show them their own hearts."

She rose from her seat and offered him her hands. He took them, not knowing how to avoid the gesture without looking stupid or rude. They were warm and smooth, like her voice, but her eyes were blazing. Intense women always made him nervous.

"You've got some sort of power, Noel. Real power—it must be real." She didn't need to add *because of what your mother was*. "If you start flashing it around campus like a new charge card, you'll bring the barkers down on you faster than you can roll dice. It was given to you for a reason, the same reason that let us meet here, now. Don't flaunt it. Let it rest. Keep it hidden until you're old enough to know evil, then use your power to fight it." Her hands tightened on his.

Noel pulled away. "When do I change my name to Green Lantern?" He saw the light in her eyes go out. "Don't worry about me. I'm not dumb enough to give free magic shows in public. I waited until no one was around before I used my spells on you, didn't I?"

"In a glass-walled building," Amanda replied.

"Oh." Noel shuffled his feet, glanced covertly through Beinecke's transparent lower walls. No one was there to press a nose to the glass, for which he was exceedingly grateful. "Anyway, don't sweat it about me turning into a big, bad, black magician."

"Very well. I won't. But I will be here if you ever need a friend; for your father's sake." She went back to examining her papers and cards. "Will you still be wanting that book?"

Noel lowered his head. "No." He left the Beinecke as quickly as he could without actually breaking into a run.

Back in the dorm, he slammed his door and threw himself full-length on the bed. Burying his head in his arms, he tried to shut out the ever-returning sight of Amanda Rhodes' knowing eyes. Who was this woman, anyway? She gave him the creeps. Where and how had she met his parents? He supposed he could call home and ask them about her, but could he trust their answers?

He couldn't. There had been too many lies.

He heard his roommates talking in the living room. Even so close, he felt distanced from them by more than space. His shoulder still ached, but he was aching worse inside. In his mind, Amanda Rhodes' face melted into Lysi's.

Why had he let that strange librarian unman him? He was going to use his powers any way he damn well liked, for good or evil! No; for evil alone. That was the only way to get more power, and that was what he wanted.

Wasn't it? It was hard to think, all alone like this. Everything got all boggled in his brain. He always knew what he wanted much better when Lysi was there.

He missed her. He could still see her smile as she listened to him talk about his mother. All the tumble of confused feelings cluttering his mind seemed to sort themselves out when he spoke to Lysi—the shock, the anger, the resentment, even all the love. Lysi knew him. She knew, but it didn't have the same meaning as Amanda Rhodes' knowledge. Amanda was *I know what you did and you'd better not do it again, you naughty little boy.* Lysi was *I know what you did and I understand why you did it.*

He wanted her back. He wanted her back desperately. He could almost feel the silky texture of her hair with its scent of nameless spice drifting over his skin, the stroke of her hands down the length of his back. He could almost hear her voice saying:

"Are you going to lie there hogging the whole bed or could you skootch over some?"

His head popped up. Lysi grinned and sat down on the mattress, nudging him over with her naked hip until she had room enough to stretch out.

"Ahhhh! Now that's much better." Wonderful things happened when she arched her back. She turned to him. "Thanks for letting me loose, Master. Many thanks. *Molto grazie. Muchas gracias. Mille remerciements.*" She went on to find many more linguistic ways of showing her gratitude.

Afterwards, when Noel was able to regain control of his fine motor skills, he saw the fateful book sitting on his desk as if it had never been gone. "How did that get back?" he blurted.

"You're asking me? You're the one who brought it. You're the one who sprang me." Lysi's lips pursed. "You're the one who doesn't have a blindworm's idea of how you did it, either—am I right?"

"I was just thinking about you and . . ."

"It's always the thought that counts, Master. Like the thought you bashed into me when you stuck me in that book to start with. A properly focused thought can do more damage than a whole cartload of curses."

"Focus?" Noel snapped his fingers. "That's what she said! She was right! So she *does* know something about sorcery!"

Slim claws unsheathed on Noel's bare chest and tickled a thin trail of blood from his skin. "She who?"

"It doesn't matter." The claws insisted that it did. Noel became annoyed. It was good—it was undeniably marvelous to have Lysi back, but he'd never met someone who called him "Master" so much and meant it so little. Imperiously he removed her hands from his person.

"We can waste our time talking, or we can spend it more wisely."

"Mmmmm. Suits me." Lysi tried to reestablish contact, only to be fended off a second time.

"I meant business." So did she. "The business of magic," he clarified. "I've been thinking. I know what I want now. I want to be a wizard, with a wizard's full power, and I'll do what I must to get it."

"You will?" Lysi's mouth began to water.

"Evil deeds. I'll do 'em, if I get more power in return. I'm through wimping out. Either I'm a wizard, or I'm nothing. I swear it." Although Noel backed this up with the inappropriate gesture of crossing his heart, Lysi knew his intentions were good.

She also knew which road was thus paved.

She was about to lob out a few suggestions for melting good conduct medals, when a high, nasty peeping sound split the air of Noel's bedroom.

"What the hell is that?" Noel had his hands over his ears.

"Shit," Lysi growled, fumbling under the covers. She pulled out a small brown bat, its red eyes flashing rapidly on and off in sync with the nerve-grinding noise it was making.

"It's my beeper." She squeezed the vermin's stomach firmly. It belched and fell into expectant silence.

Lysi got out of bed and summoned a scarlet jumpsuit into airtight contact with her skin. There was a discreet slit aft for her tail, two more topside for her leathery wings, and a V-neckline that plunged with more abandon than the Grand Canyon. Between her horns was a glittering silver hairbow to match her inch-long sterling fingernails and sequined spike heels.

"Why are you dressed like that?"

Lysi's mouth curled into a playful smile. "I'm going to a masquerade. No, seriously, come along with me and you'll find out, Master. If you've made your decision, you could learn a lot from the folks I'm going to see."

Noel sat up in bed and reached hesitantly for his jeans. "Where are you going?" His enthusiasm was well concealed, even if nothing else was.

Second thoughts are the work of Heaven and the bane of Hell. Lysi could smell one a mile off. She didn't like the way Noel had said "Where are *you* going?" instead of "Where are *we*—?" She whipped the covers from his fair and trembling body and whisked him into an outfit that was almost the twin of hers, but for the fact that it was black, needed to accommodate neither wings nor horns, and sported Gestapo boots and a vampire cape for accessories.

"You'll see, Master. And you'll like it. You meet the nicest damned people at a witches' sabbath." Before he could stall her again, she flashed them gone.

7

A Water-Bed of Intrigue

"Loosen up, Master," Lysi said through clenched teeth. "You're embarassing me."

Noel shook his head rapidly. "I don't like these people. Let's get out of here."

"Easy for you to say!" The she-demon spread her hands to describe the blue chalk pentagram holding her captive. It shone with a faint, guttering phosphorescence, like a glow-worm with emission control problems. "It may not look like much, but it's enough to hold me. Now, will you just give them what they want so we can be gone?"

"Yes, dear boy." A too-chummy arm dropped across Noel's shoulders and a weedy blond leaned in hard on him. "It's not every day we get to blood a real wizard." The speaker looked as if he had slathered his chinless face with cold cream, but as he was stark naked it soon became evident that this was the natural tone and texture of his complexion; all over.

"I'm a real wizard," came a sulky voice from the corner, where an XXX-rated movie was spooling its grainy way across the television screen. "Been one for years. You never made this big a fuss over me."

The blond turned languidly and said, "That's because the darkest magic of which you are capable, Thomas, is convincing the rubes that aliens have landed in Iowa again."

"I'm a serious journalist." By the flickering light of the motel TV, Thomas showed up as an undersized brunet with kinky hair and raggletag beard whose glasses outweighed him easily. Sitting cross-legged on the black simulated-satin rubber sheets, small pot belly bulging over the waistband of his red Playboy bikinis, he resembled a badly done hunk of plastic Buddha.

"And I am the Queen of Rumania. I don't think they're giving the Pulitzer for investigative pieces about three-headed nuns giving birth to mummified Elvis clones." The blond sighed as one who suffers mightily. "It is an evil world we live in, Noel, when something like *that* passes for a news-paperman or a wicked wizard."

"Don't listen to him." On Noel's other side, a Junoesque woman loomed up suddenly, preceded by a foot-long ebony cigarette holder. It was all she had on, besides a look of ennui. "Freddy's biggest contribution to evil has been to serve time as a roadie for a heavy metal rock band. Purveyor of live lizards to the lead singer, *pas vrai, petit?*"

Freddy gave her the shredding eye. "And what have you done to justify your presence at a witches' sabbath, my overripe little tomato?" He pronounced it *toe-maaah-toe.*

The lady swirled her ample hips into one of the patched Naugahyde vibrating lounge chairs. "I do more evil than all of you put together."

This declaration drew cries of outrage from Freddy and Thomas. The other two women present were quick to lodge protests as well.

"You never!" A stick-limbed platinum blonde, skin the color of old leather, pounded her featureless chest. "*I* run a combo fitness center and tanning parlor. Muscle strain *plus* anorexia *plus* skin cancer *plus* some off the most screwed-up self-images in the whole United States of—"

Her companion, who could barely keep her eyes open under the weight of two pairs of false eyelashes and industrial strength mascara, pooh-poohed this eloquently: "Twinkie piss. I'm in the rag trade. This year's line is pure neon stretchies. For him, her, or it. Leaves absolutely nothing to the imagina-tion. Next year we're bringing back leisure suits and hobble skirts. Plaid ones."

"I write diet books when I'm not doing journalism," Thomas provided.

"I do a little scribing of my own," Freddy said grandly. "Seven songs for the band—that's only so far—and you know what you hear when you play them backwards?"

Noel thought he did. "Satanic messages?"

Freddy's lips brushed Noel's ear as he whispered, "Satanic beyond belief. Devilish without a doubt."

"Such as?" Noel quivered expectantly.

"Such as 'You Really Want To Be a Vegas Lounge Singer

When You Grow Up, Don't You?' and 'Yes, Yes, Quit Your Job. *You* Can Write the Great American Novel.' "

"I always liked the one about 'Believe the Politicians, Believe Them All!' " the spa owner said.

Thomas was bold enough to say his favorite was the one enjoining youth to remember that when they were all grown-up they must buy their own children every last fad toy on the market the moment it came out, or risk being branded unfit parents. "That'll put the fear of Moloch into them," he chortled.

The large lady, indifferent to their objections, blew smoke rings the same blue-gray shade as her hair. "Very well. I leave the final judgment to our diabolic minion. Speak truth, Daughter of Lies! Who among us now present has done most to serve your infernal masters? I conjure thee by Azazel and Behemoth, by Lucifer and Moon-Calf, by—"

"Plenty, that's plenty of names already." Lysi waved the lady into silence, then whispered for Noel's benefit, "She can go on for hours, rattling off the roll call down yonder, if she's not stopped." Freddy overheard and tittered.

He stopped giggling when Lysi said, "It is no contest. You and no other of those gathered here have done the greatest ills on earth, Pamela Pinkham."

"Now just a bloody minute—"

"Shut up, Freddy." Ms. Pinkham puffed a double lungful of smoke into his face. He fell back, choking. At liberty, Noel approached the formidable woman. He still wore the bodysuit procured for him by Lysi, and had clung to it, as it clung to him, even during the more athletic ceremonies of the five people gathered in this cheap motel room. Now it made him feel strangely uncomfortable to be so covered next to such a boundless expanse of epidermis, an exaltation of captive lipids.

"Ms. Pinkham—" He was not quite sure how one politely phrased the question he had in mind. "What do you do that's so . . . bad?"

"Beauty advice columns for women's magazines."

"That's it?" Noel was nonplused. "That's all?"

"That is enough. Shall I recount the number of eggs that have been whipped to a froth and poured over thinning hair, at my bidding? The gallons of beer likewise disposed of? The cartloads of avocados that are mashed up and slopped onto dry skin? The hogsheads of honey and almonds converted to facial packs? The tanks of milk inundating desperate bodies? The lemon juice rinses, the cucumber compresses, the pulverized strawberries—! And all so that my devotees may look properly youthful when they go to charity concerts to feed the hungry.''

Noel was visibly impressed.

"Well, *she* has it easy," Thomas sniffed. "She's only got to convince *women* to do something stupid."

"Like convincing fish to swim," Freddy added.

Ms. Pinkham did not respond. She merely rose from her seat and crossed to the closet where the celebrants' clothing hung neatly in a row of welded-on metal hangers. She pulled a small plastic flask from the breast pocket of the smaller size man's suit, a tiny bottle from the pants pocket of the larger.

"Powdered rhino horn," she said, shaking the flask.

"Give that back!" squealed Thomas. He lunged, but the sheets had too much drag for him to get anywhere.

"Civet," she said, twirling the bottle between two fingers.

"Be careful with that! Do you know how many civet cats have to be—?" Freddy shut himself up in mid-sentence. The two men looked chastened.

"I also write an advice column in a popular men's magazine, under a pseudonym. Thus far I have ruined 3967 stereo systems, 9274 bottles of sublime Bordeaux, and 76,398,427,170 meaningful relationships. You would be surprised how many people confuse diameter with circumference, but I am not directly responsible for the inflated expectations of others. I believe the right is mine to claim this latest novice as my ward-in-wickedness. Any nay-sayers?" The Pinkham hand, large and thickly ringed with soap-scummed diamonds, fell on the same shoulder Freddy had so recently quit.

"Don't panic, Master. You won't have to sleep with her," Lysi hissed.

"Silence, Sprat of Iniquity. I heard that," Ms. Pinkham said. To Noel, she remarked, "The demon we command speaks truly there, for once. We would not dream of demanding that a real wizard join in our celebrations. His *atman* would prove too powerful and might overshadow the *ka* of our united *animae*. I needn't tell you what that would mean to the group *purusha*."

"Not at all," Noel answered. He felt ready to agree to any

amount of gibberish if the bottom line precluded his submitting to Ms. Pinkham's severe embraces.

"A *true* wizard, I said." The lady's blackly penciled eyebrows slid into a single unit just above her diminutive nose. "Our she-devil there claims you are one, but we would be fools to trust anything she tells us unsolicited. First you must prove to our satisfaction that you possess genuine magic, and then we shall do as our demonic servant has requested and train you in the furtherance of evil."

"If not . . ." Freddy slithered up to Noel again and made the little kid's gesture of slitting throats with a finger. "We don't like falsies."

The rest of the coven formed a circle around Noel, cutting him off from Lysi in her pentagram. She tried to keep an eye on him by standing on tiptoe, but even with all the force of Hell behind her this was impossible to do in spike heels. She took the philosophical attitude and settled down to file her nails.

In the center of the circle, Noel looked from face to face. "So . . . what do you want me to do?"

"Nothing too garish," Freddy said. "Let's try to keep this as tasteful as possible, in the circumstances."

"Don't do anything *yicky!*" the rag-trade lady said with a delicate shudder. "You know, like blowing up Thomas. I want to see that, I'll catch a teen-goo movie."

"O.K." Noel closed his eyes and folded his arms. He concentrated mightily and set fire to the wastebasket.

Freddy poured three cans of New Formula Coke onto the blaze. Water from the bathroom was out of the question. Both the sink and the bathtub were filled with slowly congealing lime Jell-O for the after-sabbath revels.

"Is that the best you can do? This isn't an Eagle Scout test, you know."

"Hey, I did that no hands!"

"You would be surprised what I can do 'no hands.'" Freddy countered.

"Surprised and not a little disgusted," Ms. Pinkham added. "Thermogenesis is strictly small potatoes with our group. It was one of the first gifts we requested of our personal demon in exchange for our vows of allegiance to Lucifer. We can also sour milk, afflict poultry, and slow up post office lines. You must show us something more."

Noel thought it over. He considered levitating Ms. Pinkham, but he lacked the self-confidence to attempt telekinesis of such dimensions. He toyed with the idea of slamming Freddy into the Gideon Bible in the bedside table, just as he'd done to Lysi, but when he went to fetch it, he found the drawer empty. This was hardly surprising in a motel that offered "Group Siesta Rates, Tour Buses Welcome."

In the end he asked, "What would you like to see me do?"

Ms. Pinkham had a suggestion ready. "Summon a demon."

"But you've already got one." Lysi blew him a kiss from the pentagram and waved.

"Not one for our use, young man; for your own. It took the six of us four weeks of nonstop relay chanting and skyclad dancing to bring us this one."

"We got a little cabin in the Poconos just for the event," Freddy put in.

"The six of you?" Noel counted only five.

"Leopold never could hold his soma." Ms. Pinkham shook her head over another's weakness. "He was caught in the astral backwash when this she-devil appeared and he was turned into a werewolf on the spot. I used my best influence with the AKC to obtain him papers, but he could not join us tonight. This motel has a strict no-pets rule. However, poor Leo does not concern us. You do. True wizards are on a first-name basis with Hell. They need not go through as much as we did to summon demons from the depths. I'd accept that as sufficient proof of your powers."

"Call up a demon?" Noel itched and sweated in his jumpsuit.

"More than one, if you want to be a showoff," Freddy said. "But one will do."

Noel tried to sneak a look at Lysi, but Ms. Pinkham's body effectively blocked the slender succubus from view. He took a deep breath. He was flying this one solo. His first instinct was to grab the telephone and give his mother a ring, but he didn't think that either she or his audience would see the humor in it. Fanatics could always take a massacre in better stride than a joke. He closed his eyes once more, clenched his fists, and focused his thoughts on Hell.

He set fire to the wastebasket again.

"Never believe a demon," Freddy said, slipping into his trousers. He jangled the change in his pockets. "I'm going to get some more soda to throw on the fire. Anyone want anything?''

"Yesssss. I'd like to tear out your liver and eat it whole, raw, and dripping." Goggle eyes the color of stagnant water glowed greenly as the wastebasket flames solidified into the scum-encrusted body of a demon.

Freddy dropped his trousers and his jaw.

"Yicky!" the spa owner squealed.

"Oh gosh oh gosh oh gosh oh gosh oh gosh," her rag-trade sister babbled, fingers dragging mindlessly back and forth across her lips.

"Yes, well, I'd say that proves you're a wizard," Ms. Pinkham said briskly, donning her clothing with the least wasted effort possible. All around her the others were following suit, though without the great lady's Spartan calm. Certain items of dress were inadvertently exchanged in the scuffle. The demon in the wastebasket grinned.

"Yes, yes, it certainly does. I'll be happy to use whatever influence I may to advance your career. You may feel free to look me up any time. Better yet, have your demon call our demon. We'll do lunch. Speaking of which, I am famished. Who would like pizza? Show of hands!"

Ms. Pinkham herded the coven out the door with all dispatch.

Noel's demon hoisted his bandy legs out of the wastebasket, moist chuckles welling up out of his wattled throat. On rabbit's feet he scuttled across the floor to pick up an abandoned ice-blue scrap of lady's lingerie, which he twirled overhead like a lasso. The lace and nylon unmentionable spun itself out into a spiral of cerulean light, then poured down over the demon to cover him in a medieval scholar's gown.

"Great Gorgon! Y'all see them dinks run?" He slapped his concealed furry thigh with delight before offering Noel his hand to shake. "Mighty proud to meet up with someone like you, Massster. Prouder'n a pig with a purple pocketbook, an' that's a fact. Name's Bob. Use to be a sight more to it, but the Underlords call you and y'all better be there 'fore the second syllable hits the fan." He leaned against an invisible door-jamb, the horny plates above his eyes lifting at a cocky angle. "Ssso what can I do for you?"

Noel's first impulse was to run after the outgoing coven crowd and offer to treat all hands to an extra large pepperoni, on condition no one mention wizardry in his presence again.

First impulses, however, were lately losing a lot of their zing with Melisan's boy. The more he dabbled with magic, the less frightening its results became. He had no way of knowing that the greatest challenge of Hell was not so much to keep the wicked suffering as to maintain their interest.

Therefore, Noel quickly assumed a look of cool command and said, "Take us back to my dorm. Right now."

Bob tipped him a wink. "No way, Massster." He cocked his head at Lysi. "Less'n you want to leave Sugar Baby there in the lurch."

"Get me out of this damned pentacle," Lysi demanded. *"Right now!"* She stamped her foot. For a moment Noel thought he saw a flash of black webbing, but when he looked again it was just a lady's dainty instep. He rubbed out one side of the chalk pentacle with his foot and Lysi stepped free.

"Hi, Sssweetcheeks." Bob's grin went a longer way than most. His scholar's robe rippled in oddly disturbing ways as he gave Lysi the glad eye, but Noel was not about to inquire into the underlying cause. "Long time no see. Raleel sends his—"

"You can go now," Lysi rapped out. She hooked her arm through Noel's. "Your services are no longer needed."

"Says who? Don't ssseem's I recall anyone down under getting sssaved and leaving you bosssss. I take orders from my massster. Read the handbook, Tootsss."

Lysi's scowl only made Bob snigger and hiss like an overheated radiator. "Tell him to hit the brimstone trail, Noel," she directed, expecting instant obedience.

Noel did not obey. Gently he disengaged is arm from hers and tapped his chin thoughtfully. "I'm a little new to this, Bob. I know I called you up from Hell—"

"Virginia Beach, but we won't quibble, Massster."

"Wherever. Tell me how I did it."

The small demon looked skeptical. "You mean you don't know? Sssay, what kind of half-asssssed operation is this?"

"Silence!" Noel's voice reverberated through the room. His face was tinged with a bright green aura, and when he smacked his fist into his palm, lurid purple sparks flew up. Lysi's spine went cold. Bob cringed, losing a lot of his visible insubordination. "Maybe you'd better watch the way you speak to me, Servant. If I could summon you without knowing how it's done, imagine what I can do once I do

know." His smile was slightly contemptuous. "Think about it."

Bob thought. "You centered your mind on a hellspawn, and because you didn't name names, you got me."

"Just like that?"

"Hey, you got the power." Bob shrugged. "Use it or lose it."

"What were you, top of the waiting list?"

" 'Sss one way of looking at it." The demon did not want to commit himself.

Noel was very pleased with himself. "So now you're my familiar too. Not bad. I'll bet there aren't many wizards have two demons at their beck and call."

"There's no limit to how many demons you can call up, Massster," Bob said. "There just aren't many wizards'd want to support more'n one at a time. Cossstly; very cossstly."

"Costly how?" A little of Noel's smugness flaked away. "I never signed anything, you know. I still have my soul . . . don't I?" He appealed the matter to Lysi.

"Of course you do." She snapped her fingers and returned the pair of them to more Ivy League-acceptable garb. "Don't worry about our upkeep, Bob. Our master's an excellent provider."

"I am?" Noel was fast losing his calm. "How? I haven't given you a thing!"

Lysi snuggled up and grazed his ear lobe with her exquisitely sharp little teeth. "You've given me plenty."

"Lysi's a succubus, Massster." Bob's leer was a testimony to fluoride-treatments in Hell. "They feed on libido. Sssurprised y'all didn't know that, seeing as who your kinfolk are. Your momma, she sure did have herself a reputation for pigging out on passion. Mmmm-*mm!* You jes' betcha she—"

The bolt of ice smashed into a whirl of twinkling snowflakes when it hit Bob's chest dead-center. The demon yelped and tumbled paws-over, coming to rest with his head in the wastebasket that had spawned him. He sat up and removed the basket from his head, scraping soggy ash from his cheeks and shoulders. Then he took one look at Noel's face, white and red with fury, and jammed the basket right back on.

"What'n sweet blue tunket did I say wrong *this* time?" His whine echoed eerily into the upended can.

Noel marched across the room and jerked the wastebasket

off Bob's head. "What do you know about my mother?" he barked, leveling a finger between the demon's rolling eyes. A leftover wisp of blue frost seeped from beneath the nail bed.

Bob swallowed hard. "N-n-nothing, Massster. I just know what I read on the Little Incubus' room wa— I mean, every demon knows every other demon, even the ones that turned tail on us and went mortie."

"Well, she's not one of you anymore, so you can forget all about her. Got me?"

"Almost."

"What was that?"

"I said, yesssssir. Right. Your wish is my command. Whatall d'you want? Back to your dorm, right? You got it!"

With a flick of his claws and a flitter of wine-colored light, Bob's gown belled out into a balloon that enclosed the three of them for an instant.

It was an instant that lasted an age for Noel. He heard strange, high-pitched noises, and the deeper tones of human speech muttering complicated curses. The demon's blue gown parted into emptiness. Noel groped for Lysi's hand and fell into a void, where direction was a jest and time an impossibility. Green dits flashed before his eyes. He flew headfirst through emerald-spangled black, making straight for a shining wall. Wild winds of the abyss tugged at his hair. Beyond the wall, a huge face scowled, hideous in anger, and further maledictions rolled in sonorous waves from its bulging lips. Noel screamed and crossed his arms in front of his face, but his cry was torn from his throat as he reached the glassy barricade and hurtled through in a smoking, glittering, howling explosion.

8

User Fiendly

"MASTER, MASTER, WAKE up!"

Noel cast off the veils of unconsciousness one by one. Lysi's face swam into view. She looked genuinely concerned. In a dreamy, detached way he thought how sweet it was of her to care so much about him. No commonsensical voice chimed in to caution him that demons were not supposed to be sweet.

"I'm O.K., Lysi, don't worry." He brushed his fingers through his hair, expecting to find splinters of glass. There was a mattress under him—Yale issue to judge by the lumps. He sat up in a dorm room like many others, though he didn't recognize the wall hangings as his. "What happened?"

"Ask the genius over there." Lysi did not sound pleased. Noel looked at where she pointed.

From the tilt-back swivel chair in front of his PC, Jonathan Davis gave Noel the thumbs-up sign. "Just doing like you asked, Master," he said.

It was not Jonathan Davis' way to call any of his roommates "Master." Then again, it was not Jonathan Davis' voice.

From inside the Computer Science major's angular body, the demon Bob chortled. "Hey! Hey, y'all hear that? I said *Master,* 'thout no hissing hardly 'tall. Sumbitch, but I do 'preciate good dental work. Sorcerer. Sousaphone. Cecily. Saskatchewan. Sesquipedalian. Sustenance. Hooo-*eee*, this is fine!" He slapped Jon's thigh with more Down Home relish than the usurped Mr. Davis was likely to find in his purebred Brooklynese background.

It was disconcerting for Noel to hear Bob's faintly Southern accent coming out of Jon's mouth. He jumped off the bed and gave the swivel chair a mighty spin to bring the s-spouting demon full-face with him. "What happened?" he repeated.

"Just doing like you asked, Master; brought you back to the dorm slicker'n owl shit. Grabbed the nearest astral gateway—" he nodded at the computer screen "—and popped us through. 'Course you never did say you shared these here premises with excitable types. Soon's we nip through the screen I hear a whole lotta bellering worse'n hog slaughter time. 'What did you do to my program? What kind of inter-face is this?' " Bob's mimicry of Jon's unreliable tenor was perfect. " 'You have access to these files?' "

Bob's green eyes gleamed behind Jon's wire-rimmed glasses. "I showed him what sorta access I had, all right."

"You mean you just—took over his body?"

Bob linked his fingers behind Jon's head and leaned back. "Yup."

"Well— Get out of there! Now!" Noel waved his hands sharply until Lysi made him stop.

"Master, you're not trying to get a dog off the sofa. We're talking exorcism here."

"Fine, so we talk it. How does it work? Never mind. I got him here and I'll get him out. I exorcise thee." Noel waggled his fingers in his roommate's occupied face and awaited results.

Bob held back a snicker poorly.

Noel looked abashed. "It didn't work. Do I have to say it three times? Or was I supposed to mention him by name? 'I exorcise thee, Bob' . . . I don't know, it just sounds so dorky. Maybe if I set something on fire . . ."

Lysi rubbed his back soothingly. "Sorry, Master, you simply can't do it. An exorcism is the big time, and you're just a bush-league wizard. You haven't got the power."

"Why don't I? I called him up! He's my familiar, and he's supposed to do my bidding. O.K., so I'm bidding him to haul ass out of Jon's body before I count ten or—"

"Or what?" Bob twisted Jon's usually bland face into a nasty sneer. "I'm within my rights. I was just obeying or-ders. If you'd studied any gramarye at all, you'd know that the First Law of Demonics says that familiar spirits are bound to protect their masters. That includes protection from discov-ery. It's never too late for a witch hunt. The Second Law's obedience. Well sir, I did like you said, but when this yahoo started his yowling, I had to protect you, now didn't I? So I shut him up the least fatal way I could. Ain't you proud of me?"

Noel sagged back onto Jon's bed. "I don't get it. I'm protected half past Thursday now, and you can make Jon forget he ever saw us come out of his PC. So why can't you obey me and get out of Jon's skin?"

"Because the *Third* Law of Demonics, Master dear, says every good demon shall and should grab what he can while the grabbing's good and not let go till doomsday."

"Once a demon occupies a human body, he can only leave if he feels like it or if commanded out by a person of sufficient powers," Lysi said. "Since Bob took over this one in fulfillment of his obligations as your familiar, you haven't a leg to stand on, Master."

"Squatters' rights," Bob said. "Nyah."

Noel said nothing. If Bob or Lysi had watched enough PBS programming, they might have recognized his introspective look as one Kent Cardiff often wore when pondering whether to lionize or liquidate his guest speaker.

After a time he asked, "What if I give you another command to fulfill? One where you have to leave campus?"

"I'll do it. Don't hardly have no other choice, under the rules. Yeah, even if you send me to the heart of Hell itself, Master, I'll obey. But I'll take *this* with me." Bob studied his earthly lodging one limb at a time. "Nice little body the boy's got here. Too bad was something to happen to it. Nothing in the rules say I have to protect anyone but you, y'know."

"You'll never get him out, Master," Lysi whispered. "Every familiar banks on finding an excuse for getting into a mortie's skin sometime. When that happens, nine out of ten mages feel sorry for their fellow morties, so they don't make the familiar inside do anything too strenuous, for fear it'll kill the borrowed body. It's like a demon's holiday."

"And the tenth?"

"The tenth has what it takes to pry the demon loose."

"I see." Noel lapsed back into deep thought. Bob hummed a nerve-grating little tune. His left hand began to stray over the PC keyboard until his right slapped it away.

" 'Scuse me, Master. Seems like your roommate's got fractious on me."

"Jon?"

At the sound of that name, the left hand made another leap for the keyboard, only to be fended off again by the right.

"Had to stow him somewhere," Bob explained, holding the left hand captive in his lap. "Good thing there wasn't that much to him, else I'd had to give him maybe half, maybe a whole arm. Every displaced spirit needs a different amount of elbow room. Hey! Elbow room! I like that." He slapped his thigh again, and the left hand made a break for it. It typed several strings of characters across the screen before Bob pinned it down and sat on it.

"Feisty little sumbitch." Bob erased the message, but not before Noel read his captive roommate's plea for help.

"You win, Bob," he said. He stood up. "If that's how it works, there's nothing I can do to change the rules. I'm just going to give you one last chance to get out now."

"Or else?" Jon's features were not at their most attractive when forced into a fey expression of innocence by a demonic tenant.

"Or else I'll make you get out. Not now; later."

"I've got all the time in the worlds, Master." The demon gave an exaggerated yawn. "I'll find plenty to amuse me while I'm waiting. Seems Jon-boy's squeakin' a little something in my inner ear 'bout how he'll trade all he knows 'bout these here machines if'n I give him some access time. Whatever the Hell that is." He swiveled back to face the screen.

Noel made a peremptory signal for Lysi to follow him out of Jon's room. They left the possessed body with its right hand playing hunt-and-peck on the PC keyboard while the left hand flew.

When the door closed behind them and Lysi saw that no one else was in the living room, she asked, "Why did you say that? You can't make Bob vacate. I already explained—"

"You said that the tenth magician can force a demon out of a human body. O.K. So I'm going to be that tenth magician. I need more power? I'll get more power."

Lysi tried to look solemn. "Power costs."

"You told me. Evil. So how much wrongdoing is it going to cost me to dislodge that demon?"

"Let me see . . ." Lysi whipped out a pocket calculator shaped like a small dragon. Numbers and arcane symbols flashed between its tiny jaws when she poked its belly. "Hard to say, what with market fluctuations. Yesterday's sin is today's trendy must-do. Then there are cultural differences to calculate. A good lamp-shaking belch at table can be compliments to the chef in Kyoto but get you off the A-list in Newport. Of course there is the package deal. . . ." She looked at him sideways and offered her most disarming smile.

"I'm not selling my soul."

Lysi pouted, but only for a moment. "Who asked for that, Master? I'll tell you what, you come up with some nasties to do and I'll start a running tab for your misdeeds. When you've saved up enough negative energy, I'll help you use it to oust Bob. Fair enough?" She offered her hand.

Noel did not take it so fast. "How do I know you'll tell me the truth about when I have enough magic?"

"Here." She tucked the little dragon into the breast pocket of his flannel shirt. He felt it move, miniscule claws piercing the fabric and his skin. The horned head thrust out of the pocket and smiled an LED display of zeros, then ducked back inside.

"It's—alive?" Noel nearly inserted one probing finger into his pocket, then reconsidered.

"Definitely. Machines are the province of morties. Everything *we* use is strictly organic. Oh, don't be so close-minded, Master. Cruncher will keep an accurate tally of your malfeasances, and credit them according to the fair market value in effect for your time and geographical location."

Noel pinched the pocket open a fraction. "What do I feed him?"

"Just go about your business and rack up those iniquities. That'll be enough for him. He's a workaholic." A tiny roar issued from the pocket, making Lysi smile. "And he's hungry. Got any ideas to get the old Baal rolling?"

Noel considered, fingers to lips. Then he too was grinning. "Yeah," he said, nodding his head in benediction of his own genius. "Yeah, I've got one. How about I break a commandment *and* stab Western Civilization right where it hurts, all at the same time?"

"You're going to burn that Beinecke book for me?" Lysi's eyes as much as said *My hero!*

"No," said Noel. "I'm going to burn PBS."

9

Cacodemons Are
Standing By

LYSI STOOD OUTSIDE a pay phone booth in Grand Central Station, waiting for Noel to emerge from the men's room. She was not wasting her time while she waited. She knew better than most that idle hands were the Devil's playground.

"Mister, could you spare some change so I can make a phone call?" She had change of her own, but saw no reason to use it when minor extortion would provide.

The gent Lysi waylaid snarled and tried to get past her. He used the New York Stalk, a combination of fullback's rush, hockey player's body-check, and rhinoceros' unseeing charge.

Lysi used the Gehenna Moon, an eyeblink-quick illusory dropping of every article of clothing she wore. Then, while her victim remained frozen in awe and disbelief (The girl was totally dressed. Wasn't she? He could have sworn . . .) she repeated her request. He parted company with $2.46 in coins and stumbled away in search of liquid psychoanalysis.

Lysi dialed quickly, one eye peeled for Noel's return. "Hi, Raleel? It's me, Lysi . . . Your *sister,* frog-face. Listen, I just wanted to thank you for sending Bob around. Yeah, he actually did something right for a change. Forced my pigeon's hand, is all. We're on the road to Hell with this one's soul for sure . . . Of course I'm positive. He's going to do wicked deeds with *good intentions* behind them. Say no more, right? It won't take long before he forgets all about his original reasons for wrongdoing, once he gets a taste of what real power's like. Then I can name my price, and you know what that's going to be. Daddy's as good as free. So what do you think of your sister now? . . . Stop laughing, Raleel! Ohhhh, I hope your ratings go down the pipes!" Lysi slammed the receiver, then melted it for good measure.

She came out of the booth just as Noel returned. He was

carrying a box of candy and a small stuffed bear wearing an *I Love New York* T-shirt. He passed these to her without a word.

"For me?" Lysi lifted the lid of the candy box and sniffed appreciatively. Succubi were not above bonbons.

"Souvenirs." Noel tried to act as if the gifts had materialized in Lysi's hands from parts unknown. "Your first trip to New York."

"Truth to tell, I've been here before. Ever hear of Black Thursday?"

"Yeah, but . . . I wasn't with you that time."

The two of them stood there for a time. It was hard to say which one looked more uncomfortable. Finally Noel glanced up at the gigantic clock overhanging the Forty-Second Street entrance to the station and seized on the perfect way to break the uneasy silence. "Look at the time! We'd better get going."

As he dragged her from the station, Lysi passed several garbage cans. Any one of these would have served for ditching the teddy bear. Candy was one thing—any excuse for Gluttony was fine with the Underlords—but the bear could not be turned into a mortal sin so easily. There had once been a motion before the Reform Committee to promote tackiness to sin-status, but it was vetoed at the top. Hell had its pride.

The bear was an innocent gift of the heart. It represented thoughtfulness, tenderness—and most unpardonable of all—affection. Each of these sentiments alone was bad enough in a soul one hoped to drag down. Together, they were symptomatic of inborn wholesomeness fit to gag a ghoul. To ignore such symptoms—or worse, to aid and abet them—would leave a black mark on any self-respecting demon's record, tantamount to a Miss America candidate doing the swimsuit-walk nude, gravid, and coked to the eyeballs.

Lysi knew all this. She should have thrown the bear right back into Noel's face, with a scornful laugh. (She was good at scorn.) At the very least she should have tossed it. She told herself that she had every intention of doing so. But she didn't do it, and she didn't even ask herself why.

In a television studio somewhere in Virginia, Raleel stole a vision-aided peek at his twin. She was clutching Noel's arm with one hand, the teddy bear with the other. He laughed so hard that he was almost unable to go on the air.

"So you're Lysi. Terribly pleased to make your acquaintance, my dear.'' Kent Cardiff shook the she-demon's hand warmly. ''Awfully grateful that you've consented to help us out here. Pledge Week can be such a bore, but I needn't explain necessary evils to you. Freshman English and all that.''

''It's all in a good cause, Mr. Cardiff,'' Lysi gushed. ''I simply adore educational television. Paradox is my life. And it's *so* important. If you didn't raise enough money, whatever would become of PBS?''

''I suspect we should have to descend to eating our young, or at the least strike a deal for Colonel Sanders to purchase Big Bird. It doesn't bear thinking about. Fortunately, thanks to people like you and Noel and these others to man the phones, such an outcome's most unlikely.''

His hands described the compass of the room, where tiers of desks were already being occupied by the volunteers who would answer all incoming promises of support for public television. They were about equally split between the super-fashionable and the self-consciously bohemian. There would have been no need for a fund drive at all had PBS been able to garnishee what the first group paid for hairstyles and nail-wraps and what the second group paid for pre-shabbied jeans and Third World chic.

''I'm ever so happy to help out.'' Lysi wrapped her arms around Noel and gave him a lingering squeeze. ''I'd do just about anything for the sake of culture.''

''So I see.'' Kent set his pipe to his lips and looked indulgent, all-knowing, and benevolent toward Young Love.

Lysi laughed aloud, right in his face. Kent dropped the benevolence in favor of a baffled stare.

''Would you excuse us a minute, Dad?'' Noel hustled Lysi off to an unoccupied corner of the studio. ''What's the idea?''

Lysi pressed a fist to her mouth to subdue her chuckles. Between sputters she said, ''I couldn't help it! He's such a—*tweed!* I could just see his thoughts: 'Hallelujah, Noel's finally getting some. Praise be, the boy's normal.' That's the same man who'd lock you up in a convent until age forty-three if you had an X chromosome where your Y is.''

''Don't talk about my father like that.'' Noel wasn't laughing. Suddenly, neither was Lysi. ''Apologize to him.''

''For what? Who do you think you are—?''

''I'm your Master. Do as I say.''

This was quite a change from the young man who so
recently had given her words of tenderness, devotion, and a
stuffed bear. Lysi began to protest, then stopped. Instead, a
lazy smile dimpled her cheeks. A high-handed air of command was one of the first symptoms of increasing power-hunger.

"How right you are, Master. Forgive me for forgetting
myself. I'll do as you say at once." Unexpectedly, she
pressed her body tight against his and gave him a kiss that
turned his bones to tofu. "I just love it when you give
orders," she husked.

Through a pleasantly buzzing haze, Noel saw her walk
back to his father and explain the reason she'd broken into
such inopportune mirth. At that distance, he could pick up
only snatches of Lysi's story, but he gathered it involved a
complicated, interlocking series of literary puns inspired by
Kent's pipe, and ending with a perfectly hilarious line from
one of Aristophanes' plays, which Lysi quoted in the original
Greek. Kent still looked befuddled, but at least this was
confusion on a more intellectual plane.

With his father occupied, Noel slipped away. By his watch,
there wasn't a quarter hour left before Pledge Week went on
the air. He needed to get someplace where he could set his
plan in motion.

It was an evil plan, and he was proud of it. He'd thought it
up himself, refusing even to tell Lysi the specifics. "If this
isn't good for a wad of nasty-points, I don't know what is,"
he told himself as he found the nearest men's room and shut
himself in a stall. In his breast pocket, Cruncher growled
hungrily. "Yeah, yeah, cool it. You'll have plenty to chomp
down soon enough, boy."

The tiny dragon shut up. There was silence in the restroom.
The young wizard closed his eyes and stretched his hands
forth above the waters. As he had done to summon Bob, so
now he aimed all his thoughts and desires on the creatures of
the netherworld and bade them arise from the depths. It did
seem like the perfect place for launching such a call. He'd
certainly done well enough with a motel wastebasket. His
ears strained to catch the sound of bubbling in the makeshift
porcelain cauldron before him.

In a bit, when his head started to hurt, he opened his eyes.
He was still alone in the stall. He tried a second time,

visualizing fiends straight out of Hieronymus Bosch's least repressed mental picnics. The results were the same.

A pounding came from the stall door. "Hey, you gonna be in here all day, bud?"

"No, just a second." Failure tasted sour in his mouth. He flushed the toilet for credibility's sake and came out.

"Hey, thanks a lot. Thought I was gonna lose it," said the pig-snouted demon outside. He shoved past Noel and locked himself in. His four comrades—all of the same beast-human mix—yelled after him to hurry it up, they too had needs.

"Be with you in a second, Master," a chicken-legged fiend said affably, making the O.K. sign with four-inch talons. His second face, growing just above where the feathers began, added, "There ain't no potty-stops on the road from Hades."

It took Noel about as long to get hold of himself as it took the five demons to attend to their needs. They ranged themselves in a row, leaning against the sinks, and regarded Noel expectantly. Their leader was a creature with flaky dull-gold skin and a melon-sized tarantula for a head.

"Yuh?" he inquired, hairy legs curling. Noel outlined his desires. "Yuh." The demon pumped Noel's hand with his own seven-digited extremity and motioned for his troops to move out.

When Noel spread-eagled himself on the men's room door, blocking their exit, he learned that it is possible for a tarantula's face to register annoyance. "You can't go out there looking like *that!*" he exclaimed.

" 'Smatter?"

"Those people out there aren't used to demons." *With the exception of my father,* he thought. *And I'll bet even he never saw any that looked like you.* "If you scare them off, the whole plan's ruined."

"We thought that was the idea," the chicken-legged demon said, edging to the fore. "Stop Pledge Week dead."

"Not stop it, *spoil* it. If the phone volunteers run away, they'll just postpone the fund drive. What I want is for you to use everything in your powers to discourage people from donating one penny to PBS."

"Discourage them?" The demon's nether face frowned. "We don't do discouragement," his upper face said.

"Destruction, devastation, defloration, and degradation, O.K.

But discouragement . . .'' A demon resembling a fuzzy green
bedroom slipper dipped in peanut butter scratched what had to
be his head. "Dunno."

Noel drew back his shoulders. "You'll do as I say. I'm the
master here!" He liked the sound of that. "Yeah. I'm *your*
master. I'm the one telling you what to do, so you do it."

"Awright, awright, don't dribble in your drawers." Hamster paws attached to an aardvark's body motioned for Noel to
calm down. The human face surmounting all had acne. "We'll
handle it. Just tell us what you want."

"I told you, didn't I? No more excuses. I'll expect to see
you all in the studio in exactly thirty seconds after I leave this
room. Looking normal. I mean, looking human. Now *move
it!*" Noel turned on his heel and left.

The five demons looked at one another, even though it was
not a pleasant activity.

"Tyro," said Tarantula.

Pig Snout tittered. "Probably just got his first taste of
magic and he's pigging out on power. I can smell 'em a mile
off."

"So whadda we do, huh? He didn't give us specifics,"
Hamster Paws said.

The chicken-legged demon's lower mouth blew a Bronx
cheer at the closed men's room door. The upper had more
helpful advice to offer. "We wing it. Look, what choice do
we have? He summoned us, and by the laws of Hell we're his
until he dismisses us or we fulfill our mission. I don't know
about you guys, but these *nouveaux mages* give me a pain in
the tail-feathers. He's got a lot going for him, granted, or
he'd never have drawn up five of us at one go, but he's never
been on the pulling end of the strings before. You can always
tell. Let's do what he wants and get out of here before he
really starts jerking us around."

The demon's claws clicked together and a prim young lady
in a navy business suit stood beside the urinals. She picked up
the Mark Cross attaché case at her feet. In moments, the four
other demons had effected similar changes in their appearances.

"Ready," Tarantula said from behind his nattily trimmed
black mustache and curling beard. The others echoed their
own readiness.

The young lady lifted her case and peered inside. "Are you
all right in there?" she asked.

" 'Sallright," her spare face replied.

Noel watched with satisfaction as a group of five perfectly ordinary-looking people marched into the studio with military precision, taking their places at the phones. A technician urged the rest of the volunteers to be seated and in the blink of a camera's red light, Pledge Week began.

In the first tier of desks, a grad student from Barnard began to blink convulsively. Her right-hand deskmate asked if anything was wrong. It was early in the program yet, and the phones rang only sporadically. For some reason, these sporadic rings seemed to come in on five phones only.

"I'm not sure," the Barnard student answered. She touched the corner of one eye gingerly, terrified of smearing her mascara. Her roommate had told her this was a great place to meet sensitive guys. "I think maybe I've got something stuck in my contact—"

She stiffened in her seat, eyes staring straight ahead. Her deskmate reached out to shake her, but his hand swerved back to clamp onto the handset of his phone. He too sat up straighter than he ever had in his life, despite having a posture-obsessed mother. His eyes opened wide, the pupils dwindling to pin points.

On the left side of the Barnard girl, an impeccably suited young businesswoman smirked. One by one, all up and down her row, volunteers were seizing up like unpampered Porsche engines. She knew without looking that the same was happening in the tiers behind her. Subliminal cackles of delight from her fellow fiends tripped across her mind as they congratulated her on coming up with such a fine plan. She shrugged aside their praise and telepathed Phase Two instructions to her cohorts. Under the desk, the Mark Cross attaché shook with laughter.

Now, for the first time, all the phones were ringing as the demons relinquished control of the lines.

"Hello?" The Barnard students's voice was hollow. She held her phone with all the fluid ease of a Barbie doll, and her words came out as animated as a busy signal.

"Yes this is PBS Pledge Drive why don't you send us lots of money and we will make sure to program the finest in educational stuff like all those good British dramas so you can listen to the accents and pretend you've got great taste in

literature when you haven't picked up a book in years . . .
Yes this year we will do the life of King James II the one who
burned all the innocent women as witches and who liked little
boys and William Shakespeare you know what *he* was when
it came to those young actors and maybe Lord Byron's life he
really loved his sister if you get my drift . . . And your
dollars make all this possible and we will list your name on
the TV screen so all your neighbors and your kids can see it
. . . Same to you thank you." She hung up and made several
notes on the forms in front of her. She never even looked
down at the papers.

Lysi watched the volunteer to her left go through a similar
spiel. Zombie-like he promised his caller that PBS intended to
sponsor tag-team mud-wrestling matches between a famous
political-commentary pair and a brace of film critics. To her
right she overheard a woman in a New Wave haircut demanding funds to back a special to be called "Kipling was Right:
Why the Third World Needs Imperialism So the Benighted
Heathen Don't Kill Each Other Off." The lumberjack clone
in the seat one row below hers was touting a science program
on "Sloppy Mating Rituals: Youth Wants to Know," to
preempt *Sesame Street* and *Mister Rogers' Neighborhood*.

"What do you mean where will your kids learn their
letters and numbers lady why don't you teach the little yard
apes how to read and count yourself you're not that stupid
you're just too damned lazy." He took a long pause, listening. "Yes I see thank you." He wrote something down.

Chance had seated Noel between two of the disguised
demons. His own phone rang unanswered as he listened to
first one of them, then the other, offering their callers a PBS
schedule of kung fu movies and "Julia Child Cooks With
White Bread and Mayo." *Lord of the Flies*, *A High Wind in
Jamaica*, and *The Children's Hour* were proposed as much
more educational programming for the milk-and-cookies set
than anything currently on the screen.

"Look, let's not kid ourselves," the transformed Pig Snout
said in a reasonable tone. "*You* know they're little horrors
and *I* know they're little horrors, so isn't it time *they* found
out just how rotten they really are? Maybe that'll get the
pint-sized varmints to shape up. Ain't nothing like guilt, take
my word for it."

Noel did not see the look of perplexity that slowly came

over Pig Snout's face as the demon listened to the caller's reply. He was eavesdropping on Tarantula's conversation on the merits of bringing a twenty-four episode "Life of Madonna" to the viewing public. "No, not *the* Madonna; *that* Madonna." Noel bit his lip to keep from laughing in triumph.

He bit it a sight too hard. "Yow!" Blood trickled down his chin as he patted his pockets for a hankie that wasn't there. He abandoned his post to cadge one from his father.

Kent Cardiff had just come off the side-set, where one PBS celebrity after another took turns exerting their money-making charms upon the audience. As Noel came nearer to the group of technicians, fellow performers, and assorted hangers-on congratulating Kent on his sincerity, he saw his mother among them.

"Oh, my goodness! Noel, what have you done to yourself this time?" It was too late to avoid her, much too late for him to escape her assault of maternal first aid. He was dragged into the corridor and forced to have his lip blotted repeatedly with tissues, then with a scented hankie soaked in cold water from the drinking fountain.

Through all stages of the treatment, Marguerite kept up a barrage of questions without pause for any answers. "What are you doing here? Why didn't you tell me you were coming? How long have you been in New York? Is everything all right at school? How did you cut your lip? Noel, you haven't been in a fight? Did you tell your father you were going to be here? Did you tell him not to tell me? Why do you think I'm your enemy? Haven't you forgotten all that silliness about my past yet? Why can't we be honest with each other? Are you listening to me?"

She went on like that while splashing water all over Noel's shirt and shoes. Once or twice he tried to get in a reply, but Marguerite wasn't one for long breaths between sentences. Noel's head began to throb. This wasn't the first time he'd had to endure one of his mother's tirades. It was a scolding disguised as an inquiry about his welfare, but a scolding still.

It dawned on him that he didn't care for scoldings. He wasn't a child anymore. He was a man, and more than that. How many men could claim to control the forces of Hades? Five demons even now did his bidding, a lovely succubus shared his bed, and if he did happen to have a less than cooperative familiar awaiting him in New Haven, he'd soon settle Bob's Hellish hash.

Why couldn't he take care of Marguerite?

"Mom," he said. "Shut up."

Marguerite stared at him. Then she burst into tears.

An hour and a half later, when Noel had sworn a host of oaths to convince his mother that he hadn't meant it, please stop crying, and he would be good in future, they returned to the studio. A distinctly cooler atmosphere prevailed between mother and son, all his protestations aside. Inwardly, Noel dreaded what his father was going to say. To judge by Marguerite's air of righteous determination, she was going to tell Kent everything, Noel's promises of reform be damned. As always, it would be for his own good.

"Kent, there is something I want you to hear. I know you have to go on the air again, but this won't take—"

Kent fastened the last button of his Burberry. "Can it wait until we get home, dear?"

"Home? But aren't you scheduled to make another plea?"

"Not this year. Perhaps not next." He knotted his muffler. "It's finished."

Finished! Noel's chest went tight. He hoped he could conceal his elation.

"Pledge Week is over. With matching gifts from our industry sponsors, we've got money to burn. We made twice our goal and thought it would just be hoggish to keep after people for more contributions." Kent gestured to the now-empty tiers of desks, the technicians securing their equipment. In the classy library set, Lysi sat dejected in the big leather armchair. "We let everyone go home. I never saw the like. They even refused to take the bonus gifts. I shall not understand Americans as long as I live."

Noel stole away to Lysi's side. "Where are the others?" he whispered.

"Gone. Summoned by the Underlords." The way she said it told Noel that the five were not going to be getting any medals back home. "Not even the greatest wizard's powers can hold a demon when he's called by them. And yours?" Her laugh was short and caustic.

"I *wanted* them to ruin Pledge Week!"

"As a week, it's ruined. As a couple of hours, it was fine. Besides giving PBS enough funds to dramatize the *Oxford*

Unabridged Dictionary, you've also brought untold joy to all the viewers who can't stand having their programming schedules thrown off by the station whining for contributions. Some of that bunch might even send in extra money out of sheer relief!''

"I thought demons could destroy anything. What did I do wrong?''

"You might have given them more specific directions. Instead, you left them to their own imaginations. One of the first rules of sorcery is always remember that cacodemons don't have a hummingbird's plop worth of imagination.'' She smacked her fist into her palm. *"Twice* the funds-goal!''

"But—but after what I heard, I thought—''

"Either the callers thought they'd heard wrong or else they assumed that PBS must be in real financial trouble to propose such a radical programming turnabout. They gave money to stop it. Except for the ones who gave money to see it happen and called all their weird little pals in on it too. I got some good leads for later . . .''

Lysi thumbed half-heartedly through her little black book while Noel dipped into his breast pocket for Cruncher. The miniature dragon didn't look well. It took a lot out of him to raise his head and mewl with hunger. The LED display in his maw flickered weakly, a line of zeros.

Noel just had time to revive the poor beastie with a request for keeping a tab of negative nasty-points. Cruncher brightened immediately, masticated the input, and proudly showed Noel that he was a hundred and thirty-six points on the side of the angels. Lysi saw it just before Noel jammed Cruncher back into his pocket. She moaned audibly.

"Well, Noel, aren't you going to introduce me?'' Marguerite's smile was strained to say the least. She regarded Lysi with the warmth many people reserve for the lower invertebrates. "Your father told me you'd brought a friend down with you. I assumed he meant Roger. Is this the reason you're been too busy to write? Ha, ha, ha.''

Noel felt anger rising; he could do little about it. He saw his father standing behind Marguerite and knew that any smart answer would only get him deeper into Kent's bad graces. Somehow he forgot what a potential trove of nasty-points parental wrath might bring. The returns didn't matter: he didn't want to hurt his father.

As for his mother . . . His hand found Lysi's and clasped it strongly. He smiled at Marguerite with no hint of malice. "I guess you've figured it out, Mom," he said blandly. "I'll be happy to introduce you. Lysi, this is my mother. Mom, this is Lysistrata Damon. My fiancée."

"YOUR WHAT?"

It was the first and last point of agreement Lysi and Marguerite ever had.

10

A Good Man Is Hard to Find

LYSI SAT CROSS-LEGGED on Noel's dormitory bed, watching him type up a term paper like one possessed.

"I don't know what the hurry is," she grumped. "You don't get many negative credits for cutting classes and flunking courses, but at least it's something."

Noel pulled the final sheet from the typewriter. His eyes were bleary and red, the usual effects of pulling an all-nighter to get the work done. He looked and sounded wrung out. "The kind of power I'm after won't be bought for a handful of nasty-points. I'm not going to fool around with anything less than a big score. Anyhow, I want to stay in school. There's always more chances to do something rotten when you've got a university's resources to play with."

"My, yes. You've done so much with them already."

Noel was not taken with Lysi's sarcasm. He was too tired to be taken with anything. "I've got some reading to do," he said, casting a longing look at the bed. "Do you mind?"

"Who, me?" Lysi rested a hand on her bosom. "Who am I to mind anything you do, Master? I'm just your humble and obedient servant." She vanished from the bed.

"*And* your damned fiancée!" she shouted from Jonathan's room.

At the desk, Bob turned Jon's eyes away from the book they were reading. "You wanna keep it down, Lysi? This ain't half bad." He turned a fresh page in *The Soul of a New Machine*. "Goll-eee, the possibilities!"

Lysi smacked the book across the room. "Congratulate me, Bob," she said coldly. "I'm engaged."

"In what?"

"In your ear. This is earnest. Noel and I are engaged to be married."

The imp was speechless, but the left hand of the body he

occupied did a little two-fingered can-can of joy before flipping Bob the bird. Lysi sat on the floor and leaned against Jon's desk.

"At first I thought he only said it to tork his mother. It sure did that. I thought she was going to turn back into one of us right there. But on the train coming back to New Haven, I asked to see how Cruncher had toted up the points for that one." She tilted her head back, eyes closed. "Now I know why they call it holy matrimony. He even got extra ticks for the sincerity of his feelings for me."

"So what's your problem, precious thing?" Bob pushed Jon's glasses back up to the bridge of his nose. "Make him renege. Breach of promise oughta count for something, even if it's only to a succubus. He still wants more power . . . ?"

"He says he does. He says he's going to get it. I tried convincing him to break this off. I offered him points for it, like you said." Lysi's sigh came from the depths of her being. "He told me he'd do something wicked enough for our engagement not to count against him. It stands." She flung her arms at the ceiling. "Why did he do it? Why?"

Bob toyed with the computer keyboard, forcing his left hand into cooperation. "Maybe he wants to make you suffer? . . . Nah. He'd rack up the nasties for that and they'd show on his account. Maybe he wants to aggravate his ma some more? . . . Uh-uh. Shock value's shot after the first blow. Maybe . . ." He took off his glasses and chewed the earpiece. "Maybe he loves you."

"Bite your tongue." Lysi spoke the words with horribly compelling force. Bob bit down hard and yipped in pain. "That's all I need to have working against me now, on top of everything else. Just when I thought I had him on the downward slide, too! I've got to think, Bob. Some minds just aren't geared for the big time when it comes to evil."

Bob drew back, scandalized. "All morties are equally open to devilishness. That's doctrine, baby. You ain't gonna make me listen to nothin' contradicts that. You know what they do to heretics Down Home?"

Lysi dismissed all association with unorthodoxy. "Maybe at the moment they're born, they're all equal, but I'm talking *now*. Pernicious influences. A stable home life. Parental concern. Overindulgence in the wrong sort of reading material at a tender age. My pigeon's been raised too damned nice. If I wait for Noel to come up with anything wicked on his own hook, it'll be doomsday before he tries jaywalking.''

"He summoned demons, didn't he? That oughta show he's got some spiritual decay to improve on.''

"Hunters and conservationists both trap animals, but their motives are *not* the same. It's what you do with your demons once you've got 'em that shows your inner nature. Noel has the power to command the hosts of evil, and the subconscious desire to put them all to work selling Girl Scout cookies. The will to fail; it always shows.'' Lysi shook her head. "I've got to give him some turpitude tactics of my own devising, and let him think they're his. And I've got to work fast.''

"Hey, honeylamb, not a bad notion.'' Bob's grits-eating grin looked poorly on Jon's face. "Ain't no way that boy could screw up a plan for evil that's made by a real live demon. Allus see a specialist, that's my motto. But what's the big rush? Your daddy's got whole hogsloads of time.''

"It's Noel's mother—the apostate. I think she knows what I am.''

Bob guffawed so loudly that he didn't catch Jon's left hand as it rapidly typed a message into the PC and dispatched it elsewhere. He only reclaimed it to wipe tears of amusement from his eyes. "Baby, how in this world could she know? And if'n she does, whatall can she do 'bout it? She's a mortie now; no more threat'n a good intention.''

"You wouldn't say that if you'd seen the way she looked at me.''

"That's about all morties can do, sweetcheeks. They look, they go d-uhh, and maybe if'n they're real lucky they duck in time and get to look some more. Don't you give her a second thought, Lysi. She's got nothing can touch you.''

The angel folded in his wings of glory and settled onto the tatami mat. On the other side of the shoji-screened private dining room, waiters practiced discretion in direct proportion to the tips they hoped to receive. "You didn't invite me down here just to share sushi, Melisan. Why have I been summoned?''

Marguerite/Melisan looked anxiously at the third place at table, still vacant. "I called Lura too.''

"She'll be along. She's finishing up an invisible marriage-healing mediation over in Anaheim, but she'll join us as soon as she can.'' The angel's flawless face grew even more wonderful to see when he smiled. "It's her first solo flight. We're bicoastal now. They don't trust just any novice pair to split up and work separately so soon. I am most proud of her."

"Proud, Atamar?" Melisan couldn't resist a sly sting. "Isn't that what got us into trouble in the first place?"

The angel's smile darkened. "We don't joke about that."

A sweet voice filled the air of the private dining room. "Why not? Only the damned can't laugh. Don't pay any attention to Atamar, Melisan. When he gets pompous like that, he even gives Uriel the jollies." A female angel materialized at the empty place. Her snowy wings gained an extra measure of brightness in contrast to her unbound ebony tresses.

"Oh, Lura, I just love what you've done with your hair!" Melisan leaned across the table to give the new arrival a cocktail party salute, making loud, contactless kissing noises on both cheeks.

"This?" The female angel lifted wave upon wave of black curls. "It's strictly regulation. Everyone at our level wears the natural look."

"I assume we were not invoked just to compare hairstyles," Atamar said. He rested his hands, held in an attitude of prayer, on the low table. "Why did you call us here?"

Melisan looked flustered. "I couldn't very well invite you to my home. Please forgive me for that."

"It's not as if we're strangers to your husband." Lura giggled and began to fool around with her chopsticks.

"Lura, stop that. Dignity." Atamar's eye still had the power to command instant obedience. Where the former demon had once used brute force to back up his orders to subordinates, he now relied entirely on the strength of his personality. From the shamefaced way in which Lura dropped the chopsticks Melisan noted that this was quite enough. She gave thanks for it. What she was about to ask of her former comrades would take plenty of spiritual sinew.

"I don't want Kent to know what I'm doing," she told them.

Atamar's perfectly chiseled lips pursed. "The bond of trust between man and wife is, or ought to be, inviolable. We can not be party to—"

"Stop getting so huffy, Atamar. You're not impressing anyone." Behind her hand, Lura whispered to Melisan, "I

may get in trouble for saying this, but I think I liked him
better when he was self-employed. Nowadays it's always
'What will the Thrones think? Are there any seraphim watching? Is this the way the Principalities want it done?' You'd
think he didn't have half eternity, the way he's bucking to get
us promoted."

"What's wrong with that? We are capable of greater duties
than those presently vouchsafed us." Atamar flicked invisible
earthly dross from the hems of his trailing sleeves. "Just
because we used to be . . . what we used to be, is no reason to
deny us elevation to the upper ranks."

"Atamar, what do you expect them to do with us?" Lura's
words had the ring of an old, old argument, sounded out
many times before. "Considering what we were, I think our
superiors have been very understanding. We've barely tried
our wings, we're scarcely out of basic training, and I wouldn't
call eternity a limited-time offer. Why can't you let us rise
through the ranks leisurely?"

Atamar addressed Melisan, as if his words would have
been wasted on Lura. "She means well, but she doesn't
understand. Still tainted with the touch of earth, poor child,
measuring the divine by a mortal yardstick. Nothing is impossible in our realm. Given this, and adding to it the fact that
time is meaningless to immortal beings, what difference does
it make if we obtain our highest possible heavenly post
without all that tiresome waiting?"

He looked so self-assured and patronizing that Lura could
not resist murmuring, "The Devil can argue scripture."

"What was that?" For an instant, Atamar's stainless wings
flashed the shadow of darker, more leathery pinions that once
had sprouted from the former demon's back.

"I said that perhaps if you weren't so transparently ambi-
tious, we might be a rank or two higher by now."

"Other angels want to get promoted and their ambitions
don't hold them back. Why can't I aspire?"

"Because they want to move up so that they can apply
their greater powers to do greater good works. You just want
to hear everyone say, 'Yay, Atamar.' " Lura made the traditional *whoopdedoo* spirals with her forefinger.

"Maybe if I heard it more from you, I wouldn't need to
hear it elsewhere!"

"Oh? Just where have you been hearing it lately?"

"Lura, Atamar, please calm down. I can't stand to hear you shouting at each other like this." Melisan moved in to smooth ruffled feathers, literally and figuratively.

The two angels settled down, unmollified. "It's come to a pretty pass when a mortal has to play peacemaker for us," Atamar said coldly. He turned his back on Lura, wrapping his wings about him until it looked as if a mound of Vermont snow had miraculously been transported to a New York Japanese restaurant.

"I hope you don't quarrel like that up yonder." Melisan poured herself a little warm sake and enjoyed the luxury of feeling superior. "Kent and I never disagree."

"Is that why you're sneaking around behind his back?" Lura mewed. "To avoid a disagreement?"

Melisan wore sanctimoniousness like an unbecoming mantle. "I don't want to alarm my husband. Is that a sin? I want to shelter him from an eentsy little problem which I had *hoped* you might be able to handle for me without the need to upset Kent."

"I thought you mortals called in the medical men for your *eentsy* problems." Lura took a little sake herself and studied the menu. Atamar continued to sulk.

"This happens to be outside the scope of Dr. Fitz—Say, do your superiors know you drink?"

Lura's swanlike wings rose and fell in a graceful shrug. "We have not yet been taken into the Higher Knowledge, but gossip has it that all Creation is divided into three parts: the supremely good, the supremely evil, and the middle ground. One of our consultants from G'dran—what you'd call Cygnus II or III; I'm horrid with addresses—claims that his people also recognize the existence of a realm of mortal thought as separate from that of mortal action, making for two middle grounds in their theosophy."

"Which has what to do with the fact that that is your second cup of sake?"

Lura's maddening look of condescension made Melisan long for the good old days when they had been succubi sharing a desert exile. Many was the time they had lit into one another in a no-holds-barred free-for-all, but at least then it had been a battle between equals.

No, not quite equals. In the desert she had been the one to wear wings.

Now Melisan had to listen to her one-time sister in sin talk down to her from a height of moral superiority based solely on the fact that Lura dwelled in heavenly mansions, while Melisan was still marking time in a Park Avenue co-op. Melisan resolved to lead a blameless life, go to Heaven when she died, and immediately on arrival boot Lura where it counted, devil take the hindmost.

"You see, Melisan, since we belong to the lowest ranks of heaven, we're fairly close to earthly things. We can even assume earthly form. The higher orders never do."

"Snobs," Atamar mumbled from within his plumy solitude. He emerged momentarily to snare himself a sake cup, then rewrapped his wings and sipped the rice liquor in sullen isolation.

"Because we are so close to things earthly, when we actually reside in your darling little plane of existence we can share any of your activities. Within reason," Lura amended, seeing Melisan sharply raise an eyebrow. "Which is why I will have the grilled salmon while you explain what you want of us." She snapped the menu shut.

"Lura, sweet, no one is getting so much as a strand of seaweed while you look like that."

"What's wrong with how I look?" Lura patted her iridescent robes lovingly. Their ever-shifting rainbow hues cast opal reflections into the concave surfaces of her wings.

"Waiters don't expect religious experiences as part of the lunch rush."

"Oh, is that all?" Lura made no move, yet from one second to the next she went from angelic splendor to the lesser magnificence of Calvin Klein *prêt à porter* separates. "Atamar, you too. I know you like salmon just as much as I do, and I'm getting hungry."

Atamar's wings dissolved, leaving him clothed in a white linen suit and turquoise shirt. "Contamination. You shouldn't feel things like hunger, Lura. You wouldn't, if we belonged just one rank further along in the hierarchy. Just one!" He blew an exasperated breath. "Teriyaki chicken for me. I have *some* self-control."

The waiter whispered in and out of the private room to take the order and serve the food, refilling the sake service at discreet intervals. During his absences, Melisan divulged her problem.

"Engaged to a *demon*?" Atamar gave the last word scornful emphasis. "I can see why you don't want your husband to know."

"Why? Don't they still say 'Like father, like son'?" Lura patted Melisan's hand. "Perhaps she's like us: a demon who isn't wholeheartedly for Hell. She might change, given the proper chance. You did."

"We all did," Melisan snapped.

"But we had a miracle to help us," Lura reminded her.

Atamar sank his nose in his sake cup. "Hardly that."

"Oh, you're just envious because Steve rose three ranks for helping us." Lura's laughter was too sweet to be human, her appearance notwithstanding.

"Just as we helped him to promotion!"

"Wouldn't you just love a kickback on that!"

Atamar made a point of showing Lura his back. "Melisan, do you think this demon pursuing your son is like us?"

"I don't know. I didn't have contact with her for very long. The reek of damnation clings to her—almost a familiar scent blended with it—but I sense something else about her as well; something not entirely of the Pit. Whatever it is, whether she wants to change for the better or not, how can she? And if she can't, I'm afraid she'll drag my son down with her."

"So you want us to separate them?" Lura asked.

"I want you to destroy her."

"I see." Lura spied the waiter's silhouette hovering on the other side of the shoji. "Check!" She passed him a Gold Card before Melisan could say anything. "Darling, not a word. We insist on picking up the tab. It's the least we can do since we absolutely can't help you at all with your eentsy problem. I feel just awful about it, too."

"Why can't you?" Melisan demanded. "You're angels."

"But not destroying angels. Certainly not angels capable of engaging in truly obliterative combat with supernatural opponents. We can't even work full miracles. I can't tell you how sorry—"

"Why can't we?" Atamar said.

"My love, I just explained—"

"Why can't we?" he repeated, standing up. "The angel who brought us out of the desert was just as low-ranking as we are now, yet he managed to defeat Murakh in battle."

"Defeat is not destruction," Lura maintained. "And he had help."

"Defeat will suffice." Atamar stretched out his hand to Melisan. "Will you be content if we remove this she-demon from your son's life? If we secure the welfare of his soul?"

Atamar's gaze was as masterful as always. Meeting his eyes, Melisan wondered how the former demon had ever come to resign himself to an angel's eternity of service to others. He did not look like a being created to take orders.

"It would be enough, Atamar. More than enough." Without thinking, she raised his hand to her lips.

This bemusing tableau was broken up by the waiter's return with Lura's charge slip. She made the necessary calculations and signed it with a flourish, though her face showed a decided unease. She kept stealing glances at Atamar, who was outlining his plan of attack to Melisan.

". . . unfortunate constraints. We can't initiate any physical conflict, but we can defend ourselves and our charge. Sometimes the knowledge that Heavenly forces are at work is enough to discourage lesser fiends. We shall begin at once by flying to New Haven and establishing a good cover on campus as tenured faculty."

"Tenured? As young as you two look?" Atamar nodded affirmatively. "Don't tell me you can't work miracles," Melisan said.

As they left the tatami room, Melisan overheard their waiter giving vent to bilingual spleen. Apparently the Higher Knowledge from which Lura and Atamar were still barred included knowing how much to tip in modern midtown Manhattan. Silently she prayed that at least they knew what they were doing when it came to her son.

11

Angels and Ministers of Grace

"O.K., WATCH THIS," Noel whispered.

"I'm watching." Though the night air was chilly, Lysi wore no jacket. She needed none, being what she was. In view of what Noel had in mind for this night's activities, she would have needed none even if she'd been mortal.

A burning building casts a lovely glow and throws off a lot of heat.

"Destruction of private property. Willful. Maybe danger to surrounding structures. Oh boy, just wait until Cruncher gets through digesting this." Noel rubbed his hands together, either in anticipation of all the nasty-points he was about to accrue or because he'd forgotten his gloves.

"Get on with it. Master." Lysi was wearing gloves, though she had as little physical need for them as for a jacket. All she wanted was something to cover her left hand and the ring now glittering there.

It wasn't much, as diamonds go, and it was even less when you knew it was a zircon. Ancient legends told of stones with the power to capture and enslave the highest in the hosts of Hell. That might account for the malaise Lysi felt every time she looked at the ring and recalled Noel, kneeling at her feet and inadvertently jamming the bauble onto her thumb because she kept trying to pull her hand away. It took a direct command from him, reasserting himself as her sorcerous Master, to make her hold still long enough for the ring to slide onto the proper finger. The whole scene was such unabashed mush that Noel's cheeks were crimson throughout. She saw his blushes in her mind's eye, and the memory inexplicably elicited an answering blush of her own.

It would have been a simple matter to ditch that irritating bit of jewelry. Yale had drainpipes enough, and she knew all the words to *Whoops! Uh-oh*. As she often told her *I Love*

New York teddy bear, Azathoth, she just didn't know what was making her hold onto such patent evidence of mortie sentimentality.

"He doesn't even rush through lovemaking," she complained. "I tell him and tell him, 'Sate yourself, dear. Take as little time as you want. I don't have any needs.' He doesn't listen. He's . . . so damned *tender* I could—I could—" Her skin flushed with autonomous memories. She stared past Azathoth at something only she could see, and her lips turned up at the corners in a dreamy smile. Abruptly she snapped herself out of it. "And the way he looks at me! Like he's seeing something that isn't there. How long can it take to look at one person's face? Morties!"

She hugged the teddy to her fiercely, stroking her cheek against its plush skin. Azathoth understood.

Initially she had agreed to wear the ring on one condition: Noel must do something horrible at once. Slyly she suggested that he use the one wizardly power with which he seemed to be especially gifted.

"Burn something. It's always good for a laugh."

He took her suggestion, but rather than choosing an occupied building, or even a valuable structure, he had hustled Lysi out of the dorm in the dead of night to this rundown section of New Haven where a row of deserted old houses stood waiting for the wrecker's ball.

"O.K." He swallowed hard. "O.K., here goes." Noel rubbed his hands together some more. He took a deep breath and closed his eyes tightly, fists clenched.

"You're doing everything but click your heels together and fly to Kansas," Lysis said after three minutes passed with no visible effect. "Don't you want to do this?"

"Sometimes my powers don't answer so well; not right away. Remember how Bob showed up?" Noel's eyes were still shut. "Do you smell smoke?" he asked hopefully.

"I smell cat piss. Give me back Cruncher. I don't want the S.P.C.D. on my tail for dragon-abuse. You'll starve the poor baby to death if you've switched him over to keeping a nasty-point tally for you."

"No, wait, wait! I think I've got it!" Sweat formed on Noel's forehead. A wink of flame showed in the second-floor front window of the least decrepit house across the street. He opened his eyes. "Aha! You see? I did it!"

The flashing lights of a police cruiser glided up alongside them as they did an unfettered reel of celebration on the sidewalk. One of the policemen leaned out the window. "You kids all right?"

"All right?" Noel gave him both barrels of the old Mad Scientist laugh. "I just set that building on fire and he wants to know if I'm all right!"

"You did what?"

"Noel . . ." It was not the way she'd been brought up, but in the circumstances, Lysi raised her eyes to Heaven. You got no bonus hell-bent credits for stupidity, and confession was infamous for being good for the soul.

"Hey! Look there, Charley!" A door slammed. The other policeman was out of the car and running across the street to where the old house was being devoured by swiftly spreading flames. Over his shoulder he shouted, "Look what's coming out! Radio for backup!"

Charley looked. "Shit." He called for serious assistance and ran to help his partner. Lysi and Noel were forgotten. The police were much more interested in the people streaming from the supposedly abandoned building. Three more cruisers pulled up, and not one officer spared the bewildered young couple a look. When the firetrucks arrived, it was worse.

"Come on, Noel." Lysi pulled on his arm. "No sense being a bigger jerk than you already are. Let's go home."

"But I set fire to the house." Noel looked like a man who spends his life's savings on body-building, only to have his true love leave him for a Woody Allen look-alike.

The next morning the New Haven papers were full of the biggest drug bust in state history. At least nine dealers from three competing local groups had been flushed from their mutually selected neutral meeting-place, their territory-treaty negotiations interrupted by a fire of undetermined origin. Two of those arrested as they fled the inferno were high-level snowmen. Between them, via their minions, they'd sprinkled more white dust around the Nutmeg State than a squadron of Tinkerbells.

"Cruncher died last night," Lysi said as she set her breakfast try down beside Noel's.

"Lysi, I'm sorry. I meant to—"

"Spare me. I'm so depressed that I'm actually thinking about attending one of my philosophy lectures."

"You must be unhappy." Noel prodded his scrambled eggs, looking morose. "Lysi, I didn't want to tell you this, but I think we should be honest with each other. I've been— I've been attending my classes too."

A red aura coruscated down Lysi's arms and charred every edible item on her tray to dust and ashes. It was over immediately, happening too quickly for untrained mortal eyes to catch. "What? When?"

"When I told you I was sneaking back to the dorm to destroy Luis' biochem notes. And the time I told you I was going to stand on line for that heavy metal concert and change the seat numbers on everyone's tickets to all read the same. And when you thought I was practicing invisibility and slapping Smurf magnets onto all the machines at the computer center. And remember when I said I was going to catch up on the required reading list for Necromancy Through the Ages you gave me? All those times, and others, I was in class."

Lysi bolted to her feet and tugged at her engagement ring. It refused to come off. She scowled when she saw a thin blue line of energy binding it to her finger.

"Take that spell off me, Noel."

"It's a ring guard."

"I don't care if it's a Varangian guard, I want it off, and the ring off, and the engagement off too!"

People at nearby tables were looking, and people sharing the long commons table with Noel and Lysi were moving away. Noel felt his face go hot. "You're making a scene. Sit down. Please."

"Oh, fine!" Lysi sat down again. She lowered her voice, but added an extra measure of scorn for every decibel deleted. "Courtesy to a demon! What next? You've just admitted to clotheslining Sloth. You've taken all the teeth out of Lechery by declaring your honorable intentions. You squander what little money you've got on gifts for me, so there goes Avarice . . . Noel, you're not eating your breakfast."

"I'm not suicidal."

"Right. Scratch Gluttony. That leaves us Wrath and Envy. Forget about Pride. If you had any worth mentioning, you'd have blasted me back into that cursed book by now. I am mouthing off to you, Master. Doesn't that bother you?"

Noel took Lysi's hand. "You're just upset about Cruncher. I know it's not the real you talking."

"The real me wants to know when you're going to fish or cut bait. Or do you think your roommate Jon likes sharing his body with Bob?"

"I'll get him out." Noel sounded sure of it. "I said I'd do whatever it takes to get the power." He pushed his tray away and rose from his place, a man with a mission. "Today I'm going to shoplift a pen at the Co-op."

Lysi's head hit the table with a loud thunk. She covered it with her arms. "At least if you would've destroyed that Beinecke book, you'd have enough power to make things unpleasant for Bob. He wouldn't vacate, but he wouldn't have a pleasant stay. Stealing a pen? For that, you couldn't give Jon's body dandruff."

"Is that true?"

"No. I lied. Snicking a Bic sends you straight to Hell and they give you a flipping medal for destroying an irreplaceable book."

Lysi heard a scraping sound, as of a heavy wooden object being dragged across the Commons floor. When she looked up, Noel was gone.

"Bingo." She smiled.

"Is this seat taken, young lady?" Tall and impeccably tailored, the man in rich brown Harris tweed slid Noel's abandoned tray aside and pulled up a chair. He had not expected a reply to his question. Lysi stared at a face whose inhuman perfection had few equals. Already, female students and staff were turning to gawk at him, their features displaying everything from chaste appreciation to rampant lust.

Lysi's bowels knotted. Perfection like this was old news to her. She had seen it many times, Down Home, on the ineffably beautiful faces of the Firstfallen. This face in particular—the laughable black-rimmed glasses aside—was one she knew from her father's sandy demonstrations.

"Atamar . . ."

"You know my name? Ah, but I see whose get you are." He removed his glasses and let his true vision read her to the marrow. "So. That explains it. Here Melisan thought that you were only a haphazard prospector. Interesting to see her reaction when she learns you're Murakh's whelp. How is your father?"

There was pure hate in his voice when he said that, unmarred by any human need to shield it for form's sake. An image thundered into Lysi's mind with the words, showing in an instant all the old rage her father's name could stir up in the new-made angel's breast. Such a sending would reduce a mortal to quivering, brainless terror. They weren't used to dealing with naked truths in any guise.

Lysi was only half human, and Atamar's sending simply made her mad.

"My father is just fine, thank you, and going to be finer." She tried to slam the angel with a sending of her own, but a wall of whiteness girdled his mind, keeping his thoughts inviolate.

"You forget, Lysi: I once experienced your father's present situation. Exile never improves. It either goes on, or ends. I doubt his will end too soon. I know the terms of his captivity very well."

Lysi lifted her chin defiantly. "It will end, Atamar. He'll be free. I don't have to mince words with you. We both know the price of his ticket out of the desert. I'm going to get it for him."

"With the soul of Melisan's son?" Atamar's mouth twitched, his eyes remained unreadable. "I think not."

"How do you plan to stop me? You can't destroy me or you'd have done it by now."

"Don't be so sure you know all of my abilities. I might be guarding some small surprises for later."

"Bullshit," Lysi said loudly. Heads swiveled their way, and a small, kinky-haired blond gent bustled across Commons.

"Miz Damon, I'd like a word with you." His lips worked furiously between the well-kept hedges of beard and mustache. Atamar did a professional job of concealing his satisfaction as the officious little man spoke long and earnestly to Lysi on the inadvisability of thus addressing a tenured full professor in public. He left while Lysi was trying to inject her excuses. There were too many rapt witnesses for her to dare use any magical means of escape.

Lura was waiting for him outside Commons on Beinecke Plaza. "The oddest thing . . ." she said.

"What is?"

She indicated the tent city of the apartheid protestors. "I was hovering around, invisible, waiting to see if you'd want

me to talk to Lysi with you—one succubus to another, more
or less—"

"Very much less. Don't forget yourself, Lura."

Atamar's ungentle chiding made no impression. "—when
all of a sudden I thought I saw Melisan's boy come out of that
building. He stopped right about there, stared at one of these
shanties, and the silly thing fell over."

"Of course it fell over. The boy has magic in him."

"Why would he want to do something like that with it,
though? What was he trying to accomplish?"

"Clearly this is that she-demon's influence. She's an inso-
lent lump of hubris, an audacious little—"

"Talked back to you, did she?"

Atamar gritted his teeth. "She will learn her error. Before
that, we must prevent her from corrupting Melisan's child too
deeply. If he knocked over a harmless structure for no apparent reason, it must be because he has already decided to take
the path of wickedness."

"It wasn't wicked, though. Not from where I sat."

"My dear, you have been known to become too easily
distracted when at your post." Atamar's fingers strayed to toy
with Lura's rich, dark hair, a pleasantly discordant note of
magnificence against the crisp, serious navy twill suit and
oxford shirt she wore.

"Sexist!" Lura slapped his hand down, then added in a
whisper, "I had to say that, Atamar. People who know me on
campus were watching."

"Why you had to choose Women's Studies . . . Forget it.
Tell me why you said the boy wasn't doing something bad by
knocking down the shanty. The students put them up for a
good cause. To destroy them at random—"

"The minute that tent pitched over, a nice-looking gentleman was walking right by it. He saw the tent pole hit one of
the girls inside. Poor thing, it must have hurt awfully; she
started to cry. Some men just crumble over feminine tears,
the puffed-up old chauvi—sorry, Atamar. Anyway, he tried to
comfort her, she stopped crying, they began to talk about this
and that, South Africa came into the conversation . . ." Lura
spread her hands, at a loss in the face of Fate. "He's a very
influential trustee of the University, besides coming from a
long line of alumni. Rich alumni, the kind you want to breed
in captivity. He said he was going to talk to *certain people*

about Yale's investments. I have a feeling that *certain people* are going to listen. He also got her phone number.''

Atamar's brows came together. "Where is the boy now?''

"In there.'' Lura gestured toward Beinecke. "It's a library. He's safe enough for the moment. Want me to go back in there and try to scare off the succubus some more?''

"No. Better if she thinks there is only one of us onto her. Avoid her at all costs, Lura. I might be able to use you to better strategic advantage later.''

Lura bristled. "*Use* me? Now you listen here—!''

"Go after Melisan's boy. Speak to him. Since you're still so unashamed of your former life, use all your powers of persuasion upon him to undo what that one has done. You succubi are reknowned for your persuasive abilities. I will take care of more important matters.'' Atamar's tweeds shimmered into a golden cocoon and discreetly removed him from the premises.

Lura made a mental note to persuade Atamar to stop addressing her as if she were programmable. The means of persuasion she would use on him would not be very pretty, but it might be personally satisfying. The article on "Respect: Beat It Out of Them,'' which she had clipped from a magazine in the Women's Studies department, made a reassuring crinkling sound in her skirt pocket as she walked over to Beinecke.

There was something arrestingly familiar about the woman behind the front desk. Lura could have sworn she knew her from somewhere. Her suspicions jelled when the librarian looked up, saw her, and squealed, "Oh my God, no! I'm not ready to die!''

It was an unfortunately common knee-jerk reaction among mortals who recognized an angelic visitor, and the reason why so much of Lura's normal workload was done invisibly.

"You know what I am,'' Lura said.

The librarian bobbed her head. "I can see, can't I? I remember you. You're the one called Lura.''

"Right now I'm called Professor Laura Petracca. And you are—'' she stared into the librarian's rapidly beating heart "—Why, Amanda Rhodes! Long time no see.'' She shook hands with her vigorously.

Amanda just shook. "It was—it was kind of them to send you as the one to fetch me. This is so—sudden. I know I should've called Mummy last night. I don't suppose I'll be allowed . . . ? No, that's only when you're arrested, isn't it. Poor Mummy. She always did say something like this would happen if I didn't eat my greens. I'm . . . I think I'm ready now, Lura." She rose with noble resignation, a superb portrayal of Joan of Arc en route to the stake. "Take me."

"Where? Oh, *there?* No, silly. That's not in my job description. I'm not here on your account, although it is lovely to see you again. You seem to have matured nicely. How's that delicious hunk you were hotpantsing over back in the desert? Whatsisname . . . Geordie Burns?"

" 'Hotpantsing'?" Amanda sank as her eyebrows rose, all her joints letting go now that it seemed her number was not yet up. "You said 'hotpantsing'?"

"Isn't that a verb?"

"Aren't you an angel? Do they let you use words like 'hotpantsing' up there "

Lura's laugh was divine, Amanda's reaction automatic: *"Ssshhhh!"*

"Oh, Amanda, I'm sorry. I couldn't help it. Don't you think a Creation that gave you the aardvark, the platypus, the unicorn, the echidna, and the swan, all on one dinky jug handle of the universe, could stand some variety in angels too? And our vocabulary." Lura looked at the librarian fondly. "I never thought you'd turn out to be the prudish one. Still, it's so good to see someone from the old days."

Amanda was unmoved by Lura's homecoming spirit. "Hmph. If you're that interested in looking up old buddies from your desert days, you're in luck." She shoved a flyer of upcoming events from the Yale British Art Center across the desk.

"Yes, I must be." Lura tucked it into her pocket without reading it. "However, right now I do have more immediate business here. Did you see a young man come in here, oh, say ten, fifteen minutes ago? Blond hair, blue-green eyes, about yay tall?"

This time Amanda shot out of her chair with the force of rocket-powered pantyhose. "Why that little bastard!"

"Technically. But his parents did marry as soon as they were able . . . You know him? Melisan's son?"

"Rragh!" Amanda slammed her palm to the switch controlling the panel behind her. It slid back and Lura had to leap

over the desk to keep up with Amanda as she dove into the Beinecke stacks. The librarian scorned to wait for the elevator. She paused, appeared to sniff the air, and raced unerringly up several flights of stairs and down one of the narrow rows of bookshelves inside the great glass cube.

"Now I've got you, you little fiend!" Amanda sprang forward and grabbed Noel's arm, spinning him around to face her. He held a book in his hands, though not the same one in which he had imprisoned Lysi.

"Amanda . . ." Lura tapped the librarian's heaving shoulder. "He's not really what you just called him, either. Technically, that is."

"Screw the technicalities!" Amanda had Noel by both arms now, and looked ready to start shaking him. "You came into my library, you zapped me with some spell or other, and you went into the stacks before I came to, didn't you? Didn't you?" She really did give him a good shake then.

Noel's hands came up suddenly between Amanda's to stiff-arm her grip off him. He jumped a few paces back and waved the book at her.

"Yes, I did. Get off my case or I'll do it again! I don't have to take anyone talking to me like that, not anymore. I . . . am . . . a . . . *wizard!*" He struck his chest with the book to underscore each word.

"And a very bratty one." Lura moved Amanda aside. "Hello, Noel. I'm an old friend of your mother's. Can I help you find something? Your manners, for example? You're not supposed to be up here and you are making Amanda very cross. Put the book back and come along. I'd like to talk to you about the seven warning signs of succubus addiction."

Noel backed off farther, his dark brows a straight line. "Keep away from me, whoever you are. If Mom thinks she can sic another shrink on me . . . Hey, I'm warning you, I can freeze you in your shoes with a look!"

"No, Noel. Not me." Lura's twills melted into pearly silks and shinings. "Put back the book. Come."

For a moment, Noel stared at the angel in all her beauty. Then his jaw stiffened. "Uh-uh. I don't care if it's gold or cord, it's still a string. She's not going to pull mine any more." He raised the book, opened it, and tore it in half down the spine with his bare hands. The two halves crackled into flame.

Amanda screamed.

12

Souvenir of the Crusades; Wish You Were Here

"I SAID I was sorry," Noel said. "Can I get you another cold compress?"

Flat on her back on Noel's bed, Lysi moaned and made weak brushing motions with one hand.

"I think she wants you to leave her alone," Bob said, coming in with a fresh washcloth soaked in cold water.

"But this is my room, and I've got a paper I have to work on for—" Lysi uttered a wail of animal pain.

"Y'know the old saying, master? 'Bout never mentioning rope in the house where someone's just been the guest of honor at an over-the-tree-limb necktie party?"

Noel scuffed his feet across the bare wooden floor. "All right. I'm going." He paused in the doorway only long enough to say, "I didn't know about the manuscript, Lysi. I really didn't. I'm sorry." He closed the door behind him.

"I can burn this copy of the Yalie Daily if y'want, punkin," Bob offered. "That way you won't hafta look at the story in cold, hard print no more."

Lysi scraped the dripping washcloth off her forehead. "That won't change what happened." She retrieved the crumpled *Yale Daily News* from the foot of the bed. The front page was glory-space shared evenly between the story of the exhibit of precious medieval arcana coming to the British Art Center and the late-breaking bulletin of a humble librarian's discovery.

Amanda Rhodes and Professor Laura Petracca smiled demurely for the camera as they held up the rare twelfth-century manuscript. It was a slender volume of hand-limned pages—an odd interleaving of parchment and papyrus—bound in gilded purple kidskin.

"No wonder," Lysi said, teeth clenched. "No bloody wonder. I recognize that one." Her finger jabbed Lura's face out of the photo. "Atamar's mate, double-damn them both.

Another renegade.'' She balled up the paper and pitched it at the wall. Bob grabbed it out of the air in mid-flight, using Jon's lank body with a fielder's grace that would have astonished its previous master.

He read aloud from the newspaper, not to torment Lysi, but because he never had gotten the knack of silent literacy. " 'It often happened that old manuscripts were used to cover and bind more current works,' said Ms. Rhodes, 'especially when parchment was scarce and the monkish scribe did not understand or value all of the contents of his order's library. Many times scholars have found invaluable manuscripts of great antiquity preserved only because they were used in this fashion to cover mediocre works of fleeting importance.' "

Bob lowered the paper momentarily. ''Whew! That there woman surely does mouth a heap of two-dollar words, don't she?''

''There ought to be laws,'' Lysi mumbled, chin on knees. ''The middle plane should be zoned for divine intervention and free access. It's not fair, Bob!''

''Hmmm . . .'' The imp remained noncommittal. He resumed reading aloud. " 'The newly revealed manuscript has yet to be identified. It appears to be written in Arabic. However, all faculty members specializing in Near Eastern languages who have examined the book confess themselves unable to translate it. They suggest it might be an obscure dialect or an entirely alien language transliterated into Arabic characters. Pending further study, it has been agreed to include the manuscript as a timely and priceless addition to the medieval exhibit soon to open at the Yale British Arts Center.' My oh my.''

Bob carefully folded and tore the newspaper into a ragged crown which he perched on his head. ''Got to hand it to the boy, Lysi. When he fucks up being bad, he fucks big time. Next to that whoppin' big jewel they got under 'leventy-six-ought-two burglar 'larms, our Master's done contributed the most valuable piece of Middle Ages bric-a-brac in that whole exhibit.''

A wet washcloth can be a dangerous weapon when knotted at one end and snapped. Bob yipped and hit the rafters. His paper crown came tumbling down. Lysi dropped the washcloth and grabbed it, undoing amateur origami as she tried to piece together the scraps of the torn front page.

"You coulda just said, 'Bob, honey, pass me the paper.' "

"Where is it?" Lysi had no patience with jigsaw puzzles. Bits of tattered newsprint flew. "Where's the story about the exhibit?" She tossed it all aside and grabbed Bob by Jon's shaggy scruff. "Tell me about the jewel!"

"Ease off, woman! I just know what I read in the papers." Bob weaseled loose and smoothed out invisible wrinkles on his clothes. "They're callin' it the Richard Jewel, 'counta that's whose it was—Richard the Lionheart's. Y'know, the big-shot Crusader king who just couldn't keep his hands off'n the good-lookin' minstrels? It ain't a single stone, properly speakin'. It's a big ol' gold medallion stuck all over with diamonds and rubies and Magog knows whatall trash. Worth a whole hogsload of money just for the ingredients, and historical value." Bob whistled shrilly. "Hadda do a lotta string-pulling to get it to Yale as part of this-here exhibit. Turnin' the whole place into a reg'lar medieval carnival over it, too."

"Yahoo!" Lysi threw the much-abused newspaper into the air. It exploded into a shower of red, white, and blue stars that showered down over her, sluicing away her mortal disguise. Her two lower pairs of eyes blinked in confusion as she executed a webbed-feet-over-spiked-head cartwheel. She landed in the classic cheerleader split position, crowing with joy and tossed her disguise back on.

"You lookin' forr'd to a buncha weird kids playin' dress-up all over Yale?" Bob asked. "All they do's bash each upside the head with fake swords. They're gonna be carryin' on like that all this weekend right out on"—he shuddered at the name—"Cross Campus."

"I couldn't care less if they used real steel. To hell with them—"

"Sure 'nuff hope so."

"—and their dress-up games. I'm talking about the Richard Jewel. Oh, this is it. This is golden. Not even Noel could do this wrong. Lilith's left knocker, I'll make *sure* he doesn't turn this into something decent. C'mere." She jerked Bob down onto the floor with her. "Noel's going to steal and destroy the Richard Jewel."

Jon's teeth showed in a wickedly appreciative smile. "Nice. Theft and vandalism."

"More. When you destroy something of historical value,

that's tantamount to destroying knowledge. Remember the good old days, Bob, when we could really count on a book-burning or more a week?''

''Do I!'' Bob licked his borrowed lips. ''Mighty fine festivals we had down Dis-way to celebrate. Yessir, mighty fine. Ain't seen nothin' recent like that German feller stirred up—what was it?—forty, fifty years back? Too bad we gotta kick-start such goings-on ourselves these days. Some morties just need a li'l ol' push to do things our way, some need a shove. Raleel's doing his damndest to—''

Lysi wasn't interested in hearing of her brother's efforts toward instigating more frequent library barbecues. ''Knowledge destroyed.'' She savored Noel's future sins as she ticked them off on her fingers. ''The book he offed to get at that stinking manuscript turned out to be a mis-shelving from Sterling: not rare or irreplaceable at all, worse luck, or he'd've gotten some big points for ashing it right there. Oh, well. Theft and vandalism, like you said. Also disgracing Yale. The Richard Jewel's only here on loan. Big-time academic scandal, maybe a lot of alums getting pissed off, holding back contributions, fewer worthy kids getting financial support, less cash for making improvements . . .'' She hugged herself and laughed maniacally. ''Plus the uproar when he gets caught . . . Oh, Bob, if the shame doesn't kill Melisan, I don't know brimstone from broccoli!''

''How's he gonna get caught?'' Bob asked.

Lysi winked. ''How do you think? But not until after he's broken up the jewel and pawned the pieces. We're going for the sleaze, Bob; the hard-line sleaze. Maybe I can get him to spend the money on bimbos, booze, and cheap science fiction books. That'd be a nice touch. You know, when this is over, I should write Lura and Atamar a thank-you note. If they hadn't shown up on campus, I would've futzed around for months, letting Noel find his own way to wickedness. They made me get off my duff and *do* something for damnation.''

''Yeah, well thank heaven for angels is what I allus— Aiiiieee!''

Two Furies erupted from Jon's closet, viper-whips flailing. One pried open Jon's mouth while the other yanked Bob out and frog-marched him off to the bathroom. The sounds of running water and screams were heard, then:

''I forgot the soap, Tisiphone!''

"Oh, for . . . Here, mind this." Tisiphone pushed Jon at Lysi. The succubus stared at him a moment, then sat on him for safekeeping. Jon was too bazzled to move. Tisiphone unwrapped a large, foul-smelling bar of soap—clear yellow, containing a number of highly testy scorpions—and joined her sister in the bathroom. The screams escalated to shrieks. They stopped, the furies returned with a very draggled Bob between them, and stuffed him back into Jon's body.

"No bad language in front of succubi," Tisiphone said, wagging a finger in Jon's face before she and her sister departed the way they'd come.

"Steal the Richard Jewel?" Noel rubbed his chin. "I don't know . . ."

"Do you want to do something rotten or don't you?" Lysi asked. "Do you want real power, or are you going to spend the rest of your wizardly career as a human cigarette lighter?"

"Do you want me outa this skin or not?" Bob added with a soap-bubble-rimmed grin.

"Why is Jon foaming at the mouth?" Noel asked.

"Don't change the subject. I'm offering you a one-shot chance to get everything you wanted, sorcerously speaking."

"Yes, but . . ." Noel eyed his fiancée suspiciously. "What's it gonna cost me?"

Lysi clicked her tongue. "Are you still concerned about losing your soul, Master? Golly, what a worrywart. You'll get wrinkles before you're twenty, this way. How do you know you haven't lost it already?"

"Have I?" Noel looked truly alarmed.

Lysi stretched out her left hand and let the light wink off her zircon. "Let's just say your taste in companions might be questionable in certain circles."

"No." Noel suddenly sounded as if he were reciting a memorized lesson of nondebatable certainties. "You don't lose your soul that easily, not just for consorting with demons. My father didn't. There's always the chance that a mortal can be as much of a good influence on a fiend as a fiend can be a bad influence on a mortal. Or vice versa." He scratched his head, and sounding more like his normal, muddled self, added, "She never did explain that last part."

"She?" Thin threads of steam trailed up from Lysi's eyelashes. "Who is this 'she'?"

"Professor Petracca. She was there with Ms. Rhodes when I—when I—" He looked down, ashamed of his past *faux pas de magie noire*. "She got Ms. Rhodes to agree not to report me for what I did to the other book, and we got to talking."

"That's the way to get wizardly power. Listen to improving lectures from some half-assed Yale prof." Lysi's tongue dripped sarcasm. She made no mention of "Professor Petracca's" other career. Hearing things from the mouths of angels, rather than faculty, tended to legitimize them. What Noel didn't know wouldn't hurt her plans.

"Professor Petracca has tenure."

"Full-assed, then. She also has a nice pair of legs. Why don't you see if she's got a taste for new meat? I'm sure she'll be the first to tell you that it doesn't matter what you do with your body so long as you think pure thoughts! I'll bet she'll come up with all sorts of ways to prove it, too." She turned her back on him and sobbed.

"Lysi, please . . ."

Lysi waited for him to take her by the shoulders, make her look at him, swear eternal devotion, dab off her tears. She hoped he'd do it soon, for though the tears he'd touch would be ordinary enough, the real demon's tears beneath would sear Lysi's face with acid while they lingered. Every illusion had a price, even for those who served Evil. Hell was the metaphysical beauty school of Creation.

Nothing happened. Noel never touched her, yet on her cheeks the forced tears dried one by one, with little glows of warmth, delicate as a ghost's kiss. She brushed her true skin with her fingertips and marveled to feel it unmarred.

"Don't cry, Lysi. She's nothing—a nice lady is all. I only want to make you happy. You've done so much for me."

"Like what? Like going to bed with you? Big deal! That's my job. I'm a succubus! You don't thank a fish for swimming. And you didn't have to give me an engagement ring. I'd've stayed in your bed as long as you liked. You've got *that* much power. Master."

"Then maybe I've got power enough to make you stop calling me Master."

Lysi felt a creeping sensation ride up her body from soles to throat. She wheeled around sharply. "What do you think you're pulling, M—M—M—?" The forbidden word would not come. "Why, you goatbiter!"

"Hey, boy, this here's America," Bob put in. "Freedom of speech."

"Don't you worry." Noel's tone made Bob quail. "As soon as I force you out of there, you can call me Master till you choke." He removed the last teardrops from Lysi's face, still without a touch. His sea-dark eyes were no longer so young. When she looked into them they held her with more power than she dared admit, more power than she or all the Underlords could bestow.

"I'll steal the Richard Jewel," Noel said with the solemnity of a Crusader taking his first oath. "Not because I want the power for myself, but because I think you want me to have it. You did something for me, Lysi."

"I'll say I—" He raised his hand, and she was dumbstruck. He spoke on, still holding her to silence.

"You gave me more than a good time. You gave me a new way to see myself. You let me learn what I could do standing on my own, without my parents there to tell me what to do next and how to think. It's not easy, making this decision for myself—maybe it's wrong, but I don't care. I can sort out the right and wrong of it later. I'm through taking the easy way. For now, I'm learning how to be free. I'm using the gift you gave me: myself. I've cut all the ties. I'm going to be the one who runs this life. I couldn't have done it without you there, believing that I could. That's what you gave me. That's why I love you."

He lowered his hand, restoring her to speech. His kiss was as chaste as if she were the image of an angel.

"Geeeez—I mean, Gehenna!" Bob swore under his breath.

Lysi clapped a hand to her mouth and scrubbed off Noel's kiss angrily. "All right, you say you'll do it. Super. That's all I care about, the bottom line." She said it loudly, as if trying to convince someone.

"You're right about one thing, M—M—Noel. It will cost, pulling this one off, but not your soul. You'll need additional powers you haven't got yet: bodily transportation, electronic dissociation, fifth-level defenses—"

"Fifth-level?" Bob wondered aloud. "Aren't those only used against low-ranking ange—?" Lysi stepped on his foot.

"How about invisibility, so no one sees me stealing the jewel?" Noel asked.

"For that, you have to pay more than you're prepared to give."

"And for the powers you mentioned? Won't I have to do something evil to earn them?"

"That's the beauty of it, Noel. This is the mission that pays for itself." Lysi wound her arms around Noel's neck and tickled his ankle with one bare foot. Her breath was as hot and gusty as the desert wind. "By stealing and destroying the Richard Jewel, you'll earn evil and then some. I believe you can do it. I believe in you so much, I'm willing to give you all the powers you want on credit."

She unloosed one arm from the amorous headlock she had on him. Parchment crinkled near Noel's ear. Out of the corner of his eye he saw a closely written document with a red seal at the bottom that oozed eternally melting droplets.

"An application for the charge-card of Hell," Lysi purred, her words slightly garbled as she took Noel's ear lobe between her lips and gave it a tantalizing nibble. "I'll co-sign. You get the powers you need for a limited time, then pay back with interest when you wreck the jewel."

"And I get to keep the powers?"

"Bought and paid for."

Lysi's abrupt swings from anger to lechery gave Noel some second thoughts. "Uh . . . What happens if I don't follow through?"

"Nothing worth worrying about." She nuzzled his neck. "You did say you wanted to please me?"

Noel signed.

"Steal the Richard Jewel?" The open central court of the Yale British Art Center rang with laughter. "With all the security measures we're taking, who could steal the Richard Jewel?"

"Sorry, sir, but Dr. Hack asked me to double-check everything," Geordie Burns told the guard. "It is made of gold and precious stones, after all. The experts can't say whether the most valuable single element of it is the twin diamonds or the great central pearl, and that's without counting the lesser gems. The jewel is a special loan to us for this one stop of the traveling exhibit, to be shown only at Yale. It's a double favor on the part of Dr. Henry Montgomery, who discovered it at the Wadi-al-Qibir dig: for his old alma mater and his old friend, Dr. Hack.''

"You just tell Dr. Hack to stop worrying over nothing. The display case we've got for the Richard Jewel is state-of-the art. Why doesn't he take a look at it?''

"He's doing that right now.''

Dr. Randolph Hack looked up from his meticulous examination of the display case as Geordie Burns joined him. "Well? Will it be safe?'' Geordie nodded. "Good. I wouldn't know a burglar-proof display case from a box of Cracker Jack.'' The scrawny, sandy-haired man straightened up and rubbed the small of his back with exaggerated grimacing. "I'm getting too old for this, Geordie.''

"You get younger every year, Dr. Hack,'' the younger man said fondly. "Or that's what your wife tells everyone.''

"Louise flatters me. I love it. I'd love it more if I didn't have to keep reminding you to stop calling me 'Dr. Hack' every two minutes, Geordie. We're equals now. The days of your being my faithful underling are long past.''

Geordie sighed. "I wish they weren't.''

"Well, I don't. I was a vituperative, envious, dried up old leatherback then. You had it all, as far as I was concerned: good looks, youth, a promising academic career, beautiful girls chasing after you . . .''

"I fooled you, didn't I.''

"Geordie, did you tell Louise the truth when you said your letter came back 'Addressee unknown'?''

Geordie turned his attention to one of the many packing crates disposed around the exhibit hall. "We'd better get to work. The opening's this weekend, but I want to see some of the medieval fighting demonstrations on Cross Campus Friday afternoon.''

Dr. Hack snorted. It was just like Geordie to evade mention of any painful memories. Under that well-developed physique lurked a soul that would sooner flee than fight when it came to matters of the heart. It had been convenient until he'd run away once too often. Regrets were not so easy to outrun.

"You can go and see them for me. Bunch of weird kids bashing each other with fake swords,'' Dr. Hack muttered. "They'd better not come in here with 'em. Bash this case and they'll get a nasty surprise. Throw 'em all in a dungeon. They'd love it."

"The Association for the Re-creation and Generation of History isn't a bunch of weird kids, Dr. Hack. They're serious scholars."

"They dress funny."

"Spoken like a man who never looks at himself in the mirror before academic processions. Have you seen what the regalia for some European universities looks like?"

"Geordie, they can stick ice cream cones on their foreheads and say they're unicorns, as long as they don't hurt this exhibit."

"No one's going to hurt this exhibit."

"Steal the Richard Jewel? Lura, you haven't been reading something you oughtn't, have you?" Atamar cast a searching glance around the small studio apartment on York Street that the two angels shared for plausibility's sake. When on Earth, it was well to play it mortal to the hilt, and that included a mailing address.

"I haven't read anything you'd object to."

"And this?" A paperback novel materialized in his hand. On the cover a young woman in a white negligee was having her bosom grazed over by a bare-chested man in nankeen pantaloons. "Moral contamination. It might have been worse, I suppose." He tossed it onto the couch.

"As if what I read is any of your business, Atamar." Lura's look dared him to challenge this. "That book didn't give me the idea that the Richard Jewel might be stolen, for your information. I was the one who spoke to Melisan's child in the Beinecke Library, remember. He was rather taken aback when his evil deed went awry, and I took the opportunity to sound him out. Poor soul, I never saw anyone so desperate for an uncritical ear. Ms. Rhodes and I both listened to him talk in exchange for not turning him into the authorities."

"Turning him in might have saved him from further missteps."

"Or pushed him into them. He's a good man, but he's in love and he's young and he's mixed up about a lot of things. There's the danger. A man in love isn't quite sane. He might do anything, and the wickedest thing he can do at this point is steal the Richard Jewel. It's a multi-sin job, and you don't get those very often, outside of politics. That succubus he's in love with isn't stupid. She'll set him after it, or I don't deserve to fly.''

Atamar's laugh was calculated to belittle. "In love with a succubus? In lust, you mean. He'll get over that soon enough.''

"Did you?''

"My case—ours—was different.''

"Of course. Everything the great Atamar does is different. You don't have to go by anyone's rules but your own. Everything about you is special. The only trouble is, no one but you ever seems to see it that way.''

"I don't think I like your attitude.''

"I don't think I care.''

"That does it. From now on we work this mission together. For your own good, I'm going to keep you away from these disrupting mortal influences. Look what they've done to Melisan! I want to keep my eye on you.''

For her answer, Lura went invisible.

"Lura, you get back here!'' Disembodied laughter mocked him. "Lura, I won't play your game, I warn you.''

"What's wrong, Atamar?'' her voice taunted. "Can't you get used to the fact that you're not in command of anyone but yourself any more? And you still haven't guessed why you're kept in the lowest ranks! Don't lecture me on contamination from the mortal plane! You're still fighting lower elements than that. Is it that hard to let go of power?''

"I can let go, Lura.'' He was too calm, his words too evenly stressed. "I can let go.'' He too vanished.

The apartment held silence and emptiness. A spill of time that only had meaning for mortals went by. Lines of silver light twirled into a dark-haired angel.

"Atamar?'' she called tentatively. "Atamar, where are you?'' There was no reply, only emptiness. "Atamar, I'm sorry.'' Nothing. "You're special, you know. I do love you. I know you love me, that you loved me since our exile, maybe since before . . .'' She looked all around the apartment, to no avail. On the wall hung a cheap print of "The Temptation of St. Anthony.'' It had been Atamar's little joke when they first moved in. Lura looked at it and didn't laugh.

"Why can't we leave the desert behind us?'' she asked the

echoes. ''Did you love me then because I was in your charge, bound to obey you? Is that what you need to make you love me still?''

Her words hung on the air.

''I can't give you that. If it was only my obedience you loved, I can't. All I can give—all I ever gave you—was my self; my self where it truly lies. My heart for you to hold. My soul. My love.''

Dust burned to gold, fell around her in a mantle of wings. She saw his face form above her.

''As I have given mine.''

Light melted into light, and the world sang with its bright, bright burning.

13

Shoplifters Will Be Prosecuted

"RANDY, YOU'RE OUT of your mind."

Dr. Hack continued to unroll his sleeping bag, untroubled by Geordie's comment. "Geordie, what I said to you before about us being equals . . . I am still the senior equal. I was an archeologist before you were a tadpole. And *don't* call me 'Randy.' That is Louise's prerogative, for reasons we won't go into."

"I still say you're crazy." When Geordie folded his arms across his chest and put on that hard, judgmental expression, he looked like Conan the Barbarian in one of his grander snits over the decadence of city-dwellers and their effete indoor plumbing.

"You're free to say it. I'm still staying here."

"Museum Security won't allow it. You'll trip up the night watchman."

Dr. Hack paused, leaning back on his meager haunches. "Hmm, Security . . . That does put another color on it. I shall have to speak to someone and obtain permission."

"You won't get it. For you to camp out in the middle of the exhibit is the same as saying they're incompetent. I learned enough while I was teaching at Princeton to know that you don't call anyone incompetent who's even vaguely connected with the Ivy League. And some of them are pretty vaguely connected with the Ivy League and the real world both, believe me."

"I won't question anyone's competence. I'll simply say that if Yale wants the added cachet of being the only stop on this tour to show off the Richard Jewel, they'll have to allow me my little quirks. Otherwise I ship it back to Henry's keeping so fast I'll leave scorch marks on the diamonds." Dr. Hack's tiny eyes glittered mischievously behind his gold-rimmed glasses. "If you want a child or a university to come around, threaten to take away something that they want very, very much.''

Geordie scratched his head. "I don't know," he said. "I just don't know."

Dr. Hack straightened up. "Look around you, Geordie. Really look at what we've been traveling with and lecturing about these past three months. It's not a very big exhibit, but it's an extraordinary one. I don't want to risk any of it, not only the Richard Jewel. Thieves have been known to destroy everything they can't sell just for the sheer hell of it. The tabloids would love it: 'Vandals Wreck Occult Relics. Medieval Voodoo Hoodooed on College Campus Tour. Role-Playing Games Blamed.' ''

He rested his hand on one of the larger display cases. "Amulets against the plague. Alchemists' equipment and notebooks. Astrological guides. Grimoires and bestiaries bound in the skins of God-knows-what creatures. Behind all the high-sounding decrees of Popes and Parliaments, the swords, the Saracens, even the Provençal love songs, there was another world. The high and low alike resorted to it for answers when the Church proved hard of hearing. When crops and health and prayers failed all together, all this paraphernalia let people feel that there might still be something mortals could do to stay in control and save themselves."

Geordie peered into the case. "Do you think that's a grimoire?" He pointed to a new addition, the purple-bound book of Noel's unwitting discovery.

"I think there are times a good guest must humor his host. Yale wants it in the exhibit—without a soup bone's notion even of which century it comes from—Yale gets it in the exhibit. It's only for two weeks. Your wounded academical purities will heal."

"I think it must be something akin to the rest of the items. You don't get a deliberate mixing of parchment and papyrus in ordinary books. Then there's the Arabic . . .''

"You ascribe dark designs to what might simply be the product of necessity—a sheep shortage, a papyrus surplus. However, it looks very nice there, beside those reliquaries."

Geordie eyed the two silver objects askance. Intuition was not scientific, yet as surely as he felt the new book belonged in the exhibit, he likewise felt that the so-called reliquaries belonged as far from him as spatially possible.

Dr. Hack noted his reaction. An experience they'd shared years back in the Egyptian desert had left Geordie more sensitive and less skeptical than other men of his age when it came to otherworldly emanations. Sometimes, though, his "just because" feelings could be a majestic pain.

"I'm not packing them away, Geordie, so stop rolling your eyes like a prize stallion. I kept them in their boxes at the tour stops where we had limited room, but unless you can come up with some sound reasons why they shouldn't be shown now, clam it. Reliquaries are an accepted part of medieval hocus-pocus."

"But whose relics?"

"How should I know?"

"I do." Geordie's mouth twitched. "I looked inside that one." He pointed to the gorgeously chased box shaped like a miniature pavilion. It was about the size of a corsage box. A miniature silver banner flew from the turquoise- and tourmaline-studded roof, a human head face-on etched into both sides of the metal. On the pavilion's side-panels were delicately done tracings of famous beheadings: David and Goliath; Judith and Holofernes; Salome and St. John, and more.

"It's full of skulls."

Dr. Hack looked around the deserted exhibition hall. "And he calls me crazy," he told an invisible audience.

"Open it yourself. There are two trays inside the box, one on top of the other, made out of horn. The skulls are arranged in the trays in nice even rows, each one no bigger than the first joint of my ring finger."

"And why do you suppose you're the only one to have stumbled across the portable catacombs of the Munchkins? Did you find something equally gruesome in the other one?"

"The other one's empty. Really empty."

Dr. Hack patted Geordie on the back. "Every piece in this exhibit has been cataloged, examined, studied into the ground. You're not the only one to open that pretty silver box. I did it myself. I didn't see a thing."

Geordie didn't seem at all surprised. "I know what it says in the catalog," he said. " 'A pair of twelfth-century reliquaries, probable origin the Holy Land. Original contents unknown.' "

"But you know them." Geordie nodded, and Dr. Hack sighed. "If you'd have settled down when you had the chance,

you'd feel a lot better today. Marriage is the world's first,
best holistic healer. You might have explained to Amanda
about that pushy little Princeton tart. She would have understood. She was a pushy little tart herself once. The stains
could have happened to anyone.''

"Can we please not talk about Amanda.''

"*Et in saecula saeculorum.* By all means.'' Dr. Hack toed
his sleeping bag. "I'd better get after that permission to stay
here overnight.''

"I still don't know, Randolph . . .''

"You don't know if I'll succeed?''

"I don't know whether I packed my sleeping bag in the
back of the car or if I'll have to buy a new one.''

Dr. Hack grinned. "Welcome to Camp Lionheart.''

If one discounted the offerings of one or another exotic
film society and such mundane activities as studying in the
castellated fastness of Sterling Memorial Library, there wasn't
that much to do on a Thursday night at Yale except steal the
Richard Jewel. Noel and Lysi met in Jon's room, where Bob
laboriously pecked out one character at a time on the PC
keyboard.

"Got it yet?'' Lysi said impatiently.

"Gimme time, gimme time. You think Hell's made of
modems? Takes awhile to get through, and then I gotta get us
some permission.''

"No one asked for permission to use that computer gateway before,'' Noel remarked.

" 'Snot what I'm puttin' in for, Master.'' The demon
squinted at the screen. He wasn't used to wearing glasses,
and so had used his tenure in Jon's body to make a few minor
adjustments on his landlord's eyesight. Day by day Jon's
myopia and astigmatism were fading as the world came into
sharper focus for Bob's benefit.

"What we-all need now's clearance for the power pipeline.
Y'gotta get what's comin' to you 'ccordin' to that-there contract you signed. Doncha?'' He took off Jon's glasses and
tossed them away over his shoulder with a fillip.

"Get on with it, Bob.'' Lysi gritted her teeth. Mention of
the contract she and Noel had signed put her on edge. "The
exhibit's supposed to open on Saturday, with a special private
reception Friday night. We want the Richard Jewel before

then.'' Bob tapped out a few more characters. "Can't you do it any faster?'' Her voice rose to a scream.

"Hey, don't yell at me. This here's the fastest way to contact the right department Down Home. Leastways it's the quickest way you can get them 'thout bloodshed.'' Jon's brow furrowed. "Y'all maybe got a cat handy?''

"Don't you dare!" Lysi shouted, horrified. "That is . . . We don't want to draw any unnecessary attention.''

"Suit ch'self, honey babe.'' Bob made another maddeningly slow entry.

"You know, if Jon were here—I mean really here—he could get you through in no time flat,'' Noel said. "He always liked to say that there wasn't a system built he couldn't access.''

"Do tell.'' Bob tilted his chair back. "We got a special spot for hackers down where I hail from. Ain't never seen one of 'em access his way out.''

Noel remained confident. "You never met Jon. Except briefly. I've seen him operate. 'Course if you're afraid he'll maybe show you up . . .'' He shrugged.

Bob glowered, first at Noel, then at his left hand. "Awright'' he told it. "You're so smart, you get the power station on the wire.''

The left hand capered onto the keys and typed: THAT'S 'ON-LINE,' STUPID. WHY SHOULD I DO YOU ANY FAVORS?

" 'Cause I got your body, that's why! Wanna see what I can do to it if'n you rile me, shortcake?''

"Bob.'' Noel spoke very softly. "If you do any permanent damage to Jon's body, I'll see to it that you spend the rest of eternity as a bookmark. That's one thing I know I can do already, without any additional powers. Ask Lysi.''

"Whoa! Hey, can't you take a li'l ol' joke, Master?'' Bob tried to hold up his hands in disclaimer, but the left one clung to the keyboard and had to be wrenched away. Bob addressed it again. "C'mon, Jon, show us your stuff. It'll be good exercise for you. Ring up the Underlords. I done give you some of the intro work already.''

SLOPPY STUFF, the hand replied. WASTED KEY-STROKES. IF I COULD, I'D PUKE.

"You can do better, you show me!''

WHAT'S IN IT FOR ME?

"Jon has a point," Noel said. "You're the one's always talking about price."

Out of the side of her mouth Lysi muttered, for Bob's ears alone, "Come on, come on. I want this job over and done with. I co-signed the application, and you know what'll happen if the terms aren't fulfilled. To you, too."

Bob knew. Hell was famous for bloc condemnations of incompetence. He and Lysi were a team, however loosely linked, and as a team they would be punished for failure. Noel's mother had learned that lesson centuries ago.

"You win," he told the hand. It flipped him off again. "We'll deal. You get us the power station on-line, and we'll give you . . . Whadda y'want? 'Thin reason, that is."

THIRTY MINUTES FREE ACCESS TIME DAILY.

"On this machine right chere?" Bob did not trust his rented appendage. "How'll I know you won't use that-there time to do me dirty?"

I WANT TO PLAY 'SPACE-EATERS' AGAIN. DO YOU MIND?

"For Dis' sake, Bob, you'll be right there the whole time he's on!" Lysi had a low exasperation level. "You can use the right hand to undo anything the left does."

"Oh yeah. Right. O.K., kid, we got us a deal." They shook on it. "Now get us through."

Jon's left hand scampered back and forth across the keys, and within less than thirty seconds a swirling red configuration, like a sawmill blade made of fire, filled the screen. The hand, exultant, flashed everyone the thumbs-up.

"There you go, Master." Bob kicked his chair away from the machine. "Jes' put your hands down and hit Return."

Noel stepped up to the PC. He held his hands out over the keys without actually touching them, gave Lysi a nervous grin, shrugged, set his fingers on the pad, and used his pinky to strike Return.

A deep humming welled up from the machine. Concentric waves of visible energy thrummed out of the keys. Tiny dots of force shot forth in repeated waves, like fiery tracer bullets, covering Noel with a scale-armor plating of vibrating golden light. At first his body jerked convulsively under the barrage, but as the little discs encased more and more of him, meeting and overlapping and merging into a skin of strange energies, he found the strength to stand against each new impact.

Lysi, watching, did not see her hands come together, heels and fingertips touching in a gesture that would have brought the fury of the Underlords crashing down on her head. "Oh, please . . . please let him be all right . . ." The pulsing sounds of the magic's flow left her conveniently deaf to her own heretical murmurings.

At the keyboard, Noel was all aglow. He raised one fist from the pad and opened his mouth—to scream in pain, to shout in triumph, to cry for help? No sound came.

But it was enough. The machine stilled. The golden armor sank into his skin. He turned from the PC and extended his cupped hands for Lysi to see. They held a living blue flame that shifted through the shapes of flower, bird, star, fish, sprite, snake, more. Its form and its being were entirely his to control. His face was full of a terrible, ancient, intoxicating awe.

"It's mine. It's mine . . ."

"Oh, Atamar, look!" Lura's hand tightened on her mate's arm. Her face beamed with delight which only Atamar could see. The angels walked on air midway between the gallery's floor and ceiling while the mortals below slept undisturbed amid the display cases. "It's Geordie and Dr. Hack!"

"A regular Old Home Week," Atamar mumbled. His wings rippled uneasily. Ever since they had stepped into the British Art Center, he had suffered from an unbearable case of the willies. It got stronger when they entered the special exhibition gallery, though he could not target the exact source of his malaise.

"Won't Amanda be surprised." Lura snuggled closer to Atamar, not at all put off by his jumpiness. She had put up with more than a few odd moods during their time of exile.

"Amanda who?"

"Rhodes, darling. Don't you remember her? She was the pretty one, the one we were so sure was a shoo-in on charges of illicit lust and lechery. It was just a matter of time until she led Geordie off the straight and narrow."

"Ha." Atamar did not like to be reminded of past miscalculations. "That boy's feet were stapled to the straight and narrow. Stitched. Shackled. Riveted. We never had a chance with him. Neither did she."

"He loved her," Lura said simply. "He respected her too much to take advantage of her."

"How very old-fashioned of him. I approve . . . now. Then it was a no-win situation. Even had he not worshipped the girl with such an outrageously pure passion, nothing might have happened anyway. She was a virgin in everything save behavior and imagination. She talked a good game, but such types always fold in the stretch."

"Atamar, after we've gotten Melisan's boy taken care of, I'm going to see what can be done to get Geordie and Amanda back together. The opportunity is too good to waste."

Atamar did not approve of this. "We are not cleared for mortal matchmaking. That belongs to the Highest."

"Other angels do it."

"And you have doubtless seen the latest statistics on mortal marriages? If it is not one of our own fraternity interfering, it's the mortals themselves. Give them an ounce of freewill and they're off like a sailor on a toot."

Lura smiled archly. "Aren't we colorful?"

"I'm serious. Matchmaking is the most addictive form of meddling known to angels, the closest thing to temptation we can have close to home. All the more reason to resist."

Lura did not discourage him. "First things first," she said, deftly shifting the subject without making any promises.

The angels hovered at their posts, keeping guard over the sleepers and the Richard Jewel. It was monotonous work, as any vigil tends to be, and before long Lura noticed that Atamar was not his normally dispassionate self.

"What's gotten under your gown? You're fidgeting worse than a Philistine with hemorrhoids."

"I can't get comfortable."

"Lumpy patch of air?"

Lura's pert look was met with a scowl. "I said it was a mistake to come here. We're wasting time. He won't try to steal the Richard Jewel. New Haven is a big city, with more opportunities for sin than this. We should be watching the boy himself, not a spot where he might or might not show up."

"You didn't raise any objections before we got here. Like it or not, we both know how the demonic mind works, and you agreed with me that the succubus would push him to take the jewel. What's changed your mind?"

Atamar hooded his eyes, but before Lura could pursue a line of questioning fit to make the Inquisition take notes, the gallery floor irised open in a pool of dappling light and Noel was standing with his feet a few inches from Dr. Hack's head. He wore jeans, sneakers, and a turquoise sweater that brought out the blue in his eyes; yet over that there appeared to float a second, darker garment, now glimpsed, now gone. Stars were held in its ever-moving folds, and the lick of comets' tails, and the heavy glow of the hunter's moon.

Wizardry. Lura's thought touched Atamar. He could feel her alarm. *How has he bought it? Poor Melisan!*

Atamar's eyes narrowed, searching for the boy's soul. *No. I can still see it. He has done nothing irrevocable.* He sensed Lura relax at his reassurance. He wished he could as easily lose the uncanny feeling he was getting from something in this room. He tried to pinpoint it, his more-than-mortally sharp eyes going all around the gallery, but there was not time enough for him to examine every object closely. Already, Lura was drifting down.

"Noel." Her voice was a sweet exhalation in his ear. If he heard it at all, he gave no sign. "Noel." He walked from one case to the next, Lura an unseen presence floating in the air behind him, softly speaking his name.

He paused at the case containing the purple-bound book and the two reliquaries. In the darkened gallery, he struck a spear of light from his left hand and held it high. Fire snakes trickled down the length of it, dripped onto the glass, consumed it in a whirling rainbow. No alarm went off as the glass dissolved. Lura saw tiny rings of force nipping into the security system's wires. She searched, and sensed that he had done the same to every electric outlet for alarm in the whole building.

"Clever boy," she murmured to herself, and called his name again.

He did not respond. He was too busy reaching into the open case to remove the book. "It works," he said aloud, holding the book in his hands once more, quietly marveling at his own newly granted magic. "If it worked on this case, it'll work on the one with the Richard Jewel. Unless they haven't put it out yet . . . Shit." He looked at the various display cases scattered around the gallery, then at the sleeping forms of Dr. Hack and Geordie at his feet. "No, it must be out, or these guys wouldn't be here."

Not afraid of waking them? Cocky little chatterbox. Atamar commented silently.

It's no big deal for a wizard to speak for his ears alone, and you know it, Lura shot back. *Lots of them talked to themselves like that, out loud, but so no one else could hear. It gave them courage. This one needs it.*

Noel gazed at the book as if at a long-lost adversary. "This time I'll do it right," he said. "I wouldn't have to be hanging around here now if I'd burned this up as soon as it hit the floor in Beinecke. Serves me right, not thinking on my feet. Well, better late . . ." He closed his eyes in concentration.

Oh no you don't. Lura concentrated right back at him. A strand of wizard-kindled fire followed by a strand of angel-summoned quenching chased each other all across the kidskin cover. Result: stalemate.

Noel's concentration turned into a plain old frown. He peeked at the book through lowered lashes. "Now what's wrong? I could do this before I even got these other powers." He thumbed the book open.

No—elll . . . No—elll . . . Lura put a bit of dramatic tremolo in her call.

You sound like an extra from a bad Gothic novel. Lura felt Atamar at her side. *Playing it subtle, my dear?*

I do a very good still, small voice of conscience, which is more than you're doing. I'm hoping that will be enough. That, and thwarting enough of his magic to discourage him.

And if he perseveres?

He won't. He's too nervous. He doesn't really like this kind of work. He's secretly ashamed to be doing this—to say nothing of how afraid he is of what his parents might think. If one little thing goes wrong, he'll probably leap six feet in the air and run away.

Then let's give him that one little thing and get out of here ourselves. They may not be able to hear him, but he hasn't the power to block their other senses. Behold. Atamar's wings unfurled with a report like the wind snapping a mainsail.

Geordie groaned in his sleep and turned over. His hand flopped out and hit Noel on the ankle. As Lura had predicted the amateur burglar jumped six feet. As she had not foreseen, he landed on Dr. Hack's sleeping bag.

Also on Dr. Hack. The senior archeologist gave a loud cry of alarm and thrashed out in as many directions as a fully zipped sleeping bag allowed. Noel's feet slid out from under him with Hack's unexpected body-roll and he landed flat on his back, pinning the doctor to the floor.

"What the hell's going on here? Geordie! Geordie!" Dr. Hack tried to buck off his uninvited rider, but he was a slightly built man and Noel was a healthy load. The good doctor could only twist and writhe futilely beneath him.

Noel might have had the upper hand, but he wasn't aware of it. All the powers he had taken on loan were new to him. He knew invisibility wasn't part of the deal, yet he wasn't sure what else was. Taking a ride on this human water-bed, his thoughts were all panic and self-flagellation. Why hadn't he done something more than tippy-toe around these trespassers? Why hadn't he tried sealing them in sleep as soon as he saw them? Why hadn't he learned the limits of his spells before plunging ahead with this mission? Why had he insisted he could handle all this himself, ordering Lysi to remain behind?

He was working on *Why am I such an airhead?* when he was lifted off Dr. Hack and had his arms pinned behind him by the redoubtable Geordie Burns.

"Who are you? How did you get in here?" Geordie did not shout. "What are you doing?"

"You see, Geordie? You see?" Dr. Hack wrestled with his zipper, anger and self-justification lighting up his face. He wriggled out of his canvas chrysalis and fumbled for his glasses and a flashlight. He shone the beam in Noel's eyes. "I told you someone would try to steal the Richard Jewel!"

With a nod of his head, Geordie directed Dr. Hack to turn the light onto the floor. The purple book lay where Noel had dropped it. "That isn't the Richard Jewel, Randolph. It's that new book Yale had us include in the exhibit."

"So much for state-of-the-art security." Dr. Hack sniffed, looking as regally contemptuous as he could, Fruit of the Loom underwear and all. "A pair of wire cutters and even a kid like this gets in." He picked up the book and brought the flashlight back to bear on Noel's face. "Don't I know you from somewhere?"

Geordie spoke before Noel could answer. "Cut the wires on this system and you set off a secondary silent alarm. The police would have been here by now if that had happened. If you didn't cut the wires, son, what did you do?"

By this time, Noel had recovered his composure. It might have had something to do with the borderline condescension he heard in Geordie's tone, or just the fact that he didn't like having his hands held by anyone but Lysi. "I sealed them off," he said, lifting his chin arrogantly. "With sorcery." He called up a small shrug of coercive power, only as an experiment, and when he felt the answering force of its presence inside him, he launched it.

Geordie let him go. His arms fell to his sides, and he stood with all the animation of a picket fence.

"Here now! What are you doing?" Dr. Hack's hand closed around Noel's wrist. Geordie stared straight ahead, oblivious. Dr. Hack's flashlight beam swept over vacant eyes. Once in the past he had seen Geordie in a similar state, and had rejoiced. It was another story this time.

"Now I know you," Dr. Hack said, his tiny eyes accusing. "Demon."

"Who, me?" Noel backed off. He looked at his hands, as if worried that claws might sprout any minute. It was possible. Maybe magic was like drugs, with side-effects you never counted on. It was a hell of a time to realize how encyclopedic his ignorance of the subject was.

"You can't fool me, not even with that lousy Yalie wimp disguise. You're the one who gave us all the trouble in the desert; the one who kept tripping up those five others. They weren't so bad, but you . . ." Dr. Hack screwed up his face in disgust. "Heaven only knows what you would've done to that pregnant she-demon if we hadn't intervened; her and her baby. My Louise delivered the boy, and the rest of us took care of you. I hoped we'd killed you. Whipped you right and proper anyhow, and no more than you deserved. We can do it again, if you don't release Geordie."

Noel's eyes slewed slowly right, then left. "Where's 'we'?" he asked, not unreasonably.

For some reason his mild question made Dr. Hack even more pugnacious. He brandished the flashlight under Noel's nose and clutched the purple book tighter, a male Statue of Liberty in skivvies. "Don't try scaring me. I'm not the man I was then, you fiend! I can handle the likes of you myself.

I've learned you demons are basically a cowardly lot. You run at the first sign of backbone.''

"We do not!" Noel felt honor-bound to defend his roots. "Anyhow, I'm not a demon."

"Demons are also liars."

"I don't have time for this." Noel called on the same coercive spell that had stunned Geordie, letting it build within him. Invisible to mortal eyes, the power throbbed and glowed in plain sight to immortal beings.

He's making it too strong! Lura's fists clenched.

He is angry, he has no judgment for gauging the strength of spells, and Dr. Hack acts like a tougher case than Geordie, Atamar returned. The two angels faced each other across the space between Noel and the archeologist. *You are right, Lura; it is too strong. It will do more than stun when it strikes.*

He can't mean to kill Dr. Hack. He's not that far gone is he?

Would Murakh's cub care if he was? By purpose or accident, if he takes a life, it will be the undoing of his soul. He has too much of our blood in him yet. He is too proud to imagine himself forgiven for something so great.

Lura saw a wedge of yellow fire rise above Noel's head, swing back. She stepped into human sight, one hand upraised, forbidding the blow to fall.

"Noel, stop!"

The fire fell, and wiped the angel away.

"Lura!" Atamar's cry tore from his throat. He burst into the air between Noel and Dr. Hack, groping arms closing on nothing. He rounded on Noel, wings blazing with a light too full of rage and bloodthirst to be called holy. "You deserve to burn!" His eyes streamed tears.

Noel flung up one arm to protect his face from the avenging angel. The tip of one burning pinion caught him across the midsection and knocked him into Geordie. Both went down together. Breathing hard, Atamar stood above them, hands opening and closing impotently, regretting all his lost powers of destruction.

"Not even for this!" he wailed, supplicating Heaven. "Not even where punishment is more than due? Lura! Lura!"

A timorous touch made him turn. "Atamar?" Dr. Hack whispered. "Is it really you?"

The distraction was all Noel needed. He frantically gathered in as much power as he could hold and flung it at them. Atamar vanished in an eruption of white-hot sparks, and Dr. Hack was slammed against the wall. As he slumped down, unconscious, Noel dashed from case to case until he found the Richard Jewel. He tore the glass apart as if it were gelatin, grabbed his prize, and sank back through the floor.

The gallery was quiet.

14

Stalling for Time

NOEL SANK THROUGH several floors of the British Art Center and was seeping out of the basement before he pulled up short and took a horizontal direction. It was weird, watching sewer pipes, building foundations, soil, gravel, water, nematodes and other underground muck zipping past you, knowing that it was all zipping *through* you as well. Noel thought about this too much and soon became nauseated, which in turn made him lose his sense of direction. He cast a line to the surface and did a mental hand-over-hand upwards. He came out in the middle of Cross Campus, a block past where he'd wanted to be.

In view of the hour, no one saw him emerge from the sod. The medieval façade of Sterling Memorial Library made a dumb witness, all but a few of its lights extinguished, the moon riding high behind the towers. Noel took a grateful breath of night air and patted the bulge in his jeans' pocket where the Richard Jewel reposed. He headed back to his dormitory by conventional means.

A note was waiting for him on the wipe-clean message board on the suite's front door. *Noel: Sudden call from Ohio. Sure you did great. Catch you in the morning for the full story. Don't you dare tell Bob first. Love, Lysi.*

Love? The word should have thrilled him, coming from her. She'd never used it before, that he could remember, not even when they shared the pleasure of each other's bodies. Instead, he only felt tired, indifferent, used up. He scrubbed the board clean with his sleeve and went inside. The whole suite was as still as Grove Street Cemetery, not a sliver of light to be seen coming from beneath any of the individual bedroom doors. Clearly, Bob wasn't waiting up to hear how the heist had gone. Noel was relieved. He didn't feel much like talking about it.

He started shaking uncontrollably as soon as he fastened the lock on his bedroom door. The switchplate had as good as disappeared, swallowed by the wall; he couldn't find it. His legs refused to keep him upright, forcing him to flop down backward onto his bed. He lay there in the dark, staring up at the flying reflected lights of cars still speeding by on the street below. The Richard Jewel pressed itself against his right leg, and all that had happened in the gallery pressed itself into his mind.

What have I done? Against the pattern of swooping lights he saw the apparition of the female angel, the lovely dark-haired one. She had looked like all the pictures of angels he had ever seen, yet more beautiful than they because alive: alive with the full miracle of a divine dream that a man might touch.

His touch had obliterated all that beauty in an instant.

The other one—the male—his cry of grief and pain had been real enough to still tear at the young man's heart. *Why were they there? Why—?* He saw the female's hand rise up to stop him, saw almost nothing but her hand, only a glimpse of her face. He saw the full force of his coercive spell against that angry little man in the gallery descend as she moved to block it. A spell strong enough to kill an angel. What it might have done to a man . . .

They had saved him from shedding blood, from dealing death. The bright beings had been there for that reason, for him. *For me? Was I worth it? Can I ever be—?* He closed his eyes. *What does it matter? I've destroyed them both. And what I did to those men . . . Please let them be all right. Please, I'm sorry, I'm so sorry . . .*

A teardrop slid down his cheek, into his ear. He rolled onto his right side, but the Richard Jewel grabbed him up. He pulled it out of his pocket and studied it carefully for the first time.

It too was beautiful, with an unearthly beauty distant kin to that of the vanished angels. Heavy gold, with the impressive patina of ages, its circular bulk more than filled his palm. At the top there was a loop with the scratch marks of a lost chain. In the center, a huge pearl gave off its own milky light, caught and cast back again by the facets of the two matched and matchless round diamonds guarding it. He saw his own contorted face reflected in the great pearl's belly.

Smaller rubies picked out the medallion's circumference. Arabesques of sapphires, topaz, and emeralds played across its face, skirting the three king gems. The second-hand light of street lamps was enough to let Noel see what he had stolen and what he had promised to demolish.

"I don't want to," he said to the Richard Jewel. "I can't. If I have to pay for what I've done so far, O.K., all right, I deserve it. Who was I kidding? I'm not cut out for wizardry. If this is what it takes, I haven't got it. What was I trying to prove? That I was mad at my mother? For what? She was born what she was, no choice about it. When one came her way, she chose to be something better. I had nothing but choices, and what did I do with them?"

The two diamonds seemed to stare up at him, mutely weighing his guilt. He thrust the Richard Jewel under his pillow. *I'll take it back in the morning.*

Morning came sooner than he wished. His dreams were haunted by a fair-faced angel stepping out of thin air, admonishing hand upraised, and falling into all-consuming fires of his creation. Though he woke, and slept fitfully again, she was always waiting for him just the other side of sleep. Once, her face became his as she fell. Once, it changed to Lysi's.

He woke up once and for all to find that he was sprawled naked on top of his covers, though he thought he'd gone to sleep fully clothed. His crossed hands clasped the Richard Jewel to his heart. Gray predawn light made the twin diamonds look even more harshly accusing. It was the last sight he needed after a hagridden night.

"Get *out* of here!" He threw the Richard Jewel at his door.

It smashed through the wood, crunched into what sounded like plaster, and made final impact on a substance Noel couldn't identify just going by the report thick gold made hitting it.

"Ohhhhh, shit." The splinters on his door were still smoking, rimmed with the blue gleam of expiring sorcery. He'd loosed his temper and his magic at the same time. This was no time to search for a robe. Noel ran out of his room and saw the rough crater the Richard Jewel had dug right through the sitting room wall. A sheen of white tile filled the other side of the hole.

"The bathroom. If it went through there into the next suite . . ." Noel didn't want to think about it. He opened the bathroom door and hoped for the best.

"Cover thy nakedness, lad," said the dark man who was perched cross-legged on the sink. "It is not seemly."

"Let the lad be," said the other, a redhaired giant. He lowered his foot from the toilet seat rim and strode across the room to clasp Noel's hand in hearty greeting. "My brother sees unseemliness in too many places. He is over-nice, even for a Saracen." His blue eyes looked Noel up and down, twinkling with high spirits and appreciation. "We know not where we are, and it may be that your garb—or lack thereof—is the custom of the country. I would not offend against it."

So saying, he kicked off his soft leather boots, reached up under his blue silk tunic, pulled an unseen ripcord, and dropped his hose. He was just stepping out of these when Noel gasped, "My God, who in Hell are you?"

The big man's russet eyebrows came together. "What talk is this that couples our Lord's name with infernal things? Boy, do not presume on your fair looks with me. I will have no blasphemers about me."

"My brother prefers not be outshone in that field by his retainers." The dark man's face was unreadable, yet there was a pleasantly dry bite behind his words. He stroked his thin mustache and chin-beard by turns, black eyes dancing beneath blacker brows. "Is that not right, Richard?"

"Richard?" Noel came near to strangling on the name. "*King* Richard? Of, you know, England?"

His apparent disbelief angered the redhead more than any other form of blasphemy. "Aye, and Duke of Aquitaine as well! And if I have been stripped of my crown, is that any reason to strip me of my proper titles? By the Holy Sepulcher, have we fallen in among ignorant barbarians?"

The dark man shrugged. "You will grow used to it, my friend. My people did when your Franks arrived unasked in our midst."

"Bridle your tongue, infidel! At least the years have proven which of our two faiths has conquered. See the lad! You hear he does not speak your heathen language, nor wear the turban."

"Nor much of anything else. Yet we speak his tongue, and it is neither of ours. Pact not with certainties, my lord *sic et non*." The dark one's face remained dignified, but Noel could tell he was enjoying himself.

Noel grabbed a towel from the bathroom rack and hurriedly wrapped it around his middle. King Richard's face fell momentarily, though what might have been a muffled chortle from his companion made him cover his true emotions with bluster. "Have you no breeding, boy?" he roared. "If you know me for a king, why do you stand in my presence?"

"Perhaps you might command more of your due respect if your hose were refastened, my brother." The dark man could not repress a slight smile. "Although I would not insist on ceremony too much with this youth, were I you. Who shall bow? The king, or the sorcerer who freed him?"

"Sorcerer?" Richard's voice was harsh with incredulity. "This stripling?"

"A strange country, as you say, may breed strange vessels of power. Do you see anyone else present? Yet we are free of our bright prison."

"Bah! He may be the real magician's servant, if that."

"As you will. For myself, I have always found caution to be a good first counselor." The dark man slid from the sink, his gauzy trousers making a pleasant hissing sound. He made a low obeisance before a dumbfounded Noel. "Had I the lands and men I ruled in life, Noble One, I should now lay the half of them at your feet. Failing this, you must accept only the humble thanks and service of Salah-ed-Din."

Noel's knees had a clattery conference. "You can't be. You——" His whole hand shook as he pointed a finger at the kneeling man's turbaned head. "You're dead."

"I do not argue the obvious, Noble One."

"And so's he." It took a lot out of him, but Noel managed to point at Richard too.

"Cut down by a barbed shaft in a siege like many others. A fool's errand, hounding down rumors of an ancient treasure unearthed on my lands." Richard did not relish the memory. "A handful of old coin, no more, but my life's price."

"Then how can you be here?" Noel squeaked.

"Oh, that," said Salah-ed-Din. He shrugged.

"Black treachery, blacker sorcery, a dying mage's curse," Richard elaborated. "One of *his* folk." He jerked his head at Salah-ed-Din.

"Of a certainty. One of your Frankish wizards would not be able to bind a gold ring to a courtesan. One of ours was sufficient to bind the souls of two kings after death." From within one of the flowing sleeves of his robe he produced the Richard Jewel. "In this." He placed it in Noel's unwilling hands.

The two diamonds were gone, empty black holes still warm to the touch. The great central pearl and the other stones were intact. Salah-ed-Din laid it in Noel's palm.

"You see, Noble One, I sent this unworthy gaud as a gift to my brother-king."

Noel blinked. "I thought you two were enemies."

"So we were, in the field," Richard said, doing up his hose. "But we were good knights and chivalrous, who saw no reason not to recognize each other's worth as men."

"When I heard that Richard lay sick in his camp, I sent him melons, iced sherbets, and the services of my own physician. Right was on my side. I could afford to be magnanimous, for in the end my people would win the day." Salah-ed-Din drew a deep, mournful breath. "Alas that Nazim the Dark did not see fit to understand such refinements. He was a fanatic—even more so than my dear brother Richard—"

Richard growled something scurrilous as he re-dressed.

"—a shame that he was as great a mage as he was a fanatic. He viewed any peaceable gesture toward an enemy as the mark of weakness. Weakness must be punished, and so when he heard of the jewel I had ordered sent to my brother, he placed a great curse of binding on it and sealed its power with his blood. He died, wreaking that enchantment. As we had shown ourselves so willing to come together in life, let our souls be imprisoned together after death." Salah-ed-Din lowered his eyes. "So it came to pass."

"Oh. I'm sorry." Noel was sincere.

"Sorry, lad?" Richard's hand was heavy on his shoulder. "Sorry, now that we're as good as free? Go and fetch your master, and be quick about it."

"I don't have a master."

"What? No master? Then you mean it was of a truth you who—?" Richard was thoroughly rattled.

Noel tied the Richard Jewel into one corner of his towel. He then took his toothbrush from the holder and set fire to the bristles, an eloquently silent demonstration. Richard hit the floor, kneeling. "My lord." He grasped Noel's hands, charred toothbrush included, and wedged his own between them. "I am your man and swear you fealty before all men."

Noel yanked his hands away. "Look, just get out of here and we're even, O.K.?"

The crusader-king and the Saracen lord exchanged a speculative look whose meaning the years had not changed much. "Your desire is ours," Salah-ed-Din said smoothly. "You have but to say the word."

"Go. Begone. Goodbye. *Adios.* Leave."

Richard puckered his lips. "It's not working, my lord. We are still with you. It is not my place to direct a great wizard in his black arts, but might you not do well to consult your gramarye?"

"I told you: GO!" Noel indicated the door. The kings did not stir from the bathroom floor. "Listen, if you're willing to wait, I'll slip on some clothes and walk you part of the way."

"Allah is great," Salah-ed-Din piously intoned. "Your skills are such as to allow a living man like yourself to partway traverse the path to Paradise? I am content."

"To where?" Noel bit his lip.

"You have freed our spirits from the gems, Noble One, yet in breaking that barricade a little of the stones' earthly nature clung to our souls and hardened to the fleshly shells you see. All we now require to be gone is for you, in your infinite kindness, to cut these second ties of earth and release us utterly."

"You mean . . . kill you?"

Richard was happy to set him straight. "Oh, you can't kill us. We're already dead. It will take wizardry to finish the job that barbed arrow started on me." He indulged in a hearty laugh.

He cut it short when Noel said, "I can't. I mean, I don't think I can. I could try . . . What am I supposed to do?"

"You, a mage, ask our counsel?" This did not sound right to Richard. "Must we teach you your trade?"

"Profession," Salah-ed-Din corrected.

"Bugger your niceties!" The cords on Richard's neck stood out when he shouted. "We have been granted only the freedom of a jest. Not dead, not alive, must we spend eternity thus? A curse upon the day my mother bore me!"

"Shut up before you wake my roommates," Noel hissed.

"A bit too late for that, Noel." Bradley sidled into the bathroom and gave all present a Boy Scout salute. His leather shaving kit was tucked under one arm, his monogrammed terry kilt slung over the other. He looked right at the two kings on the tiling and did not even do a double take.

That was more than could be said for Richard, who swallowed something large and invisible at sight of yet another naked young man.

"Thought I'd take a shower, as long as I was up, but I see you've got first go," Bradley said. "No rush." To the kings he added, "I can't tell you how much I am looking forward to this weekend's events. My parents and I caught your group down in Maryland one summer, I believe. What with all the horses, you threw in a jousting demonstration besides the usual swordfighting performance. Unless that wasn't your group? *Do* you do mounted combat?"

"Do I look like a common foot soldier?" Richard growled.

"I wouldn't have the dimmest what a foot soldier's supposed to look like. I just enjoy watching your shows. Now, if you ever decide to add some seafaring demos to your repertoire—I think I saw some Vikings tossed in with the rest—I'm your man." Bradley touched the brim of an unseen commodore's cap and smiled at Noel. "Shame you didn't mention you were into this historical re-creation thing earlier. I might have given it a try, though damned if you'll catch me in tights. Still, I don't mind sharing the facilities. Knock on my door when you're done." He left.

"A madman." Salah-ed-Din made a sign against the evil eye. "He babbles as if he knew us, yet Allah witness, that is not so."

"He thinks you're part of the Yale Medieval Weekend," Noel explained wearily. "The way you're dressed."

"We seem to be the only ones who are dressed," Salah-ed-Din said. "Perhaps my brother Richard was correct." Richard was still gazing fondly at the bathroom door. "Were we to strip ourselves bare, we might make sense of this mad world into which we have awakened." He reached for his sash.

"Don't do that!" Noel grabbed Salah-ed-Din's wrist. The Saracen gave him a deadly look that made him let go immediately.

"Noble One, you had but to ask." He spoke ice. "Not to lay hands on my person. For the love I bear you and the faith I cherish that you will ultimately free us, we will say no more of your rash behavior." A slender dagger flashed into Salah-ed-Din's hand. "Also, you are very young."

The bathroom door slammed open and a bloodcurdling shriek wrapped in green pajama bottoms flew over Richard's head. He landed in a crouch, pivoted on his heels, and kicked out at the dagger. It flipped into the toilet. A few more terse yells and Salah-ed-Din lay immobilized under his assailant's foot. Richard started up to his brother-king's rescue and got a swift kick to the ribs that threw him into the shower stall. He grabbed one of the taps as he went down. Fortunately, he was only drenched in cold water.

"Luis, have you gone nuts?" Noel turned off the shower and hauled a spluttering Richard out.

"What's the matter? You like getting mugged in your own bathroom?" Noel's pre-med roommate was breathing hard after his exertions, but looked proud of himself. He sneered at Salah-ed-Din. "You don't want to play with sharp stuff around here, mister. Some of us Yalies know what to do with your kind of garbage, and I'm not even black belt."

"Belt?" Salah-ed-Din echoed, staring in wonder at the elastic waistband of Luis' pajamas. "I see no belt at all."

"Let him go, Luis. He's—These are some of the medieval re-creation guys. I said they could use our toilet."

Reluctantly, Luis complied. Salah-ed-Din sat up slowly, not deigning to brush off the signs of his defeat. "So why'd he pull a knife on you?"

Noel passed another towel to Richard before fishing the blade out of the commode, wiping it dry, and letting Luis look at it. "It's part of the costume. He was just showing it to me. Everything's cool."

"O.K." Luis didn't look as if he believed it, no matter what he said. He addressed Salah-ed-Din: "Hey, I'm sorry if I jumped to conclusions. No hard feelings?" He offered his hand.

The Saracen stared at it imperiously, then said, "If you are not belted, what keeps your pants up?"

"Uh . . ." Luis inched to the door, then dashed.

"This is truly a land of unholy witchcraft," Richard said, giving his drenched hair and beard a rubdown. "Mere striplings best seasoned warriors in combat, bare hands against drawn steel."

"Luis knows karate, that's all. I think you two had better leave before anything else happens." He gave Salah-ed-Din his dagger back. "To you." He hoped the kings would take a hint.

"But where are we to go?" Richard was a big man. When hopelessness struck him, it did all the greater damage. "This is a strange land, and the ports of Heaven and Hell alike are closed to us. Were our sins so great to merit such cruel condemnation? Must we become eternal pilgrims, like the Wandering Jew?''

"Cheer, my brother." Salah-ed-Din embraced Richard's sagging shoulders. "It may be we shall find that legendary man and engage in an endless debate on the merits of our three faiths. A war of words should please you better than no battle at all, and beguile the hours of eternity." He smiled, but it looked forced.

Noel felt a hard pain in the pit of his stomach. "I'll help you," he said.

"How, Noble One? Have you not said that such knowledge lies beyond your grasp?"

"A week ago, I couldn't have set you two free from the Richard Jewel even this much. I can—I can find out how to do the rest. This is Yale, after all. We've got a great library, and then there's the Beinecke. You never know what kind of strange stuff they've got in there. There's this woman, a librarian I met, who's up on all this occult stuff from when she was a lot younger. She might be able to help out. Hey, I got 790 and 785 on my S.A.T.'s."

Now, both of the kings were smiling more naturally. "By the Holy Sepulcher," Richard said, grasping Noel strongly by the shoulders. "You have a fighter's heart, my lord. I am in your debt ten times over. Say what you would have of me."

Noel shepherded the kings into his bedroom. "I don't think you'd better stay here." He was thinking of Bob, still cloistered contentedly in Jonathan's room. He did not want to discuss the success of his mission quite yet, especially since he was now set on undoing as much of it as possible.

He doled them out ten dollars apiece. "Wander around campus for today, all right? This is all the cash I can give you, but it'll be enough if you want a little something to eat in the middle of the day."

Salah-ed-Din stroked his beard. "I do not know whether we shall have need of food, dead as we are. But I would like a cup of coffee."

"Meet me on Cross Campus this evening at—Oh heck, how would you know what time it'd be?—at moonrise."

"Give us a timepiece, tell us how it works, and we shall know the hour right enough," Richard said. "What we know not is where this field of the Cross may lie. Have you a map, my lord? I *am* able to read." He sounded piqued. "And write. I was a maker of songs, in my time, and occasionally I washed without being requested to do so.''

Noel handed over his watch, directions for its use, a map of the campus, instructions to rendezvous at six o'clock, and an apology. He hoped this would be enough to get them on their way before Bob discovered them. He was wrong.

"Noble One, might not our garb excite suspicion?" Salah-ed-Din asked. He spread the sides of his magnificent garnet-colored silk robes like wings.

"Not this weekend, thank God. If you hang around Cross Campus most of the time, no one'll even look at you twice. Just stay out of—give me that map back—*this* part of town, and *these* buildings, and you'll be fine. Now I've got to get dressed. Wait and I'll walk you out of the dorm.''

The kings sat in solemn conclave on Noel's bed while he slithered into his clothes and stowed the Richard Jewel in his pocket. King Richard never took his eyes off him, which made him feel like a stripper in reverse. Salah-ed-Din became enraptured with the elastic on a pair of his discarded underpants and had to be convinced to leave them behind. Richard needed similar convincing when, on their way out, they crossed paths with Roger in the living room. He was en route to the shower, and wearing about what might be expected.

"I could bide here until the hour you named, my lord," the English king said, sinking down onto the sofa and following Roger's retreating form closely. Noel hauled him up and out of the room without more argument.

He left them in front of Sterling Memorial Library, after pointing out that Cross Campus was just across the narrow street. Already, a number of young people were toting tent poles and rolled canvas across the grass, getting ready to set up their medieval weekend encampment. One man knelt apart, lovingly setting out different pieces of body armor on a soft ground cloth. The kings, especially Richard, watched with interest. Soon they strolled over for a closer view. Noel took advantage of this distraction to scamper.

A sense of responsibility did make him stop long enough to holler back at them. "Try to stay out of trouble until six, O.K.?''

They waved. They smiled. They were far across the grass. They couldn't hear a word he said.

15

Fancy Running Into You

Dr. Hack was pretty sure that walls shouldn't tilt in that treacherous way when an honest man was trying to get to his feet. He touched the back of his head, groaned, and decided he would feel much better if no one touched him ever again anywhere on his body as long as he lived.

"Randolph, are you all right?"

It was one of the stupider questions he'd heard of late, and he groaned again, louder, to communicate this. It had the undesired effect of causing Geordie to try rubbing his back. He yelled with pain and swatted the younger man away. He was still holding the purple book, which added heft to any swat. Geordie grunted.

"Oh, it's you." Dr. Hack tried playing it innocent. He'd known it was Geordie when he hit him. Personal pain always made him cranky. "Sorry. I thought it was the kid, sneaking up."

"The 'kid' is long gone." Geordie stretched a few final kinks out of his bones. Being stricken zombie-like left him stiff in the joints. "So is the Richard Jewel. What are we going to do?"

Dr. Hack used up the full U.S.M.C. standard vocabulary three times and was going through the fourth recitation before he stopped himself and said, "Let's not panic. There may be a way out."

"Sure. Notify the police and tell them to start tracking down the suspect. If they can find him. If they can hold him once they do. That boy has magical powers; dark ones. I should have suspected, sensed them, done something to ward them off—"

"Like what, Geordie? You and I, we've had more than a nodding acquaintance with the supernatural, but that doesn't mean we can do anything about it or against it. Resign yourself: We're mortals, which is just another way of saying *victims*."

Geordie leaned on the ravaged display case which had once held the purple book and still contained the pair of silver reliquaries. "I can't accept that."

Dr. Hack patted the younger man on the back. He spoke less vehemently. "Your acceptance doesn't change a thing. You didn't see what that so-called boy did. For all your seeing teensy-tinsy skulls that aren't there, you didn't recognize him for what he was; I did. He's a demon, Geordie. He's the same fiend we all fought in Egypt."

Geordie's head came up sharply. "We defeated him then."

"With help," Dr. Hack reminded him. "The help of others like him, the help of an angel—" His hollow chest inflated with a deep sigh. "Why they ever teach children that angels are all-powerful . . . The fiend's grown stronger. There was an angel here—two of them—and he destroyed them both, as simply as breathing. One was—"

"Atamar!" Geordie's ears pricked up suddenly, like a hunting hound's.

"Well . . . yes. How did you know?"

But Geordie was not listening to Dr. Hack. He was staring down into the display case, head cocked, face a play of recurring doubt, sparking hope, mounting excitement. "Atamar, what—? Yes. Yes, I think it—Dr. Hack! Dr. Hack, come here!" He scooped the bannerless reliquary from its velvet display-cloth and held it securely in two hands. "Dr. Hack, come here, I want you! Bring the book!"

Dr. Hack had a healthy mistrust for any form of incipient mania. Geordie's exultant commands had the opposite of their desired effect. He backed away, slowly at first, then dropped the book, spun around, and ran. Out of the corner of his eye he saw Geordie fall swiftly to one knee, snap up the book, and strike its purple-bound binding smartly against the reliquary's side.

"Going somewhere, Dr. Hack?" asked Atamar, blocking the exit with his wings. Dr. Hack screamed shrilly as momentum carried him face-deep into the angel's snowy plumage.

Lura reeled him out and plucked a few of the smaller feathers from his gaping mouth. "Tsk. You're molting out of season, Atamar. All this tension. If we don't watch it, you'll be bald-winged as a bat again before this job's done." She cradled Dr. Hack affectionately in her arms. "Hello, Dr. Hack. Long time no see. Oh, Geordie, you'll never guess who—"

"Not now." Atamar took charge in no uncertain terms. He helped Dr. Hack to stand unassisted, then motioned for Geordie to bring the reliquary to him. The angel studied it from all angles. "Remarkable. What force."

Dr. Hack dared to creep up on the angel's starboard beam and remark, "It's a reliquary. Probable origin the Holy Land."

Atamar's laughter set the miniscule silver bells on the box a-jingling. Like its companion piece, it too was crafted in the shape of a pavilion, but free of any decoration save the bells. "Holier than you know. This is no reliquary, as you would style it, but a refuge of great power, a safe-house of the spirit. I had not thought any such existed outside of the Valley of Cloud. They are usually in the keeping of higher beings. No offense."

"I don't understand."

"It's a hidey-hole," Lura explained. Atamar gave her a disdainful look. "Well, it is! Its true name is *syialim,* in the most ancient of the known tongues from beyond farthest memory. It's a nexus of great forces, proof against all magic but its own. There are only so many of these in Creation, and as Atamar says, most lie safely within Solomon's Tomb in the Valley of Cloud."

Atamar's face stole a little radiance from the silver box's sides as he rotated it slowly on his fingertips. "When the boy cast his spell, all Lura could think of was flight. To think is not always to do, yet this *syialim* felt her fear, read her desire, and drew her inside to safety in the instant before the blow fell."

"No," Lura corrected. "The instant it *did* fall. The *syialim* pulled Noel's spell in with me, or else it would have fallen on Dr. Hack. That would have been awful."

"It certainly would have," Atamar said, and Dr. Hack gave him no argument. "The same happened when the boy turned his magic on me. Some say that is how these *syialim* maintain their own powers, by absorbing the spells that pursue those spirits that they shelter."

"Of course there's a catch," Lura said. "You can't—"

"You can't get in or out just because you want to." Geordie volunteered the information like the class Bright Kid who will give the answer or die of a bad case of *oooh, me, me, me!*

Lura did not like being upstaged. It was lucky for Geordie that time had spared him his disarmingly boyish grin. "I was the one who heard you calling from inside." He shrugged. "I can't help hearing what I hear. I'm a sensitive. Atamar said it needed something magical to break the box's hold, so I grabbed the one thing that wasn't locked up in a case."

The scientist in Dr. Hack was not content. "Highly empirical of you, Geordie. We didn't even know *what* that stupid purple book was. Might've been a bunch of recipes."

"Well, I'd say we know what it is now."

Atamar gave the gallery a cursory once-over and sniffed. "The only piece of real magic in this entire pitiful jumble sale. Except for that, if we stretch a point." He pointed at the sole object remaining in the case.

Dr. Hack took out the other silver box. "Is this one, too? A—a see-a-whatever?"

"*Syialim*. Smile when you say it," Atamar suggested. "Or don't bother. That one is a reliquary."

"Probable origin the Holy Land," Lura added.

"Original contents unknown," Dr. Hack finished for her. "I know, I know."

"No, you don't," Lura said. "The original contents of that one are still intact."

Atamar concurred. "It's full of skulls. Tiny ones."

The angels had to preach silence, patience, and calmness to Dr. Hack for a good ten minutes before he stopped shouting and his natural color returned. Geordie looked smug.

Atamar cut off Dr. Hack's attempted questions about the second box with an imperious wave of his hand. "When I have leisure, I shall gladly tell you all the bedtime stories you want. Presently, Lura and I have a mission to perform for an old friend. Whether she'll remain a friend after the shameful way we've bungled things so far . . . Well, Melisan will just have to show some understanding."

"Melisan?" Dr.Hack's watery eyes lit up. "I *thought* that kid looked familiar! And there I went, thinking he was a fiend."

"If Lura and I do not have better luck soon, he well may end up in that calling. Time presses. Farewell."

"Hey! Hold it a minute!" Dr. Hack grabbed onto Atamar's

left wing. It oared forward, dragging him with it. "Melisan's kid stole the Richard Jewel."

The angel's perfect brows rose. "So? That was his purpose. Ours is to stop him from any further such escapades."

"So, we want it back. Can't you, you know—" he played wind-your-bobbin with his hands "—work us a little miracle for old times' sake?"

Atamar silently consulted Heaven for a little extra patience. Lura wrapped her wings around Dr. Hack in a perfumed embrace, by way of consolation. "It doesn't work that way, dear. Not on our level. With the power Noel has, we couldn't wrest the jewel from him except if he were willing to part with it."

"Then at least fix these cases! We'll tell everyone we won't be putting the Richard Jewel on display until the big cocktail party reception tonight. That will buy all of us a little more time."

Atamar looked self-righteous. "I am an angel, not a handyman. You have to do something for yourself."

"Fine, then let us do something for you. See that door? When it opens this morning and the case for the Richard Jewel is found broken open like that, and this one too, there's going to be a hue and cry that will rock Yale to its roots. Geordie and I won't have any choice but to tell the authorities who's responsible for the theft—leaving out certain details. As the boy's guardian angels, I'm sure you'd rather have the chance to find him, talk things out, reason with him calmly, convince him to get back on the right track without a black mark on his record. Because once we name names . . . ."

"Blackmail."

Dr. Hack's eyelashes were sparse, but he batted them charmingly.

Atamar strode over to the Richard Jewel case. A touch of his hand restored the glass to wholeness. He did the same for the other broken case, though it too was empty now.

"Dr. Hack," he growled, "you would have made an admirable demon." Lura giggled.

"I'll take that as a compliment." Dr. Hack stuck out his hand. "Partners?"

"Partners." Atamar took Dr. Hack's hand as he changed to human form. "For old times' sake."

"For all our sakes." Geordie laid his hand on theirs.

Lura became Professor Petracca and sealed the pledge as well. "For Melisan," she said. "And for Noel."

"For Noel."

16

Certes, These Be Parlous Times Fer Sherrr

THE YOUNG MAN laying out the plate armor told King Richard that he liked his garb. The slender woman who came over to help with the setup added that she thought it might have been a little more authentic if it had been made out of natural fibers instead of polyester.

"I know it looks a lot like silk, and it's cheap to make and easy to clean, but you could settle for a little more outlay and a little more upkeep and not look so . . ." She struggled to find a courteous word to the wise.

"You'd look more authentic, is what my lady Iseult is saying," the young man supplied.

"Authentic? *Moi?*" The effrontery of these commoners—to say nothing of their bizarre vocabulary—caused the king to lapse into his mother's tongue. Richard snorted loudly and stalked away to where a couple of other youths were rehearsing a demonstration of swordsmanship. He watched them have at each other with taped-up rattan weapons, a deeply puzzled expression on his face all the while.

"I didn't mean to offend him," Lady Iseult said, twirling a lock of her long blond hair around one finger.

"Ah, my lady, that is just his way," Salah-ed-Din said, taking in all her charms from beneath discreetly lowered eyelids. He did not know the proper name by which to call preshrunk designer jeans, yet if left to his own lexical devices he would name them Paradise. Like many another man of faith, he yearned for entry thereto.

It had been centuries in the Richard Jewel, and he was not a man to share King Richard's tastes.

"Might I trouble thee to comment upon my own miserably inauthentic garb, my lady?" he purred.

Lady Iseult sized him up and found more than his garb

satisfactory. "Yours look fine. You're not planning to fight, are you?"

"My interests lie in other fields."

"Is this your first event?"

Salah-ed-Din's eyes sparkled. "In truth, I have known others. Yet none so graced by the living presence of beauty as this."

Lady Iseult blushed. "I guess you're from a different fief. We don't talk so—um—forsoothly around here. I like it, though. You from Taprobana?"

"My father was a man of Kurdistan, but my sultanate—"

"Kurdistan? Where's that fief? Anyplace near Scarsdale?"

Salah-ed-Din did not comprehend her words. Neither did he desire to waste time in listening to explanations that would serve no purpose in the afterlife he shortly hoped to reach. He smiled his warmest, most ingratiating smile, and said that as his fief was indeed a distant one, he would be even more her servant if she would deign to show him around the encampment.

"I'd be delighted. Come with me. My fief's got our tent up over there by the wall. We're the Fief of the Singing Dragon— you know, Bridgeport? I'll just slip into my garb first. You mind waiting?"

"For now, Fairest One, I would be content to let still more centuries pass."

Salah-ed-Din was further contented when the lady told him he did not have to wait for her outside the tent while she changed. "We're all in this one lousy tent together for this event, and anyhow, most of us have gone skinny-dipping so much during the Wars that it's no big deal. Besides, I always need help with my lacings."

The tent flap fell shut. The Saracen lord learned the meaning of *unisex* and found it good.

Richard paced out the dimensions of Cross Campus, seeking his lost companion, and grew angrier with each passing minute that did not yield up Salah-ed-Din. "Perfidious infidel," he growled in his beard. "Mussulman swine! Mohammedan dog!"

"Hey! Who are you talking to, man?"

A persistent tapping on the small of his back made Richard turn around. He saw no one until he looked down. A curly-haired man glowered up at him from a wheelchair and almost lost his skullcap.

"My affairs concern you not, sirrah," the king replied. He found it hard to sound as cold as he would have liked. He was too fascinated with the odd contrivance in which the young man was seated. The urge to touch and tinker beat strongly in the Lionheart.

"The hell they don't. First, you're blocking my path. Second, I wouldn't talk so loudly about Mohammedan dogs if I were you. Someone might hear and take offense. Like me. Some of my best friends are definitely *not* Muslims, but that doesn't give anyone the right to use a person's religion like it was a dirty name. I should know." He readjusted the hairpin anchoring his skullcap.

Richard stared at the young man from one angle, then another, then made a slow circuit of the chair. The man waited until the king was directly behind him, then gunned it into reverse. Richard grunted as a handle rammed his thigh.

"By the Holy Sepulcher, what devilment is this?"

"Oh, can the medieval shtick. I'm not impressed. You want to fight, stop playing around with those silly little swords. Do it for real. Maybe then you'll find out how serious it can get."

"Do you think it is mere play to face another man with steel?" Richard gritted.

"Not when the steel's an M-16. Hey, c'mere where I can see you." He beckoned to Richard. The king came around the wheelchair and crouched beside it, curiosity getting the better of his wounded pride and sore thigh.

The young man searched Richard's face before he spoke. "That's better. You know, up close you look a lot older than the rest of these weirdos. Could be I've been shooting off my mouth for no good reason. Again. Maybe you were just doing something in character, talking about Mohammedan dogs and whatever. Maybe this whole medieval bit's just a hobby for you. You sure look old enough to have been in the war."

"As I was."

"No kidding? If that's the way it is, I'm sorry I made a big deal out of it, but some things just make me hit first and ask questions later. I guess it's a leftover from hearing too many redneck bastards over in 'Nam say 'dirty Jew' like it was one word."

"You are a Jew?" An old pain crossed Richard's face.

"What's the big surprise?" He flipped his skullcap in a mock salute. "Matt Pincus. There were a few of us over there. Where were you stationed?"

The young man had a strange way of phrasing things, yet Richard believed he understood his meaning. One soldier should always understand another. "I was at Acre. In the Holy Land," he added, seeing his companion's puzzled look. For his part, he wished that royal pride would have let him ask where this land of 'Nam lay.

"How'd you wind up in Israel? You regular Army, or U.N. peacekeeping forces, or what? I got to see Jerusalem for my bar mitzvah. *That* was a trip! You don't mind my saying so, you look old enough to have been there when the Six Day War hit. Remember when they took Jerusalem?"

"Who took it?"

Richard's vehemence was no less startling than the question itself. Matt grew suspicious. "You on something, man? Do yourself a favor, clean up your act. I saw enough of my old buddies killed by that shit over in 'Nam and back home too."

"I know not this 'Nam, nor your buddies. Jerusalem I know, to my shame. I stood upon the heights and saw it, but I would not enter therein. If I might not save the Holy Sepulcher, I did not merit to see it."

The young man's finger strayed casually to the motor controls of his wheelchair. "You know, you look all right, but you sure don't sound it. Maybe you had a worse time of it than I did. I mean, I may be in this thing, but at least I've got all four wheels on the ground, if you know what I'm saying. And I'm finally finishing up college. I've got an idea. Let's you and me go get ourselves a cup of coffee and talk, O.K.? One G.I. to another. Maybe later I can put you on to this really good veterans' support group I know . . ."

The wheelchair shifted into low and Richard trailed along beside it, his thoughts on Jersualem and fabled 'Nam.

Salah-ed-Din felt like a beardless youth, a mere suckling, a lackwit as, for the hundredth time, the merchant of the Great Bazaar asked him whether he carried proof of membership.

"I understand you not, Gracious One," he said, trying to contain his irritation. He regretted his impulsive gallantry to the lady Iseult. She had taken him to this Great Bazaar and asked him if he minded picking up a few provisions in one sector of the vast, roofed arcade while she looked elsewhere. He had agreed readily, partly to serve his lady, partly because he had missed the bustle and roar of life that always attends merchants and their doings.

The woman who served him was obviously one of that breed of hawkers who will leave all else behind at a moment's notice to make a sale. Did she not appear to have leaped up from her midday meal to wait upon him? Even now she still chewed a mouthful of it. Salah-ed-Din could not blame her for a wish to better herself and purchase the finer things. That one small bit of food in her mouth must have been tough as old leather. She had been chewing the same bite these past ten minutes.

"Your card. Do you have a Yale Co-op card? If you do, you get credit for your purchases at the end of the year. A percentage." She raised her voice slightly and enunciated every syllable. "Mon-ey-back-you-know-mon-ey?"

Salah-ed-Din nodded sagely. "I know money." He produced his ten-spot. "Cards I know not."

Although in some respects the merchant behaved as one eager for his custom, she was distinctly unsatisfactory in others. She picked up the bill, looked from it to the mysterious apparatus on the counter before her, and said, "You're short."

Salah-ed-Din glared at her down the full length of his hawklike nose. Some impertinence was expected from professional hagglers, but never personal insults. His fingers itched to hold his dagger—to show it to her, no more—but memories of Luis' mad, incredible attack checked him. Who could tell what black arts this bazaar-wench commanded, insignificant though she seemed?

This was in truth a land of monsters and miracles. Had not the divinely generous and loving lady Iseult shown him the sorcerous contrivings of the wizard Aerosalah and his magical canisters? These might contain the mists of a thousand gardens or the foam of an enchanted sea with which, for some reason, the ladies of this land preferred to anoint their heads. Even now his beard exhaled the penetrating essence of musk with which Lady Iseult had spritzed it in a moment of high spirits. Some of her companions who came into the tent and caught her at her play muttered darkly of Aerosalah's mortal battle with O-zoan, probably a rival wizard, but Salah-ed-Din had experienced enough of magicians' grudges. He turned deaf ears and took no sides.

Ah, but who could stop his ears from all he might hear in this bewitched and bewitching country? Were there not the awe-inspiring Black Discs of Eblis? He had watched his lady purchase several of these in a nearby shop, and witnessed how an uncanny machine released their hellish secrets. Who was the mage had forged the equipage that allowed a man to overhear the rantings of lost souls and the infernal harmonies of Ahzi Ahzbaan, of Daoud Lirot, of the Severed Heads That Yet Speak?

If the merchant-woman said he was short, so be it. She was entitled to her opinion, especially if she might have the occult power to back it up. He as not a vain man. Circumspection was the new ruling passion in the Saracen's life. That, and strawberry tofutti. There was room for neither in the grave.

"A thousand pardons. If my appearance does not delight thee, Mistress of the Eternal Cud, then I shall withdraw it from thine eyes." He touched brow, lips, and breast reverently and departed. He pocketed the ten first, then abandoned four sacks of Chips Ahoy!, a jar of Cheez Whiz, two boxes of Ritz crackers, and half a dozen bottles of Gatorade.

"I'm not letting *my* kids play those games," the cashier said aloud, shaking her head. "No way. Next!"

Matt waited for Richard outside the Yale Gay Student Alliance office. "Thought you weren't ever coming out," he said when the English king finally emerged. "No pun intended," he added.

Richard no longer looked confused. He had been promoted to stupefied. "I know not 'pun,' friend Matthew, yet for all that, it seems I know not anything. Into what manner of den did you thrust me?" His voice quavered, and his eyes rolled in cold-sweat fear when he glanced back at the closed door.

"I thought it might help you to talk to those guys, that's all. You told me you always felt you screwed up your military career because you had these—uh—leanings. I can dig guilt. Gums up your head pretty bad unless you shake it. If you're going to function like a normal man, you've got to sort out the stuff that's really your fault from the stuff that's not.

If *I* tell you it's O.K. to be gay, you gonna believe me? Of course not. I'm straight. What do I know from what you're going through? So I figured as long as you're visiting Yale, take advantage of all our wonderful facilities and talk to some people who'll understand where you're coming from and help you out.''

He leaned forward on his armrests. ''So did they?''

Richard sat down. There was no chair available, but it was immaterial to him.

''What times are these?'' he asked the world in general. ''I did penance for my sin, warred with it, married at my mother's command to overcome it, fought my way to the Holy Land so that I might be fully absolved of it, and now what do I have to show for it?'' His huge fingers uncurled, revealing a slip of paper.

Matt tilted his head to read it. ''The address of a gay bar. They give you that in there?''

''A stripling who overheard me speaking with the counselor did. He too said that he liked my garb. Friend Matthew, tell me again who holds Jerusalem,'' said Richard. ''I can't believe that, either.''

Salah-ed-Din used a rolled-up newspaper like a baton and hailed Richard from the steps of Sterling. The Lionheart crossed the street to meet him, first looking both ways. In spite of his precautions, he was almost run down by a Datsun. He hurled a lusty curse after it.

''By my sword, I would I knew whether those unholy armored things be creatures or creations! Nay, if I but had a sword worth wielding, I should face them down and slay them no matter what their nature.''

''Calm yourself, my brother,'' Salah-ed-Din said. ''They are but wagons powered by the fumes of Eblis. Great is their power, greater the sacrifice they exact, often turning on their masters.''

''How know you this?''

''I know but what I read in the papers.'' He unfurled the newspaper he carried and showed Richard a front-page photograph of a bad pile-up on I-95. The Lionheart crossed himself fearfully.

''Is such always the wage these people pay for all the wonders that serve them?''

The Saracen shrugged. "Who can distinguish truth from tale? I have seen and heard much in the few hours since we parted. They speak indifferently of flying over vast oceans, of harnessing the sun, of walking upon the face of the moon, of being destroyed by fires more powerful than any in Hell, kindled at a button's touch. Yet, with this I see representations of children who perish of hunger, elderly people who wander the streets like cur-dogs, youths with the mark of unknown diseases clouding their eyes, death in guises more horrible than the countenance of an *ifrit* . . ."

"A curse for every blessing," Richard muttered. "An evil and a wonderful time in which to live."

"Still . . ." Salah-ed-Din smiled faintly.

"And yet . . ." Richard answered his smile.

"Come, let us break croissants and drink what passes for *qahwe* in these degenerate times," the Saracen said. "I do not have to meet with the lady Iseult until three this afternoon. We are going to view the latest Woody Allen. She claims he is a cinematic wizard."

"I have never heard of that sort," Richard admitted. "However, there is much I would discuss with you. Indeed let us go to take refreshment while we may. My squire Matthew has sworn he will conduct me to Pisa after he is released from his scholarly obligations. I should like to see the Italian lands again."

Salah-ed-Din was properly awed. "To Pisa? Do I understand you aright, my brother?"

"As rightly as I understood him, albeit he spoke some mystic words that I could not fathom, enjoining extra cheese and banning anchovies save over his dead body. This is worse necromancy than Velcro, I vow. Ah, welladay! We are as babes here, though kings by right."

"But we are learning swiftly for babes, are we not?" Salah-ed-Din gave Richard a wicked, conspiratorial grin.

"That we are." Richard grinned back, no less wickedly. "And the longer we stay, the more we may learn. I have suddenly a great thirst for knowledge upon me, my lord. It would be shame to depart this second life ignorant of all its marvels. Let us spare our young magician friend the burden of releasing our spirits for a while yet."

"It would be a courtesy to him. He was much troubled by his inability to break the second portion of the spell binding us in these bodies. Our decision will ease his mind." Salah-ed-Din was a most plausible speaker.

"Paradise has awaited us these many ages. It may wait a few days longer. Or a few decades."

"You share the sentiments of my heart. I insist upon buying the coffee for us both."

"On condition that it be decaf cappuccino, brother," the Lionheart said.

Salah-ed-Din bowed acquiescence, and arm in arm the kings strolled away. Richard paused only long enough to toss Noel's watch into a trash bin.

17

Book 'Im

"WE COULD DO this a lot more efficiently if you'd drop your disguises and fly over Yale until you spot him," Dr. Hack told Atamar. "This is a dam—a mighty big campus. Who knows where he is?"

The four of them were walking down Wall Street, past the Law School, Lura and Atamar in their professional disguises. Geordie brought up the rear, toting a backpack that held the silver *syialim* and the still-unfathomed purple book, both brought along at Lura's just-in-case request.

"I know what I'm doing. Do not attempt to give harp lessons to a seraph," Atamar lectured. "It only wastes your time and annoys the seraph."

"Atamar wouldn't know which end of a harp to blow into if there were neon signs hung on it," Lura said. "For pity's sake, darling, why do you give yourself such airs? You're no more a seraph than a silverfish. Give the man honest answers, not platitudes."

"If I told him I had a fixed plan, he would want to argue about it. Wouldn't you, Dr. Hack?"

"If I thought it was half-assed, yes."

Atamar considered the little man whose soul he had once tried to steal in the days when he was still a demon. "I think I liked you better when you were afraid of me. You were not half so impertinent."

"But you're one of the good guys now. Why should I be afraid of an angel?" Dr. Hack asked.

"It is human nature to fear most what you know least, that is why."

Lura made a face. "Go back to platitudes, Atamar."

"Hey, look there!" Geordie's strong hands closed on the two men's shoulders. Lura followed his gaze down the street to the next block, where the Beinecke Library stood in splendor. Noel Cardiff was coming from the other direction, right for them.

"The little bastard! What luck!" Dr. Hack had to be held back before he sprinted off with a loud *tallyho!* As he struggled in Atamar's subtly concealed waistband grip, Noel made a sharp right into Beinecke Plaza and was out of sight. He was much too preoccupied to notice the group of four people watching him from a block away.

"*Now* we follow." Atamar led the party across High Street. When they reached the other side, Dr. Hack balked.

"What did you stop me for? Just so you could be the boss and say when we do what? I could've caught him!"

"A dog may catch a car, but—"

"—he can't drive it. Enough, Atamar." Lura cozied close to Dr. Hack while her mate sulked and bristled. "Remember what Noel did to you last time?" she prompted sweetly. "He might try the same sort of thing if you scare him again, poor lamb. I'm afraid Atamar hasn't been *quite* straightforward with you, Dr. Hack. Luck had little to do with our finding the boy just now. This is no haphazard search. We've been trailing him by our own methods all day. Tell the man, Atamar."

"Why I didn't say No in the first place when you picked Women's Studies . . . mortal notions . . . liberty, equality, sorority . . . no respect for rank anymore . . . too big for your britches . . . and don't tell me angels don't wear britches or . . . All right. We have been tracking Melisan's boy by—by—*scent*'s the nearest word for it, though the true nature of that angelic sense is not something I'd expect a mortal to understand."

"Just say you smell more than we do. I *think* my wretched mortal brain can accept that." Dr. Hack smirked.

Atamar did not see the humor. "It is unfortunate that we must take up Noel's trail where we have a distinct starting point and follow it sequentially and methodically all the way through from there. That's why we've had to wander all over campus, starting at his room. He's been a busy boy today."

"But if you're following him, why was he coming towards us just now?" Geordie asked.

"Backtracking to the rare book collection is my guess. The trail here is hot, most recently made. He went into the Beinecke several times today already."

"We know. You dragged us in and out of there every time," Dr. Hack said. "Here I thought you didn't have your halo up full wattage. Why didn't you tell us you were playing the bloodhounds of heaven?"

Atamar pointedly ignored the sting. "Which leads me to believe that Noel is looking for some*one* rather than some*thing* in that building."

"Or looking to avoid someone," Lura suggested. She drew the others behind a high granite wall at the corner of Wall and High. "Guess who's coming right up the same way Noel did? And she looks mad."

"The succubus." Atamar's teeth clenched.

"Awww, you peeked."

"Dr. Hack, you will have your chance to confront Noel. I want you to go back into the Beinecke. We will be with you, but unseen."

"Scared?" Dr. Hack pushed his spectacles up the bridge of his nose.

This time it was Lura who was not amused. "Noel doesn't know that Atamar and I survived his magic. If we remain hidden, we can do much more, strategically speaking, on two fronts." She ticked them off on her fingers: "Conscience and guilt. I know it's not fair to turn the big guns on a kid, but it may work. All that the succubus can bring to bear is the promise of making Noel feel really good."

"We, on the other hand, have the power to make him *stop* feeling really *bad*." Atamar preened himself. "There is no competition."

"You know, Atamar, I think *I* liked *you* better when I was afraid of you," Dr. Hack said. "At least with evil beings you know what to expect."

"And that is their very limitation." Atamar and Lura joined hands and stepped backward, right into the high granite wall.

Amanda Rhodes was setting up a new public exhibit of rare books in the Beinecke's first-floor display cases when Noel burst upon her. "Miss Rhodes!" In his joy at finally locating the librarian, he forgot where he was and shouted her name.

"*Ssshhhh!*" Amanda never forgot. Her shrill hiss drew more attention than had his holler. People wandering about on the upper level of Beinecke stopped to lean over the railings and see what was going on down below.

"Boy, am I glad to see you." Noel clasped both her hands fervently. "Every time I stopped in here to look for you, they kept telling me you hadn't come to work yet. I was afraid you weren't coming at all. It's nearly four, and I've got to meet them at six. You're the only one who can help me with this."

"Oh, is she?" Lysi's frigid words tinkled through the air. "How nice. Here I thought I was your helpmate."

Noel's mouth went slack with dread as he faced the beloved of his heart. "Hello, Lysi. Back so soon?"

"Where have you *been?*" Lysi demanded. She thrust her arm through Noel's as if she were hooking a large game fish. She would not loose her hold until he was safely netted, gaffed, in the boat, and beaned with an oar for good measure.

"I had things to do." Noel would not look her in the eye. He pretended to be enraptured with the contents of the exhibition case on which Amanda had been working.

"You're telling me! Well? Did you do it?" Noel nodded. "Yeah? For real?"

Amanda Rhodes was not accustomed to being overlooked. This black-haired creature was doing just that, relegating her to the role of furniture, not even extending the courtesy of an *excuse us* while she interrogated young Cardiff. It brought back hard memories of another semisweet young thing, whom Amanda had found in Geordie's office at Princeton. In Geordie's chair. On Geordie. The chippy added insult to injury by acting as if Amanda were not there, until she established her presence by dropping her *Hittite Limericks* dissertation on the hussy's bleached blond head.

One Ivy League hussy was much like another. Amanda knew the type. In earlier years, pre-Princeton, in another situation where a rival female was in danger of hogging the spotlight, Amanda had never hesitated to wrench it back where it belonged.

"Miss, you are creating a disturbance," Amanda said smoothly. "I will have to ask you to leave. Or I'll call Security," she added. Half-measures were for the timid, the bourgeois, the New Money. She was none of the above.

Lysi made a face. "Come on, Noel. Let's leave the mummy to dry out in peace." She tugged on his elbow, but Noel didn't move.

"I have to talk to Miss Rhodes."

"Why?"

"I just have to."

Dr. Hack glided across the floor like a bad summer-stock vampire. "What a coincidence," he breathed into Noel's ear. "I want to speak to Amanda, too. And you, boy."

Noel's midair pirouette would not give Baryshnikov any sleepless nights, but it served. Dr. Hack looked satisfied as the color left Noel's face when he saw the older man.

Ah, ah, ah, Dr. Hack. Naughty. It's not nice to make someone squirm, and it's worse to enjoy it. Lura was a glowing presence in the archeologist's mind.

Atamar was less of a glow, more of a hard, bright spark. *How many times do you think Hack's been able to make anyone squirm but himself? Give the man his tiny pleasures, Lura.*

"Dr. Hack!" There was a very tiny amount of pleasure evident in Amanda's greeting.

"Why so surprised, my dear? I'm the one who should be. I never expected to find you again. But . . . if you're working here at Yale, you must've seen the notices about the exhibit we're shepherding?"

"I did."

"You knew we were here? Geordie and me?"

"Yes."

"Were you planning to look us up later?"

"Never."

"I see." Dr. Hack looked wise beyond his wisdom.

"Well, I don't." Lysi was impatient. "Come along, baby. We're interrupting the Mouseketeers' Reunion." She gave Noel's arm a few more pulls, all with the same lack of effect.

"I want to talk to Miss Rhodes," he insisted, raising his voice. The watchers on the upper level leaned in closer over the railings, enjoying the free show.

Amanda heard duty call. No Rhodes ever heard that clarion summons in vain. "*Shhh!* This is a library."

"And this is a private conversation," Lysi sneered. "And I am Noel's fiancée"—she stuck her ring under Amanda's patrician nose—"and you're not. So butt out. Go catalog something, or count fines, or knit a tea-cozy, or whatever it is you librarians do with yourselves. Take this other old fossil with you." She indicated Dr. Hack.

Amanda pressed her lips together. She could hear Dr. Hack fighting a losing battle with the giggles. A gulf of uncounted years yawned between her age and the good doctor's, yet this eighteen-year-old cowpat of arrogance had dared to lump them together. War was declared, and no Rhodes since the Crusades ever left a war poorer than he joined it.

"Noel, if you wish to speak with me, I can give you fifteen minutes right now. In private. That's you and me alone, but only if you'd like." She raised one brow.

"Oh gosh, yes, please, that's just what I want!"

Amanda shut and locked the glass case with finality. Her mother had taught her that *noblesse oblige* demanded that she refrain from gloating over her victories, but Mummy hadn't run into too many soot-headed little trollops who made nasty remarks about a person's age. Amanda could not resist directing an emphatically exultant look at Lysi as she took Noel by the arm and he went with her willingly.

The succubus wasn't about to accept defeat just yet. She scuttled around and positioned herself in front of Noel and Amanda while Dr. Hack watched, snickering into his fist. Lysi folded her arms. "I don't think you know who you're dealing with, lady."

"If you mean I do not know *with whom* I am dealing— never end with a preposition, child; it shows bad breeding— you're wrong. I am a sensitive. You're a demon." Lysi gasped. "And a snip. And I am also a lady, but that is not my name, thank you. And no, I may not have any magic *per se* to use on you, but I know Noel does. Dr. Hack, if you are going to stand there like a schoolgirl nursing a dirty joke, you might as well come along and have coffee with us, too. I don't know what this boy's problem is, but it might turn out to need a man's insight." She linked arms with the two of them and gave Lysi a tight little smile.

"We won't be needing you, dear. Why don't you go home and wait for your first wrinkle, or read *Cosmo*, or take your penicillin, or whatever it is you nymphet demons do with yourselves?"

She bore both of the men away with her, around the corner and through the sliding stack-access panel. The librarian on duty made a moue of disapproval at the sight of so many civilians being admitted to the Holy of Holies, but could do nothing about it.

Her disapproving snit would have skyrocketed into scandalized squawks had she been able to peek into the coffee room and see Lysi already waiting there.

"Did you think you could keep me out?"

Amanda disdained to rise to the baiting. She poured coffee for Noel, Dr. Hack, and herself. "When one puts a flea collar on one's cat, one merely hopes for the best. How do you take your coffee, child?"

Lysi snapped her fingers, and a steaming cup appeared in her hand. "I don't need you; not for anything. Neither does Noel."

"Noel seems to think differently," Dr. Hack said. He was not a dense man, and his brief encounter with Lysi was all it took to tell him that here was the motivating force behind young Cardiff's midnight shenanigans at the British Art Center. On behalf of his still-aching head, he would delight in helping Amanda cut the little demonic slut down to size.

He assumed a confidential, paternal tone, resting his hand lightly on Noel's shoulder, and said, "Tell us what's troubling you, son." He had patented it during the many wearisome summers he'd spent chaperoning adolescents through the paces of a "genuine archeological dig" for Marmota Tours, Inc. It had fooled no one then, but there had to be a first time. "Is it . . . because you stole the Richard Jewel?"

Noel nodded.

"You got it?" Lysi's imperious interruption nettled Dr. Hack. "You got it and you didn't tell me? Or Bob? And I thought you were playing hide-and-seek all day because you screwed up again!"

Noel pulled a length of doubled twine from the pocket of his down vest. Heavy gold glinted at the end of the line.

"Hey, you were supposed to destroy it, not carry it around for a souvenir."

"It is destroyed." Noel removed the medallion entirely and showed the two craters where the enchanted diamonds once had glittered.

"That's bad," Lysi admitted, "but you're going to have to do better. Or worse."

"I believe he has. You did more last night than steal the Richard Jewel, didn't you, Noel? You destroyed something more," Dr. Hack said softly.

Oh, good jab, Dr. Hack! You're a natural. Lura's mind tagged Atamar's. *Scrim effect. Now.*

Oh, for—That's so melodramatic, Lura.

Mortals eat melodrama with a spoon. Hack's set him up

for a guilt trip. Use it while it's hot, instead of twiddling your pinions. It'll work! Humor me.

Two angelic forms fogged in and out of sight for the most fleeting of moments, a brace of celestial ghosts. Lura threw in the phantom of a voiceless wail and conjured tears of sorrow and compassion to her eyes as she gazed upon Noel. The angels' appearance was brief, but it was long enough for Noel and Lysi to see them and stiffen, for different reasons.

"You did *that?*" Lysi embraced him madly and covered everything she could reach with kisses.

He pried her off. "Yes. I did that."

"Oh, baby! I don't know how you did it, but offing angels—especially those angels—we are talking Bounty City. You want extra power now, all we have to do is send the news to the Underlords and—"

"LEAVE ME ALONE!"

Of all the . . . Shouting like that. Doesn't the little wimp know how to handle impudent females?

Atamar, the next time I hear a mortal say 'When pigs fly,' I'll be thinking of you.

"I don't want more power," Noel said. He rolled the Richard Jewel between his palms. "I was wrong to want any in the first place. I'd give it all up right now, if I didn't need magic to accomplish one last thing." He put on a brave smile, but his eyes pleaded with Amanda for help. "That's why I've come to you, Miss Rhodes. You're my friend, and you know this library. If what I need is anywhere, it's here, in one of the really rare books: a spell for freeing souls."

"Freeing souls? At Yale?" Dr. Hack couldn't keep his voice from scaling up in disbelief. "Doing charity work among the junior faculty won't restore the Richard Jewel, son. I don't see how—"

Noel explained. Dr. Hack drained his cup and waggled it weakly at Amanda, begging a much needed refill. In vain. Amanda too was *hors de combat* after hearing Noel tell of how the entrapped spirits of the kings had bloomed to life in a Yale freshman's bathroom.

"Are you crazy?" Lysi yelled. "You're talking about doing a—a—good deed." Her lips writhed around the words. "A biggie. Do it, and you'll lose all the magic you've already bought, maybe even the powers you had before—"

"Before you came angling for his soul?"

Dr. Hack had tried the patience of an angel. Lysi was less well-supplied with that virtue. Without warning she hurled a curse and a blanket of sizzling destruction at the self-satisfied older man.

It struck a cool blue shield and sputtered out.

Lysi snarled in frustration. Dr. Hack was speechless.

"Thank you, Noel," Amanda said. The sudden, short battle of sorceries had flummoxed her too, but her upbringing was stronger than her nerves.

"Was that you protecting this insect?" Lysi's eyes burned.

"I'm glad I could." It was a statement of fact, spiritless. "I've done enough harm with my magic. And he was telling the truth, wasn't he? You've been after my soul all along."

"Is that all you think we demons do? Rake in souls as if they were baseball cards? Collect 'em! Trade 'em! Share 'em with your friends!" Lysi laughed. "That was never our main purpose on earth. To serve evil, *that* is what underlies our existence. I didn't need your soul to do that. I had bigger plans for you. With your magic, and still being the master of your own soul, you could have done more wickedness than a legion of soulless sheep. Free men do greater harm than slaves; always have. You could have held the world! With a few helpful hints from me on how to manage it once you had it. Now that's more than penny-ante evil. And you could cap it all by repenting of your misspent life whenever you wanted to. You could. Your soul would still be your own. You wouldn't risk a thing and you'd have everything you desired out of life." She wound herself into his lap. "Including me."

Noel couldn't help drawing her into his arms. The sweet, familiar scent of her hair brought tears to his eyes. Her hard words were only words. She was more than what she spoke. His mind was incapable of going anywhere but back to those hours of loving they had shared. Loving. He refused to call it anything less. There had been something intangible beneath the pleasure and the fire that made it more than skin touching skin, a tenderness answering his own. He named it in his heart, though his reason protested:

She is evil!

She was. She confessed it readily. She was born of evil and she served evil. How could something evil know love? How could he feel love for her in return? Impossible.

His heart fought back, denying impossibilities.

"Why should she bother with your soul, boy, when it's your mother's she's really after?" Dr. Hack asked.

Dr. Hack clamped his lips shut, startled. That hadn't been his voice coming from them, but the others in the cramped coffee room would have to assume it was. No other male was there to be seen.

Just relax, Hack. I'll handle this, Atamar directed.

Try to make it sound more like him this time, Lura sent. *They're none of them stupid.*

Dr. Hack dropped his jaw, which Atamar promptly repossessed and used to advantage. The archeologist heard himself suavely explaining to Noel just whose daughter Lysi was, and why there was nothing at all haphazard in her concentrating her attentions on him when there were so many other Yalies to drag down. Noel's mind crowed *I told you so!* His heart murmured something else, too soft to be immediately heard.

Reason won. Noel put Lysi away from him. A new determination showed in his whole bearing. "I was right," he said. He did not sound happy about it. He gave the ruined Richard Jewel to Dr. Hack. "When we've freed the kings, this will look just the way it did before. Hold onto it for me until then."

Dr. Hack watched the medallion twirl back and forth at the end of its improvised twine chain. In his own voice he mused, "Maybe I can tell the people at the grand opening reception tonight that the diamonds popped out and will be replaced as soon as possible."

A shriek tore from Lysi's mouth. Amanda shushed her and was backhanded into the table for her officiousness. "You snakedung!" The mortals present all looked at each other, wondering whether Lysi's epithet was a collective noun or an individual insult, and if so, whose.

"Give that here!" This time there was no question that she meant Dr. Hack. "Give it to me now, or you're worse than dead."

"Lysi . . ." Noel tried to touch her, but was violently shrugged off.

"I'm not letting them ruin you, Noel. You're mine, and I'll fight for you if I have to. You're worth more than any mortal I've ever seen. Your powers are fit to challenge Virgilius himself! If you think I'm going to let you throw all that away just so you can spend the rest of your life as a human meringue, you don't know me." Again she demanded of Dr. Hack, "Give me the Richard Jewel."

Dr. Hack pressed it to his concave chest. "Why?"

"I'm going to destroy it, that's why. I'm going to shatter it to atoms. Care to come along for the ride?"

"Not really." Dr. Hack's clasp loosened. He was no hero, and he didn't notice the angels making any moves to back him up. He was passing the amulet to the succubus' waiting hands when Noel came between them. He reclosed Dr. Hack's fingers around the gold medallion.

"I asked you to hold this for me, to keep it safe," he said. "If something happens to it, maybe the kings' souls can never be freed. Until I know, or until I can release them, you have to help me. Don't be afraid. Protect it and I'll protect you." He took Amanda by the hand as well. "And you."

Lysi giggled shrilly at the three mortals who stood in a row before her. "Your power against mine, Noel? You're a fledgling! Everything you've done so far—everything you've done *right*—has had my hand guiding it. On your own, you're nothing. You need me to tell you which end is up."

"On who, child?" Amanda inquired easily.

A creature half-ape, half-reptile, threw its scaly arms around the librarian, dragging her from Noel's side. Amanda screamed as beartrap jaws lunged for her throat.

Noel raised his hand. The foaming jaws gnashed closed on nothing. Amanda peeped out from behind the young man's back while Lysi's monster jumped up and down, yowling over its badly bitten tongue. The succubus cursed vigorously and sent it back to regions unknown.

"I suppose that will learn me," Amanda whispered.

"Nice, Noel," Lysi said. "You're gaining speed, but that was never a substitute for skill. Give me the Richard Jewel and I won't hurt your friends. Let me destroy it as it should have been destroyed and we can begin to enjoy ourselves, you and I. You will have powers you never knew existed. Time will be a toy for you, space a joke, age and illness unthinkable. When you tire of your own dreams, you'll only have to say the word and the dreams of others will be torn from them, laid before you for inspection like silks at a bazaar. You'll just need to choose, and step into fantasies that begin where wonder ends. And I . . . I will be with you

through it all. You know what I can do. You know what I can
make you feel. You don't know the half; not yet.''

Dr. Hack took a glassy-eyed step forward and had to be
pulled back by Amanda and Noel.

Hard to believe she's half mortal, Lura commented.

Not at all. That's the more creative half, Atamar replied.

"No, Lysi," Noel said. "I know enough. I know what I
want now, and what I don't want. I've had enough of living
other people's dreams. It's time I had my own."

"Then have them!" The succubus' shout smashed her
illusion of mortal form. She stood unveiled at her most
monstrous—webbed feet, spiked hair, a double row of breasts
with eyes whose stare led into darkness. "Have them, and dig
your friends their graves!"

Molten streams, black and reeking, gushed from her palms,
pouring across the short length of floor between her and the
three mortals. The table, the two common chairs, the coffee
maker, all were consumed as serpentines of green fire rappelled
up from the dark flood and overran them. The blackness
flowed over Amanda's shoes. She gave a strangled cry of fear.

And stopped. She lifted one foot, then the other from the
murk. They were untouched, unchanged. Dr. Hack too was
studying his feet. Noel's head was bowed, hands clasped,
eyes closed. Multihued ripples spread outward from his feet.
The noxious flood sparkled and dissolved. He looked up only
when he heard Dr. Hack's admiring, "Son of a Minoan bitch."

"I won't let you hurt them," Noel said, looking Lysi in the
upper eyes. Twin auras of rosy light clamped themselves
around Dr. Hack and Amanda.

Atamar—

What?

Where's his?

*He hasn't enough power for that. Full protection . . . You
know what a drain that is.*

Can't we help? Can't we give him a shield too?

*What we have to lend the boy is not magic. We can only
defend him if he is attacked.*

If we're quick enough. Oh, Atamar!

Be calm. Perhaps the demon will not—

"Haven't you forgotten someone, Noel?"

—notice.

"I could kill you," Lysi said, talons flexing. "I could rend you to bits of meat, or slash your belly open like a gutted fish, or turn you into a handful of ashes. You might fight back, but your strength has limits. Mine doesn't. I've been foolish. It was your mother I wanted to undo all this time. I didn't need to get your soul, although it would have been a nice touch, for my father's sake. But if I kill you, her only child, she'll taste the bitterest bite any mortal parent can ever know. Lose you and she loses all. Faith can be a fragile thing, in the face of death; despair seductive, comfort afterwards elusive. She will fall, once you are gone.''

A plasm formed around the she-demon, the gathering of hellspawned might. Her neck elongated, split, split again, branched into nine sinuous trunks, each ending in a leering parody of her human face. Her body compacted, crouching in on itself to form a lion's forequarters, the cloven-hoofed haunches of a bull. Her father's slash-mouthed face irised open across her chest, tongue flicking out to touch Noel.

That light touch tore through cloth and skin to leave a diagonal needle-track of blood across his chest.

"What is to stop me from killing you?" Murakh's face rasped with Lysi's voice. "What is to save your mother from despair then?" the she-demon's nine faces asked.

Atamar . . .

Hush, Lura.

The angel stepped into Noel's body as into a cocoon, his unseen wings closing once over the boy. They opened, and Atamar stepped backward out of human skin.

What did you do? Lura asked.

Watch.

Noel's eyes remained open. The magic came easily, without any effort of will or concentration. Two shapes of gilded light blew softly from his lips to settle on his waiting palm. There was no distinguishing mark on them, yet it was miraculously clear that they were male and female. They poised, touched, and joined in a lilting dance. It was honey-sweet, fire-bright, brief as a mayfly's existence. Lesser lights bloomed from their circling sway and scattered on the air.

Noel raised his other hand over them, and the shadow it cast shriveled one away.

The other froze. For a moment it darted here and there across the magician's hand, seeking. At last it sank down, and cold crept over it to mask the greater portion of its light.

Lysi watched, as fascinated as the others. When this last happened, her smile was cold, satisfied.

But the light was not gone. In the heart of the dim glow, a spark lingered and took fixed shape. Too small for unaided eyes to see, it grew within the shell of the lone, bereaved figure in Noel's hand. It kindled, it moved, it danced a dance of memory shared, joy yet to share, promises that only fools could doubt who never looked into their own souls or out of their own hearts.

The lone figure left leaped up and danced with the inner flame she carried until both of them whirled away into the last shadow.

What magic did you give him, Atamar?

No magic. Only the power to remember what he has always known.

Noel spread his empty hands.

"Kill me, and you kill only me."

"Well, then I'll be satisfied with that!" Lysi raised her fists. A line of lightning sprang taut between them. Noel inclined his head.

"Noel, don't! Fight her!" Amanda grabbed Dr. Hack's hands and threw a child's London Bridge over Noel. The protective spells he had laid on them flared brashly.

Noel gently undid their interlaced fingers and left the circle of their arms. "The magic is to save you. It won't shield me. And she is right: My powers are limited." He gazed at Lysi. "I'm yours."

The silence of his surrender filled the room.

"Bastard!" Lysi tore the lightning to frayed crackles of white light. They arced over her head and flashed her from sight. Amanda and Dr. Hack could only stare.

The door opened. The other librarian came in. She wrinkled her nose at the smell of ozone, then gawked at the devastated coffee room.

"What—what—?"

"I told you we should always keep a pot of Sanka going too, Louise," Amanda Rhodes remarked with aplomb as she pulled Dr. Hack and Noel out the door. "Some people just can't handle caffeine."

18

Hello, Crusader.
New in Town?

Where do you think she went? Lura asked her mate as they hovered over the main entrance to Sterling Memorial Library, directly above the heads of Noel and Amanda.

To Hell, for all I care.

I wonder why she didn't try to kill him? She could have tried.

She might have sensed our presence, or suspected he was up to something. An empowered mage giving in without a fight? Highly questionable.

Were we so suspicious when we were demons?

Every being tends to measure others against its own standards. We were demons. Deceit was our business, distrust our hallmark.

Still, I wonder . . .

Lura's sigh drifted down as a warm summer breeze, totally out of keeping with the season. Autumn dusk was falling on the pavilions and pup tents sparingly placed on Cross Campus. On the central fighting ground, a modified melee was winding down. A few Yalies stopped to watch, but most students were in their colleges, having dinner. So were most of the Association for the Re-creation and Generation of History people. Cookfires were not permitted by the University authorities, but Berkeley College had sponsored a medieval banquet in their dining room as their mite toward an authentic weekend.

Amanda sniffed the air. "Something smells good." Her eyes moistened with longing and dreams of gravy.

"Go get yourself something to eat if you're hungry, Miss Rhodes," Noel said. "I can wait for them here."

"And miss the chance to meet Richard the Lionheart in person? You are talking to the original Robin Hood groupie, dear. I can't believe all these nasty modern stories about the man. Sheer sensationalism."

"Uh-uh." Noel spoke with authority.

"Oh? He really was . . . ?" Amanda clicked her tongue.
"Another girlish dream shot to hell. Why are all the good
ones off the market?"

"You couldn't have him, anyway. He's dead."

"You forget: I have a degree from Princeton. We do not
carp over details like death, especially if he'll buy me a gin
and tonic first." She chucked Noel under the chin. "Smile,
dear. I'm not being this obnoxious for nothing. I'm trying to
get you to stop moping. I know we didn't have any luck
finding a grimoire in Beinecke, but something will turn up.
Something always does, at Yale. I'm here to help you break
the news to the kings, so they won't blame you alone. Oh,
come *on*, Noel. It's no fun standing vigil with Eeyore. I'll
take to pinching your cheek pretty soon if you don't cheer up."

"What's to be cheerful about? Where are they? If something happened to them—"

"When were they supposed to be here? Six? I don't think
promptness became a virtue until Victorian times. Everything
that wasn't any fun became a virtue then. Well, it's seven
now. Dr. Hack must be in his glory." Amanda looked off in
the general direction of the British Art Center. "The exhibition reception's well under way."

"You could go there."

"And do what? Munch stale cheese, sip bad wine, and
hide from Geordie Burns?" Amanda sat down on the chill
stone steps of the library.

Noel sat beside her. "What have you got against him? You
just about bit his head off when he tried to talk to you outside
Beinecke. Dr. Hack told me what happened between you two
at Princeton, and—"

"How kind of Dr. Hack to mind his own damned business."

"It really *could* have been all her fault. Dr. Hack said she
was real aggressive, and Professor Burns seems like a nice
guy."

"Too nice to say, 'Excuse me, miss, but you appear to
have mistaken my pants for someone else's'?"

"I just think you should give him the benefit of the doubt,
that's all."

"Just the person qualified to give advice to the lovelorn.
Noel, might I point out that your own history of *affaires du
coeur* hasn't been anything to write home about?"

"That's different. Professor Burns isn't . . . a demon."

"No; just a rat."

"Yeah, but he sounds sincere, and a second chance—"

"The day you give that webfooted floozy of yours a second chance is the day I'll give one to Geordie Burns! Now, shut up and keep your eyes peeled for those two kings."

Noel sighed and rested his chin on his hands.

"Maybe they couldn't tell time after all."

"Oh my God, Sal, would you look at the time?" The lady Iseult leaped from the hotel bed, dragging the sheet with her. "I'm supposed to be part of the after-banquet entertainment in Berkeley at eight!" She padded into the bathroom and turned on the shower full blast. Clouds of steam puffed into the bedroom.

Salah-ed-Din stretched, enjoying the sensuous feel of cool sheets against bare skin, then followed her. She welcomed him into the tub, and for a time they had better things to do than speak. At last he struck the pelting drops of water from his eyes and said, "You are the fairest and most generous of women. Had I a hundred hearts to bestow, still you should be the most favored of my brides."

"Brides? Plural? You planning on founding a collection?" Her laugh ended in a gargle. Humor in the shower was a chancy thing.

"I speak in all sincerity."

"Sure you do. Forget it. I'm only eighteen, for God's sake."

"Despite the fact that you are past your first bloom, I yet find you fair. I would have you and no other be the mother of my sons. This batch."

The lady Iseult wrinkled her nose. "That's cute, but let's get real. I hate kids."

Her simple eloquence made the Saracen lord sit up straight and bang his back on the faucets. Suppressing a curse, he turned off the rushing water. "Lady of my soul, it may be I did not hear you aright. I have tendered you a heartfelt offer of matrimony, according to the Prophet's law. I have asked you to bear my children. This is a great honor."

"Who for?" She played with the dripping strands of his beard, braiding and unbraiding them delicately. "Sal, I like you and all that, but I've got to tell you, you do come on a little bit strong sometimes. Too macho, you know? I don't think you mean half the things you say.''

"You question my honor?" His face would have scared off a storm cloud.

"No, but . . . Asking me to marry you all of a sudden when we hardly know each other—"

"You grant me the favors of your body and disclaim acquaintance? What must I do to know you, then?" She tried to embrace him, only to have her hands struck away angrily. "I desire answers, not blandishments!"

"Well, excuse me for living!" The lady Iseult clambered out of the tub, toweled herself off, and threw on her garb before Salah-ed-Din managed to dry himself and put on the first layer of his clothing. Oddly enough, this time she required no help with her lacings.

As she put the last few touches to her toilette she said, "You know what your problem is? You want everything on your own terms; no compromises. Who died and left you king? We were doing fine, but you get marriage into your head, and then when I brush it off you act like I was tossing aside the biggest God's-gift-to-women favor since winter-weight pantyhose. I don't know if you're really stupid or just playing dumb, but for your own good, you'd better drop this instant proposal bit before you find your next lady. It sounds damned phony. If you think we women are all still so freaking desperate to get married that we'll fall over dead with gratitude when someone asks for our hand, you're living in the Dark Ages! And I don't mean just at A.R.G.H. events, either. Have a nice life, O.K.?''

She flounced out the door, leaving Salah-ed-Din to ponder the eternally fathomless ways of women and the best way to pay for the hotel room when a ten-spot was all he had.

"Don't tell me it's nine already!" The doll-like woman with the overdyed raven pageboy bob wrung her hands in mock distress. "I could stand here looking at these relics for *hours!* Simply *hours!*"

"You can always come back and do that tomorrow," Dr. Hack suggested, attempting to lure her away from the case where the Richard Jewel reposed. "They do want to close up now, though."

The woman's scarlet claws tightened on Dr. Hack's arm,

cutting off the circulation. "But I couldn't begin to get as much out of the exhibit without someone *knowledgeable* to explain it all to me."

Dr. Hack preened. "I'll be giving lectures on certain notable objects—the Richard Jewel included—at scheduled times during the run of the exhibit."

"Oh, how nice. And when does Professor Burns speak?"

Dr. Hack's smile crumbled.

An old song, eh, Hack? Atamar's chuckle prickled. *One you know well, words and music. Praise be, it doesn't move you to thoughts of mayhem anymore.*

"Oh, shut up," Dr. Hack mumbled.

"I beg your pardon?"

"I said, Professor Burns' lectures will be on the same schedule as mine. You can pick up a copy on your way out."

Still the lady lingered. She cast searching eyes around the gallery, dwelling long on each of the scant few late-stayers. "I wish I could have just a few words with Professor Burns right now. I have *such* a horrid memory, and I have *so* many questions that I'd love to have answered before I forget them."

I don't think she'll forget the one that goes 'Your place or mine?' too soon. Lura's laughter was heady as a gust of jasmined air.

"Write them down," Dr. Hack said, steering her toward the elevators. "Bring them to the lectures. Professor Burns has gone for the night."

"Oh? Where?"

Dr. Hack pushed the Down button, gently pushed his charge into the car, and said, "To a massage parlor," just as the doors closed.

"That wasn't nice, Randy," Lura said. She was leaning against the wall opposite the elevators, dressed as befit a tenured academic with good legs. Atamar, impeccable in a dark-blue pinstripe, raised a glass of champagne in the good doctor's honor.

"I don't care. And don't call me Randy." Dr. Hack jabbed his glasses back up the bridge of his nose. "He's got his gall, running out almost the moment this reception began, leaving me to cope with a tank full of strokies."

" 'Strokies'?" Lura lifted a brow.

"Mortals who realize their own importance, but suffer

from the chronic need to have it justified," Atamar said. "They measure this by the amount of stroking they receive wherever they go—be it for their money, their talent, or merely their nuisance value if provoked. Figurative stroking, only. To the ego. Literally, you couldn't get most people to touch them on a bet."

"When I catch Geordie . . ." Dr. Hack growled.

Lura tried to soothe him with a variety of small attentions. "You must forgive him, Randy. You know he's suffering from a broken heart. But don't you worry. I'll fix that right up, you just wait and see."

Dr. Hack looked at Atamar, who looked helpless. "I've given up disputing the matter with her. She is determined. She even gave me a theological argument—something about the Affinity of Souls principle in action—and when I woke up, she claimed I'd agreed with her."

Lura got huffy. "The Affinity of Souls principle is an accepted tenet. Those meant to meet and mate, must. Like calls to like, even among inanimate objects, and especially those touched by magic. That's why wizards' laboratories are always so chock-full of mystic doodads. They're mutually attracted. Souls which have experienced the supernatural are even more susceptible. Though time, distance, and circumstance may separate them, still they find each other."

"Then why do I keep losing half-pairs of socks in the laundry?" Dr. Hack asked.

"Amanda didn't seem to be expressing much affinity for Geordie Burns' soul today," Atamar pointed out.

"She will. She must. She can't help it. It will take time, but they will be together again." Lura crossed her hands on her bosom and would not be gainsaid.

"That's what I get for letting her watch *Casablanca* again," Atamar confided in Dr. Hack.

"Maybe I shouldn't have tossed all those mateless socks," the older man mused. "Maybe it is just a matter of time . . ."

"We have time for just one more performance, and then they're going to call the cops," said Lord Baudouin de Borne. The Berkeley students cheered and pounded their water glasses on the table. Some took knives and drummed with the handle butt-ends, a fun alternative to applause that they had picked up quickly from the A.R.G.H. members in their midst.

Matt Pincus seized an unattended dagger from his dinner companion and got into the spirit of things, hammering his approval on the festive board until it was debatable whether the table or the dagger would give first.

"You know, Rick, this Middle Ages stuff isn't half bad."

Richard tore his dagger out of Matt's hand long enough to stab a can of Miller Lite to the heart. He poured it down his throat and wiped his spattered beard on a silken sleeve. "You speak truth, friend Matthew. It lifts my heart to have decent fare in my belly again."

"I'm sorry about the pizza."

Richard clapped his hand to Matt's shoulder. "A true soldier faces many foes. Some come bearing pepperoni."

The percussive applause died. A short, heavyset youth in dagged mulberry velvet took the entertainer's chair. The usual arrangement of the Berkeley dining room tables had been changed for the feast, with several tables laid end-to-end at the head of the hall for a royal dais and the rest arranged in rows perpendicular to, but not touching it. This left a clear space between the A.R.G.H. dignitaries and the other revelers. It was the best they could do for a stage. Thus far it had hosted several solo musicians, a belly dancer, two excellent madrigal groups, a jester, and *The Palace of Passion,* a morality play having none.

The feast's last performer held a lute in his lap, and proceeded to tune it impatiently. Richard winced at the rough handling the instrument underwent. The harpist who had begun the evening's entertainment had lavished the proper reverence and care over the last-minute adjustments to his song's sweet partner. The harp had responded in kind, giving back as much tenderness in its music as it received from its lord's hands.

Richard might not know the love of women, but he did know love. He had been more than a king, in his first lifetime; he had been a troubadour, a servant of love. His heart knew, if his mind did not, that all the fine-faced and strong-limbed young men in the world could never dethrone his one true passion. Lady Music was mistress of his soul.

The lutanist decided enough was enough, and struck a harsh chord. A few people grimaced. Some coughed. Many did not notice.

Richard sprang to his feet, jumped onto the table, charged

up the length of the board, scattering feasting gear as he ran, and leaped upon the startled player. He wrestled the lute from his hands and sent the young man flying from his seat with one expertly placed kick. Before anyone could applaud or object, he rested his foot on the chair, the lute on his knee, and drew his fingers over the strings. The instrument complained, but softly, as it recognized that here was one who would gently guide it to fulfill its purpose in Creation.

A few turns of the pegs and Richard's second pass over the strings brought a plaintive, exquisitely sweet reply from the big-bellied lute. His voice, deep and resonant, took up a song:

"I seek in shadows, longing for the light;
 I wander lost in an eternal night;
 I serve a dream that ever farther flies,
 Nor sees the prison where her captive lies.
 Return, return, and break thy servant's chain!
 Who loves a dream shall never love in vain.
 Though wiser men than I my choice decry.
 They dreamless sleep, they hopeless men must die."

He ended with a chord perfect in its simplicity and stood down. "My own work, *extempore*. I apologize for its many faults." He crossed to where the lute's owner waited, open-mouthed, and tried to give him back his instrument.

The young man would not take it. He turned on his heel and walked away, wiping at his eyes.

Richard shook his head. All around him people were doing covert things with their eyes, their noses, and their napkins. Even his friend Matthew was similarly occupied when he returned to his seat in a more conservative manner than he had left it.

"Is aught wrong?"

Matt gave his streaming eyes one last swipe. "Nothing, man. Not one damn thing." The girl seated next to him was unashamedly sobbing. "How'd you *do* that?"

"I have some small repute as a singer."

"No, it wasn't just the song. I mean, the song was all right, but when you stood there singing, something happened. It was like—like you opened up a door. All the special times, all the beautiful things we'd ever lost, all the stuff we used to believe in—I mean *really* believe, like a kid does—it was all there on the other side and you were telling us it was O.K. to go back through. Not run away from what's real, but go back and see that just because something beautiful's gone, it's not lost forever. It lives—the glory, the dreams, the heroes, they're all there, just waiting on the other side of that door for us to remember them the right way and bring them back through to *our* side again. I saw something, Rick. I saw what's under all the fake fights and the weird get-ups and the medieval hoorah these kids are into. It's a vision. It's a dream that can be real. I actually believe it, I saw it, I *feel* it . . .''

Matt grabbed Richard's hand and laid it over his own heart. "Here. And I swear to God, I never thought that after 'Nam I'd ever feel like believing in anything again. Especially not heroes. It wasn't just the song. It was you. You sang, and you were wearing a robe of light. How'd you do it, Rick? How?''

"A robe of light . . .'' King Richard took his hand away from Matt's heart and knelt before the chairbound man. He laid both his hands on his comrade's legs, lips moving in cadenced Latin. He waited, his soul demanding the miracle.

It was as it had been with Jerusalem. Of this too he was unworthy. He might draw near, but never achieve that which he most desired. Richard stood, eyes downcast.

"It was but a song.''

He left the hall.

"Women!'' Geordie Burns spat. He shoved his empty glass back at the bartender. "I give up.''

"Then you sure as hell picked the right place to give up on them,'' the barman said, pouring him another tot of bourbon.

Geordie knocked it back in two swallows. "Nah,'' he said, leaning on one elbow. "Yale's co-ed now.''

"I don't mean Yale. I mean here.''

Geordie took a whiskey-hazed look around the bar. He saw nothing unusual. There was fairly heavy traffic, but that was to be expected on a weekend night at eleven o'clock. The men sat in pairs at the little tables, or crowded up to the bar for drinks, or drifted away to lean against the walls and watch the passing scene. Geordie felt like doing that himself. Since the row with Amanda, he had recognized himself as a philosopher who must devote his life to the deep thoughts of the universe. Discoursing on Being and Non-being was easier to do than trying to talk sense to a stubborn woman. His first philosophical observation had been *in vino veritas*. This bar was the third he'd patronized in the search for Truth.

The only thing keeping Geordie from moseying over to the wall and helping prop it up was his need to cling to the bar for support. He had an aversion to falling down drunk in a public place. Judging from the dubious looks many of the other customers were giving him, they expected nothing less than a full-face sprawl. He would not give them the satisfaction.

"Women!" he said again, and motioned for the bartender's attention.

"You are troubled by them, friend?" The big redhead at Geordie's right elbow hadn't been there a moment before.

"Drive me crazy. Can't tell themselves which way they're gonna jump next, then they want you to *know*—not guess, *know*— an' be there when they land."

"I too have often found them hard to comprehend." The redhead's huge shoulders heaved with a sigh. "My mother, above all. For all that I was her favorite, she would not stint from keeping me in leading strings even when I was a man full-grown."

"Mothers are nothing." The bartender was diplomatically ignoring Geordie and it made him testy. "I'm talking *women!* You ever figure 'em out?"

"I confess, I have not expended much time in that endeavor. I have no use for feminine prevarications. Yes or No, that is how I like my answers. *Sic et non.*"

"*E pluribus unum.* Where'n hell is that barman?" Geordie banged on the bar. "I want another drink!"

The barman came back. "You'd better go now, sir. You've had enough."

"Says who? I only had two drinks."

"Here."

Geordie tried to look ferocious, but he had the type of good looks that do not show hostility well. He resembled a pugnacious angel out on a toot. "So what if I had a drink someplace else? That a crime? I can pay. Shoot, I'm a fucking tenured full professor. You should pay *me* to drink here!"

He laid the case before the redhead. "Now look, let's ask a nunprejudiceserver. A real hunnerd 'cent American he-man such as like what made this country great and he knows when a man needs a drink.'' He sized up Richard's garb. ''So he dresses funny. He's still a man! And an American! And the Constitution says it's cool to wear weird stuff as long as you vote! What's your name, Shorty?''

''Richard Plantagenet.''

''S'O.K., we'll listen to Canadians too. Richie, am I drunk? Or what?''

''There are times a man stands in need of drunkenness.''

''What'd I tell you?'' Geordie pushed his glass across the bar. ''Same again.''

''Son,'' the bartender said quietly, ''I think you're in the wrong bar for what you want.''

''I *want* another bourbon!''

The barman looked up at Richard. ''Brother, you look like a decent guy. You're not one of our regulars, but you seem to be trustworthy. Get this jerk out of here. You can tell same as I can that he doesn't know where he really is. It'd be a damn shame if the sharks got him. We got our share of those.''

Richard surveyed the room with a trained eye. ''Indeed.'' He slipped his brawny arm under Geordie's. ''Come with me, friend. Let us take our custom where it is wanted.''

''Richie, you're a prince, a real—Say, did you know you've got a lute growing out of your back? Oughta see a doctor 'bout . . .''

Still gibbering moistly, Geordie Burns slumped against Richard's broad, silk-covered chest. His knees gave way, his head lolled back, his eyes rolled up, and his brain checked out for a short vacation. As he slipped into oblivion, he was swept off his feet and carried away by the late King of England.

The bartender wondered whether he had been wise.

19

Glad We Could Have This Little Talk, Mom

"MY BUNS ARE numb," Amanda announced, rocking from cheek to cheek on the Sterling steps. Noel flinched noticeably at her blunt turn of phrase. "Well, what do you want me to say?" she snapped at him. "*J'ai la derrière glacée?* It sounds like a flipping dessert. Where *are* they?"

"I don't know. You can go home if you want." Noel hunkered down, digging his chin into the collar of his vest.

"Ha! You've said that to me every fifteen minutes for the past six hours. And except when I went for the pizza, have I gone yet?" She fell silent, then added, "I don't know why you won't take my suggestion and do something more than just sit here, waiting for them."

"That's what *you've* been saying to *me* every fifteen minutes." *Have I done it yet?* did not need to be said.

"You're not helpless. If I had your magic, I'd be using it to find the kings instead of letting them come find me."

"I told you and told you: I don't know how to work a spell like that."

"Oh, come *on!*" Amanda slapped her knee. "If they were ordinary people, I'd accept it. But they're not; they're souls that have been steeping in sorcerous suspension for centuries."

"How does being that change anything?"

"I told you, I used to study the occult. And I'm a sensitive, even if I'm not a very good one. Every being has his own special aura, and when he's been touched by magic, it's that much stronger. Those two must have auras a yard wide! I'll bet even I could sense them, if they were near enough."

"Then why don't you do it?"

"Hmph. Maybe I will." Amanda's eyes squinched shut. "Should've tried this six hours ago." She began to hum tunelessly. Noel watched the proceedings with the jaded eye of the very young who always know better. The hum caught on a jagged, "Oh my!" Her eyes startled open.

"Got anything?" Noel smirked.

"You—you are a very fresh young man." Amanda shivered and glanced covertly down High Street, in the direction of Grove Street Cemetery. "A scoffer. Your impertinence must be what's interfering with my aura-reception."

"Nothing. Just like I thought. You should leave."

"No." Amanda was firm, though she still looked troubled. "We are in this together."

"I don't want a nursemaid," Noel mumbled to his collar. "It's almost midnight. Go home."

"At midnight? 'Tis the very witching hour. Graves do yawn. The dead do walk. Weirdos do accost you for spare change. You can't get a cab. I don't leave until you do, and I think—I think we had better leave now."

"I said I don't want anyone else telling me what to do! I don't need a keeper!" Noel shouted.

"Shut the fuck up or you'll need a doctor," came a faint, sleepy call from one of the Cross Campus tents.

In a much-dampened voice, Noel repeated, "I don't need a keeper. I know you knew my mother and father, but that doesn't mean you owe me anything. I can take care of myself, believe it or not."

"Oddly enough, I believe you. You have great powers, Noel. You could turn any assailant into Kentucky Fried Mugger with a glance. I'm not so gifted, as I just proved. I feel safer hanging out here with you, freezing my gazongas off, than I would trying to get home alone. I'm the one who needs the keeper."

She looked sincere, and a little frightened. In spite of her severe hair style and utilitarian glasses, Amanda Rhodes was a fetching woman in her prime. Her artful confession of vulnerability gave her a most attractive softness. Noel's doubts melted.

"I guess—I guess the kings are all right. Maybe they thought I meant tomorrow night. Maybe they got lost. Maybe they fell asleep and won't wake up until morning." He stood and stretched the stiffness from his bones. "I'll walk you home, Miss Rhodes."

"Oh! *Would* you?" Amanda's eyelashes fluttered like

dragonflies on speed. "But . . . you won't just come back here again, will you?"

"Why?" Noel was instantly on guard. "Why should you care what I do? I can take care of myself. I can—"

"I couldn't stand it if you did, and the kings came back, and I wasn't here to meet them! It's silly, but it means *so* much to me. Being here to meet them. With *you.*" Her wounded, innocent expression was intended to make him feel like a cad. It did.

He gave her his hands and helped her up from the steps. "Where do you live, Miss Rhodes?"

"On Mansfield Street. And please call me Amanda." She put her arm through his in Lysi's old proprietary way.

Suddenly Noel felt extremely hot, and not just in the area covered by his down vest. Miss Rhodes was approximately twice his age, although if you went by appearances rather than numbers, she wasn't quite ready to join the All-Bran Generation. Her body seemed to bump against his every second step, and not just by chance. His right hip declared its independence and bumped back exuberantly. During his second week at Yale, the Law School Film Society had shown *The Graduate.* Spots swam before Noel's eyes as he walked Amanda down High Street toward Grove. They were the leopardskin pattern on Mrs. Robinson's underwear.

The Egyptian Revival entrance arch of Grove Street Cemetery faced them from across the road as they came to the end of High Street. The moon was bright enough for Noel to read its inscription aloud: "The dead shall be raised."

"When Yale needs the room," Amanda appended. "Let's cross over."

"You don't mind walking past a cemetery at midnight?"

She squeezed his hand. "Around here the two biggest dangers are getting run over by a jogger or being attacked by some streetslime creep. I can dodge pretty well to avoid the first, and as for the second . . ." Her trust and adoration were in her eyes, and they were focused on him.

Noel's chest expanded and felt tight, all at the same time. "Don't worry, Amanda. I'll take care of you." He held the masterful bass tones almost to the end of the sentence, when his natural tenor slipped in. He strode across Grove Street, his lady on his arm, as if he were going forth to conquer the world.

Noel the Conqueror slammed on the brakes when his lady kept right on striding up to the wrought-iron cemetery gate and commanded, "Open it." When he balked, she stamped her foot. *"Now!"* All her erstwhile softness was gone.

"But it's closed."

"I never get your limits, Watson. Open the gate, and do it while the street's still deserted. We're going in."

"Why?"

Amanda clapped her hands to Noel's face and pulled it close to her own. Balefire danced on her glasses. "If you fool around with a lot of stupid questions and some witnesses stroll by and we lose our chance to get in there before it's too late, I'll be angry. Do you want me to be angry with you, Noel?"

He had seen her angry. The tragic face of Geordie Burns floated in his mind's eye as once more Amanda gave him a tongue-lashing that drew blood. *Be warned by me,* it seemed to say. *She's capable of more of the same for you, young man. Much more. Save yourself. Give her her own way.*

Noel twisted out of her grasp, held onto the cemetery gate's iron bars, and slagged them to a black pool on the sidewalk. Amanda picked her way over the cooling metal. "Put it back the way it was," were her offhanded directions as she entered the graveyard.

Noel was breathing heavily when he caught up with her on the picturesquely named Cedar Avenue, where Eli Whitney and so many other New Haven worthies were buried. "I did what you said. The gate's back up like nothing happened. Now will you tell me what we're doing in here at this hour?"

"Finding your royal friends," Amanda said calmly. "Before it's too late."

"You keep saying 'too late.' Are they in trouble? In here?" He dug his fingers into her wrists. "You did sense something before, didn't you? Why didn't you tell me?"

"Naturally you would have believed me right away if I'd told you, 'Noel, something wicked's going on in Grove Street Cemetery; something supernatural'?" His blush made her smile. "I thought not. Which was why I fell back on the old 'I is jes' a poo' he'pwess ittoo girlie, big 'trong mannums he'p me, pweez?' " She made a hawking sound in her throat. "Putrid tactics. They worked on Geordie too, for a little while. Not long, to his credit. We were both young then."

Noel was outraged. "You . . . shi—sneak!"

"I admit freely to being a shisneak. Thank you for control-ling your choice of words, dear; it's the mark of a gentleman. The important thing is, it worked. There is something evil happening in this cemetery, and the only beings with auras big enough to send out such strong distress signals must be the kings."

Noel cast frantically around the nighted cemetery. "Where are they? If anything happens to them, I'll never be able to restore the Richard Jewel! I'll be a dark wizard for life!"

"Be grateful for all your powers, dark and light. We may need them. This way." She led him up Cedar, down Myrtle, and over onto the narrower Holly Avenue.

Although Noel had no idea where Amanda was taking him or what her final goal was, he sensed a change in the air the nearer they came to the West Wall of Grove Street Cemetery. He knew nothing of auras, but he did know when a place started to give him the heebie-jeebies.

The West Wall was special. It was here that grave markers from the seventeenth century had been propped against the thick stone wall, moved from their original places on the New Haven Green, part of which had been the colony's original burying ground. Old Campus fronted the Green, and perhaps Yale or the city of New Haven did not like to be reminded of mortality. Perhaps there was truth to the rumors that nineteenth-century medical students used the grave markers as handy signposts for digging up a little extra credit for their anatomy courses. For whatever reason, the gravestones were trans-ported to Grove Street Cemetery and the bodies remained where they had been buried originally.

The exception to the rule was the scrawny corpse now seated atop one of the transplanted markers, glowing with an unhealthy green light, and shaking a bony finger at the she-demon miserably huddled at her feet.

I told you so, girl! The cadaver's jaw hung open, its binding-band in moldy tatters, but the voice still emanated from the unmoving, lipless mouth. *I told you so!*

The she-demon bowed her spiked head. "Yes, Mama." Her fingers played with the bronze saucer between her knees, the unnameable contents still smoking.

Amanda stood as one paralyzed until Noel jerked her backward and down. They crouched in hiding behind a substantial tombstone. "The kings, huh?" he whispered ferociously.

"Shhh!" Amanda hissed back. "I said there were strong auras in here, and strong evil. Two out of three—"

Unseen metal hinges screamed in the night as the corpse slid from the tombstone and stood full-height over the kneeling succubus. *Mortal blood can be the making or the destruction of true evil, my daughter. Often it is not even needful to deal with Hell for this to be so. Ah, the hopes I had for you two children! Demon's gets, witch's cubs, humankind's ingenious cruelty bound to blind, devilish power, what could stand before you?* She raised her shrouded arms to the sky and the stars tumbled into cartwheels of crimson flame.

"We've done what you wanted us to do, Mama," Lysi said.

You? The dead witch's scorn slashed the night air. *Your brother, yes, but you?*

"I've done my best . . ."

Do you call it your 'best' when now you summon me from the halls of Hell to tell me that you have failed? *That the mortal stood helpless before you and you did not destroy him while you might?* A bitter wind blew through the corpse's ragged winding sheets. Moonlight winked through fire-blackened bones. *You never got compassion from* my *side of the family.*

"Mama, please . . . I need your help. That's why I called you."

Oh, certainly. That's the only time you ever think to call your poor old mother. Why am I surprised?

"I need to know—I have to find out *why* I couldn't kill him. It's not natural. I never choked before. Is something wrong with me? Do you think maybe he's got a shield up that's so subtle and so powerful that it turned me away without my noticing it was there? Mama, an incident like this could ruin my whole career!"

Hands with a little flesh still clinging to them reached down and raised Lysi's face. The dead witch could not smile, but her disembodied voice sounded less incensed than previously. *There's the daughter I know. A professional. Let me look at you, dear one.* Lysi stood up for her mother's inspection. *Don't slouch! Four tits is no excuse for poor posture. That's better.*

"I wouldn't have troubled you unnecessarily, Mama,"
Lysi said as she pulled her shoulders back. "I had to talk to
someone about this, and I couldn't very well lay it before the
Underlords."

The cadaver snickered. *I should say not! What those bump-
kins in New Ramah did to me would be small potatoes indeed
beside what the Underlords would do to a succubus who
backed off from a sure kill. Ha! It would make the punishment
of your sire's old foes look like a holiday by comparison. You
couldn't talk to Raleel about it either, I suppose?*

"My precious brother's been too busy with his career to
help. And if he weren't busy, he'd be the first one to go
tale-bearing to the Underlords. I'd do the same, if he screwed
up."

There was a chalky, pulling sound as the dead witch wiped
a hypothetical tear from her cheek. *It does a mother's heart
good to hear that her children are at each other's throats.
Don't you worry about a thing, Lysi. We'll come up with a
perfect lie to tell the Underlords, just in case word gets back
to them. Meantime, I will search your memories and learn
what went wrong. It's nothing we can't handle, little girl. I'll
fix it so you can kill him for sure next time. Now, let me look
into your eyes . . . Think of that nasty incident . . . Let your
mind just—Aaaaaaagggghhh!*

"Let my mind scream?" Lysi asked.

Bitch! Lysi's head snapped with the force of the witch's
blow. She was knocked from her feet. The bronze saucer
spilled. Small worm-white shapes scrabbled up out of the
anointed soil and flung themselves, clinging to the cadaver's
ankles. *You dare to come to me with* that *in your heart?
Haven't you sense enough to hide your shame? Or can't it be
hidden? Is it so deeply rooted in you that your spirit confesses
it to any eye? Do you not even attempt to deceive me, to
conceal it, to spare your mother this undying pain? You . . .
love him?* Contempt and disgust infused the witch's words.

Lysi did not speak.

That a child of mine should come to this! The white shapes
at her feet made sympathetic glubbing sounds. She kicked
them. The effort caused her skull to topple off her spinal
column and roll across the autumn-crisped grass. One of the
white things fetched it back. *I'll never be able to hold my*

head up in Gehenna again, she said, repositioning said item. *Better if you had never been born.*

"Mama, I'm sorry. I'll do something about it. I'll go far away. I'll never see Noel again. I'll—"

I don't think you heard me, dear. The witch's voice was syrupy. Points of purple flame floated in the empty eye-sockets. *I said it would have been better if you'd never been born. When I give my opinion, I always like to put some teeth into it.*

She pointed at the earth. A Jacob's ladder shot from her finger, splitting the ground. The white things cowered, meeping. Out of the spreading fissure came a hooked beak the color of tarnished silver. Five ophidian eyes stared lidless above it. First one yellow lion's paw, then a second, caught at the smoke-roiling edge of the rapidly opening abyss. A third paw joined them, this one redly dripping, its claws still sunk in a marginally recognizable morsel of demon-flesh. The monster opened its maw, exhaling a cloud of fungal air whose stench bowled Lysi over into a convulsively retching ball.

Behind the tombstone, Amanda caught a whiff. She turned pale green and was decorously ill on the grass. She was still reliving dinner when Noel called in his power.

It flowed over him like a cascade of cool strength, sealing him from harm. A waterspout of white light jetted him high in the air. The magic in his blood and bone hastened to answer the one demand of his will—*Save her!* All else was detail. Amanda would have told him that the servants always saw to details in her house. Sorcery was his servant, and now it leaped from his fingertips to obey its master.

Silver curved in his hand, a bow wrenched from the moon itself. A string of starlight bent it. He summoned three shafts of fire to his palm, braided them with a single word, forged their unity into the shape of an arrow, nocked it to the bow, pulled back, and let it fly down the night.

Its flight was true and straight. It lodged in the hellbeast's central eye. The monster's scream tore up the earth, shook minute cracks into the West Wall. Winged skulls and cherub heads carved in the old tombstones moaned. The three grasping paws lost their hold on Earth. The beast skidded back into the Pit. As it went down, one paw struck out in dying frenzy, crushing the quivering white things at the dead witch's feet, hooking an ivory talon through her trailing cerements. Shriek-

ing, clattering, hurling impotent curses, Lysi's dam was dragged
back home.

The light beneath Noel faded, lowering him gradually to
the ground. He watched the silver bow turn to powder in his
hands and blow away over the graves. He heard Amanda
groaning behind the tombstone, then saw her haul herself up
over the top of it, one hand at a time, like the vampire's
entrance in some B-movie horror flick.

"What happened?" she asked groggily.

Noel went over to where Lysi still lay, curved in the fetal
position, shaking in every limb. He stroked the air over her
once, restoring her to human semblance, then gathered her
close. She locked her arms around his neck and sobbed
without tears until he kissed her.

"All right, all right," Amanda grumped. "You go to all
that trouble, I suppose I can give Geordie a second chance
too."

20

Came the Dawn

LYSI KNOCKED MEEKLY at the bathroom door. "I'll be out in a minute, Noel!" Amanda called. "Think sustaining thoughts!"

"It's not Noel. It's me." The bathroom door opened. Amanda gave the succubus a cool, sour stare. "I mean . . . it is I."

"It's a little late for good grammar to save you, young lady." Amanda briskly towel-dried her hair. It fell into lush, crinkly curls that flattered the uncompromising angles of her face.

"Could we talk?"

"Come in." Amanda shut the door and waved Lysi over to sit on the edge of the tub. She positioned herself on the closed toilet lid and crossed her legs. "Speak."

"Noel's mad at me."

"I can't see why. You tried to buy his soul, your pal is still squatting in his roommate's body, you came close to killing him, you totally mucked up his head until the poor boy doesn't know what he wants . . . Men are such fragile creatures . . . They carry grudges for the silliest reasons."

"But he saved me." Lysi laced and unlaced her fingers. "That must mean something."

"As you spared him."

The succubus looked up. "Is that all there was to it? Paying off a debt?"

"That's how he'll explain it to you, and to himself. But in reality? I don't think so." Amanda scrunched her fingers through her still-damp hair. "I think he loves you as much as you love him—pardon me for eavesdropping, but your mother *is* rather the strident sort."

"If he loves me—"

"*If* you can get him to admit it. Today. This morning.

After he's had a chance to get some sleep and dredge up all the things you've done to him and driven him to do. It's very dangerous to give some people time to think things over. You should have wormed your way into his sleeping bag as soon as I unrolled it, and not given him a chance to think. Instead, you camped out on the couch in the next room."

"Crawl in with him, in someone else's apartment!"

"What is this world coming to," Amanda asked the light fixture, "when librarians must turn pander for modest demons? He loves you, but his mind's telling him he'd be a fool to take you back after all your satanic monkeyshines. What that boy needs is an excuse to tell his brain to stuff it and let his heart do the talking. I know. I've wasted years waiting for my excuse to take Geordie back. Thank God you and Noel finally gave me one! Second chances can be contagious."

"If he loved me enough to face my mother's spells last night, a few hours' sleep won't make a difference." Lysi reassured herself. She got off the bathtub rim and opened the door. Noel was standing in the archway, leaning on the jamb. His jaw was set in the manner of a man with an urgent mission. "Noel! Oh my darling—"

" 'Scuse me." He pushed past her and sidled around a departing Amanda before shutting the door on them. When he came out shortly afterward, Lysi tried to resume her interrupted effusions of love.

He turned her arms aside, his a jaw still set. " 'Scuse me. Gotta dress. Find the kings. I'll be looking around Cross Campus. Later, O.K.?"

"I told you," Amanda said, brushing out her hair. "But you wouldn't listen. You're almost human, Lysi. Tough luck. Now what are you going to do?"

"Follow him to Cross Campus," the she-demon stated. "Make him see he's wrong about me."

Amanda set aside the hairbrush. "You don't know when you're licked, do you?"

"Does any human?" Lysi smiled shyly. "On-the-job training's the best way to start a new career. What about you? Are you coming?"

"Me, miss this? Who are you kidding?"

"*Whom.*" Lysi raised one didactic finger.

Amanda raised a different one, and the two of them fell into a very human attack of the giggles.

• • •

Geordie awoke to a severe pounding in his head. He ached all over, and something was wrong with his eyes. The ceiling of his hotel room was rippling and had turned from stark institutional white to stripes of blue and yellow. The mattress underneath him felt fuzzy and as if it had been stuffed with rocks. He rolled over, trying to get comfortable.

"Hey! Watch it!" came a baritone complaint.

Geordie bolted straight up, away from the man onto whom he'd tumbled. He then doubled over, to keep his brains from spilling out of his ears. He groaned, but it only came out as a hoarse, dry whimper. His lips grated against each other like mating Gila monsters and he longed for hospital food to take away the bad taste in his mouth. With a great deal of respect for his battered senses, he looked around him. He was one of several large, sleeping-bagged lumps inside a tent. He didn't know about the others, but he was naked.

"You are awake, my friend?"

Geordie turned slowly toward the voice and saw the big redhead from the night before. He too was stark bare, without even the hint of a sheet to cover him. He lounged on a pile of clothing. Geordie recognized some items as his own, others probably belonging to—what was this big guy's name again?—Richie?

Richie was smiling. He looked mighty pleased about something. Richie . . . It was coming back now . . . Rich—Richard Plantagenet? As in King Richard? As in the violated Richard Jewel? As in *that* King Richard? As in . . . ?

Geordie reached over and fingered the crumpled tunic under Richard's elbow. It was silk. He remembered the lute. He remembered Richard's reputation as a troubadour. He remembered many more facts about Richard's other reputation. The true nature of that last bar he'd visited the night before came crashing down on Geordie's head, along with fragments of his skull.

Richard's hand fell atop his and pressed it warmly. "A good day to you, my lad. I pray regret does not beset you."

This time Geordie's groan had some meat to it. The king looked troubled.

"Ah, but I see it does. Your pardon, dear friend. I shall be out on Cross Campus if you need me." He dressed and was gone out the tent flap before Geordie could ask any questions, or even wonder whether he really wanted to hear the answers.

"He didn't come back to the room?" Atamar asked.

"Not at all," Dr. Hack replied.

"I knew it. You can't deny the Affinity of Souls principle without something awful happening." Lura dunked her donut and sighed over the frailties of mortals. "I knew we should have trailed him, Atamar."

Atamar moodily munched an English muffin. "The whereabouts of Geordie Burns are not vital. The work I had to do last night was." He tapped the cover of the purple book significantly.

"Well? Can you tell us what it says?" Dr. Hack asked. He leaned closer to Atamar. Since Lura was seated between them at the luncheonette counter, this was a pleasant experience.

"No," said the angel.

"I thought angels knew it all."

"Some do. Some don't. Someday I might. For now . . . no."

"Why don't you just flitter off back Up There and ask someone who does know it all for a little help?" Dr. Hack's thumb indicated the ceiling fan as a source of omniscience.

"How will I ever come to know more than I do now if I am not willing to learn? Sloth is not a virtue." He thumbed the book open. "What is written on the papyrus sometimes yields a name that I can read: Richard the Frank, Salah-ed-Din, Ba'ouji . . . the name Nazim the Dark recurs more frequently than the rest. I wish I knew more, but there are pitiful few linguists in our part of Heaven."

"I'm not surprised." Dr. Hack got up to pay the check. "Let's forget about the book and concentrate on finding Geordie. I just wish I knew where to start looking."

"Try Cross Campus," Lura suggested.

"Why there?"

"That's where the Association for the Re-creation and Generation of History is having its weapons demonstrations this morning. It's the most interesting event going on at Yale. He won't be able to help but hear all the clashing and banging. It will draw him like the hapless moth to the flame!" Lura's eyes shone as they always did when she overemoted.

Dr. Hack questioned Atamar with his eyes.

"She wants to see the fighting herself, and this is the best excuse available," Atamar translated. "We might as well. I can work on the book some more while she watches men hit each other and sweat."

"Why not, then?" Dr. Hack's thin shoulders rose and fell. "For lack of a better suggestion, Cross Campus it is."

21

Plantagenets Do the Darnedest Things

ON CROSS CAMPUS, the ill-assorted group of seven was making so much noise that the A.R.G.H. Field Marshal had to intervene.

"Gentles, your pardon, but I'll have to ask you to keep it down. Ugolino di Napoli just died."

"My sympathies," said Atamar.

"You want him brought back?" Noel asked. "You've come to the right people." He gave Lura and Atamar a nasty glare.

The Field Marshal was not accustomed to hearing such bizarre statements from non-A.R.G.H. members. He opted to skirt the issue of their mental stability and plowed on to do his duty.

"Ugolino is not one of our best fighters, good sirs, but he makes up for it by losing spectacularly. Very realistic death scenes, highly touching last words. Except this time, he had to shout his way through a beautiful leave-taking speech in his lady's arms, and still the spectators could barely hear him over the noise you were making. He was supposed to be bleeding to death from a series of major cuts, inflicted by the Displaced Knight. It just didn't sound natural for a man who's lost that much blood to have the strength left to bellow."

Geordie managed a wistful smile. "Who can say what's natural for any man to do until he finds he's done it?"

"Indeed." The Field Marshal looked at Geordie askance and decided that a little inauthenticity on the field of honor was better than a lot of time reasoning with oddballs. With a low reverence, he departed.

"Geordie . . ." For what seemed like the twentieth time, Amanda tried to take him by the hand, only to have him pull away from her, eyes averted. "Darling, I said I forgave you for that little slut back at Princeton. I was wrong to just run away from the whole scene without hearing your side of it. If you say nothing happened, nothing happened.''

"Nothing happened," Geordie told the sidewalk. "Why should it?" he flung his head back and loosed a loud, bitter laugh.

Dr. Hack turned to Lura. "Touched," he said.

She disagreed. "He's just a little upset—and a lot hung-over—but I don't think he's crazy."

"I meant you," Dr. Hack said. "You and your Affinity of Souls. Now that she's willing, he's checking out. They've got about as much chance of getting back together now as—as—well, as those two."

He jerked his head to where Noel was carrying on a heated argument with Atamar while Lysi clung to his left leg and sniveled. A conservatively dressed older couple strolled past this strange tableau, and paused for a moment.

"Yalies," the man opined with a short, wet sniff.

"Well, at least it's nice to see that this generation of co-eds is going back to the proper values," the woman remarked.

Noel found it difficult to holler at an angel while a demon clung to him so closely. His subconscious was allergic to allegory. Aside from an occasional shake which did nothing to dislodge the diabolic barnacle, Noel tried to ignore her.

"—could have told me you were still—"

"What do I have to do to convince you that I've changed?" Lysi wailed, drowning out his words. "How can I prove it?"

Noel was out of patience. "Demons don't change!" he shouted down at her. The quieter voice of afterthought made him add, "Except my mom. And you two." He looked at Atamar and Lura.

"Gerial, too," Atamar supplied. "And Horgist, insofar as he's no longer an active demon. Then there was Nevrac, Shamanu, Ixtacatl, Petrus Cornelius, Odoacer—all before our time, though—Annette, Moondoggie, Chet—"

"Stow the roll call!" Noel stamped his foot, or tried to. "If there's any justice, you and your partner ought to be slammed back into demonhood. You *lied* to me!"

"Fibbing to the stainless young! The ultimate sin!" Atamar threw his hands up in mock horror. "And when did this particular doom strike?"

"In the British Art Center. I thought I'd killed you, but all the time you've been alive."

"*Nostra culpa,* though hardly classifiable as a lie *per se.*
Lura, dear, Noel wants us destroyed after all, in the name of
truth. Shall we oblige?"

Under Atamar's superior brand of sarcasm, Noel retreated
from anger to the sulks. "Well, you could've come and told
me you were all right. I was worried."

"We did what we thought best for you, Noel." Lura's
hands were a sweet burden on his shoulders.

"We did . . . postpone telling you that we were still
around, I admit it." Atamar did not seemed troubled by this
oversight. "We were busy."

"And you *did* almost destroy us."

"Thanks. That really makes me feel better."

"You want the truth."

"No, Lura; he *claims* he wants it." Atamar could raise
simple scorn to a sublime art.

"If you come with me to the British Art Center, I can show
you the *syialim* that saved us from your spell." Lura answered Noel's puzzled look with a full explanation of the
strange silver box and its arcane powers. "So you see, dear,
your only misdeed has been to steal and mar the Richard
Jewel, and that's easily righted. We've always been here to
help you, Atamar and I. Let us help you now."

"You really want to help me? Great, fine, super. So help
me find a way to free the spirits of the kings and fix the
Richard Jewel!"

"Oh," Lura said. "That."

"Sorry," said Atamar. He didn't look sorry.

"You can't do it? But you're angels! Do a miracle!"

"We are not empowered to intervene in situations where a
mortal has done wrong. He must correct his own misdeeds."

"If they can be corrected," Geordie mumbled.

"Few things are irrevocable," Atamar said, with a frosty
pursing of his lips for Geordie. "Pride and self-pity are the
hardest to get around—the one feeds on the other—but if you
truly wish to change what you have done with your life—"

"You know it!" Noel's fists clenched. "I've got to undo
the harm I did. I don't want to be an evil wizard anymore, but
as long as I'm in debt to Hell for my additional powers—"

"You're not, baby!" Lysi switched her grip from Noel's
pants leg to his belt, getting instant attention. "Honest, you're
not in debt to anyone."

"I'm supposed to believe anything *you* tell me?" Noel's laugh was as bitter as Geordie's, though more subdued.

"According to the terms of the agreement you signed, you got the added powers on trust, contingent on your doing something wicked. O.K., you stole the Richard Jewel, sort of wrecked it, almost obliterated two angels—"

"Since when does Hell recognize the conditional mode?" Atamar asked. "The only thing the boy did purposefully wrong was steal the jewel, and by returning it to Dr. Hack he negated the desire to do wrong *a posteriori,* if not the misdeed itself *de facto.* Ergo he has not sinned *de jure. Actus non facit reum, nisi mens est rea.*"

"He and the one lawyer we've got Up There are like *that,*" Lura told Dr. Hack, crossing her fingers.

"If my memory serves, Hell is strong on willful self-damnation, not happenstance evil. You did not fulfill the terms of that agreement, Noel."

"But then why—why do I still have all this extra magic?" Noel patted his pockets as if that were where he kept spare spells.

The angel's gaze slued around to rest on Lysi, silently directing her to speak. She got up from her knees. "It was always yours. You just didn't have the confidence to tap it. I thought that if you got a taste of wickedness, you'd like it and come over to our side on your own hook. In the end, selling me your soul would be a formality." She raised her face, already streaked with tears that burned angry red stripes down her cheeks. "I'm glad you didn't, Noel."

He turned away from her, staring at his empty hands. "It was always mine. The magic was always mine . . . ."

Lura tapped Lysi gently on the back. "A trust agreement with Hell requires a co-signer," she said in the succubus' ear. "Was it you?" Lysi nodded. "And now that it's void?"

"My spirit's fate is tied to his."

Lura's mouth curved up on one side. "I think that was always so, dear, contract or no."

Atamar drew Noel a little apart from the others. "The magic is yours, and so it will always be. No soul was ever condemned for holding magic, nor sanctified because it was hollow of all human feeling. If Lura and I could work a miracle for you, if we could free the kings and restore the

Richard Jewel, and you having all the power you do, would you want that? Truly?''

Noel thought a while. "No," he said. "I've been saying and saying that I don't want someone else telling me how to live and what to do. If I want to live my own life, I'd better be ready to sweep up after it."

"Elegantly put."

Noel stuck his hands in his pockets. Pretending great disinterest he asked, "So there's no help you two can give me with the kings? None at all?"

"I never said that. We are always available in an advisory capacity."

"Advice like on how to find them? It'd be a start."

"By all means." Atamar vanished, though not in his usual way. This time he knifed into the mob surrounding the cordoned-off battleground. A huge man with a shield that bore no device was battling a woman who fought with a poleaxe. The weapons were rattan, well-wrapped with duct tape, and the fighters wore safety padding under their armor, but the sound of weapons striking home still made the audience wince and cheer by turns.

"Geez, Vin, this is almost as good as watching pro wrestling," said one spectator to her mate.

"No way," he replied. "It's all rigged."

At this moment, the female fighter left a bad opening in her guard and the man took full advantage of it. She fell with a crash, and was immediately helped to her feet again by her opponent.

"Victory to the Displaced Knight!" the Herald boomed.

The winner doffed his helm. Sunlight blazed red-gold on King Richard's hair and beard. Atamar stepped in from the sidelines and grabbed him by the arm, hustling him through the press to where Noel waited.

"Come back here! We still need him!" the Herald called, and gave dignified chase. A dark man in more-than-authentic Saracen garb trailed after, a sardonic smile on his lips, and a wheelchair-bound man in a yarmulke brought up the rear.

"Here," Atamar said. "My first piece of advice to you is use your eyes." He presented Noel with the kings, the Herald thrown in for good measure. The latter was sweating profusely.

"You've got to come back into the lists!" he insisted to Richard. "We're on a very tight schedule, and we've never had a fighter like you in an arms demo before. The word has come down from their Highnesses: Sweep the field completely, and they will award you a prize as if this were a true tourney. Just one more match, and if you win that, you're our new champion!''

"Way to go, Rick!" Matt Pincus called, giving his friend a boxer's overhead handclasp victory sign. He tooled his chair up to where Geordie and Amanda stood, and said, "Hey, Burns, you left your real clothing in Rick's tent. You want me to get it back to you before it grows legs? This is New Haven, man, not Camelot. Stuff walks away."

Geordie just made a wounded sound deep in his throat.

"That's the most I've been able to get out of him too," Amanda said.

King Richard gazed appealingly at Noel. " 'Tis but a final bout, my lord. In all this strange land, I have at last found a dear, familiar occupation."

"Bashing people on the head," Dr. Hack said *sotto voce*. Lura sniggered.

"I swear by the Holy Sepulcer, I shall return as soon as I have fought this last match."

"Oh, go ahead," Noel sighed. "You might as well. I'm no closer to getting you released than I was last night."

King Richard's face was transformed with gratitude. "My thanks." He strode back to the lists with the Herald bustling after.

"Released?" Matt had good ears. "He mean like from an institution or something?"

"Alas," Professor Burns replied. Matt could not know that the object of Geordie's pity was purely self-centered.

Salah-ed-Din acted as if he were fifteen minutes late rather than over fifteen hours. "It rejoices my eye to behold you again, my lord. And your noble friends. Ten thousand pardons for any small delay that has kept me from your side, but I was unfortunately detained by—''

"I don't want to hear about it." Noel cut him off with a sharp wave of the hand. "Lura, Atamar, if you want to help me, don't let this one out of your sight. I'll keep an eye on Richard myself. When this bout is over I'm taking both of them, locking them in my room, and not letting them out until I've found the way to release their spirits once and for all." He stalked into the crowd.

The Displaced Knight was the A.R.G.H.'s new darling. Noel had to admire the way he wielded sword and shield, until he remembered that King Richard hailed from a time when a passage at arms was as regular an event in a man's life as watching weekend football. The Crusades were Super Bowl Sunday, and Richard had been one of the best damned quarterbacks the British ever fielded. It wasn't his fault that his backfield let him down. Saracen-1; Franks-0.

Richard's final opponent was a man a full head taller than himself, and outweighing the king by pounds. He was no slouch as a fighter, either. The A.R.G.H. did not dance through their arms demos. Real blows were struck, real pride was on the line, and if no real damage was done, it was a testimonial to smart safety procedures, scrupulously followed. Just outside the battlefield's cordon, a chirurgeon was treating one of Richard's previous foes for a series of bruises and a badly sprained wrist. Noel hated to think what the results of battle would look like if the men used real weapons, though he saw more than one genuine blade at a nonfighter's waist. Others were displayed on ground cloths and tables at intervals around Cross Campus while attendant A.R.G.H. members lectured the crowds on medieval weaponry.

Richard's sword scored on his opponent's shield arm. The man promptly dropped his shield, voluntarily immobilizing the stricken arm. Richard tossed his own shield aside, and the crowd lauded this demonstration of chivalry. The fight went on until Richard relieved his opponent of the use of first one leg, then the other, in succession so quick that the English king had to drop to his own knees to keep the contest even. It ended with a touch of Richard's sword to the other's chest, the big blade wielded with impossible ease and grace more proper to a rapier than the monstrous steel of the Middle Ages. A champion was made.

The man keeled over obligingly and the crowd went wild. A.R.G.H. members and mundanes together surged through the ropes to hoist Richard onto their shoulders and carry him in triumphal procession once around the perimeter of Cross Campus. Noel was nearly trampled when he tried to struggle through to reach the king. High above the sea of nodding heads and waving arms, Richard the Lionheart's bosom swelled with a feeling he had done without for much too long. It intoxicated him more than love, invigorated him more than battle-madness, fulfilled him more than any passage of music.

You are king! cried the burning center of his soul. *For this you were born; you are king! They are yours, these brave fighters, and will follow you joyfully to all the ends of the earth. Take back the life that is your birthright, Lionheart. You are king!*

Noel finally caught up with Richard when the procession set him down on the steps at the High Street end of Cross Campus. He elbowed his way up to the king, but his words were overridden by the Herald's booming voice as he proclaimed the Displaced Knight the victor of the day's combat. A man in dagged green satin and a lady in Renaissance brocade, both wearing heavy silver coronets, came forward to award Richard his prizes. The man presented him with a sword and praised at length his performance in the lists. Richard heard none of it. He hefted the blade, getting the feel of it, gauging its sweep and reach with greedy eyes.

When the lady took a thick gilded chain from the velvet pillow proffered by a page and made as if to hang it around Richard's neck, the sword licked out and struck the links from her hands. The lady uttered a small cry of shock.

"Mockery!" shouted the king. He thrust his sword at the sun. "By the Holy Sepulcher, I'll have none of it!"

Noel scurried forth to grab Richard's left arm. "What are you trying to do, get yourself arrested? You're coming back with me right now."

For his pains, a mailed hand closed on his face and shoved him backward. He tumbled into Lysi's waiting arms.

"Serve me as I merit, or keep your apings from my sight!" Richard wheeled on the coroneted couple. They were unable to move. Light spilled down the king's blade, poured over him, made him burn with the fine, untamed brilliance the eye can see fully only in dreams. The man in satin stared, hypnotized as Richard's swordpoint danced in spirals a finger-length from his eyes.

"A man fights for the right to wear a crown," said Richard. "Or he bestows it where it has been earned."

Swallowing dryly, the man reached up and removed the coronet from his head. He held it out, not knowing whether to dare place it on Richard's head himself or not. Richard resolved his dilemma by snapping the circlet from his hands, raising it high so all might witness, and setting it on his own flaming hair.

"A Richard!" he shouted, the brightness around him growing, and the cry came back from uncounted throats. Rattan swords stabbed the air, and true steel blades snatched up from the displays, and clenched fists too.

"A Richard! A Richard!"

From somewhere in the mob a lone voice sneered, "What'd I tell ya, Roz? 'S all staged, y'know?"

"Oh my God," Noel said, through bruised lips. He clambered up and made a second, more tentative approach on the king. This time he kept beyond arm's reach. "Hey!" Richard did not hear. The cheers were too loud, too savory. "Hey, over here! It's me; your *sworn lord!*"

The Plantagenet's leonine head turned slowly at that. He observed Noel coolly, and Lysi too when she came up to stand beside him. "And have you come for me at last, to banish me from this dear-won second skin?" A frown-line between his brows deepened to a valley. "You mistake. I reject your overlordship and recant my oath of fealty. A God-fearing king owes no allegiance to one who traffics with the powers of darkness," he intoned. "Be gone. I will not entrust my spirit to a wizard's hands again. I will have no further doings with you, nor all your unholy sorceries."

"I think he's trying to say he likes it here," Lysi murmured.

"Oh yeah?" Noel's smarting face made him fighting-mad. "Well, I say it's time to stop playing and come with me. You know what sort of powers I've got. You're not a fool. Are you going to try matching strengths with me, or are you going to obey?"

"The big guy's good," came a harsh whisper from the spectators, "but the kid . . . psheee. They ever say 'Oh yeah?' in the Middle Ages?"

"Shhhh, Vin. 'S not his fault they didn't get him a costume. Give him a break, huh?"

"Obey you?" King Richard's glowing aura began to throb subtly as he clasped both hands around the pommel of his sword and lifted it majestically to the heavens.

"This blade is but the smallest portion of my strength, Magician! You will not tear my spirit from me this time, not with all your black arts. I am needed here, needed more than ever I was before the gates of Jerusalem. I call a new Crusade! I summon the hearts too brave, the spirits too noble, the souls too great to bear the petty bindings of this puling age. *There* is my strength!''

His sword swept in a wide arc over the upturned faces of the crowd. ''*There* is might greater than any your foul magic will ever command. True hearts, strong arms, souls pledged to honor the power of a dream! Who will answer for me? Who will stand beside me? Who will fight at my side this hallowed day?''

Heatless flames burst golden from the sword, cut back across the crowd, rose in a mighty wave that crested into a surge forward, an armed charge of those whose spirits had no choice but to answer Richard's call.

''A Richard!'' cried the king, and led his cheering followers in a mad rush from Cross Campus, over High Street, and through the bronze and oak doors of Sterling Memorial Library. Noel and Lysi dived into some nearby shrubbery, out of the path of this onslaught.

''Don't you idiots bloody well *dare!*'' Amanda's hot librarian blood was up. She sprinted after the crowd. ''You can't go into the stacks without a pass! No food permitted inside! No drinks! No swords!''

''Rick! Rick! Wait for me!'' Matt Pincus shouted. ''Atta boy, don't let them lock you up anywhere!'' He gunned the chair too hard. It lurched forward and swiped Amanda off her feet. She belly-flopped across his lap and rode up the handicapped access ramp into Sterling, like a deer tied to a hunter's fender. A pair of chivalrous knights, concerned for the health of the prone lady's skull, held the double doors wide for the lastcomers before slamming them shut.

''Amanda!'' Geordie dropped his listlessness in an instant. It wasn't fast enough. By the time he reached the library doors, they were fastened tight. Laying an ear to one, he heard the scrape of heavy objects being shoved against them.

The siege of Sterling had begun.

22

It Seemed Like a Good Idea at the Time

LYSI LEANED HER elbow on Noel's shoulder as they sat in a row with Lura, Salah-ed-Din, Atamar, Geordie, and Dr. Hack, watching the police cars drive up. Several men with bullhorns were trying to get the crowd to move back while roadblocks were set up, but no one was willing to give up a good spot unless physically pushed away by the men in blue.

"All I did was tell him to come with me," Noel said.

"Ordered him. Master, you're going to have to learn to choose your words more carefully," Lysi said. "Kings can be touchy."

Noel was too depressed to reply.

"Men called him Richard *sic et non,*" Salah-ed-Din mused. "Yes and no, no middle ground. Allah witness that when he says 'No,' he means it."

A policeman with the father of all bullhorns stood before the doors of Sterling. "THE FUN'S OVER, KIDS. COME ON OUT NOW AND NO ONE'S GOING TO GET HURT. THE LIBRARIANS YOU LET OUT THE SIDE DOOR SAY YOU WERE REAL POLITE TO THEM, SO MAYBE WE CAN GET YALE NOT TO PRESS CHARGES. YOU COME OUT NOW AND IT'LL BE BEST FOR ALL OF— "

Sklang! A black-fletched arrow protruded from the bullhorn's bell. The man dropped it and ran. The policemen who had been standing in the open scattered to crouch behind their patrol cars.

"Who the hell fired that thing?" one of them whispered. "Where from?"

His buddy shrugged. The big window over Sterling's front door was stained glass, solid.

"Up there," a young woman said, down on her haunches with the two policemen. "The tower, see? They've sent an archer there. He's good."

"I'll say he is," the first policeman mumbled. "Say, how do you know what they're up to inside? If you're one of them, why are you telling us their tactics?"

"I know little enough about their tactics, Officer, except for the fact that I overheard their leader calling for suggestions from his men. He's not a local, I gather, and doesn't know the building. Several of his men happen to be women, and a number of both sexes are Yalies who know the inside of Sterling very well. I overheard one of them vote for putting the archer in the tower just as I was being escorted out the side door. As for why I'm telling you this, I am a reference librarian and you asked a question."

"Yeah, well, what else are they up to in there?"

The librarian sat down on the curb. "They've barricaded the front doors with some of the card catalogs, and if they're smart, they'll do the same with the side entrances and the passage into Machine City from Cross Campus Library."

"Say what?"

"Machine City is right under the first floor of Sterling. A stairway in the middle of the main corridor goes down there. It's full of vending machines. They will have to eat, you know, if they dig in for any length of time. Cross Campus Library is right under Cross Campus, where all those tents are right now. See those two cement-fenced stairwells behind us, going into the ground? They'll take you down to C.C.L."

"Great! We can get 'em from that way!"

"I wouldn't count on that." The librarian clasped her hands in her lap. "Cross Campus Library is a weak spot to defend. They'll cut themselves off from it entirely, barricading the connecting passageway, as I said. These are not children playing dress-up, Officer. They are educated, intelligent fighters."

"Fighting with what? Swords against guns?" the policeman spat.

"Swords and brains," said the librarian. "You would need heavy artillery to breach the doors and walls of Sterling, not .38's or .45's, or even a Clint Eastwood special. Not that it makes a difference. Yale won't tolerate a shoot-out in the O.K. Corral. Besides, they have a hostage."

"*What?*"

"Yes, one of the Beinecke librarians, Amanda Rhodes."

"But they let the rest of you go!"

"Because we wanted to leave. She refused. Someone has to look out for the welfare of the books, she said. Those Beinecke people," the librarian sniffed. "They do take themselves seriously. Have a nice day."

Noel and his group were situated near enough to overhear this exchange. "Poor Amanda," Lura said. "So loyal, so devoted. You don't find a woman like that every day." This last was projected with great force at Geordie. He merely choked on a sob.

"Do you mind telling me why you're auditioning for the title role in *Lucia di Lammermoor?*" Dr. Hack demanded of his colleague. Distastefully he pinched one of Geordie's satin sleeves. "How did you wind up wearing this?"

"Stains on my regular clothes. Don't ask me how they got there. Please don't; it's too painful."

"Painful stains? Geordie, you're being a twit, but medical science might have the cure. Where were you last night?"

"With King Richard." Geordie looked Dr. Hack right in the eye. "Yes *that* kind of 'with.' "

"Oh." Dr. Hack ran his tongue over his front teeth. "So . . . who looks good to you in the Bowl games?"

Inside Sterling, King Richard was ranting and raving before his pickup Council of War. His father, Henry II, had never studied modern management techniques, yet got good results by throwing himself down on the floor during high-level meetings, foaming at the mouth and chewing the rushes when things didn't go his way or one of his Council gave him bad news. Richard had learned a lot from his father, but there were no rushes on the floors of Sterling.

"What do you mean, it's indefensible?" he bawled. He had chosen the main Circulation Desk as a fitting platform from which to deliver his harangue to the troops. The placid, painted countenance of a lady in white robe and blue veil backed him. Our Lady of the Circulation Desk had seen worse tantrums, although thrown in softer voices, as when graduate students could not find the tome they needed for a dissertation on *Advanced Understated Glottal Fricatives in Fragmentary Dravidian Subdialects*.

One of the thirty-odd A.R.G.H. members who had followed Richard blindly in his assault on the library came forward. The king was still in armor—borrowed plate, but still an imposing sight when worn by a man who had spent the better part of his life wearing metal. It was wise to kneel to such a man, even when you yourself were wearing armor and carried a real sword in your belt.

"My lord—" He bent the knee to Richard. "My lord, there aren't that many of us left, and this building's no castle. It wasn't meant to be defended. Even with the doors locked and blocked off, there are still a heck of a lot of windows on the first floor, in the basement . . . There's an ornamental moat on a couple of sides, and I think there are windows you can reach if you drop into it."

"Who's going to do the dropping? The cops?" A woman stepped to the fore and bowed curtly to Richard. She leaned on a rattan poleaxe, but her sheathed shortsword was genuine, as were her twin daggers and the pride of her collection, a mace. "We haven't got the numbers, my lord, that's true. A lot of the people who came charging in here with us charged right out again when they realized what they'd done."

"Let them go," Richard declared. "We have use for none but the valiant."

The kneeling man said, "We'll serve you as courageously as we're able, my lord, but all the valor in the world won't hold off our assailants forever. I'd say we should retreat to the stacks and try holding those, if it comes down to it. That's the best we can do, seeing as we don't have the troops."

"If truth be told," the female warrior said, "we don't have technologically superior weaponry, either. That would worry me, if this were an ordinary battle. It's not; but we'll lose it if we think in ordinary terms. I say we don't lose."

Richard dropped to a crouch on the wide, semicircular desk and leaned forward on his toes. "Speak on, my lady. How shall we face our foes?"

"Use what we have that they don't: the unexpected; the advantage of place; the unknown; and the fear of all three salted with a little cheap grandstanding."

The king rocked back, rubbing his chin as the woman warrior outlined her plan in detail. "My lady, I do not understand all you say," he said. "Still, proceed with my blessing. Had God but granted me wisdom and ten women such as you, Jerusalem should have been mine."

"We don't need Jerusalem now, my lord," she replied, tossing back her fine, dark hair. "What we need is a bullhorn."

•   •   •

The phone call from inside Sterling came as a surprise to everyone on the outside. Atamar's lip curled when he saw the leaders of the besieging forces trade astonished glances at the news.

"Did they expect twentieth-century folk to parley from the ramparts or send out a messenger? Do they think they're dealing with real medievals? Pah! Next they'll be hosting a witch-burning."

"Ahem," said Lysi.

"Oh, sorry, my dear. Nothing personal."

The police entered into a brief, brisk debate, at the end of which a strong-jawed officer walked into the middle of High Street, holding a bullhorn over his head and another to his lips.

"O.K., HERE'S WHAT YOU ASKED FOR! NOW HOW CAN I GIVE IT TO YOU IF YOU DON'T OPEN THE—"

An arrow whizzed down from the north tower, landing not far from the officer's feet. He froze to the sound of rifles being cocked in the ranks behind him, orders being barked. The barrels lowered by degrees as he moved forward again and picked up the arrow. A length of sturdy line was attached to the shaft. He tied the bullhorn to it and watched as it was reeled in, then bolted. Before long a regal voice blasted across the campus.

"SOLDIERS, WE BEAR YOU NO ILL WILL. I AM RICHARD PLANTAGENET, FREEBORN MAN AND CHRISTIAN KNIGHT. MY MEN AND I WILL RENDER UP THIS BUILDING GLADLY, IN EXCHANGE FOR CERTAIN TRIFLING CONCESSIONS ON YOUR PART."

"Here comes the sting for a one-way to Cuba and a sack full of green," one veteran told his mate. "They never change."

"IMPRIMIS: A GRANT OF LAND TO BE HELD BY ME AND MY DESCENDANTS, IF ANY, IN FEALTY TO THE OVERLORD OF THIS REALM. MY CHIEF COUNCILOR SUGGESTS SAUSALITO, BUT WE WILL NEGOTIATE. SECUNDUS: FREE PASSAGE THERETO FOR ME AND ALL THOSE FAITHFUL KNIGHTS WHO NOW SERVE ME, AND ANY WHO WISH TO JOIN WITH US, AND OUR GOODS AND CHATTELS, NOT TO EXCEED THE CAPACITY OF A 747. THE SWINE, SHEEP, AND BREEDING CATTLE MAY BE DELIVERED TO US AT A

LATER DATE. TERTIUS: THAT YOU BIND YOURSELVES
BY SOLEMN OATH TAKEN UPON RELICS OF THE
SAINTS THAT YOU MAY BE DAMNED TO THE FIRES
OF HELL FOR ALL ETERNITY IF YOU SPEAK US FAIR
NOW AND SEEK TO DISOWN YOUR PROMISES LATER.''

Silence smashed Cross Campus flat.

''ONE MORE THING!'' The voice issuing from the bull-
horn changed. Now it was identifiably female. ''NO ONE
SENDS KING RICHARD BACK ANYWHERE HE DOESN'T
WANT TO GO! WE'RE NOT KIDDING. WE'VE GOT A
HOSTAGE, AND I DON'T MEAN AMANDA RHODES. I
MEAN, YES, I DO MEAN HER TOO, BUT WE'VE GOT
A BIGGER ONE THAN THAT. WE'VE GOT STERLING,
AND WE'VE GOT A COUPLE OF BOOKS OF MATCHES,
AND WE KNOW HOW TO BRING THE TWO TOGETHER.''

There might have been more the lady intended saying, but
the sound of a scuffle, amplified by the bullhorn, garbled it.
A man's voice came through next—not the king's:

''—CRAZY OR SOMETHING, JAEL? WE'D NEVER
BURN A WHOLE LIBRARY FULL OF—''

There were more blips of sound, and the woman was back
on the air:

''—TELL *THEM* THAT! LET THEM SQUIRM!''

''BUT IT'S NOT THE HONORABLE—''

''GIVE ME BACK THAT HORN, THORIN, OR YOU'RE
HISTORY!''

Further tussling broadcast itself over the slack-jawed faces
of the assembled police force, until Richard's voice came on,
chastising his overexuberant followers in terms that made
squadroom-hardened men blush and rookies quake.

''YOU HAVE OUR TERMS! WE GIVE YOU UNTIL
NONES TO REPLY.''

The air went dead.

''Nones?''

''I think that's the day after Tuesday on the medieval
calendar.''

Dr. Hack took didactic pleasure in informing the police that
Richard wanted his answer by around three o'clock in the
afternoon, canonical time.

A car from the local television station pulled to a stop on
the College Street end of Cross Campus, disgorging a crew
like a circus funny-car spewing clowns. Microphones bloomed

in front of every pair of idle jaws. Lysi got one in the teeth and covertly poached the wires while the castrated newshound urged her to tell the audience her gut feelings about the human drama being played out right before her very eyes.

"And how about the hostage?" he rapped out. "Has anyone heard anything from her yet? Is she still alive? Have they shown any proof that they haven't killed her already?"

Dr. Hack had some experience in dealing with the media. He moved Lysi to one side and took the dead-calm, emotionless, lecture hall approach. It was the second-best way to drive newsmen nuts, the first being silence.

"Amanda Rhodes is all right."

"How can you be so sure? Those people in there, they're not exactly living in this century, wouldn't you say?"

Dr. Hack smoothed nonexistent strain lines from his brow and replied patiently, "Precisely. Which is why I trust them when they say that they still have her. Warfare in the Middle Ages was a get-paid-as-you-go affair. Most medieval soldiers went into battle with the intention of taking as much booty as they could lug home. Hostages were part of that booty. You couldn't ransom a dead hostage."

"So it's kidnapping added to trespassing! You heard it here first, ladies and gentlemen." The reporter swerved to face the minicam, too busy distorting the facts to see the frantic signals his crew were giving him about dead audio. "Fanatics have captured an innocent Yale employee, a young woman named Amanda Rhodes, a librarian, and are holding her for ransom in Yale's Sterling Memorial Library. But is it Amanda Rhodes they are holding hostage, or is it Yale itself? Could this be their symbolic way of criticizing some of academia's more medieval practices? Is it a cry for a new era in higher education? Or is it simply that the failures of the present have compelled otherwise stable human beings to take refuge in the fantasies and fripperies of the past? In all this, the tragic figure of Amanda Rhodes dominates any possible negotiations. Will she emerge as heroine, symbol, or . . . martyr? This is Dave Nicely, for—"

"Amanda! Amanda!" The minicams swung to the shout like sharks homing on a bloodspill. Geordie Burns had pushed his way between two reporter-beset police, trampled over a prowl car, leaped from the hood over a barricade, raced across High Street, and swung himself over the stone lip of the moat fronting Sterling. In the pit, glass smashed; a basement window being broken. A hail of arrows from the north tower drove back the policemen who tried to follow him.

Five minutes later, the woman was back on the bullhorn:

"THANKS FOR THE SECOND HOSTAGE, GENTLES. THANKS A LOT."

"You've really lost your mind, Geordie, do you know that?" Amanda tried to get comfortable, but there were only so many ways you could fluff up a folio World Atlas. Open, the huge book was about the size of two sofa cushions end-to-end, and nearly as thick. She and Geordie had been remanded to the upper stacks in the Geography section. They sat on the floor at a dead end between two ranks of bookcases, the only thing between their seats and cold stone being the atlas.

Matt Pincus was assigned as their guard. He didn't carry steel, but he'd helped himself to a fire extinguisher. As he'd told them once, he gave no second chances, and he knew to aim for the eyes.

Talking was permitted. Amanda had done nothing but talk about Geordie's foolhardiness ever since. "Why did you do it? You go from not saying one word to me, to doing a one-man Charge of the Light Brigade. You could've been killed! Why?"

"I couldn't stand it, Amanda. I had to do something. I had to know whether you were alive or dead. I had to see if you were all right. I had to try to rescue you."

"Unarmed?" She regretted her sarcasm at once. The first spunk she'd seen in him for some time wilted and was lost. In a kinder tone she added, "It was brave of you, Geordie. Not many men would try that for a woman who—who hasn't exactly been fair. I'm sorry about Princeton. I overreacted, but I was so hurt . . ."

"I told you, she came after me. What you walked in on—"

"Pride," Amanda said. "That's what blew the whole incident out of proportion. Pride, and not enough pride. It's a bad combination. I could never believe that someone like you could honestly care for someone like me, no matter how many times you told me you did. It was too good to be real. I wanted you ever since that desert dig, remember? I dreamed about you back then . . . wonderful dreams.'' Her smile was a girl's again. ''How many times do dreams come true? When I came into your office and saw her with you, the dream was over; it was time to wake up. But I was too proud to let you be the one to say we were through, so I said the words. Then I ran away before you could say anything more.''

She touched his hand. ''There's more to be said now, and I can't run away from it. I do love you, Geordie. I still do love you.''

''Don't.''

''Why not? A word from you won't change how I feel. I think, though . . . I think you did love me, once. It wasn't all a dream.''

''I did.'' His voice was rough.

''If that's changed—you don't have to tell me why—I can accept it. Can't you accept the fact that I love you?''

''I love you too, Amanda. That's why I have to get out of your life. If we get out of here.''

Amanda searched his face and found it earnest. She turned to Matt. ''You're a man. You translate what he said into English.''

''He said he loves you—''

''That I understood.''

''Well, I didn't understand the rest of it myself.'' Matt gestured at Geordie with the nozzle of the fire extinguisher. ''If I had a woman I loved who loved me, I'd say that *out* of her life was the wrong direction.''

''Then you don't know what love is!'' Geordie snapped. ''I do, and I refuse to let Amanda marry a lie! Look at her! Amanda, take off your glasses, please. Now undo your hair. And would you mind unfastening the top button on your blouse? . . . The top two? . . . Maybe one more?''

''Whoa!'' Matt cried truce. ''I'm in a chair, but I'm not dead. Two's plenty. Ms. Rhodes, you're one beautiful lady.''

''Oooooh, thank you.'' Amanda's simper dripped sugar and scorn. ''My ambition is to work with small animals and drunks. Now do I get voted Miss Congenialty, or do I have to muss you up?'' To Geordie she said, ''What is the point of this, besides torturing an innocent man?''

''I want Matt to see that you're a healthy woman with— with healthy desires.''

''She's got some of the healthiest desires I've ever seen,''

Matt concurred. "You've hit paydirt, Burns. Do you know what I'd do to be in your place? When this is all over, take the lady dancing and remember how you rubbed my nose in it. I hope it makes you feel real proud."

"How can you say that when you were in the same tent with Richard and me last night?" Geordie's anguish echoed through the stacks. "You know what happened!"

"You threw up."

"No, no, I mean what happened between Richard and—" his voice became a whisper "—and me."

Matt Pincus laughed out loud.

"I don't think this is all that hilarious," Geordie protested. A quick look at Amanda's shocked face backed up his judgment.

"That's because you weren't there last night, man." Matt wiped a tear away as he reined in his laughter. "I was. Oh, baby, that was a show. All Rick could do was keep hauling you out of the tent every time you started to heave. You got some on yourself the one time he wasn't quick enough. Poor guy had to strip himself, and you, and stuff you in that sleeping bag so in case you lost it again, you wouldn't get it all over the clothes. There he sat, buck naked, trying to do your laundry, with one sock for a washrag and water from a canteen. Got the smell out, but I bet you've got a few stains left."

"But—but in the morning—he was so *nice* to me!"

"He's nice to everyone, including people he's going to total in combat. It's called chivalry." Matt got serious. "Look, you know Rick's gay and so do I. So what? Maybe what you don't know is he's a man of honor; a righteous man. You think he'd take advantage of you when you didn't know what was going on? Burns, you've got a pretty face, but Rick wouldn't force himself on an angel if the angel wasn't willing."

"So that was why—Oh, Geordie!" Amanda's arms were around him, and he responded happily. Matt watched their embrace for a little while, then cleared his throat.

"There's only one way out of this row of stacks. I can guard you two much better if I, uh, go down to the end and keep an eye on the staircase too. Don't get funny ideas." He wheeled backward and around the corner.

The funniest idea Geordie and Amanda got was to open a second monster atlas and make it in Massachusetts.

23

Read Any Good
Books Lately?

"IF ONLY I didn't feel so helpless!" Noel pounded his fists on updrawn knees, then dropped his head between them, covering it with his arms. Lysi tried to comfort him, and he hadn't the strength to reject her.

"See?" Lura said smugly. "Affinity of Souls in action. The same as what made Geordie break into Sterling when he heard Amanda was imprisoned there."

"Result: they're both hostages. What a useful principle the Affinity of Souls is, to be sure," said Atamar. He returned his attention to a more worthy subject, the inscrutable purple book. Let the New Haven police and the University officials hold one conference after another, it was all a waiting game now, and to wait was to fill hours with idleness. Atamar had never ranked Sloth as his favorite Deadly Sin, even when he'd been a demon. Now he absolutely abhorred it, both in himself and in those around him.

A languid sigh from Salah-ed-Din grated on the angel's concentration. "Can't you find something to do besides deep-breathing exercises?"

"What would you have, my lord? You and I appear to be the servants of one master, yet our young employer sets you the task of warding me and gives me no such occupation. I might almost wish that when Richard took that castle, I had charged at his side. Alas, we were ever opponents, despite our fine manners, and the custom of enmity goes beyond the grave."

Atamar grunted and got back to the book. The letters danced before his eyes, making light of his every attempt to pierce the riddles they wove. He still recognized the four proper names—Richard the Frank, Salah-ed-Din, Ba'ouji, and Nazim—but they were Arabic written in Arabic. The rest of the text was scribed in the same characters, yet made no sense when read as Arabic. Atamar scowled and tried reading a sentence or two aloud, to see if that helped.

"I never shared Richard's bed, and who says so is a liar!" Salah-ed-Din shouted.

"Who said—?" A young hypothesis began to form behind Atamar's flawless face. He turned to a page at random in the purple book and read off a sentence with Richard's name in it.

"Ah well, there the motherless son of a debauched camel does not lie, but exaggerates," the Saracen lord allowed. "Richard did have a temper. But seventy-two pages executed in one night because one of them showed up with a head-ache? Foul calumny. There were not seventy-two pages in the whole of Richard's camp that he should squander them so freely."

Atamar thrust the book into Salah-ed-Din's lap. "You wanted a task? Read this, if you can."

The Saracen gazed into the book, then gave Atamar a look reserved for simpletons. "Why should I be unable to read this? I am well versed in Arabic." He looked back at the text and his brow furrowed. "This is not Arabic."

Atamar smiled. "Tell me another."

"It is my own tongue, Kurdish, transliterated into the Arabic script. Moreover, it is a dialect thereof that I have not heard since childhood. I remember that Nazim the Dark and I, before our sorry rift, would often bemuse my more inquisi-tive courtiers by carrying on conversations that only we might comprehend." He chuckled, thinking back. "Why do I even dignify this language by the Kurdish name? It became a bastardized garble, a borrowing of many tongues. My boy-hood language was but the backbone."

He turned a parchment page, then a papyrus one. All his light manner fled. "Truly, seeing the libelous excretions of Nazim's black spirit, I do not wonder that he chose to record his ravings against Richard and myself in this hidden tongue. Had he not been mad, he should have been ashamed. Ha! Do you see?" Salah-ed-Din jabbed at a sentence. "Here he tells of how, for our sins, he intends to bind our spirits, though he has not yet settled on the exact spell." He flipped ahead in the book. "And here he speaks of the enchantment, though he questions the severity of sacrifice it will cost him to do it. He is afraid to die. Ah, Nazim, Nazim . . ." Salah-ed-Din sorrowed over the lost sorcerer. "Was it worth your life, to keep the Frank and myself from Paradise? You were once my friend, until a fanatical fire burned all sweetness from your soul."

The Saracen passed the book back to the angel. "This is the final journal of Nazim the Dark. It pains me to read so much hate, and know that I was half the cause. He was a good man, while he still heard reason, but his family was murdered by the Franks—not Richard's troops; the French. I can not blame him for the evil that twisted into his spirit. It destroyed my friend before he ever destroyed himself."

Atamar held the book in two hands. His head lolled back, his eyes closed. The purple cover paled to blue, a red ghost-book hovering above it. This image rose over Atamar's head and opened to pages of gold, an otherworldly butterfly. It lit on the angel's face and trickled between his parted lips like richest wine. When Atamar raised his head and opened his eyes again, he was very pale.

"You were right. There was much hatred there." He gave the blue book back again to Salah-ed-Din. "Read what remains."

Reluctantly, the Saracen did as the angel bade him. The book had shrunk in thickness by more than half, the remaining pages shining silver. Salah-ed-Din forced himself to read what the vanished wizard had written there.

When he was done, he found that he could smile. "No just man builds a prison without doors, no lock exists without a key. Nazim speaks of the agony of his heart. He can not in conscience lock away two brave souls from the face of God forever. Praise Allah, some humanity still dwelled in Nazim's blinded spirit! He writes of how the last binding may be undone, though he tries to make it sound as if he is gloating over an impossibility."

"An impossibility which his own words make possible?" Atamar asked.

"Even so. Three things must be found to free our spirits: A wizard of some skill . . ."

Mightily amused, Atamar glanced sideways at the totally dejected Noel. "That we have."

"The Richard Jewel . . ."
"That we can get."
"And Richard."
Atamar was silent.

24

A Pair of Kings Beats a Full House

THE LADY JAEL sat at ease in one of the library's filing carts, sharpening her liege-lord's sword. The cart was particularly handy for this purpose, being a combination chair and podium on a wheeled platform. This miniature portable desk was normally used by the Sterling Library personnel for making the updating Grand Tour of the card catalogs. This time a blade, rather than a card file, rested on the small table-top, but the wheels underpinning the whole structure were still good for getting a girl where she wanted to go in a hurry.

Where Lady Jael wanted to go was to Richard's side, especially when she heard the rumor that Thorin of the Broken Axe poured in her ear. "He's afraid of a magician?"

"That's why we're here," Thorin said. His large brown eyes were solemn, giving him the look of a battle-ready basset hound. "He's scared the kid's going to make a move on him and make him go *poof!*"

"What kid are you talking about?"

"The magician; the magician's a Yale freshman."

"Son-of-a-gun, I knew they had a better Liberal Arts program than Mount Holyoke. I should've transferred."

Thorin chastised her. "This isn't a joke, my lady. Our liege-lord's fear is very real to him. What concerns him, concerns us."

"Thorin, lighten up. It's all gossip. King Richard's not afraid of anything. Look around you. He's *home*." Jael leaned back in the file-cart chair and took in the great main hall of Sterling with open arms. Dying sunlight still made the large stained glass window beautiful. To either side of the hall, a row of heraldic banners were displayed from gray stone balconies. The two other fighters who had been assigned to patrol the hall, besides Jael and Thorin, paced back and forth along these narrow walkways. They were archers—

not in a class with the tower man, but still formidable. From the elevators behind Our Lady of the Circulation Desk's bailiwick, Richard could be heard issuing commands.

"Does that sound like a worried man?" she asked.

Thorin rested one hand on his hip. "I just hear the whispers. And you saw the kid, remember? The skinny blond who lit our liege-lord's tail-feathers after he took the crown? Hell, he's the one who caused the big charge, if you want to point any fingers. One minute I'm having a good time, doing O.K. with the huckstering, showing this Meryl Streep clone how to fasten a unicorn pectoral, and the next I've slapped together as many arms as I can tote and I'm trampling police underfoot to get into this rockpile! Tell me that's not sorcery at work! It sure wasn't in my biorhythm chart for today."

Jael hopped down from the file cart with Richard's sword. "I'm going to put a stop to these rumors. Bad for morale."

"When the S.W.A.T. team shows up, we'll discuss morale."

"They won't. Yale won't let them. What big-gun American university would? Bad publicity, Thorin. They're going to stand on their academic *droit de seigneur* and mouse this whole incident."

Thorin wasn't buying. "They tear-gassed students in one of the Yale colleges, once. Why should they spare us? We're not even matriculated here!"

"Get real. That was in the 60's. It was in to overreact. These times, they like to wait on a problem long enough so it has the chance to go away."

"Who said that?"

"Either Charlie Brown or Jimmy Carter; I forget. But we're not going anywhere until King Richard says so."

"That's another thing." Thorin leaned on the cart. "Do you really believe he's who he says he is?"

"I was at the banquet." Jael's gaze grew misty. "I heard him sing and play. It was no common song. I saw him fight in the lists—I fought him and lost, and I'm good. You see a bout differently when you're in it. He wasn't playing with that sword; he knew it like a brother. That's when I knew that he wasn't an ordinary man. You and I both heard him speak when he took the crown. His words transformed the world, melted back the mundane, opened a gate to let the dream glide closer to us all. He can say he's King Arthur, if he wants to. I'll follow him."

"Yeah, I know." Thorin sounded hoarse. "So will I."

"But I won't let him be afraid!" Jael's dark eyes snapped. "I'm taking the rumors back to the source, and if there's any truth in them at all, I'm going to do something about it."

"If they're true, what can you do against a magician?"

"Neutralize him." Jael veered suddenly and swung Richard's sword into the file cart. It sheared through the support holding up the chair, which hit the floor with a crash. She studied the edge and found it unharmed. "Any way I can," she said, going to seek her king.

"Shake hands?" Noel couldn't believe it. "That's all you and Richard have to do?"

Salah-ed-Din bowed. He and Noel were seated on the grass of Cross Campus in a circle with the remnants of their group. "So it is written. We must clasp hands in amity—a thing we never did in our lives—and Nazim the Dark claims that his spirit will confess itself defeated. I quote:"—he opened the book to a page which he, Atamar, and Lura had nearly committed to memory— " 'Then shall the beneficent being, whose Name of Power is Ba'ouji, come forth in his might and breathe the breath of freedom upon them.' "

Lura pried the lid off a cardboard cup of coffee and passed it to Noel. "Ba'ouji is a djinni, dear, one of King Solomon's best servants. If anyone can break a wizard's binding, he can."

"You know him?"

"By reputation only." Atamar flipped the Richard Jewel high into the air and caught it on the fall. "He's been tied up these past several centuries. In this." He tossed the medallion up again and slapped it onto the back of his hand when it came down. "Heads or tails, Hack?"

"For God's sake, be careful with that!" Dr. Hack sloshed scalding hot coffee into Lysi's lap as he started up in an abortive effort to grab the Richard Jewel away from the angel. Lysi didn't even blink. She flicked her jeans once and they were dry.

"Don't fret, Randy," Lura said. "I left a nice simulacrum in its place at the British Arts Center. No one but us knows that the real thing's gone."

"Ba'ouji will free the kings if they shake hands, but first you must free Ba'ouji, Noel," Atamar said.

"If I can find him. Where is he?"

Again Salah-ed-Din read from the dead wizard's journal:
" 'That magician bold and wise enough to seek entrance
where no doors may be, in the sea-born palace, the place of
milk and snow, of frost and moonlight, the precious abode
built in travail upon a grain of sand, he alone may find the
mighty spirit and name him by his Name of Power, thereby
summoning him into the waking world.' "

Noel succeeded where Dr. Hack failed. He grabbed the
Richard Jewel from Atamar. "The pearl!" He stared at the
huge, luminous sea-gem at the medallion's heart. "He's in
the pearl the way you two were in the diamonds!"

"Very good, dear." Lura came near to patting him on the
head.

"Very good? Nazim did everything but spell out the word
'pearl' for anyone who could answer why the chicken crossed
the road." Atamar never dispensed casual flattery. "If you
can tell us how you propose to release the djinni, since you
know where he is, I will be the first to praise you."

"From what Salah-ed-Din just read, it sounds like the djinni
will appear on his own the minute the two kings clasp hands."

"Were I you, *sidi*, I would not place my implicit trust in
the words of any magician, least of all Nazim the Dark."
Salah-ed-Din laid a finger beside his nose. "There is always,
as you say, a catch."

Lysi moved nearer to Noel. "He's right. The djinn are
powerful, but they can be mean mothers. Nazim doesn't say
anything about how to dismiss Ba'ouji once he's appeared
and done his job. You'd better take precautions."

Noel had a skeptical expression. "You're the expert?"

"The djinn are first cousins to demonkind. How far do you
trust demons?" she asked with a straight face. "If you want
to control the djinni once you've summoned him, draw these
on the ground first." Lysi thrust the flattened coffee-shop
bag into Noel's lap. She had scrawled a series of arcane
symbols on the brown paper. "And try saying these words."
She pointed to four lines of sound effects for a malfunctioning
blender. "You'll have him."

"Sure I will." Noel wadded up the bag and batted it across
the circle. Lura caught it and smoothed it out.

"These are real, Noel," she said, giving it back to him.
"Lysi's on our side."

Noel did not want to discuss it, so he jammed the bag in his back pocket. Still, he was not persuaded. "If she wants to help me out so much, she can do it by getting her sidekick imp out of my roommate's body, packing up shop, and hitting the road." He spoke as if Lysi were not there to hear every word. "She's a traitor, and nothing she can do is ever going to make me see her any differently."

"A traitor to whom? To you?" Lura's eyes grew tender with sympathy. "Or to herself?"

"She never betrayed herself and she never would. She's too selfish for that."

"Is that why she did not strike you down when she had the opportunity?" Atamar asked. He had vanished from his place in the circle and materialized beside Lysi. Now he put his arm around her. There were more tears on the she-demon's face, but the angel's touch healed their burning paths. "You have little vision, Noel. You're still trapped behind your own eyes, prisoner in your own skin. You can't feel any wounds but those that scar your own feelings. Before you call any being— demon, mortal, or divine—to account for a failing, see how innocent of it you are first."

"Don't talk that way to him!" Lysi lashed out, throwing off Atamar's arm. "Noel isn't selfish! He cares about me! Or . . . he used to." She linked her hands in her lap and the little teddy bear souvenir of their New York junket appeared. She held it to her heart.

Noel made a great business of gagging, until Atamar's hard stare made his cheeks burn. "Butt out, Lysi," Noel muttered. "I'm not making the same mistake twice. I'll handle the djinni without any help from you." He stood up and brushed grass stains from the seat of his pants. "The first thing I'll do is get Richard."

"Just like that?" Dr. Hack snapped his fingers.

"Hey, you're talking to a wizard here." Noel grinned confidently. "One touch and those big bronze doors cave in like potato salad. Don't get up, Dr. Hack. This'll be over before you can work all the kinks out of your bones." He sauntered toward Sterling, whistling.

The bullhorn blasted down from the north tower just as Noel got to the police car barricade at High Street.

"HEY! WE WANT TO TALK TERMS SOME MORE," the female voice announced. University officials chattered with law enforcement personnel while waiting reporters tensed to spring at the first opening.

"GO AHEAD," said a man in a dark-gray suit. "WE'LL LISTEN."

The four words hadn't stopped echoing back from Sterling's walls when the spokesman was nailed by a video Valkyrie in plum Ultrasuede. "By 'We'll listen,' do you mean Yale as a whole or yourself as an individual? In which case, aren't you misleading them by utilizing the word 'we'? Are you going to take their demands seriously, thereby bowing to medieval terrorism, or are you merely going to compromise your ethics by promising to hear them out, while in reality turning a deaf ear to what they're trying to say?"

He got to say "Uh," then was overcome by the tower bullhorn. "WE'RE WILLING TO CAVE ON A COUPLE OF OUR PREVIOUS DEMANDS. FORGET SAUSALITO AND THE 747. ALL WE REALLY WANT IS A GUARANTEE OF FREEDOM FOR OUR LIEGE-LORD, RICHARD PLANTAGENET."

The spokesman raised his bullhorn. "IS THIS PLANTAGENET YOUR LEADER?"

"YOU GOT IT."

"ALL RIGHT. COME OUT NOW, AND I CAN PERSONALLY PROMISE YOU THAT YALE WON'T PROSECUTE EITHER YOUR—UH—LIEGE-LORD OR ANY OF YOU, PROVIDED THAT NO DAMAGE TO STERLING IS FOUND AFTER YOU VACATE, AND THAT THE HOSTAGES ARE UNHARMED. A FEW QUESTIONS, A SHORT INSPECTION OF THE PREMISES, AND HE'LL BE AS FREE AS THE REST OF YOU."

"OH NO HE WON'T."

"LISTEN, YOU CAN TRUST ME."

"WE'LL TAKE THE CHANCE. BUT YOU'RE NOT THE ONE TO TELL US RICHARD CAN GO FREE. SEND FOR THE MAGE, AND THEN WE'LL REALLY TALK."

The spokesman lowered his loudspeaker. "Send for the what?" he asked a policeman.

"The mage," Noel said, coming up on the gray suit's left. "It means magician, sorcerer, wizard . . ." He cleared his throat. "Me."

He suddenly knew just how Lady Godiva must have felt. Eyes could have weight, goggling eyes most of all. He staggered under the load of incredulous stares now piling onto him. He decided to deal with doubters in the most efficient way. The gray suit's silk rep tie turned into a lizard and scuttled up the man's sleeve. As the University spokesman did a freeform Highland fling to remove the ad-libbed reptile, the badges of every policeman near Noel began to spin and throw off blue and white sparks.

While New Haven's finest slapped at their chests, Noel stepped into the middle of High Street and looked up at the façade of Sterling. A shell of protection enclosed him, his more prudent version of wearing an arrowproof vest while waving the white flag of truce.

"I'm here," he said, and his unamplified voice still carried where he willed it.

"SO YOU ARE. IS HE THE ONE, MY LORD?" There was a short, muffled exchange between the female speaker and a man's voice, then she resumed. "MY LORD KING RICHARD SAYS YOU ARE. RAISE YOUR RIGHT HAND, MAGICIAN!"

"Why?"

"YOU ARE ABOUT TO SWEAR AN OATH AND BIND IT TO YOU BY THE VIRTUES OF YOUR OWN MAGIC. MY LORD KING RICHARD TELLS ME THAT SWEARING ON HOLY RELICS WOULDN'T STOP SOMEONE LIKE YOU."

"What am I swearing to, if I agree to swear at all?"

The lady in the tower chuckled. "WE HAVE TWO HOSTAGES HERE, AND A VERY HIGH TOWER. YOU'LL AGREE. YOU WILL SWEAR THAT YOU WILL NOT USE ANY OF YOUR POWERS ON MY LORD KING RICHARD WITHOUT HIS DUE CONSENT. THAT'S NOT MUCH TO ASK."

Noel's right hand was in the air and the words of an improvised oath were tumbling out of his mouth before he heard Atamar's desperate cry within his mind: *Noel, swear nothing! Even if they try to throw the hostages down, Lura and I could—Oh, Helicarnassus! Too late.*

The Yale spokesman had evicted the lizard by this time. He shouldered Noel aside and took over. "YOU'VE GOTTEN YOUR OATH. YOUR LIEGE-LORD DOESN'T HAVE TO WORRY ABOUT THIS—ER—MAGE ANYMORE. NOW COME OUT OF THERE!"

"NO," said the lady. She ceded the bullhorn to Richard.

"THE LADY JAEL IS NOT EMPOWERED TO CHANGE MY TERMS!" the Plantagenet thundered. "THEY STILL STAND. IT LACKS AN HOUR OF NONES. USE IT WELL, ELSE WITNESS THE GREATEST FIRE SINCE THE SACK OF ROME!"

Station Lionheart went off the air.

The University spokesman looked at Noel. "So you're a magician. A Yalie mage. Bibbedy-bobbedy-boola-boola." He began to laugh like a hyena. He was till laughing when a couple of his colleagues led him away, purring soothing promises of a nice cool drink at Morey's.

"That was rash, ill-considered, and stupid," Atamar said, taking Noel by the elbow. "We did wrong to tell you that your powers were your own. Now you value them too cheaply and toss them away without thought."

"I've still got them, don't I?" Noel asked the angel anxiously.

"What good if you do? You can not use them against Richard, by your own oath, nor can Lura and I intervene. He may well get all he asks for from these University people or else he may stay in that building long enough to force their hand. I can't predict whether he'll push them to violent means. If he does, the innocents who followed him in there will be the ones to suffer. And the hostages."

"My fault again."

Atamar did not dispute it.

Lysi got Lura's attention. The two of them moved out of earshot. "I could do it," the succubus said. "I could use my powers to force Richard out of there."

Lura's face brightened, or an instant only. "Noel must do this for himself, or all the virtue of the deed is lost to him. Why do you think that Atamar and I can't do more than advise him, protect him to a degree, fetch and carry minor objects that might aid him?" She looked rueful. "There are the Hounds of Heaven, and then there are the Gofers."

Noel and Atamar rejoined the others. Noel sat down hard on the grass and would not talk. The marks of guilt and remorse were evident even to mortal eyes. To Lura's, they positively blazed. She was angry, but her anger was directed only at her mate.

What have you been saying to him?

The truth. He seemed so fond of it.

The truth to a mortal? To one so young?

He isn't a child.

Children can take the hard truth and fear it, hate it, reject it. When they are grown they seize it as proof that all life is worthless, and that only those who lose all hope lose all pain.

Which in a way is itself the truth.

A partial truth is worse than a lie! I won't let him give up!

On life?

On himself. That is the more important of the two.

"Think, Noel," Lura urged in his ear. "You're not beaten yet. Your magic's not all of you. Use what you still have to defeat Richard."

He looked as if he would have liked to laugh in her face. "He's locked up safe in a building I can't get into without magic. He's got an army of followers. He's got a sword and no hesitation about using it. Without my magic, what have I got? Good S.A.T. scores?"

"You have us. All of us." With a gesture, Lura included Dr. Hack, Salah-ed-Din, and even Lysi. "Open your eyes, Noel. See the stronger magic."

Lura yipped as Lysi clutched her by the hair and yanked her backward. The she-demon stood splay-legged above Noel. She no longer implored his pardon or tried to touch his heart. Instead, scorn colder than the sink of Hell pulsed from her every word, gesture, and expression.

"You couldn't see spit if it was in your eye, little man. Stay where you are and sulk; it's all you're good for. I'm tired of trying to wiggle back into your good graces just so I can try for a second grab at your soul. Hell doesn't need any wimps. You're right, Noel: You're nothing without your magic. You're nothing without some greater force telling you what to do every step of the way. First it was your mommy, then it was me, now it's this pair of celestial pigeons. Let King Richard go. He may be dead, but he knows what he wants and how to get it better than you do." She squatted before him and let her tongue loll out to her knees. "I'll bet he'd even score higher on the S.A.T.'s."

Noel's teeth gritted together. His hands formed hawk's claws, and a ram's head the color of his eyes slammed into Lysi's chest, toppling her onto the still-sprawling Lura. Noel leaped up with a shout:

"Salah-ed-Din!"

The Saracen lord made his most graceful bow. "I am here to serve the eventual freer of my soul."

"You do want to be released?"

"I have savored what there is of life this second time, and found that like all things, it is sweeter in the memory than the deed. So long as my soul may cherish remembrance, I go willingly into the yet-to-come."

"Come with me. I have an idea of how we're going to make that coward Richard see things your way."

"Never say that to his face, sidi!" Salah-ed-Din wiped the words from the air between them. "Fear does not govern him, but the desire to keep a new crown, however small. He is a valiant man, a man of honor, chivalrous by his own lights, and no coward, but a true king."

"Yeah." Noel's teeth flashed. "That's what I'm counting on."

"Give him the bullhorn or I'll turn you into a toad," Noel informed the policeman. The man still carried the smudge marks of a Catherine-wheeling badge on his breast pocket. He gave the bullhorn to Salah-ed-Din without demur.

The Saracen quickly learned how to manage the newfangled apparatus and hailed the library, demanding parley with Richard himself. It didn't take long for the English king to blast his response from on high.

"SAVE YOUR BREATH, FRIEND PAYNIM, IF YOU COME TO SWAY ME FROM MY COURSE. HERE I AM; HERE I STAY UNTIL I HOLD THE DEED TO MY NEW REALM IN THE PALM OF THIS HAND AND FLY THE FRIENDLY SKIES THITHER."

"TRULY YOU SHALL FLY, MY BROTHER, AND YOUR SHAME SHALL FLY WITH YOU."

A roar from the tower rent the sky, a bellow of outrage loud enough to need no bullhorn to amplify it.

"HOW DARE YOU? IS THE GREAT SALAH-ED-DIN BECOME THE LICKSPIT OF THAT STRIPLING MAGE? COME TO ME, AND TOGETHER WE SHALL DEFY HIM TO HIS TEETH!"

"A TOOTHLESS DOG CALLS ALL MEAT FOUL. OUR DAY IS SPENT, RICHARD. THIS SMALL WORLD HOLDS NO TRUE SPACE FOR KINGS SUCH AS WE WERE.

THIS IS THE TRUTH, AND I AM PREPARED TO PROVE THE RIGHTNESS OF MY WORDS ON THE FIELD OF HONOR. IF YOU DO NOT HAVE THE SINEW TO BACK YOUR OWN CAUSE IN THE SAME MANNER, THEN REMAIN IN YOUR STONE BURROW. IT IS THE WAY OF RABBITS AND JACKALS TO HIDE.''

"CALL ME COWARD, YOU MOTHERLESS SWINE? YOUR FOLK WERE EVER READIER TO FIRE UPON MINE FROM AMBUSH, FOR FEAR OF MEETING CHRISTIAN KNIGHTS IN OPEN COMBAT!''

Salah-ed-Din's face turned dusky red as his jaw tightened, yet his words remained measured. "I DO NOT FEAR TO MEET YOU ON ANY TERMS. NAME THEM, IF YOU DARE, AND LET THE COMBAT DECIDE ALL!''

Silence came from the tower for a while. Once more there were the ragtags of several different voices picked up by the bullhorn, and then Richard spoke.

"HEAR MY TERMS: AT THE HOUR OF NONES, ONE DOOR OF THIS BUILDING SHALL BE UNLOCKED. ENTER FREELY, YOU AND ALL YOUR TROOPS TO THE NUMBER OF THIRTY. I AND MINE WILL AWAIT.''

"TROOPS?'' Salah-ed-Din looked to Noel. "YOU KNOW I HAVE NONE. I WOULD MEET YOU IN SINGLE COMBAT—''

"MY MEN HAVE BOUND THEMSELVES TO MY SERVICE. NOTHING WILL DETER THEM FROM FIGHTING MY FIGHTS. I CANNOT ANSWER FOR THEM SHOULD YOU TAKE THE ADVANTAGE IN A SINGLE COMBAT. FOR YOUR OWN SAFETY, COME WITH MEN OF YOUR OWN.''

"BUT WHERE AM I TO GET—?''

"THAT, AS SIR MATTHEW OFTEN SAYS, IS NO SKIN OFF MY NOSE. TAKE MY TERMS OR LEAVE THEM. UNTIL NONES, AND WHEN THE GREAT DOOR OPENS, ENTER PREPARED TO FIGHT, TO SURRENDER, OR TO SEE THE BOOKS BURN!''

25

Boxed Set

THE POLICEMAN TRIED it one more time. He wasn't going to force a point with a kid who could make Nature do a headstand, but he was losing patience.

"Why *can't* the Arab use my men as his troops?"

"Can any one of them handle a broadsword?" Noel countered. "In fact, forget swords; can they follow battle orders?"

"They can shoot straight. How about that?"

"Great, if they're going down Hogan's Alley. I'm telling you, one whiff of gunpowder in that building and Richard cries foul and torches the place. He doesn't have many fighters, but I'll bet he's placed them strategically at least one every couple of floors in the stacks. That's a lot of little fires to put out, providing you can fight your way through to all of them."

"So what do you want us to do? Just stand here like idiots?"

Noel took a deep breath and let it out slowly. "Go over to the Payne-Whitney Gymnasium and bring me back every fencing foil they've got."

"*Yes*, Master!" The policeman made an exaggeratedly sweeping bow. "*Right away*, Master! Your wish is my goddam command, Master! You want them gift-wrapped?"

"I want them here. If we ever do get the thirty together, we may need them. I'm going to the British Art Center right now. Bring the foils here and hand them over to the lord Salah-ed-Din. By the way, don't call him an Arab. He's a Kurd."

The policeman went off, cursing under his breath. "Fencing foils? Gonna Zorro those loons in there to death? Arabs! Kurds! Kid wizards! Fencing foils! Jesus! Cagney and Lacey wouldn't put up with this shit."

A microphone whisked into Noel's face as he tried to leave. Salah-ed-Din was already hemmed in by newshounds who wanted his historical perspective on the present situation in the Middle East. He was treating them all with gracious courtesy and saying a few choice nothings in a great many words. They ate it up, every mouthful. Rather than compete for a piece of that pie, the lady in plum Ultrasuede had decided to go for the youth-interest angle, with both fangs.

"Tell us, Mr. Cardiff, when did you first discover that you had the power to strike terror into the hearts of normal people? Wasn't the temptation to use your magic for pure self-gratification overwhelming at times? Have you devoted yourself to the cause of doing good out of personal ethics, or is it merely the psychic relic of a juvenile desire to play Superman?"

"I'll talk to you later. Right now I've got to—"

His attempt to sidestep her was blocked. She spoke a few sentences directly at the minicam before resuming the attack. "There you have it, ladies and gentlemen. Omnipotence is a heady brew. Already we see the marks it leaves. We may deplore Noel Cardiff's abuse of his powers, but who among us can safely say that our own children, if given similar carte blanche with the paranormal, would not fall into the same mold as this young man? Do the supernaturally gifted have to subscribe to the laws of common courtesy, or can they trample on anything they please, including the American public's right to know? Mr. Cardiff, how does it feel to hold so many adults on a leash?"

Lysi stepped out of a shadow behind the reporter and her crew and aimed two fingers. The woman's eyes flew wide in horrendous realization. She kicked off her shoes.

From the knee down she had the shaggy legs and paws of an Irish setter. For her, Maude Frizon and Perry Ellis had just passed into history. The man with the minicam knew a human interest twist when he saw one. Her assistant was on the spot with a microphone to ask her how she felt in the face of personal tragedy. Her anguished howl followed Noel for the better part of a block.

"Took you long enough," Dr. Hack grunted when Noel came into the exhibition hall. "Well, look around. This is one of the finest collections of medieval arcana in this country."

"Everything for the boy-sorcerer on the way up." Atamar looked pleased with Noel, for once. "We shall find our answer here if anywhere, while Lura helps Salah-ed-Din amass the basis for his soldiers' armaments."

Noel drifted over to the nearest display case. "I still think we'd do better to talk to some of the leftover A.R.G.H. people; ask them for volunteers to be Salah-ed-Din's troops."

"Do you also think they'd fight their friends? It's not a demonstration this time. Anyone who truly wants to fight is already inside Sterling. The A.R.G.H. people who followed Richard are the bravest of their brave. They must know that this battle will be real. If I know the Lionheart, he wouldn't force anyone to stay with him who wanted out. You can't coerce a good fighter, and you can't call a last-minute draft on loyalty. If you're going to get some troops for Salah-ed-Din, you'd better start looking for the recipe for bringing back the dead."

Noel looked at Atamar. "Isn't that illegal?"

The angel pursed his lips. "First let's see if it's possible, then if it works, and then whether it was legal."

Dr. Hack checked his watch. "And let's hurry. It's twenty-to-nones."

Some time later, Noel pushed a pile of books away. "It's not working!"

"What do you mean? We found the Hydra spell for resurrecting soldiers in the Salamanca grimoire and every other one since." Dr. Hack spread his hands over the array of open books dotting the floor. "It's a standard!"

"Yes, and every one of them says the same thing: You need some part of each dead man to use in the spell if you're going to bring him back."

"That is logical," Atamar said. "Not even magic can call something tangible out of nothing, but it can transform. The original object should be akin to what you wish to make of it. The silk-purse sow's-ear example holds true. That's why I told you to requisition those foils. They'll make lovely swords, battle axes, even shields and bows and arrows; all weapons."

"You need men to make men," said Dr. Hack.

"Am I supposed to raid the Grove Street Cemetery?"

"That," Atamar said, "would not do. Your magical power can't turn a sword into a plowshare, nor the remains of a man of peace into the body of a warrior."

"Keep looking," Dr. Hack directed. "Maybe one of these books has a Circean spell for making fighting men out of bad-tempered animals. If you find that, I know a number of cats who'd give Richard a battle he wouldn't forget." He started from the exhibit hall.

"And where are you going?" Atamar asked.

"Where angels fear to tread." Dr. Hack winked. "The men's room."

The good doctor was just finishing his business when the air above the urinal sparkled, swirled blue, and Lysi floated cross-legged at eye-level with Dr. Hack.

"Got time for a word?" she asked casually. Dr. Hack startled so badly that he stumbled into one of the sinks. "Hey, get a grip on yourself." Lysi tilted sideways to pick up a piece of toilet paper which she waved like a flag. "I come in peace."

"You'd better leave the same way, young lady," Dr. Hack said huffily, trying to locate and adjust his zipper while maintaining eye contact. "Our friend Noel can't use his magic against Richard, but you're another story. I can't believe you actually turned on him that way."

Lysi wore a complacent smile. "I was good, wasn't I?"

Dr. Hack gazed at her for a time. "I see . . ." A puzzle-piece fell into place in his mind. "Yes, you were very good. Convinced me."

"You know I had to do it. He wouldn't take any direct help from me."

"You still care for him?" Lysi nodded. "Too bad he'll never believe that. I fear you're succubus *non grata* with Noel forever."

"Sometimes 'forever' gets called on account of rain, Dr. Hack. The important thing is, I love him. I'm going to continue to help him any way I can as long as I don't interfere when he tries to help himself. I don't want to cripple his spirit that way."

"Commendable, my dear. It still doesn't explain why you're loitering in the men's room. It's a pretty sure bet Noel needs no help in here."

"But he does need the bones of fighting men."

"Don't tell me; you've got a wholesaler on the line?"

Lysi grabbed Dr. Hack's shirt collar and drew him to her, not too gently. "I need an agent; someone credible to show

him where the relics he needs lie. You *will* help me?'' she
cooed as she gave the material a clockwise twist.

"Agckh," said Dr. Hack, which she took for consent.

Back in the exhibition hall, Noel sat tailorwise on the floor
with an iron-bound grimoire in his lap. He slammed it shut
just as Dr. Hack returned. "Not a thing!"

"Look again. You might have missed something, especially as you don't read Latin," Dr. Hack said dryly.

"This one was written in French, which I do read." Noel
got up, hauling the weighty tome with him. "You can look
for yourself if you don't trust my word." He dropped the
book into Dr. Hack's unready arms.

"Whoof! Nothing in all these pages, eh?" A calculating
look crept into the archeologist's small eyes. He peeked
cautiously at one particular glass case on the display floor. It
had not been disturbed by their search for a fitting spell, since
it contained no books. He hefted the grimoire and ran a finger
around the thick metal strips binding the cover's spine and
edges, the rust-speckled clasps. "By gad, you're right, Noel.
Let's get back to Cross Campus and force those costumed
ninnies into Salah-ed-Din's service. Even if we found Circe's
own Week-at-a-Glance, it'd probably be written in Linear A.
Come on, let's blow this pop stand!"

Using both hands, he flung the heavy book away.

Given the law of gravity, it should have hit the floor almost
at once. Instead, it curved upward, banked right, spread its
covers like an albatross' wings, and sailed calmly into the
closed display case. Glass and wood didn't stand a chance
against iron hinges and bindings. The case crashed over, and
two silver boxes jounced and rolled across the carpet. One
came to a stop unharmed, but the other cracked open with a
sound like many marbles spilling out.

"Yick!" cried Noel.

"What?" Dr. Hack saw nothing but the boy kneeling
beside the open box and holding his thumb and forefinger
apart as if they described something with the dimensions of
an acorn. The archeologist blinked, squinted, rubbed his eyes
and cleaned his glasses, but still saw nothing there.

Not so Atamar. He placed his hands on Noel's shoulders.
"Why didn't I think of this before?" Now, he too knelt and
gathered unseen nuts. He spared a moment to pick up the
silver box and turn it slowly in his hands, studying the

interior with a hawk's eye. "We are saved, Noel. Carry them in this."

Noel scooped up handfuls of air and dropped them into the box. A musical pattering sound answered.

"In the name of Marcel Marceau, what are you two doing?" Dr. Hack shouted.

Atamar slapped Noel on the back. "Run ahead and begin to call them. Here, take the Salamanca grimoire; it's the slimmest one that holds the spell you'll need. I shall remain here to explain things to Dr. Hack, but you have no time. Hurry!"

Noel did not wait to be told twice. He didn't even wait for the elevator, but took the same route out of the British Art Center as he'd used the night he'd stolen the Richard Jewel. The floor had no sooner re-solidified than the angel looked at Dr. Hack and said, "You did everything but exclaim, 'Whoopsy-daisy' when you tossed that book. You're no actor."

Dr. Hack smirked. "The kid's no critic."

"You're also no magician. How did you make it fly?"

"Obviously it was our dear Lura's beloved Affinity principle in action. Like calls to like, soul to soul, and magical object to— "

"Bushwah calls to bushwah. What's the truth?"

"You'd better ask the special effects department." Dr. Hack snapped his fingers. "Lysi!"

She appeared mounted on a chimera whose lionhead jaws closed snugly around Dr. Hack's hand. "Snap your fingers for me again, and Bubba will snap something for you." She dismounted and shooed the monster back into the realm of nightmares. Dr. Hack flexed his hand tenderly.

"I never suspected," Atamar said. "You *are* sincere."

"More than you'll know."

The angel took the she-demon's hand and looked into her eyes. "And do you know what you are daring? Your own sire once was charged with punishing five demons who were slipping out of Hell's grasp into humanity, and more. If you persist in this course, the Underlords might well name someone else to fill your sire's ancient role. As a demon, you will be helpless to defend yourself against such an infernally appointed enemy."

Lysi was unafraid. "I'll risk it."

"For Noel? He doesn't want you now."

"So?"

"He wouldn't care if anything happened to you."

"That's his concern. I'm not responsible for anyone's feelings but my own. You won't change them, silvertongue."

"If you believe he'll change, you're a fool. You don't know mortals. They can be mulish."

"In love as well as hate. His heart is more stubborn than his mind. One day he'll realize the truth about me. I can wait for that. I'm half a mule myself." She smiled bravely.

To her astonishment, the angel smiled back. "The other half's pure jackass; I know your sire. What a joke it would be on him— on all of them!—if the Underlords sent a fiend to chastise a wayward succubus and he only found . . . a mortal girl."

Lysi's eyes were full of hope. "Oh! Could you do that for me? If I weren't a demon anymore, maybe then Noel would believe—"

"I want to. Whether I can . . . There is a price for miracles too, Lysi," Atamar said softly, squeezing her hand. "I pray that for your sake we will earn it."

26

Battle Royal

"I FEEL LIKE a jerk," said one policeman to his right-hand neighbor in line.

"And I feel like they gave me the Nobel Prize. Shut up and keep your foil stretched out the way he told you."

The next man down on the right said, "I wouldn't mind standing around here holding this thing, but it's almost three. That's nones, right? So we should be getting ready to rush the building the minute they open that door."

"Right, and have the whole library burn down around our ears. Yale'd really like that."

"Well, I wouldn't mind so much if someone'd only tell me what the hell that woman across from us is doing. She takes a step, bends over—"

"Yeaaah." His neighbor was an avid observer of human nature when it had good legs.

"—puts something down, stands up, moves over a step, does the whole routine over again, and there's *nothing there!* So what's she doing? Planting daisies?"

Lura overheard this exchange and gave the foil-toting policeman her most charming smile. "I'm laying out the skulls of the noble vanquished, Officer."

"Sure, lady, sure." To his neighbor, he whispered, "Body like a *Playboy* fold-out, mind minus a ball bearing."

"Well, I don't expect someone of *your* sensitivity to see them," Lura snapped. She went back to placing one knob of nothingness in front of each policeman.

"Hey, I'm plenty sensitive! You ask my wife! Five minutes' kissing on the couch minimum before we do *anything* else! I even watch Donahue!"

Lura straightened her back, the policeman's clamor no more than a cricket's chirr. "There's the last of them, Noel," she said. "Are you ready?"

Noel nodded. "I have the Hydra spell by heart." He touched the fingers of both hands to his brow. Lura saw the throbbing gleam of blue light already gathering at the tips. The alien cadences of medieval Latin rolled from his lips, and the light spread. It oozed over his knuckles, down to his wrists, and cinched itself there in two massive bracelets of sorcerous power.

"Hold your weapons steady." His voice seemed to come from very far away, a dark, hollow hill where the light of day was less than a legend. The police tried to do as they were told without letting their arms shake too much. The officer who was such a fan of Donahue was not doing well.

Noel began to walk down the line of policemen. At the far end, Salah-ed-Din waited, and beyond him, Sterling. Noel spread his arms to either side, his fingers starring out. Rainbows whipped around his wrists, tiny sea-green serpents wove through his fingers, their silver eyes and fangs glittering. A wizard's ghost-robe floated from his shoulders. He wore the sun, the moon, the dying stars caught up in a veil of night.

He paused in the middle of a step. His left hand touched one outstretched fencing foil, his right hand pointed down to something no one but a few might see, something that Lura had placed very carefully on the grass of Cross Campus. Heatless fire shot from the guard of the first foil to its tip. The policeman stared in fear and wonder, but kept his hold. The fire slid up Noel's left arm, lanced across his chest, and plunged down the right to strike the green space at which he pointed.

Whiteness glowed in the grass. A miniature human skull grinned with embered eyes, visible to all. It rose up from the earth, and there were other bones dribbling down from it, the spine a stem that branched into arms and legs, finger bones and toes tinier than needles of frost on a windowpane. Flesh wound itself around the naked joints and limbs, a blood-rose that the air itself breathed onto bare bone. Clothing followed, a gauzy white fall of unmelting snow, a harder chrysalis of leather and metal. And all the time, the body grew and broadened, grew and breathed, grew and stood a warrior full-grown—in less time than a man's mouth could open to deny that such an uncanny thing was happening.

The Saracen fighter took his bow and quiver from the hands of the policeman opposite him and made the triple reverence.

One by one, down the line, Noel worked this same transformation. Men sprang up from the earth as if from nothingness. Ancient weapons, sharp and deadly, flashed in the
sunlight where slender fencing foils with bated tips had been
before. Round shields opened like mushroom cups in the
grass, budding from the same magically transformed matter
as had formed the swords. Salah-ed-Din beamed to see his
army grow, then frowned as he looked more closely at the
men.

"Allah witness that I know that face, and that one, and
likewise . . . *Inshallah,* I believe I know them all!"

"You should," Lura said. She showed him the silver box.
Its small pennant had snapped off when it rolled from its
display case, but the designs on the sides of the box were still
plain, as were the curlicued engravings framing each scene of
decapitation. "Nazim didn't seem to think that this message
needed so much hiding. It's plain Arabic, and it tells of how
he took the heads of fifty of your men who died valiantly,
fighting the Crusaders."

"Fifty! *Bismillah,* I am honor-bound to lead only thirty.
How will we dispose the rest?"

Lura shrugged. "Noel will have to tell us that." She
watched him continuing along the line, leaving chain-mailed
warriors and dumbstruck policemen in his wake. "Your old
boyhood chum was quite a collector. He caught their spirits
the same as he caught yours and Richard's, binding them into
their own skulls, made small and stored in this box."

"But for what purpose?"

"To use them against you, perhaps. To have a guard of
proven worth if he ever felt he needed one. I can't say for
sure. Nazim the Dark was not an easy man to second-guess."

"He was worse than any slaver, this I realize." Salah-ed-
Din's brows came together. "May Allah grant that the terms
to free their spirits are the same as those affecting Richard
and myself. I shall fight the better for it, if it buys these noble
souls their final freedom."

Noel was almost to the end of the line when a bloodcurdling scream and a strangled cry made him wheel about. The
officer who had boasted of his finely honed sensitivities stood
transfixed, eyes bugging out, a damascened scimitar held
stiffly before him. Blood trickled down the blade. Little
wonder; the body of a dead Saracen was impaled on the steel.

"He tried to jump me!" the policeman babbled. "He leaped out at me, shrieking something wild. Frisk him; I bet you find a dagger."

"It was a *battle cry,* you moron!" his neighbor hollered at him. "He just wanted to get his hands on his own sword, like these other guys!" He jerked his thumb at the mass of fighting men already milling around, examining their restored bodies with approval, evaluating their armaments, marveling at their surroundings.

"I didn't mean to do it!" The policeman dropped the dripping scimitar, the body still hanging from the blade. The two no sooner hit the earth than a sunset-colored haze descended and dissolved them both to white dust. It blew away with the exhalation of a thousand gardens.

"Of course," Salah-ed-Din said. "He has found his own road to Paradise. He died in a holy cause, on *jihad.*"

"Twice," Lura added.

The policeman stumbled groping toward Noel. "Please don't do anything to me! It was self-defense, I tell you!" He never heard the crunching sounds under his feet.

"Stop right where you are!" Noel shouted, but the man was deaf with fear. Little puffs of white light formed at every crunch his feet made. They sailed into the sky, trailing human voices raised in joyful song. Noel ran to meet the policeman halfway and shove him off to the sidelines before he destroyed any more of the precious skulls that he could not see. A number of his fellow-officers dropped their foils and tried to calm him down.

"Hurry, *sidi,*" Salah-ed-Din exhorted Noel. "I must speak to my men before we can attack. The hour is almost upon us."

Noel himself was walking unsteadily now. He lurched into Salah-ed-Din and hung panting on the Saracen's shoulder. "There. That's all of them."

Lura made a quick count. "Twenty-eight," she announced. "See, Salah-ed-Din? Your honor's going to be just fine. You're even spotting Richard two points. At least the ones who didn't make it are free."

"Freedom they deserved, and freedom that these shall earn more gloriously," Salah-ed-Din declared. He took up his own sword and shield. Hailing his troops in their own tongue, he began to speak. They heard him out and raised a great cheer whose reverberations had not wholly faded when the Harkness Tower bells struck three.

The left-hand door of Sterling swung inward, a marked invitation. Salah-ed-Din gave the rallying cry, and the fighters charged. He himself was caught up in their rush and swept from sight into the building. The door slammed as soon as the last man was through.

"You know," Lura said, "I wonder if that was wise?"

"A headlong charge into a closed-in place that's enemy turf?" Noel stooped to pick up one of the discarded foils. He ran the blade across his palm and was holding a light, flexible sword. He touched its tip to the earth and a shield was there for him. His misty wizard's-cloak twinkled into a short-sleeved shirt of light mail, though his head remained bare. "Twenty-nine," he said when he was fully armed.

"You're not supposed to fight, Noel."

"Not with magic against Richard. No deal about using regular weapons. Or using magic on other people, come to think of it."

Lura was doubtful. "An oath's a sacred thing. Don't try weaseling through too many loopholes or one of them could turn into a noose."

"O.K. No magic against anyone. But I'm still going to use this." He lifted up the sword.

Lura's hand closed around his on the hilt. When she drew it back, her fingers enclosed a twin blade. She needed no shield or armor. "Thirty," she said of herself, and started for Sterling.

Noel caught her by the crook of the arm. "They've got enough front-door callers. You come with me."

Pleasantly bemused by mortal heroics, the angel obeyed.

The first man through the library door was almost to Our Lady of the Circulation Desk when an arrow from the side balcony thupped between his shoulder blades. He pitched forward onto the stone floor, cracking his skull. Blood pooled beneath him.

"Oh my God," breathed the archer, looking down at what he had done. "I killed him."

"Gunnar, get down!" The shout from his mate on the opposite balcony was almost too late. Gunnar ducked just as a

Saracen arrow whizzed past his head. Two more swiftly followed.

"Do not slay them!" Salah-ed-Din bawled. "Your souls shall answer for theirs! Take them alive or drive them out, but let them live!"

No one but the Saracen troops understood him. Gunnar crawled along the balcony on his belly as if his life depended on it. From the corner of his eye he saw his companion archer firing one bolt after another into the mass of warriors below. Some glanced off conical helms, some lacked the force to penetrate chain mail and leather armor, some missed the mark entirely.

One Saracen paused long enough to tear a file drawer from the upended card catalogs so recently used to bar the front doors. He tied it to a long rope which he unwound from around his waist, then swung it over his head in circles until it had enough momentum to fly up and over the balcony railings. He never found out whether the improvised weight would sustain him in his planned scaling attempt. Gunnar's friend shot a cloth-yard shaft into the man's upturned face and pierced his eye.

The Saracen screamed and pawed at the length of wood protruding from his brain before he too toppled over. "Jesus Christ." The second archer turned pasty white and dropped his bow. He was still down on his knees retching when a pair of Salah-ed-Din's men found a way onto the balcony and made him their prisoner.

Salah-ed-Din raised his hand and barked the command to halt. The only sound in the great main hall of Sterling was the distant scrabble of Gunnar's fleeing feet. All waited, listening. In the silence, the bodies of the two slain warriors melted away.

"Where are the others?" Salah-ed-Din's voice echoed strangely in the quiet library. "Where is King Richard?" He dispatched men to search the first floor of the library. These returned to report encountering no one. There was a tense moment when they heard footsteps coming up out of the stairwell in the middle of the hall.

"Don't shoot, please!" Lura called in badly accented Arabic. She and Noel presented themselves to a displeased Salah-ed-Din.

"You will dishonor me."

"You're entitled to thirty fighters," Noel said.

"Thirty!" The Saracen lord laughed without joy. "Thirty to fight ghosts. We have met but two of the foe. One escaped, one is here." He motioned for his men to bring the captured archer forward. "He will tell us nothing."

Noel looked hard at the archer. *"Roger?"*

"It's a hobby," Noel's roommate grumbled. "I'm Basil Archangelos of Mytilene. What's it to you?"

"Rog, this isn't playing around anymore."

"You're telling me? I just killed a man! Shit, I feel rotten." He looked ready to throw up again. "So what're they gonna do to me for it?"

Noel weighed truth against a whopper. Strategy won.

Roger was the color of a frog's belly by the time Noel finished outlining the finer points of Oriental tortures awaiting the close-mouthed. The white was showing all around Lura's eyes when he was done, and Salah-ed-Din was smothering his laughter with a violent coughing fit, but Roger was ready to talk.

"He's got hardly anyone down on the main floor. Most of us are up in the stacks, guarding the way to the roof."

"Richard's on the roof?"

"With the bullhorn. He figures he can blast it down one of the vents if he wants to give the command to set fire to the library." His face fell. "None of us had the heart to tell him."

"Tell him what?"

"Come on, Noel, you know me. You know how I feel about books. Do you think I'd ever willfully destroy one? Ten? Hundreds? A whole library full?"

"You wouldn't," Noel agreed. "But those crazy friends of yours are straight out of the Dark Ages. Who knows what they'd do?"

"They'd tell you what made the Dark Ages so damn dark was not enough books, that's what they'd do." Roger stuck out his chin. "They know what they owe to books more than a lot of the sitcom slaves out there. They know you can't solve any problem in thirty minutes, less commercial breaks. They know that the past wasn't perfect, but they also know how to look through the histories for past mistakes so they'll recognize them if they come around again. They'll do a lot of things, but they won't hurt books. Not even for King Rich-

ard. Now that you know we don't really have any aces except
the hostages, why don't you go tell the cops?''

Noel remembered what he had been willing to do to one
precious book, and was chastened. Salah-ed-Din took over
the interrogation.

''My heart is glad to hear that past folly instructs as well as
past wisdom. Your people have no desire to destroy books?
Know then that mine have no wish to destroy life. These
officers of law who wait outside are too bewildered by what
transpires here. In their panic, they might react too violently,
and irredeemable harm might be done. No, we shall call on
none save ourselves for help. We seek but to win through to
the Lionheart and make him see reason. My men have been
instructed not to take lives.''

''I—I saw your men die. Don't the others want to . . .
avenge their comrades?''

''Their true bodies died long ago. The death of these
present shells grants long-deferred release to their spirits, and
once your king and I take hands, we two men of war shall
also learn the lessons of the final peace. Vengeance? My men
will have only thanks for those who give them the grace of
freedom through an honorable death.''

''What will you do to the king?''

''I must see if I can persuade him, face to face, of the
uselessness of his present course. Our age and all that made it
dear to us has passed. I will use nothing but words to force
him to comply with what is best.''

Roger was vastly relieved. ''Then I'm with you. Follow
me, and— ''

Wood groaned. An under-oiled wheel squeaked. A mullioned
window fronting on the library's interior courtyard creaked
open. Shadows moved in the alcove where the card catalogs
were kept.

''—say, what did you do with your other prisoners?''
Roger stopped in his tracks suddenly, en route to the elevators
and stairways leading to the stacks.

''What others, if your fellows are above?'' Salah-ed-Din
asked.

''You mean you didn't check out this floor first?''

''He did,'' Noel said. ''All the rooms. They didn't find
any—''

''Just the rooms? Didn't you look in the courtya—?''

"A RICHARD! A RICHARD! A RICHARD!"

Four file carts rumbled out of the alcove, each pushed by two brawny A.R.G.H. members, with a third seated firmly on the chair, dust mop couched straight out over the desktop. The Saracen troops stood rooted with amazement as these unlikely juggernauts bore down on them. Three fell at the first onslaught, with a mop to the solar plexus. The fourth cart rider missed his mark and had to be wheeled about by the runners for another try. This time, instead of using his mop point-on, he wielded the weapon in a sideways sweep and knocked two Saracens from their feet at one go.

"Go for it, Bishop Potiphar!" one of the other cart riders yelled merrily, and instructed his own runners to get up speed for another run. He copied the battling bishop's strategy and took out another paynim.

Now the runners from two of the carts drew their swords and laid about with the flat of the blade, making sure their downed foes stayed down. Steel clanged on the Saracen helmets, leaving the paynim stretched insensible on the floor.

Noel gave a loud, inarticulate shout. It lacked the commitment of a set battle cry, but at the moment all he could think of was "For God, for country, and for Yale!" He threw himself on one of the cart riders whose runners were otherwise occupied and dragged him off. The man fought back, but the mop was useless at close quarters. So was Noel's sword, given that he was too scared to risk drawing it. It took skill to strike with the flat only, skill Noel knew he didn't have. The two of them rolled around on the floor for long, awkward minutes, until the combat was decided by Salah-ed-Din, who bashed the A.R.G.H. man over the head with his shield.

Noel pulled himself up off the floor. The Saracens had recovered their wits—those who hadn't had them knocked from their heads. There were two carts still in action. A Saracen waited right in the path of each, gaping as if helpless to move. The jousters cheered their drivers on to greater speeds, but at the last moment, both Saracens dodged aside, whipped out their blades, and sliced off their foes' dust mops nearly to the root. The disarmed carts continued past in a blur and rammed into the Circulation Desk.

After that, Salah-ed-Din's men used force of numbers to overpower their assailants. One of them had even recovered a dust mop and was grinning wickedly as he gave his enemies several bashes of their own medicine. Motes flew, and strong men begged for quarter. They were remanded to the unofficial jailers' care.

"To the stacks!" cried Roger, and the diminished troops fell in behind him.

Salah-ed-Din split his men up between the elevators and the stairs. "I trust your good faith, friend Basil Archangelos of Mytilene," he said, "but I do not trust these flying boxes. I make you responsible for these four soldiers, great swordsmen all. Convey them to the roof, where Richard waits. It may be that they can defeat him and hold him captive until we have climbed so high by simpler means. Let Allah decide whose shall be the glory."

Roger bowed smartly to the Saracen lord and waved for the four to enter the elevator with him. Their faces were a study in strictly controlled fear and suspicion as the doors slid closed. The motor whirred, the indicator began its ascending sweep.

Every electric light in Sterling went out and the elevator's emergency bell shrilled an alarm.

"They had someone at the power switch," Noel said.

"Allah is great," Salah-ed-Din replied piously. "May He grant Sir Basil the gift of a facile tongue wherewith to explain this situation to four very frightened and displeased men. Who has brought torches?"

At that moment, the lights came back on but the elevator remained stuck. "Can they do that?" Noel wondered.

Lura got a better grip on her sword. "As Allah wills it," she said. "And the circuit breakers. My lord Salah-ed-Din, send a couple of your men down into the basement for Sir Reddi-Kilowatt before he plays any more tricks with the electricity."

Following Noel's suggestion, the three Saracen warders led their prisoners down into the comparative comfort of Machine City, their hands a-jingle with the spare change Lura had given them to buy refreshments. They were soon joined by two more of their party, the proud captors of the A.R.G.H. man who had been listening for the sound of an elevator in motion and had then thrown the switch.

They all settled themselves quietly, but not for long. Between the Saracens' inability to fathom the mystic workings of the coffee machine and the A.R.G.H. people's naturally courteous curiosity about their hosts' arms and armor, the fighters soon evolved a common ground for communication and a makeshift language of handsigns and facial expressions to see them through.

The floor above them was more peaceful. The stunned Saracens had been laid out as comfortably as Lura could manage, all in a row with their heels toward Our Lady of the Circulation Desk. They remained only semi-conscious. One of them finally did sit up. He touched his head and moaned.

Then he rubbed his eyes. Had he died and come into the Prophet's promised Paradise after all this time? Waves of dusty golden light were emanating from the mural of the white-robed lady, and as he watched, he saw her step down from her place in the painting and ride a ramp of sunshine to the floor.

"Salaam aleikum," she said. Silver bells pealed out and twin flocks of doves burst from her billowing sleeves.

The Saracen's yowl of terror roused his mates from their painful slumbers. The six of them ran down a side hall and took shelter in the Periodical Room.

"Tsk," the vision mused. "Maybe the pigeons were a bit much." A gilded cheval glass materialized before her. She checked the drape of her robe and raised the hem of her veil so that more of her face showed. Lysi winked at herself in the glass and conjured an olive branch to her fingers. "Perfect."

She began to rise slowly, with proper celestial dignity, through the many floors above.

It was a greatly reduced force that commenced climbing the stairs. They met no opposition on their way to the second floor, but once there, Noel suggested that some of the men take the stairways that were inside the library stacks themselves. Salah-ed-Din considered it.

"We have accounted for fourteen of their people, by my reckoning. I would imagine Richard will keep his archer in the high tower, which makes fifteen that cannot touch us for the moment."

"Richard's not waiting up on the roof alone, either."

"You speak truth. His pride as a king and his wisdom as a campaigner would not allow him to leave himself unguarded.

Let us say that he has four with him, at most. Hmm . . . and the one below, Sir Reddi-what?"

"Never mind. So there are only ten of his men in the stacks. There are more of us! And there'll be more yet when your men on the first floor regain consciousness."

"Aie, but how will they know where to find us? We must not count upon their help."

"We still outnumber Richard's forces. We can take the chance of splitting our own party, and they don't know we're *not* trying to kill them. When they get their first look at your men, they'll see they're up against the real thing."

Salah-ed-Din's warriors didn't understand anything Noel said, but they gathered from his tone and loving looks that he was complimenting them. Smiles shifted the scars on their leathery faces and showed off all the failings of medieval dentistry. More than one of their number was missing an eye, and the stitched socket made those men look as if they were winking obscenely. It was a more terrifying sight than when they grimaced in battle.

"Very well, we shall do as you say." Salah-ed-Din set aside seven of his men to go into the stacks and told the remainder to stay by him. "Lead these for me, *sidi*, I pray," he said to Noel, indicating the seven warriors. "They would not know which way to turn among so many books."

"But I don't speak their language. How can I command them?"

"I'll go with you." Lura took a definite step into the midst of Noel's party. The Saracens began to stomp and whistle their appreciation. Lura put an end to that by bellowing a few juicy phrases in Arabic. The men blushed and rolled their eyes at each other, staring at her with awe. "I don't care how long they've been without a woman," Lura said prissily. "If you can't expect some self-control from the dead, what is this world coming to?"

"Salah-ed-Din," said Noel, "when you reach the top flight, on seven, wait for us. We'll meet there and go on to the roof together."

The Saracen was solemn as he replied, "We will not tarry forever, for who knows what awaits us both in this ascent? Shield yourself with your powers, *sidi*, that you at least may survive."

"I'm not going to use my magic in here," Noel said. "Not until we've taken Richard."

"Your oath but forbade you to use your powers against him, not against others."

"I'm not taking a chance. If I use magic at all, I might forget myself and keep on using it indiscriminately. I won't break my word and I won't dishonor yours."

Salah-ed-Din clapped his hands to Noel's shoulders. "Allah strengthen your arm. You are my son in spirit. Defend yourself from harm, or know that my heart will break should anything befall you."

Noel tried to shrug off the Saracen's praise. "What could happen to me? All these fighters on my side, experts with their weapons . . . We're only going after a bunch of weekend warriors. They won't stand a chance."

On the flight of stairs between the third and fourth floors, Salah-ed-Din was almost crushed by a book-cart sent hurtling down the steps from above. He flung himself to one side, but three of his men were not fast enough. Their shrieks of pain echoed up the stairwell. The armored man and woman who had shoved the cart peered over the railings at what they had done.

"Ah, shit, I can't believe I did something like that," the man said. "I quit."

"Before you quit, go find me a first-aid kit," the woman snapped. "I've got Red Cross training. Hey!" she called down the stairs. "Hey, we're sorry. We were just trying to scare you off. We surrender! Peace, O.K.? *Shalom?* Uh, wrong word, but— "

"Beauteous One, peace is never the wrong word," Salah-ed-Din called back.

"What's this stuff underfoot?" Noel asked as his shoes crunched on small blue crystals. His party had entered the second-floor stacks and were now climbing the narrow, twisting stairs connecting all seven floors of books, plus an equal number of mezzanine levels. Salah-ed-Din's route only touched the whole-numbered floors.

Lura sniffed. "Uh-oh. We get out on *this* level and take the regular stairs for a flight."

"Why?"

"Save your breath and do it."

She turned and ordered the Saracens to retreat. They were not accustomed to having a woman command them, and proceeded to contest her orders. Lura wasted no time in debate, but elbowed her way past them, dragging Noel along. Their shrill chatter was cut off by a yell from the floor they'd been approaching.

"Surrender in the king's name!"

One Saracen gave an exultant battle cry and charged up the stairs, followed by the rest, scimitars waving.

"I warned you!" the voice hollered, and something pungent splashed down the stairs.

Fumes rose from the blue crystals as the liquid hit them, fumes that choked and burned the life out of the first two men in line and sent the rest flying, holding their headwraps over their mouths and noses.

In the hall outside the stacks, Lura and Noel were waiting for them. "What happened?" Noel panted.

"What generally happens when you pour bleach on crystal drain cleaner. You get chlorine gas. They must've found a janitor's closet. That can be the same as an arsenal, in the right hands." She questioned the coughing men. "We lost two," she told Noel grimly. "We should be glad we didn't lose more. What do you think of weekend warriors now?"

Noel was silent.

One of Salah-ed-Din's men exclaimed the Arabic equivalent of "Now *this* is more like it!" as a group of four A.R.G.H. warriors presented themselves on the fifth floor landing, prepared to do battle. The Saracen looked hopefully to his lord for instruction.

"They are brave and honest fighters. We will meet them in honor." Salah-ed-Din designated four of his braves to accept the challenge. "Remember, do not kill them."

Even hampered by this stipulation, Salah-ed-Din's men had the advantage of years and practice. Two of them disarmed their men after a very short set-to, one by a blow to the wrist, one by hooking a foot behind his opponent's ankle and shoving him backward.

"Foul! Foul!" cried the A.R.G.H. man so overcome. "I want to appeal this match to the Field Marshal."

"Fool, I *am* the Field Marshal!" said the gentle nursing an injured wrist.

The other two pairs of fighters looked well-matched until one of the A.R.G.H. men, wearing the heavier partial-plate armor of his chosen century, took a misstep and fell down a flight of stairs. The clangor of his fall distracted his fourth companion in arms, and she was disarmed and captured.

"You fought well," Salah-ed-Din told the four. "You are worthy of your arms." He summoned one of his men to him. "Convey them downstairs to join the others. Treat them with all deference."

As the prisoners were being led away, one stopped and made the triple reverence to the Saracens. Salah-ed-Din gave him the thumbs-up sign back.

Noel heard the ruckus of Salah-ed-Din's men beset by the A.R.G.H. fighters several flights above. "They're ahead of us. We'd better get back into the stacks and hurry, or Richard's troops will be able to bag us all in one place."

They left the main stairway. As Noel opened the door leading into the stacks, he remarked, "You know, it sounds weird, but I hope whoever released that poison gas didn't get a whiff of it himself."

"Why, thank you," said the fighter who was waiting just inside the door, sword drawn. Two other fighters stood behind him, leaning against a bookstack. "That's real nice of you to think of me. *En garde.*"

Noel gasped and drew steel without thinking. He stuck his sword straight up in front of his face and made a gawky downward slice. The swordsman jumped back, and Noel's Saracens threw themselves into the breach.

"You could have killed him," Lura said as she and Noel watched the three pairs square off. All six fighters had sense enough to take their quarrel away from the door, out into the central area of the stacks where there was room to maneuver a blade. This left Lura, Noel, and two other Saracens free, though the Saracens would have been pleased to uneven the odds in their countrymen's favor. A sharp reprimand from Lura scotched that.

"Who, me? Kill a guy with a sword?" Noel looked offended. "*He* could've killed *me.*"

"In a pig's eye. I can't be aggressive with this—" she extended her own sword "—but I can defend the bejeepers out of you."

"I don't need to be defended!"

"You couldn't win a cole slaw match opposite a cabbage, using that sword. But have it your way. Everyone always seems to think he knows better than an angel." Lura flounced past the embattled swordsmen, and the two unemployed Saracens went with her. Noel had no choice but to follow her to the stack stairwell. Before she ascended, she shouted some Arabic instructions to the fighters.

"What was all that?" Noel demanded.

"I told them where to bring the prisoners when they took them, but not to bother about it if they got killed themselves. I do hope they don't. It makes these poor A.R.G.H. people feel *so* guilty, and bloodstains are so difficult to get out of one's garb." The angel floated up the stairway.

Salah-ed-Din and his last three men were almost to the seventh floor when he heard the shouted warning, *"Gardez l' eau!"* and the excellent acoustics of the stairwell likewise brought to his ears the hissed *"That's only for throwing chamberpots, dimwit."*

He did not have time to reflect on the hidden meaning of this exchange, for just then the floodgates opened and a gout of water with the force of a charging bull knocked him from his feet and down on top of his followers. Salah-ed-Din's head struck the stairway wall. Purple and orange flowers bloomed before his eyes. Through the haze of pain he saw several young people in mixed medieval garb standing at the top of the flight, waving white wands the length of a big man's arm. Another group was just laying down the dripping nozzle of a firehose.

"What witchery is this?" the Saracen lord muttered. "It is not Richard's way to play a double game."

While he gathered himself out of the shards of pain, he saw his men already on their feet. He had been as much the scholar as the warrior, but these fellows knew only the sword, and were that much more resilient than he. They pounded up to attack the wand-wielders.

Then Salah-ed-Din saw one of the A.R.G.H. men fling his wand. It shattered on impact and exploded in a blinding flash.

It was hard way for a simple Saracen soldier to be introduced to the miracle of fluorescent lighting. The first soldier up flung his arm across his eyes, but it was too late. Other wands were flying, and from a box on the landing, more were being passed out to waiting hands.

Salah-ed-Din's heart sank within him. All of his men were now dazzled by the exploding wands. Some bore the gashes of flying glass on their faces. Richard's folk halted this phase of their attack and started down the stairs. Whether they would be as apt with their blades as with these ungodly devices was moot. Richard still remained on the roof, and Salah-ed-Din must reach him, though it meant abandoning his men to their fate.

Draggled as a shipwrecked rat, the great king crept unheeded down the steps and slipped off at the sixth floor.

"Good God, what happened to you?" Noel was moved to offer Salah-ed-Din a steadying arm, which the king rejected proudly. "You were supposed to meet us on the main staircase, but here you are sneaking up behind us through the stacks. We could've hurt you!"

"The main staircase is still Richard's," Salah-ed-Din said coldly. "Allah will it that it does not guard the way to the roof, or we will still have hard fighting."

"No, the stair to the roof's inside the stacks, but—Where are the rest of your men?"

Salah-ed-Din's eye was the icy gold of a hawk's. He did not deign to answer the question.

"I guess we'll still have some hard fighting up there, if Richard's got guards with him," Noel said. "All we've got is two."

Salah-ed-Din moved to embrace the two soldiers left to his command. They spoke to him of the perils that they had passed, while he gazed at them with a father's cherishing eye. When they had done, he returned his attention to Lura and Noel.

"Ali and Yusuf have told me that you acquitted yourself bravely and wisely, *sidi*. Your spirit is valiant even when no otherworldly power touches it. Come, we shall yet prove its mettle. Lead me to the lion's lair."

The heavy fire-door to the roof opened slowly. For a time

it hung there, unmoving, the doorway divulging no sign that anyone but a ghost had moved it.

Richard the Lionheart was not a patient man. "Come forth! Come forth in all your strength, my enemy. We do not fight from covert as you paynim do. Come in your numbers against us! We await!" At his side, Thorin of the Broken Axe, Lady Jael, and Matthew Pincus stood poised for what might come. Behind him, tied wrist and ankle, but still managing to play a mean game of touchy-feelie, Geordie and Amanda sat making truffle-eyes at each other.

Ali was the first through the door. He leaped onto the roof with a falcon's scream. Lura stepped out next, more demurely, followed by Noel and Yusuf, who looked somber but ready to fight. Salah-ed-Din came last.

Richard and his party stared and waited for more. None were forthcoming.

"*These* are your numbers?" Richard wondered aloud.

Salah-ed-Din inclined his head. "Even so."

The Lionheart beamed. "Sausalito, here we come."

27

The Weaker Sex

"WELCOME TO MY little world." Richard enjoyed irony. The newcomers looked down and saw that a goodly portion of Sterling's rooftop was covered by a medieval city in miniature, a tinsmith's fit of whimsy done in the days when labor was cheap and craftsmen liked their little jokes. Yale was dotted with similar examples, from the gargoyles on the Law School to the quote from *Scaramouche* carved into the Hall of Graduate Studies' wall. Here atop Sterling, a metal city had sprung up to knee-height, some of the buildings covering vents and pipes, some there just for show.

Salah-ed-Din contemplated this micropolis. "Truly you have found a kingdom worthy of your rule, my brother."

The angry color rose to Richard's face. "Do not mock me, infidel. I shall yet have a realm again."

The Saracen's eyes showed only pity. "A worthy realm awaits us both. The fool lingers at the feast long over, while the torches smoke, the meats grow cold, and the laughter of lovely women turns to keening. The wise man knows the fitting hour to depart."

"I will not go!"

"So says every man. Do you fear the unknown so deeply?"

"I fear nothing. I died shriven of my sins, all of them forgiven for my part in the Crusade, after leading a life of honor."

"My lands saw your honor. I heard the cries of the fatherless, I smelled the smoke of your burnings, I looked into the faces of the dead. Were these what wiped away your sins? Ah, you grow pale, Lionheart. Your soul recognizes truth. Will you linger in this diminished world and add to the burden of sin already on your soul? Depart while some measure of virtue still clings to you. No king is mightier than the mud that drags down all.''

Richard shook a fist at Salah-ed-Din. "You found this new life just as sweet as I!''

"For a time. As our new friends would say, this is a nice place to visit, but—"

"You envy me for the crown I won and seek to coax it from me with lies!''

"What does a crown mean in these times, Richard? I envy you nothing, but my spirit is bound to yours. I want my freedom.'' The Saracen drew his straight Toledo blade. "I will fight you for that, man to man. You cannot in honor refuse the challenge.''

King Richard looked sly. "What good would it do for you and me to fight? You know we can not die a second time. I offer you a pact: Let two of our people fight, a trial by combat to decide the question. I will abide by whatever you say, if your man wins.''

Salah-ed-Din thought about it. "Done. I choose—"

"No, no, my friend. *I* choose. That too is part of the bargain.''

"An unfair part!''

"You ask much of me. Give me at least leave to defend my point. Come forward, mage. You are my choice.''

Noel stepped gingerly between two tiny tin houses. He felt the pulse in his throat beat faster. "King Richard, I'm not a fighter. I've kept my oath, I won't use my magic against you, I won't even turn it against your followers. Be reasonable!''

"I am most reasonable. Do you see the champions from among whom I must choose your opponent?'' He indicated Thorin, Jael, and Matthew. Thorin looked the most formidable, until Noel saw that the big man carried no weapon but a broken axe. Then a stiff breeze blew, whipping Jael's heavy cloak closer around her small body. Thorin yelped and doubled over, cupping his hand to his eye.

"Damn! Something in my lens again . . .''

"Well, that narrows it.'' Richard's mouth twisted. "Hardly a rank of titans. Do you wonder that I choose you rather than one of Salah-ed-Din's men? We must give my poor follower some chance of victory.'' The king paced back and forth on the rooftop. "I will not insist on this match if you refuse, mage. But if you refuse, so shall I. Friend Matthew! Show him what you hold!"

Matt held up a pocket lighter and lifted the roof of one of the little houses. "Better agree or—or I drop this down, lit!" He flicked the lighter on as he spoke. His voice wavered and the flame jiggled, but Noel didn't want to find out whether this wheelchair-bound man shared the A.R.G.H. people's respect for books.

"Do you still hesitate, magician?" Richard worked a note of ridicule into his voice.

"You wouldn't ask me to fight him, would you?" Noel pointed at Matt.

"I would not. He might have the advantage, being a seasoned soldier. You may guess who remains." He nodded at Jael, who stood wrapped in her cloak, eyes downcast.

"Fight a *woman?*"

"In trial by combat it is for God to decide the rightness of the cause. Do you doubt that He can give the victory to what vessel He pleases, however frail?"

"O.K.," Noel said dubiously, gazing at the small woman. "If that's how you want it, I'll fight."

"Good," said the lady Jael, tossing her cloak from her shoulders. The sun danced over her armor. She drew a dagger from her belt and juggled it hand to hand before catching it by the tip and throwing it. It whizzed past Noel's head and sheared off a few split ends. "I was afraid I wasn't going to have anyone to play with."

They moved away from the tin city, onto an open space. Noel had his sword out, but Jael chose her mace. They circled warily, Jael's mouth in a bright, feral grin. She took a clumsy swing at Noel and laughed when he jumped backward, fanning his sword wildly in her direction. She made a few more swings, less deliberately awkward this time. The mace's spikes grazed Noel's legs, tearing his jeans, drawing blood.

Noel, I won't let her hurt you. Lura's voice was in his thoughts.

Nor I. I am here for you, too. Atamar's mental call joined his mate's.

I don't need to be protected! Noel's mind shouted back.

Are you going to shelter me all my life? When are you going to let me prove myself on my own?

Only you seem to think that something needs to be proved, Noel. You confuse being independent with being alone. Lura's thoughts were sad.

Have it as you like, Atamar added. *We will not intervene.*

"Come back here, mage," Jael taunted. "You're going to go right off the roof if you keep backing away from me like that." She made a wider swing at him and when he leaped away he felt the coping press against his back.

He ducked under Jael's next swing and rolled to one side. The mace crashed down a foot from his head. Sweat chilled his brow, even more when he looked up and saw by her laughing face that the miss had been on purpose. She was in complete control of the weapon. He got into a crouch and made some random stabs and swipes with his blade. She beat each one down, and on the last, she struck the sword upward, out of his hand. It spun over the parapet and plummeted into the street.

"Now," the lady Jael said, not even breathing hard. "I think that settles that."

Salah-ed-Din bowed to King Richard. "You said that if my man won, you would do as we asked. You did not name the conditions of your own fighter's victory."

"First, the jewel must be given to my hand. I do not like the idea of that wizardling holding anything that touches my fate."

"*Sidi* . . ."

"No!" It was a sob. Noel's hand clutched a heavy shape worn beneath his light mail.

"You must honor what we have promised."

"Tell her to kill me first; that's how you'll get it."

"Do not tempt me, boy!" the Lionheart roared. "If I so instruct her, my lady Jael will not hesitate."

"Oh, won't she?" Noel shot back. "She could've killed me while we fought, but she didn't. She wouldn't! There's some things your people won't do for you, King Richard. If they do any harm, it's because this is all a first-time thing for them. They never saw a real war. Fighting's all clean, on film, sealed under glass on a screen but never up close where you can smell how people die!"

"You question the loyalty of my people?" Richard looked about to succumb to a fit of choler.

"Question them yourself! Forget about killing me; just hand her that lighter and tell her to drop it down the pipe!"

King Richard straightened his shoulders and laughed. "Is that all? My lady, to me!" He stretched out his palm and Matt swiftly laid the lighter there. Richard could not mark the look of relief on the chairbound veteran's face. He handed the lighter to Jael. "Show this whelp his error."

Jael stood there holding the lighter in one hand and her mace in the other. She flipped the lighter open and struck it to flame. The tin house was still to one side, the pipe into the bowels of Sterling uncovered. She took a step nearer to it, then another.

She flung the lighter down from the roof's edge and fell to her knees before the king.

"I can't."

"None of us could," Thorin said, coming to place his arms around her.

King Richard looked at Matt. "And you, my friend?" It was despair given words.

Matt shook his head. "Not books. Not me. I've done my share of destruction, and it still burns. Don't ask for any more, if you really want to call me your friend."

The king drew in a long, shaky sigh. He was alone. "A dream," he said. "A dream whose hour has passed." He looked down at the miniature houses around his knees, then up at the Saracen lord. "Indeed, you spoke rightly of the fool who lingers. The feast is done. Let us depart."

"Give me your hand on that, my brother," said Salah-ed-Din.

Noel plucked the Richard Jewel from the inside of his shirt just as the two kings joined hands. He felt it grow warm and saw the great central pearl begin to send forth wave after wave of liquid light. "Ba'ouji . . ." he breathed, and the light surged up into the sky, a monument of cloud against the blue, a man-shape with the eyes of a panther and tusks of a wild boar. The might of the sea and the sky, the fires of the earth and the beasts that would not tame, all made him.

AS IT WAS BIDDEN, SO LET IT BE DONE!

The djinni made a dome of his huge hands above the kings, and their bodies fell away into dust. Two stars whirled and burned with the ecstasy of freedom.

GO.

Their splendid fires engulfed all, consumed the two Saracen warriors on the rooftop, penetrated the building beneath, gave blessed release to every captive soul still within. The lesser sparks rose up and bound their flames to the spinning hearts of the living stars. They soared into the welcoming embrace of the heavens and were seen no more.

28

Mark of Genius

"I'LL TAKE THAT for you, Noel," said Geordie, appropriating the Richard Jewel. He gazed at it with satisfaction, and the twin diamonds stared back rudely. "Look at this beauty, Amanda; it's as if nothing happened."

Amanda draped herself across Geordie's shoulders, but she wasn't all that interested in the Richard Jewel. Noel had never seen a librarian simper and mean it.

"So here you are!" Dr. Hack stumbled through the roof door and rushed over to examine the restored, recovered medallion. "It's mad downstairs. Police everywhere, librarians bitching and moaning, and all those medievalists swearing on a stack of Bibles that they'll help move the furniture back where it was and clean up the mess. Some excitable type's caterwauling about a security deposit. Let's stay up here where it's fairly safe." He winked at Noel. "Fine work, boy. Damned fine work."

The lady Jael approached Noel circumspectly. "Excuse me. I hope there's no hard feelings about the fight?"

"You didn't kill me. No hard feelings." He gave her a half-smile. He was feeling too empty for anything like resentment or anger to seed inside him.

"Good, because . . . you can use your powers now my lord King Richard's gone, and we need them for a couple of little things."

"I can't use them to hide you and your friends from the cops. It'd hardly be the right start for me. I guess I'm going to be what they call a white wizard from now on."

"Oh, these are perfectly innocent things; details. First, we'd appreciate some help getting Matt down from here. It's pretty steep steps. Richard carried him up, and Thorin and I brought the chair, but we figured you might be willing—"

"Sure, sure, no problem." He gestured, and suddenly

Matt's chair sprouted the wings of Pegasus. The veteran's mouth dropped open in happy awe as he touched the new switch on his control box and felt the chair lift up, then soar and bank wherever he steered it.

Noel waved away Matt's shouted thanks. "Anything else?" he asked Jael.

"Just one thing. I know you'll think I'm being silly, but it does bother me. Make him go away." She pointed, and Noel turned to see the still-looming cloudy figure of Ba'ouji. His massive, foggy body blended in well with the normal clouds in the late afternoon sky. In the dying light, few of the party remaining on the rooftop noticed him, and no one in the street below, until he chose to speak.

WHERE IS MY MASTER? The djinni's voice was the crack of summer thunder. WHERE IS NAZIM THE DARK, WHO BOUND ME TO THE HOUSE OF PEARL?

Noel searched the roof for Lura, but she was gone. *You did say you wanted to handle things yourself?* Atamar's words tickled his mind.

"Yeah, and I will, too," Noel muttered. He presented himself boldly to the djinni. "Nazim the Dark is dead! You have served his purpose."

The djinni did not crack a smile. In view of his peculiar dental structure, this was a plus. His head descended and the great nostrils noisily snuffed up Noel's essence. SAY YOU SO? YOU'RE A MAGICIAN TOO, FROM THE STINK OF YOU. WELL, ONE YOKE SITS AS WELL ON THE OX'S NECK AS ANOTHER. WHAT WOULD YOU HAVE OF ME?

Noel was taken by surprise by this question. "Uh—nothing. You're free, Ba'ouji. You don't have to stay in that pearl any more. You can do whatever you want."

The djinni's eyes widened, their pupils cross-slashes of black on a ground of deepest green. BUT I LIKED LIVING IN THE PEARL. IT WAS PRETTY. I WANT TO RETURN. PUT ME BACK, MAGICIAN.

"I'm sorry, I can't do that."

NAY? BUT YOU HAVE THE POWER!

"I might, but I mean I *can't* do it, because it would be wrong. How can I justify imprisoning another being?"

I DO NOT CARE TO ARGUE JUSTICE! MORTAL ABSTRACTIONS MAKE MY HEAD HURT. I WANT YOU TO LOCK ME AWAY IN THE PEARL!

"I told you, I'm not going to. My conscience won't allow it. I'm through with compromising my morals. No more, not for anyone. Look, I'm really sorry about this."

YOU SHALL LEARN 'SORRY!' The djinni's fist tore a ball of lighting from the sky and pitched it straight downward. Noel clapped on a shield, but the projectile never met it.

Riding his new-given wings into the djinni's face and brandishing one of Jael's spare swords, Matt Pincus shouted, "Leave him alone! Get out of here, you big bastard!" and got the full impact of the fireball. The white wings crumpled in flames and the wheelchair crash-dived.

The djinni cocked a cloudy eyebrow. MY ERROR.

And more than that, Child of Night. A silvery voice rang out over the rooftop. The sun's dawning glory shone around the modestly robed lady who trod the highest vaults of the sky and wagged her olive branch reprovingly at the djinni. *Begone, by all the powers I command. Begone back into the pearl, if that is your desire, yet know that there you shall slumber until Solomon himself awakes in the Valley of Cloud and calls you to his service again.* She shook the branch once more for luck, and vanished.

Ba'ouji trembled in the spill of light from the lady, and dwindled to a chittering white sphere that zipped across the rooftop and buried itself in the heart of the Richard Jewel. Geordie dropped the medallion as if it had suddenly turned into a young cobra, but the djinni was already inside. Amanda clicked her tongue, picked the jewel up, wiped it on her skirt, and gave it back to her beloved.

Dr. Hack looked over the parapet on the High Street side of Sterling. "Yep," he reported. "They saw her, too. I never saw so many people get flattened by a hit-and-run miracle in my life. You'd think this was Mecca, the way they're all down on their knees. I'm staying up here forever, where it's sane."

"We're not." Noel had him by the arm. "We're going down to take care of Matt."

"Don't you think it's a little—" Dr. Hack saw the look in Noel's eye. "Let's go. You're the magician."

The roof was deserted. From the emptiness, two angels shimmered into sight. "All-ee, all-ee outs in free!" Lura caroled.

"*Must* you be so arch?" Atamar asked. To the air, he called, "Lysi, come here. Please."

The she-demon materialized with a smug expression on her face. "Did you like it? A heavenly visitation is one of my best numbers. I got lots of practice using it to annoy Daddy. I was going to use the rig on Richard if he wouldn't listen to reason, but Noel handled him just fine."

"He did. There is hope for the boy." Atamar gave Lysi a speculative glance. "For you too. I think we shall be able to arrange the transformation I spoke of earlier. You have helped us, and all is now restored to balance."

"When can you make me mortal?" Lysi clapped her hands together eagerly. Her medieval robes became more mundane streetwear. "I want to tell Noel! If he sees that I'm *not* a demon any more, he'll— Oh, could you please, please transform me in front of him?"

Atamar executed one of Salah-ed-Din's most flowery bows. "The lady's wish is mine."

"This is perfect!" Lura cried. "The Affinity of Souls works, just like I said. See? Hurry, Atamar. I can't wait to see Lysi in his arms."

But when Lysi and the angels came down into the street, they found Noel's arms were already full. He had thrown up a shell of force to seal himself off from everyone, and he cradled Matt Pincus' ruined body to his chest as he wept.

Atamar . . . Lura's thought begged her mate for an explanation.

He has magic, but none to heal a hurt so great. The man is on the point of death. Shall I open Noel's thoughts? He remembers your words, Lysi, of how djinn must be controlled. He sees himself again as he discards your spells, the spells that might have restrained Ba'ouji in his rage. It was that man's life he threw away, out of his own pride. He knows this, and it will kill him.

Lysi stood straight and stiff as a spear, watching Noel as he rocked and mourned. She saw Matt's soul hover on his lips, still clinging, yet ready to fly at any moment. Her mouth set. Her command cut into Atamar's mind.

Save him.

She was gone. The angel could not argue, dared not follow her. Lura was at his side, and her eyes told him that they shared the wonder and the pain of Lysi's choice. Their bodies turned to air. They sailed from either side, through the walls of Noel's shell, and unperceived by anyone, coaxed a frightened soul back into a body that was undergoing great transformations.

"I . . . feel . . ."

Matt's voice shocked Noel into dropping his shield. The man's eyes opened by degrees.

"I feel . . . weird. What happened?" He pushed himself up, out of Noel's arms and looked around. "Where's my chair, man?" Noel dumbly indicated the smoking twist of metal nearby. "Oh, for . . . Do you know how much those things cost?" He slapped his thigh for emphasis.

He froze. He slapped it again. He slapped the other one. He concentrated on his feet and started to laugh when the right, then the left one, wiggled. "Hey! Hey, get me up!" he shouted. Noel helped him stand, placed himself so that Matt could lean on him, but the veteran shoved him off and made a lurching, stumbling, glorious walk into the arms of the waiting paramedics. "He did it! He freaking did it! That kid over there—"

Uh-oh, thought Atamar as the crowd converged on Noel.

At least he'll have a career, Lura replied. *Something to keep him busy while we find Lysi. If she deserved our help before, she deserves it now a hundredfold.*

I say we'd better stay close to Noel. If these people think he worked the miracle, he's going to have a lot to handle.

Oh, Atamar, you're such a wrinklemonger. Noel told you he wants to take care of himself. I think he can. I have faith in him.

So do they. Atamar indicated the crowd. *That's the trouble.*

Epilogue

Plus Ça Change . . .

BECAUSE IT WAS the agreed-upon time for Jon's handfast spirit to have a go at the computer, and because Bob found round after round of playing *Treasure of Blood Valley* boring past words, the imp decided to take this opportunity to check in with the boss. Besides, he didn't really understand computers, but he understood kissing-up.

"Swear t' Gorgon, it's true. This place 'uz jumpin' with all kindsa folks, lookin' ta get in on Noel's 'miracle healing' powers. Sweet sumbitchin' Satan, that boy 'uz past ripe for the pluckin' when your letter got here . . . Yeah, I tole you, din't I? You make sure you put in a good word for me, see? Don' wanna be an imp forever . . ."

Jon's left hand struck a few keys, then picked up the mouse. Bob gave it a sharp look, but as it appeared to be doing nothing more than mindless doodles, still unrealized on the screen, he went back to his call.

"Sure I'm sure. Heard him slam outa here this mornin' with a suitcase. Din't even call his ma, din't tell nobody where he's goin'. He's been so damn upset these past coupla days, he hasn't even had the time to roust me outa this body . . . Nohow, boss; I like it in here, and not even you got the pull to get me out . . . Yeah? You gotta catch me first. You let me know when he comes down there and if he takes the bait. Never did trust the females to get it right . . . Hey, your mother's the exception, awright? . . . Nah, I ain't heard diddly from Lysi. Like she blunked off the face of the earth, no such luck . . . Sure, I'll keep you posted. Take care now, y'hear?"

Bob hung up the phone and watched Jon's hand at its labors. He yawned a mighty yawn and closed his eyes. The hand hit some more keys, then made five fast passes with the mouse.

"O.K., Handy-Dandy." Bob stretched the rest of Jon's body. "Playtime's over."

The enraged hand sprang. It hit one key, and on the screen a string of eldritch words scrolled their unappealable sentence while the mouse-drawn pentagram flashed into visibility and sucked the screaming imp out of Jon's body.

"Whew," said Jon as he studied the screen. Bob's face, distorted by his last howl, was held in the pentagram's center. Very punctiliously, Jon saved the file.

The phone rang just as he was labeling the software. "Hello . . . No, sorry, no one named Bob here." He hung up and laughed, then went to get a pizza the way *he* liked it for a change.

Under the brilliant, wholesome, inspirational smile of "Sometime" Joseph Lee, the secretary tapped busily away at her typewriter. The intercom buzzed and she answered. "You can go in now, Mr. Cardiff."

The man behind the desk looked strangely younger than the man in the big blowup photo outside. Noel rubbed his hands together nervously, but his malaise was doomed. "Sometime" Joseph Lee was famous for setting folks at ease. He pumped Noel's hand, had him sit down in one of the plump blue leather chairs, and fixed him a nonalcoholic cocktail personally.

"Nothing like a little something to wet the whistle, now is there?" He raised his own glass in a toast. "To your most wonderful gift, son, and to the force that guided you to me. To us. To our mission."

Noel put his drink down. "I've come because your letter—it seemed like you knew what I've been going through. I had to see you, sir, but your mission . . . I'm still in school."

"Sometime" Joseph Lee let Noel bask in the warmth of his smile until well-done, then he said, "Isn't the way of sweet healing the best lesson you can learn in your troubles, son? Now, I know what you're thinking. You're thinking, 'Who's this man I hardly know to going telling me I've been guided here by anything but my own will?' Well, son, I'll tell you why I come on so strong. It's my way of testing you. I want to see if the fire of truth in my words will make you strong or melt you down. And if I'm saying too much, too fast, why that's just my way. See, I'm tired of folks who always go around saying they're gonna change their ways. I say to them, 'When are you going to give some *di-rec-tion* to your life?' and you know what they say? They say, 'Sometime, Joseph; sometime.' Now I'll tell you, there ain't no 'sometime' down in Hell! So what's it going to be for you, son? You gonna hem and haw and act all shy, waiting for your sometime? Or are you gonna put yourself in these two hands and let us work together to use your gifts for the purpose they were intended?''

Noel was a man in a daze. His right hand rose of its own will and was soon clasped between both of ''Sometime'' Joseph Lee's.

''You won't regret this, son,'' he said as he ushered Noel out. ''First time I get you up before our television faithful, first healing you do, you are gonna feel a warmth inside you that'll tell you better than I ever could that you've put yourself in the right hands.'' To his secretary he added, ''Patty-Jo, you call up Brother Beau and tell him to look after our young friend here. Keep the light on you, honey.''

Reverently, Patty-Jo told him to keep the light on himself too. As he closed the door, he heard her telling Noel what a privilege it was to work for a man like ''Sometime'' Joseph Lee.

He shut the door and locked it. The intercom buzzed. ''It's your mother on line three, sir.''

''Sometime'' Joseph Lee punched the button and picked up the phone. As he perched his elegantly suited rear on a stack of letters from faithful watchers, he reflected on what a good idea it had been to buy Mama that cellular phone. It went where wires couldn't. It was a hell of a lot better than speaking with her face to face.

''Mama? . . . Yeah, he got here . . . Hell *will* I screw up the way Lysi did! 'Kinda question's that, y'old witch? You know me . . . Later.''

He hung up and smiled. Layer by layer the features of one of America's rising televangelists melted away. The broad face of the demon Raleel laughed and laughed.